The
Baker's
Daughter

Also by Sarah McCoy

The Time It Snowed in Puerto Rico

Sarah McCoy

The
Baker's
Daughter

a novel

BROADWAY PAPERBACKS / NEW YORK

BROADWAY

Copyright © 2012 by Sarah McCoy
Reading Group Guide copyright © 2012 by Sarah McCoy

All rights reserved.
Published in the United States by Crown, an imprint of the Crown Publishing Group, a division of Random House, Inc., New York.
www.crownpublishing.com

Broadway Paperbacks and its logo, a letter B bisected on the diagonal, are trademarks of Random House, Inc.

Originally published in hardcover in slightly different form by Crown Publishers, an imprint of the Crown Publishing Group, a division of Random House, Inc., New York in 2012.

ISBN 978-0-307-46019-6
eISBN 978-0-307-46020-2

Printed in the United States of America

BOOK DESIGN BY ELINA D. NUDELMAN
COVER DESIGN BY CHIN-YEE LAI
COVER PHOTOGRAPHY BY MYLES WICKHAM/MILLENNIUM IMAGES LTD.

10 9 8 7 6

First Paperback Edition

For Brian
Zahlen bitte, mein Schatz.
Ich liebe Dich.

prologue

*L*ong after the downstairs oven had cooled to the touch and the upstairs had grown warm with bodies cocooned in cotton sheets, she slipped her feet from beneath the thin coverlet and quietly made her way through the darkness, neglecting her slippers for fear that their clip might wake her sleeping husband. She paused momentarily at the girl's room, hand on the knob, and leaned an ear against the door. A light snore trembled through the wood, and she matched her breath to it. If only she could halt the seasons, forget the past and present, turn the handle and climb in beside her like old times. But she could not forget. Her secret pulled her away, down the narrow steps that creaked under weight, so she walked on tiptoe, one hand balancing against the wall.

In the kitchen, bundled dough mounds as white and round as babies lined the countertop and filled the space with the smell of milk and honey, and promises of a full tomorrow. She lit a match. Its black head flamed and licked the candlewick before fuming to nothing. She preferred the candle's burning ribbons to the electric bulb, buzzing bright and incriminating high above. Armed soldiers patrolled outside their doors; she couldn't risk inciting curiosity or waking her family.

She bent to her knees beneath the rising bread, pushed aside a blackened pot, and groped in the darkness for the split in the floorboard where she'd hidden the new letter. Her palms, callused from the rolling pin, snagged on the timber planks. Shallow splinters embedded in her skin, but she did not take notice. Her heart pounded in her ears and radiated heat through her arm and fingertips until she heard and felt the crackle of the paper she'd bunched into the crevice earlier.

It had arrived in the day's mail, sandwiched between a receipt from their local miller and a long-since-forgotten edition of *Signal Magazine*: its cover torn off; its pages watermarked beyond legibility, except for a pristine BMW ad boasting an aluminum bicycle for the "modern" rider. This tiresome correspondence made the letter's delicate handwriting and old-fashioned wax stand out. She'd recognized it at once and quickly tucked it into her dirndl pocket before anyone in the post office could catch a suspicious glimpse.

At home, her husband had called to her, "What's the news?"

"Nothing new. Buy or pay." She'd handed him the magazine and bill. "Take, take, take, the world never stops." She shoved her hands into her pockets, gripping the letter tight.

Her husband grunted, tossed the disintegrated magazine into the trash, then slid a pointed blade across the top of the miller's note. He retrieved the receipt and held it close, summing the numbers in his mind and nodding in agreement. "As long as it keeps on turning, man will wake with hunger each morning. And thank God for that. Otherwise, we'd be out of business, ja?"

"Ja," she'd echoed. "Where are the children?"

"Out doing their chores," he'd replied.

She'd nodded, then retreated to the empty kitchen to hide the letter until it was safe.

Now, with the sickle moon hanging high above like a fishbone, she crouched low and brought the candle to the ground. The letter's waxy seal had been cracked by her earlier clutch. Fragments littered the tiles. She carefully swept them into the base of the burning candlestick, unfolded the paper, and read the familiar script. Her hands trembled with each weighty word, the sentences tallied; her breath came faster and faster until she had to cover her lips to keep quiet.

The candle flame arched and quivered. A blue vein pulsed in its core. The air had changed. She stiffened on the floor and listened to a faint rustle of movement on the other side of the kitchen. A mouse, she prayed. A stray dog sniffing at the back door. An alpine gust or passing ghost. Anything but someone. She could not be discovered. Not with this letter in hand.

She scooted farther beneath the countertop, crumpling the paper into her lap and hugging the iron pot that stank of yesterday's stewed onions. She waited for the flame to curl upright and steady, staring so hard that her eyes began to burn. She closed them for relief and saw scenes like old photographs: girls with matching bows at the end of plaited pigtails sitting beneath a fruit tree; a boy with limbs so thin they looked like bent reeds on the river's edge; a man with a face marred by shadows swallowing chocolate that oozed out a hole in his chest; a woman dancing in a bonfire without smoldering; crowds of children eating mountains of bread.

When she opened her eyes, the flame had gone out. The black of night was lifting to velvet blue. She'd fallen asleep in the hiding place. But morning was coming, and it would no longer be safe. She crawled out, bones creaking and popping.

She carried the letter with her, hidden in the flimsy folds of her nightgown, and once more took the steps on tiptoe, past the girl's room; through her bedroom door, she slipped back beneath the covers; her husband abided in dreamlessness. Slowly and with great precision, she reached around the bedside and pushed the paper beneath the mattress, then rested her hand on her chest.

Her heart felt foreign, as if someone else's thudded within, moving ceremoniously, while the rest of her lay numb and cold. The clock ticked on the bedside table—*tick, tick, tick* without the *tock* of the pendulum swing. Her heartbeat filled the balancing pulse. In her mind, she read the letter's words to the rhythm of the metronome. Then suddenly, the clock erupted in clattering shouts. The hammer struck the bell again and again.

She did not flinch.

Her husband rolled over, pulling the blanket with him and exposing her body. She remained rigid as a corpse. He switched off the alarm clock, turned back to kiss her cheek, and rose. She feigned deep sleep. The kind that, when true, gives glimpse to eternity.

Soon enough she would join him in the day, keeping silent what she knew and welcoming the white-hot sun as blamelessly as possible. She would tend to the children, scrub the dishes, wind the cuckoos, and sweep the floors. She would bake bread and glaze the buns in melted sugar.

one

*R*eba had called Elsie's German Bakery every day for over a week without getting through. Each time, she was greeted by a twangy West Texan voice on the answering machine. She took a swig of orange juice to coat her voice sunny and sweet before the beep.

"Hi, this is Reba Adams from *Sun City* magazine. I was calling again to reach Elsie Meriwether. I left my number in my last two messages, so if you could ring me back . . . that'd be great. Thanks." She hung up and threw the cordless onto the couch. "P.S. Get your head out of the oven, and pick up the damn phone!"

"Why don't you go over there?" Riki pulled on his coat.

"Guess I don't have a choice. My deadline is in two weeks," Reba complained. "I thought this would be an easy, *fun* one to write. An hour on the phone, send the photographer to take some shots, and I'd be done. It's just a feel-good profile." She went to the refrigerator and eyed the caramel cheesecake Riki was saving for tonight. "Christmas-round-the-world with a local slant."

"Uh-huh." Riki jingled his car keys. "Well, that shouldn't be too hard. We got Texas and Mexico—what else matters?" He smirked.

Reba rolled her eyes and wished he'd hurry up and go. The happy anticipation of his departure made her sadly nostalgic. Once upon a time, his presence had incited waves of giddiness, like she'd drunk too many glasses of wine. The smart-aleck remarks had been cute in a cowboy way; his dark looks and Spanish accent made everything feel exotic and aflame, brazen and irresistible.

While doing a story on immigration, she'd followed him around his border patrol station, barely able to keep her pen steady enough to take notes; the vibrations of his voice down her spine carried through to her fingertips like a tuning fork.

The station tour and interview ended where it began, at the entrance. "We're just everyday guys doing our jobs," he'd said and opened the door for her exit.

She'd nodded and stood for an uncomfortably long moment, unable to convince her feet to move out of his dark, magnetic stare.

"I may need a little more info—would you be available later?" she'd asked, and he'd promptly dictated his cell phone number.

A few weeks later, she lay naked beside him, wondering who was this woman that possessed her body. Not Reba Adams. Or at least not the Reba Adams from Richmond, Virginia. That girl would never have slept with a man after knowing him such little time. Scandalous! But this girl felt shiny new, and that was exactly what she wanted. So she had curled her body around his and leaned her chin on his tanned chest, knowing full well that she could get up and leave anytime she wanted. The power of that made her light-headed with satisfaction, but she didn't want to leave, didn't want him to either. There and then, she prayed for him to stay. He had, and now she felt like a migrant bird tethered to a desert rock.

She jiggled her foot anxiously. Her stomach growled.

"See you later." Riki kissed the back of her head.

Reba didn't turn around.

The door opened and shut, and a cool draft of November air swept round her bare ankles. After his white-and-green US Customs and Border Protection pickup passed the front window, she pulled the cake from the shelf and to keep them perfectly symmetrical, she cut slivers from each of the three remaining pieces, then licked along the blade of the butter knife.

Midafternoon, Reba parked out front of Elsie's German Bakery on Trawood Drive. The shop was smaller than she'd imagined. A carved wooden sign hung over the door: *Bäckerei*. The smell of yeasty breads and honey glazes hovered in the air despite the blustery wind sweeping round the Franklin

Mountains. Reba pulled her jacket collar up under her chin. It was a chilly day for El Paso, a high of 63 degrees.

The bell over the bakery door chimed as a dark-haired woman and her son tottered out. The boy held a pretzel, studded with salt and half chewed.

"But when can we have gingerbread?" he asked.

"After dinner." She took his free hand.

"What's for dinner?" The boy bit into the knotted middle.

"Menudo." She shook her head. "Eat, eat, eat. That's all you think about." She pulled the boy past Reba. Sweet cinnamon and allspice clung to them.

Reba marched into the shop, ready to finally get answers. A jazzy, big-band tune played overhead. A man reading the newspaper sat in the corner with a cup of coffee and a slice of stollen. A slim but sturdy woman with silver-blond hair worked deftly behind the display case, sliding a tray of crusty rolls into a basket.

"Jane! You put the sunflowers seeds in when I say to put caraway!" yelled someone from beyond the curtained doorway dividing the café from the kitchen.

"I'm with a customer, Mom," Jane said. She pushed a graying bang behind her ear.

Reba recognized her Texan twang from the answering machine.

"What can I get you? This is the last batch of *brötchen* for today. It's fresh." She nodded to the basket.

"Thanks, but I—well, I'm Reba Adams." She paused, but Jane showed no flicker of recognition. "I've left a few messages on your machine."

"A cake order?"

"No. I'm a writer for *Sun City* magazine. I wanted to interview Elsie Meriwether."

"Oh, I'm sorry. I usually check the messages on Sundays, but I didn't get around to it this past weekend." She turned to the kitchen. "Mom, there's someone here for you." She tapped her fingers on the register to the beat of the jazz trumpets, then tried again. "Mom!"

A pan clattered. "I am kneading!"

Jane gave an apologetic shrug. "I'll be right back." She pushed through the curtains, revealing steel kitchen appliances and a wide oak baker's table.

Reba examined the golden loaves stacked in baskets on the open shelves: *Roggenbrot* (Light Rye), *Bauernbrot* (Farmer's Bread), *Doppelback* (Double-baked), *Simonsbrot* (Whole Grain), Black Forest, Onion Rye, Pretzels, Poppy Seed Rolls, *Brötchen* (Wheat Rolls). Inside a glass display case were neat rows of labeled sweets: Marzipan Tarts, Amarettis, three different kinds of *kuchen* (Cake: Hazelnut, Cherry-cheese, and Cinnamon-butter), Almond Honey Bars, Strudel, Stollen, Orange *Quittenspeck* (Quince Paste), Cream Cheese Danishes, and *Lebkuchen* (Gingerbread). A paper taped to the register read: "Celebration cakes to order."

Reba's stomach growled. She turned away from the case and focused on the willowy leaves of the dill plant by the register. *You can't, you can't,* she reminded herself, then dug in her purse for a roll of fruit-flavored Tums and popped a disk. It tasted like candy and satisfied the same.

Another pan clattered, followed by a stream of choppy German. Jane returned with fresh flour on her apron and forearms. "She's finishing up some tarts. Cup of coffee while you wait, miss?"

Reba shook her head. "I'm fine. I'll just take a seat."

Jane motioned to the café tables, noticed her dusted arms, and brushed the wheat airborne. Reba sat, took out her notepad and tape recorder. She wanted to make sure to get print-worthy quotes now and avoid another trip. Jane wiped the glass case with something lavender scented, then continued to the tables around the bakery.

On the wall beside Reba hung a framed black-and-white photograph. At first glace, she thought it was Jane standing beside an older woman— Elsie, perhaps. But their clothing was all wrong. The young woman wore a long cape over a white dress, her light hair swept up in a chignon. The older woman at her side wore a traditional German dirndl embroidered with what looked to be daisies. She clasped her hands in front and gave a meek glance, while the younger cocked a shoulder to the camera and smiled wide; her eyes bright and slightly indignant to whomever behind the camera.

"My *oma* and mom—Christmas 1944," said Jane.

Reba nodded to the photograph. "I can see the family resemblance."

"That was Garmisch before the war ended. She's never been one to talk much about her childhood. She married Dad a few years after, as soon as the military nonfraternization laws lifted. He was stationed there eighteen months with the Army Medical Corps."

"That sounds like a good story," said Reba. "Two people from totally different worlds meeting like that."

Jane flicked the cleaning rag in the air. "Isn't that the way of it?"

"What?"

"Love." She shrugged. "Just kind of hits you—BAM." She squirted lavender and wiped the table.

Love was the last thing Reba wanted to talk about, especially with a stranger. "So your dad's American and your mom's German?" She scribbled a helix on her pad and hoped Jane would simply answer her questions, not ask any more.

"Yup. Dad was Texan, born and raised." On mentioning her father, Jane's eyes brightened. "After the war, he put in to get stationed at Fort Sam Houston and the army gave him Fort Bliss." She laughed. "But Dad always said anywhere in Texas was better than Louisiana, Florida, or the damned North, for God's sake." She shook her head, then looked up. "You ain't got family in New York or Massachusetts or anything, right? Can't tell by accent these days. Have to excuse me. I had a bad run-in with a Jersey pizza baker. Left a sour impression."

"No offense taken," said Reba.

She had a distant cousin who went to Syracuse University and ended up staying in New York for keeps. Her family couldn't imagine how anybody could stand the cold winters and conjectured that the bitter temperature imbued itself on the people, too. Reba had only visited the Northeast a handful of times and always in the summer. She was partial to warm regions. The people in them always appeared tanned and smiling—happy.

"I'm from down south. Virginia. Richmond area," she said.

"What's a 'Ginia girl doing out here?"

"Lure of the Wild West." She shrugged. "I came to write for *Sun City* magazine."

"Well, shoot. They recruit that far?" Jane flipped her cleaning rag over her shoulder.

"Not exactly. I thought I'd start here and eventually make my way to California—L.A., Santa Barbara, San Francisco." It was a dream that still made her restless with hope. Reba shifted her weight in the chair. "Two years later, I'm still here." She cleared her throat. She was doing all the talking when what she needed was for Jane to start.

"I understand, honey." Jane took a seat at the café table and set her lavender cleaner on the ground. "This is a border town, for sure, a transient, crossover place, but some never get to crossing. Stuck in between where they were and where they were headed. And after a few years go by, nobody can recall their original destination anyhow. So here they stay."

"That's quotable." Reba tapped her pen. "But you've lived here awhile, correct?"

"All my life. Born at Beaumont Hospital on Fort Bliss."

"So where are you headed if you're already home?"

Jane smiled. "Just 'cause you're born in a place don't make it home. Sometimes I watch the trains go by and wish I could jump on. Watch the planes scratch the blue and wish I was inside. Mom's always called me a daydreamer, a stargazer, a rambler—whatever I am, I wished to God I wasn't. Dreaming doesn't do me a bit of good."

two

THE LEBENSBORN PROGRAM
STEINHÖRING, GERMANY

DECEMBER 20, 1944

Dear Elsie,

With news that Estonia has fallen to the Red Army, I write this letter with mounting anxiety for our good German forces and a heavy heart for the loss of our men. The compound here at Steinhöring and all the adjacent apartments have covered their windows in black. A handful of the girls lost family members—fathers and brothers. In addition, a number of Lebensborn companions perished, one of whom fathered my own twins. Poor Cristof. I only made his acquaintance the one time last spring. He was not yet twenty-two years old, skin still soft as a nectarine. Far too young to die. It makes me furious—this continued waste of life, this warring. I understand there is no better way to die than for the cause of our Fatherland, but I curse the foreign devils that spilt Aryan blood. We will not be trampled. This will only light a fire to our communal torch and Germany will be victorious! As the führer said, "The confidence of the German people will always accompany their soldiers." And our confidence will remain steadfast.

Instead of wallowing in despair, the Program is committed to making the upcoming holidays the most spectacular ever. I am helping to organize the decorations for the Julefest feast. Already we have a number of commended officers who have accepted the Program's holiday invitation. Our soldiers need companionship and support now more than ever. We are foraging the local communities for whatever meats and vegetables we can procure, and I'm determined to provide good <u>quality</u> bread and pastries like those in Papa's kitchen. I have yet to find a baker who can match the Schmidt recipes and feel as though I've swallowed hardened mud after eating the things these Steinhöring bakers make. I miss home and our family so very much.

With the birth of the twins, I have had little time to spend with Julius. I hope to do so now that the babies are in the Lebensborn nursery. I'll only admit this to you, sister, but I worry for them. They are both smaller than Julius was at birth. I hope that is simply a consequence of sharing a womb and soon they will grow round and healthy as any Aryan child. I can't be perceived as producing inferior offspring. Already, it has taken far too many years to conceive again. The only reason I was allowed to stay was because I proved to be a faithful daughter of the Reich.

The officers enjoy my company, though I will not and could not tell even you the things I have had to do to remain by Julius's side at the Program. Some of these men, while outwardly dignified, have debauched expectations in the bedroom. You are a virgin, Elsie, you do not know, and I pray every night that a compassionate German man will make you a wife before a mistress. That was the hope for Peter and me. I think of our last Christmas together when he asked for my hand by giving us the kitchen cuckoo clock and placing the gold band on the wooden figurine's head like a crown. What a glorious Christmas Day! The cuckoo chimed and out came the ring. Mutti and Papa were so proud. How simple and happy life was then.

How are the Christmas preparations coming? Does the bakery continue to have many customers despite the lack of rations? One of the girls here has family in Berlin, and she said there is barely a burnt crumb to be had. Berliners are bartering gems and gold for unleavened bread and dried pork skins. I suspect these rumors are lies spread by spies to scare the faithful. Things are in short supply here, but one can still buy a sweet cake and a stein of dark beer on any given day. What is it like in Garmisch? How are Mutti and Papa? I must write them soon. I send them my love and the same to you.

Heil Hitler,
Hazel

SCHMIDT BÄCKEREI
56 LUDWIGSTRASSE
GARMISCH, GERMANY

DECEMBER 21, 1944

Dear Hazel,

Good Saint Thomas Day! The bäckerei is so busy this time of the year. With only the three of us to knead the dough, work the oven, stock the shelves, and manage the till, I can't find a moment to enjoy the Christmas cheer. And then there are customers like Frau Rattelmüller who make it almost unbearable. Such a pest! Always complaining and making rude remarks about my hair being a mess or I'm lazy or asking if I still have yesterday's dirt under my fingernails. (Which I do not. I scrub them every night!) She makes such a scene to Mutti and Papa, still treating me like a child. That's the donkey chiding the other for having long ears. She's acting so peculiar lately.

She used to come round at the normal hour like everybody else, but not anymore. 5:30 in the morning and she's at our back door, peeping in the windows, banging her cane when she knows good and well we've always opened at six o'clock. I believe she's gone senile. Not to mention that a dozen brötchen is a gluttonous amount. Doesn't she know there's a shortage of flour and milk! You should see the SS rations Papa has resorted to using. The powdered milk and flour bake hard as brick. Many customers have complained of finding pebbles in their rolls and almost breaking a tooth. So now I have the added chore of sieving all the supplies we receive. Frau Rattelmüller swears if she cuts her gums and dies of infection, her blood will be on our hands. But it'll take more than a pebble to bring down that old witch. I suspect she'll be showing up for the next century munching her way through all our bread and bang-bang-banging that ridiculous cane. We'll never be free of her.

This morning I was fed up to my ears, so I woke up early with Papa and forced myself out of bed despite the chill. (It's colder this winter than last. Too cold for even the snow to melt into ice on the eaves. Remember that December we ate icicles dusted in sugar. You told me that snow sprites dined on them every night, and I believed you because I wanted to-.-.-. even though I knew there were no such things.) I was downstairs with a tray of hot brötchen when Frau came hobbling up the street in her long coat and cap.

Before she had a chance to knock her cane, I opened the door. "Good morning, Frau Rattelmüller." I smiled wide as Lake Eibsee. "Your brötchen has been waiting for you. Dear, dear, I pray it isn't cold. You must've been visited by the dream gnomes to have slept in so late." I looked over my shoulder to the cuckoo for emphasis. "Why, you are almost a minute past."

That sent Papa into a fit. He laughed so loud it echoed round all the pans in the kitchen and made Frau mad as a honeybee. She bought two loaves of onion bread instead of her usual. Mutti said Papa ruined a whole batch of lebkuchen with his salty tears. But it was worth it. How I wish you had been here! You would've laughed yourself to crying like you used to do when Papa wore his jester cap in the Fasching carnival. Mutti was not so pleased. She told me not to play with the old woman. She's hanging by a thread, she said. But I told Mutti that Frau has been playing with me for far too long already. Besides, this is wartime. Who isn't hanging by a thread!

Mutti, being Mutti, pulled out the currants that very minute and made thomasplitzchen buns to take over to Frau's as a peace offering. She's there now as I write.

I wonder what you're doing in Steinhöring. I miss you terribly. Can you believe you've been gone six Christmases? Feels like an eternity, and this war seems even longer. There's nothing new here. The *Zugspitze Mountain* is a bore. Nobody's skiing this season anyhow. I wish we could go back to sea. Remember that summer trip to the coast of *Yugoslavia* when we were girls? Walking the pebble beach and eating cold cucumbers in the sun? We were so happy then. It feels a hundred years ago. Not that we could go back now. War, war, war. It's everywhere, and I'm sick of it.

On to happier tidings: Did you hear the news? Our friend *Josef Hub* was promoted to lieutenant colonel and transferred to the Garmisch SS. He is rumored to dispatch information from the Mountain Troops to Reichsführer *Himmler*. Imagine that! But he's not like the others. His rank hasn't changed him a bit. He still comes to the *bäckerei* and eats raisin kuchen with Papa every Saturday. *Mutti* swears he has the bluest eyes in the country, but I told her there are plenty of perfectly blue eyes all around. She's just partial to Josef for all he's done for us.

How is *Julius*? You said they enrolled him in a special kindergarten for future officers. Papa nearly burst his buttons when I read that part to him. He's so proud. We all are, of both of you.

Don't worry about us and the *bäckerei*. The SS rations are small and of poor quality, but they are more than any other baker in town. Josef and Papa have a deal. The Gestapo bring SS flour, sugar, butter, and salt to the back door on Sunday afternoons, and Papa takes a cart of bread to headquarters each Monday. Business couldn't be better. I know I shouldn't complain about the long hours when so many of our countrymen are facing harder times than us.

Did Mutti tell you? I'm going to the Nazi <u>Weihnachten</u> party. Josef said it is time I attend one. He gave me the most beautiful ivory dress. Though the tag has been cut out, he said it came from Paris. At first I thought I oughtn't to accept, but he gave Mutti an iridescent clamshell compact and Papa a rosewood pipe. So I assume these are our Christmas presents. Quite extravagant! Not having any family of his own, Josef dotes on Mutti and Papa like his own parents, God rest their souls. His company has been a godsend, and I hope it means more sacks of sugar and presents! The dress is proof of his good taste.

I'll have Papa take a photograph before I go to the party. I want you to see the dress. I'll write again at Christmas. I hope you get this letter soon. Mail is moving slow these days.

Heil Hitler.

Your loving sister,
Elsie

three

SCHMIDT BÄCKEREI
56 LUDWIGSTRASSE
GARMISCH, GERMANY

DECEMBER 24, 1944

*E*lsie, hurry! You don't want to keep Herr Hub waiting," Mutti called from downstairs.

Elsie fumbled with the buttons on her kid gloves. She'd worn them only once—years before at her First Holy Communion. They made everything she touched feel like newly risen dough. At communion, she'd kept them on when the Lutheran minister handed her the chalice. The smooth cup against gloved hands felt truly divine; the bite of red wine, not so much. She'd instinctively put a hand to her mouth after tasting the tart sacrament and stained her right fingers. Mutti thought it a sacrilege and soaked the gloves in water and vinegar for nearly an entire day. Still, the index finger retained a slight blush.

Elsie dabbed a last bit of rouge on her bottom lip and smeared it round, checked that all her hairpins were hidden and blinked hard to make her eyes glossy bright. She was ready. It was her first official Nazi event—a coming-out party—and she couldn't make a better appearance. The dress, ivory silk chiffon trimmed in crystal beading, hung at just the right angle so as to give the illusion her breasts and hips were rounder than their actuality. She puckered her lips at the mirror and thought she looked exactly like the American actress Jean Harlow in *Libeled Lady*.

Her older sister, Hazel, and she had spent one whole summer holiday sneaking into matinee showings of pirated Hollywood films. *Libeled Lady* was a favorite of the owner who also operated the reel. He ran it twice a week. Elsie had just completed an abridged English language course in *Grundschule* and eagerly plucked familiar words and phrases from the actors' lines. By the time school resumed, she was performing whole scenes for Hazel in their bedroom adorned in Mutti's feather hats and fake pearls. So accurate in her English clip with its musical up and downs, Hazel swore she could've passed as the American blond bombshell's doppelgänger. That was before Jean Harlow died and the Nazis closed the cinema for displaying American movies. The owner, like so many, had quietly disappeared.

Shortly thereafter, the *Bund Deutscher Mädel* was made mandatory, and Elsie and Hazel participated in replacing all the beautiful theater posters of Jean Harlow and William Powell with stark images of the führer. It was their local BDM's community service project, and Elsie had loathed doing it. In fact, she hated most everything about the BDM. She failed at all the "wife, mother, homemaker" training activities except baking, and she detested that her Saturdays were spent in group calisthenics. While Hazel thrived and grew more popular, Elsie felt oppressed and stifled by the uniforms and strict codes of conduct. So at the tender age of eleven, she begged Mutti to work in the bakery. She'd overheard her papa discussing a new assistant to work the front of the shop, taking orders and helping customers. She'd eagerly jockeyed for the job. It would mean a reprieve from the BDM for her and save their family from paying out their earnings. While Papa agreed, he championed the national agenda and made Elsie promise to learn the Hitler Youth's Belief & Beauty doctrine from her older sister. She had, to some extent, but then Hazel became engaged and the BDM forbade participation of girls who were married. When her pregnancy was revealed, she moved to Steinhöring. The BDM didn't admit mothers, either. Thus, by the time Elsie reached the proper age to practice the principles, there was no one to teach her, and the war had made her participation in the bakery paramount. She didn't see the value in the BDM's "harmonic cultivation of mind, body, and spirit" if her family was struggling to make ends meet.

Now, a few hours before an official Nazi party, she wished she'd paid more attention to the BDM lessons of her childhood. It was like trying to conjure the taste of a fruit you've seen in paintings but have never eaten. She wished Hazel could give her solid advice. Elsie's only instruction on the art of glamour came from those faraway memories of a starlet sashaying about the silver screen. Tonight was the first time she had ever been escorted by a man, and she couldn't afford to make a mistake.

"You dance divinely," she whispered in English to the mirror and visualized William dancing with Jean, the image all silver-tipped and shimmering.

"Elsie!" Papa called.

Elsie quickly pulled her burgundy cape over her shoulders and took one last look in the mirror, liking the sophisticated woman she saw, then she proceeded downstairs.

At the base, Mutti, dressed in her best edelweiss-embroidered dirndl, swept crumbs out of sight. The rough broom bristled the burnished floor.

"I doubt Josef's attention will be on the *doppelback* crumbs. Leave the mice a Christmas present."

Mutti stopped sweeping when she saw her and put a fist to her hip. "Ach ja, you'll stand up well with all those fine girls this evening."

"Freilich!" Papa came from the kitchen. "You'll make Josef proud." He put an arm around Mutti's shoulder, and she eased into his side.

"I promised Hazel I'd send a photograph," explained Elsie.

Papa went to find the Bosley camera.

Mutti adjusted the folds of her hooded cape. "Be sure to laugh at his jokes," she said. "Men always like that. And try—try to be temperate. The führer praises this in women."

Elsie groaned. "I know, I know. Now stop fussing at me, Mutti."

"Please, dear, try."

Elsie yanked away. "Papa, did you find it?" she called out.

Mutti kept on, "Don't act like a gypsy or Jewess—unpredictable spirits. Remember your sister in the Program. Remember the bäckerei. Herr Hub has been so generous." She cleared her throat. "We'd be as bad off as the rest if it wasn't for his kindness. Look at Herr Kaufmann. The Gestapo came in the middle of the day and packed him off to one of those camps. And all he did was refuse to have his son join the *Deutsches Jungvolk. One cross word—that's all it takes, Elsie.*"

Papa returned with the Bosley. "I'm not sure the film is good." He opened the shutter and wound the knob.

"Kein Thema." Elsie sighed.

Mutti worried too much. Like most women in Germany, she wanted her children to be proper, her marriage to be superlative, and her household to be a paragon of decorum. But try as she may, Elsie had never been proficient in the set standards.

"He'll be here any minute. Papa, hurry." Elsie arranged herself beside

Mutti and prayed to God she wouldn't let them all down this night. She wanted them to be proud.

"Look," said Papa. "Two of the three finest women in Germany. You'll be a good wife, Elsie. As the führer says"—he paused and lifted a stiff palm to the air—"'Your world is your husband, your family, your children, and your home.' Mutti and Hazel are excellent examples."

Within the last six months, Papa had begun perpetually referring to her as wife material and quoting the führer with every reference. It wore on Elsie's nerves. She'd never understood why people quoted others. She tried never to quote anyone. She had ideas of her own.

"Gut. I understand. I'll be on my best behavior. Now take the picture."

Papa looked through the back of the camera lens. "Luana, get closer to your daughter."

Mutti scooted in, smelling of dillweed and boiled rye berries. Elsie worried the scent would stick, so she squared her shoulders hard to keep a margin between them.

"Ready?" Papa lifted his finger over the button.

Elsie smiled for the camera and prayed Josef would come soon. She was anxious to have her first glass of champagne. He'd promised.

"*It's so beautiful,*" said Elsie as the driver pulled up to the Nazi banquet hall on Gernackerstrasse.

The timbered lodge was ornamented with heart-carved balconies and colorful frescoes depicting shepherds in lederhosen, jeweled baronesses, and angels with widespread wings. From each window, red-and-black swastika flags joined their flight, fluttering in the alpine breeze. Cascading lights had been masterfully strung over the snow, illuminating icicles and casting a stunning corona about the structure. Its frosted eaves looked like piped sugar on a lebkuchen. A fairy-tale gingerbread house. Right off the pages of the Brothers Grimm.

"*You* are beautiful." Josef laid his palm on Elsie's knee. His warmth emanated through the wool cape and chiffon dress.

The driver opened the door. A burgundy carpet had been placed over the snow to keep the attendees from slipping or ruining the shine of their boots. Josef took Elsie's hand and helped her from the cab. She hurried to step out and let the swathe of ivory and crystal gems hide her feet. Although Josef had purchased her dress, she had no shoes to match.

Reluctantly, she'd borrowed Mutti's nicest pair of black T-straps, which still looked worn after an hour of buffing.

Josef took her gloved hand and threaded it through the crook of his arm. "You shouldn't be nervous," he consoled. "Not with such a pretty German face. They will love you the moment they see you." He touched her cheek with a leather-gloved finger. Her stomach jumped—the same lurch she felt when the pretzels were a minute from baking to brick. She knew exactly what to do then, rush to pull them from the fire and cool by the window. But here, dressed like a film star, she hadn't a clue. So she took a deep breath. The smell of burning pine air stung her nose. Her eyes watered. The lights ran together, and she gripped Josef's arm to keep steady.

"There, there." He patted her hand. "Just smile."

She did as he said.

The door of the lodge swung open and strains of violins cut the wind. Inside, the doorman took her cape. Exposed to the lamplight, the crystal beads cast miniature rainbows against Josef's uniform.

"Heil Hitler, Josef!" greeted a stocky man with a poof of a mustache above his lip, and the remnants of some sticky food caught in the sprout.

Elsie wondered what other bits might be lodged there and tried to hide her repulsion.

"Who is this?" he asked.

"May I present Fräulein Elsie Schmidt." Josef clicked his heels. "And this is Major Günther Kremer of the SiPo."

Elsie nodded. "A pleasure."

Kremer turned to Josef. "Charming." He winked.

"Günther and I have known each other for many years. He was one of my men in Munich. Is Frau Kremer here tonight?"

"Ja, ja. Somewhere." He waved over his shoulder. "No doubt discussing her pewter spoons or some such nonsense. Shall we have a drink?"

Down a corridor lined with Nazi flags and fir trees covered in candied fruits, they followed Kremer as he chatted about the wine and food and glitterati in attendance. Elsie wasn't listening, too caught up by the brilliance of the scene. It was everything she'd dreamed, exactly like the lavish ballrooms and festive parties in the Hollywood films of her youth. Her pulse raced. Oh, how she wanted this world: Josef's world of power, prestige, and uncensored euphoria. It dripped off everyone and everything in the room, like fruit glaze on a strawberry tart. For this moment, the dust of the baking board and black cinders of the oven were forgotten; the smudge of labored coins and soiled ration coupons in her palm, washed clean. By

Josef's side, she could pretend to be one of them, a royal princess of the Third Reich. She could pretend the world outside this place wasn't full of hunger and fear.

The corridor opened to the grand banquet hall. Long white tables striped the floor with silver candelabras at each fourth chair. A string quartet sat on a platform, their bows moving back and forth in perfect unison. Couples spun in slow circles on the dance floor like miniature figures on clock gears. The men wore SS uniforms, a background pattern of tan dress coats and beet red armbands. The women highlighted the scene in vibrant dress shades, plum and apricot, orange and cucumber green—a harvest of young and old.

A fleshy brunette in a scarlet lamé dress examined Elsie from head to toe, pausing at her feet. Elsie followed her gaze to the toe of Mutti's T-strap. She quickly scooted it back under the hem. A waiter approached with a tray of bubbling blond flutes. Josef handed one to Elsie.

"Here you are. I always keep my word. But be careful. One never knows the effect of champagne until you've tried it."

Champagne. Elsie's mouth went wet. She'd only ever watched as screen stars sipped and grew giddy on the beverage. She hoped it would have the same magical effect now. She took a glass and marveled. She'd never known its color: light gold, like the wheat shafts just before cutting. She guessed it would be as sweet as honey and as filling as bread. She licked her lips and drank.

The tangy bubbles bit hard. Brüt dry. A mouthful of baking yeast bloomed in water. She gulped to keep from spitting back into the flute but was not quick enough to hide her expression.

Josef laughed. "You'll get used to it."

"Try another sip and then another. If you don't love it by the third, I'll drink the rest for you." Kremer chuckled. The buttons of his coat strained against his portly stomach.

Despite herself, Elsie recalled Mutti's advice and forced a dainty laugh. He was Josef's comrade, after all. She wanted him to like her. So she did as he instructed and drank again, attempting to finish the glass and be done entirely.

"Prost! It looks like you've got yourself a strong fräulein," said Kremer. "How about a dance while Josef gets you another?"

Elsie held Josef's gaze. "I'm not very good," she said.

"No matter." Kremer took Elsie by the elbow and led her to the dance floor. "I promise to go slow." He pulled her close and placed one hand on the small of her back while clasping her gloved fingers. His stiff uniform pushed the dress's crystals into her skin, a thousand nails tacking them together.

Elsie looked over her shoulder at Josef. He smiled and lifted her empty glass. When he turned to call the waiter, Kremer slid his hand down the back of her chiffon.

Elsie pulled away. Her cheeks flushed hot. "Herr Kremer!"

He grabbed her hand and yanked her forcefully against him. "Hush. It's a party. *Don't* cause a scene, fräulein." He smiled a toothy grin and spun her deeper into the dancing crowd. "I wanted to speak with you privately. You see, there are those who find it odd that someone of Josef's stature would take up with the uneducated daughter of a common baker when there are far superior options, including your own sister."

She winced at his mention of her academic record. While Hazel had attended *Gymnasium* and graduated at the top of her class, Elsie had stopped early of graduation from *Hauptschule* to work full-time in the bakery. Though she'd just met Major Kremer, he obviously had great knowledge of her and her family.

"There are so many spies these days. Everyone suspects beautiful, new faces." He leaned in and examined her face uncomfortably close, his hot breath like rotten eggs.

Elsie sharply turned her cheek. "My family has known Josef for years."

"Ja, and who knows how many secrets you have already gathered to pass on to our enemies."

"I am not a spy!" she hissed. "My papa bakes bread for the Nazi headquarters in Garmisch. My sister is in the Lebensborn Program."

"I am not curious about them. I am curious about you." He sucked his teeth.

They moved in circles on the floor. A woman with peacock feathers in her silver hair wriggled her nose when they bumped elbows. Elsie swallowed hard. Her head reeled. She was a loyal German, but how else could she prove her allegiance? All she had was her word.

Kremer's uniform stank of sweat and cigarettes. Champagne bubbles came up her throat. She wanted to slap him, to cry out for Josef, but the sharp pins of Kremer's Security Police uniform reminded her of the possible consequences, not just for herself but also for her family. So she gulped down the sourness.

The song ended. The quartet removed their bows from the strings, stood and bowed.

"Here you are, dear."

Startled, Elsie jumped and knocked the glass from Josef's hand; effervescent wine fizzed over them.

"I'm sorry." She wiped droplets from his uniform lapels. The starch kept them from soaking in. Her dress was not so fortunate. The champagne streaked the ivory hemline.

"No harm." Josef took her arm. "I know a cleaner who can get anything out with lye soap and a boar brush." He kissed her hand.

"Thank you for the dance. It was a delight." Kremer clicked his boots and left with a smirk.

The quartet leader came to the podium. "Ladies and gentlemen, if you would take a seat, we would like to begin our Weihnachten presentation."

Josef led her to the middle of their banquet table. At the far end sat Kremer beside Frau Kremer, a dark twig of a woman with wan cheeks and a sharp nose. She caught Elsie's stare and narrowed her eyes.

Elsie turned her chair toward Josef to avoid her. "Josef," Elsie began. Her voice shook, so she cleared her throat to steady it. "I need to speak to you about—"

"Look, look!" He cut her off and pointed to the stage. "We have a surprise. Do you like music? Wagner, Hotter, Clemens Krauss?"

Elsie's fingers had gone numb. She undid the mousquetaire buttons of her gloves and pulled at the champagne-soaked fingers. "Ja, but I've never been to an opera."

He furrowed his brow and *tsked*. "I should send you some recordings then."

Elsie didn't own a record player but hadn't the composure to explain that to him now. She took off her gloves and felt instantly naked, the air over her palms intrusive. She laced her fingers together in an effort to buttress herself.

"Josef," she tried again.

"And now!" announced the bandleader. "A short musical performance for your dinner entertainment." He lowered the microphone, set a small footstool before it, and took a seat with his violin.

Josef tapped his index finger against his lips. "Later," he whispered.

A murmur of curiosity rippled through the crowd, then fell silent as a stout SS-Gefolge woman with a shock of white hair down the center of her crown led a boy, no more than six or seven years old, up the platform steps. He wore a simple white linen shirt with matching gloves, black trousers, and a bow tie. He might've looked like any boy dressed for Christmas Eve if his hair hadn't been cropped to his scalp, the color of his skin so sallow that he seemed featureless, a walking apparition. The woman instructed him to step onto the stool, and he did so with lowered head. Then, he looked up with eyes as big and brilliant as springwater.

The leader played a long, high note on the violin. The boy, with fists at his side, took a deep breath, opened his mouth, and sang. His countertenor voice rang out through the corridors. Everyone quieted their conversations and turned. Pure and smooth as new butter, it took Elsie's breath away. She'd heard the Christmas hymn her whole life, sang it herself, but never before had "Silent Night" sounded like this.

"All is calm, all is bright . . ."

The violin fell away, but his voice remained.

"Only the Chancellor steadfast in fight, watches o'er Germany by day and by night . . ."

Before he'd finished, the dinner service began. Waiters clinked china plates on varnished trays and poured jewel-toned wine into waiting goblets. Conversations resumed. A woman laughed too loud.

"Always caring for us . . . always caring for us . . ."

Elsie closed her eyes.

"Wine?" asked the waiter from behind.

"Silent night, holy night . . ." The boy's voice never faltered or strayed from its perfect pitch.

A lump rose in Elsie's throat, brimming emotions she'd tried to suppress earlier.

"He has an excellent voice," said Josef.

Elsie nodded and blinked dewy eyes. "Where is he from?"

"He sang to the arriving detainees at the Dachau camp," explained Josef. "Sturmscharführer Wicker heard him and had him sing at a handful of his dinner parties. Everyone seemed to enjoy it. He has a unique voice, mesmerizing if you aren't careful to remember from where it comes."

"Ja, unique." Elsie collected herself.

"Brings us greatness, favor, and health. Oh give the Germans all power." The boy finished.

The violinist came to the microphone. "I quote our führer: 'All nature is a gigantic struggle between strength and weakness, an eternal victory of the strong over the weak.'" He clicked his heels together and raised his bow in party fashion. "Guten appetit."

The bubbling crowd broke into a cacophony of clanking silverware and chatter. The violinist began a new song to which the boy sang, but Elsie could barely make it out above the dinner crowd.

"Is he a Jew?" she asked Josef.

"His mother was a Jewess singer. His father, a Polish composer. Music is in his blood." Josef pulled a brötchen roll apart and spread butter on either half.

"My nephew, Julius, sings. Hazel says he's rather good."

"We should have him sing for us some time." He laid one half on Elsie's plate. "Tonight is this boy's last performance. He's going back to the camp tomorrow. With everything going on in the Ardennes . . ." He crunched his bread and swallowed hard. "I apologize. That is no subject for Weihnachten."

She'd first heard about the camps years before when the Grüns, a merchant family that sold the best soaps and shampoos in the area, vanished in the middle of the night. Elsie had visited their store at least once a month. Their son, Isaac, was two years her senior and the handsomest boy in town. He winked at her once when she bought honey milk soap. Secretly, she'd imagined him while lying in her warm bathtub, the steam rising like a fragrant veil around her. The memory shamed her now. Though Jewish, they were well liked in the community. Then one day, their store was boarded up and marked "Juden," and they were gone.

A week later, while waiting in line at the meat shop, she overheard the shoemaker's wife whispering to the butcher that the Grüns had been sent to the Dachau camp where they were sprayed with lye water like cattle and didn't need shampoo because their heads were shaved. The image sent Elsie running out the door. When Mutti asked for the lamb, Elsie said the butcher hadn't any, though there were clearly half a dozen in his pen. She never told her parents or anyone about what she heard nor did she ask about the Grüns. No one spoke of them. And while the shoemaker's wife was not prone to gossip like the other town wives, Elsie chose not to believe her. Now, however, she could not deny the shaved head of the little boy.

Josef sniffed his wine, then sipped. "I have something else I'd like to discuss." He reached into his uniform jacket and pulled out a small box. "When I saw it, I knew it was a sign." He opened the lid, revealing a gold engagement ring studded with rubies and diamonds. "I think we'd be very happy together." Without waiting for an answer, he slid it on her finger.

The waiters interrupted, setting large platters between the candelabras. The snout of a roasted piglet faced Elsie; its eyeballs were cooked blank;

its crispy ears perked and listening. Bowls of creamy potatoes flanked the swine with white sausages at the rear, a ghostly tail. Though it was the most food she'd seen in all her life, Elsie's stomach turned with distaste.

"Will you be my wife?"

A ringing commenced in Elsie's ears. Josef was nearly twice her age, a friend of her father's, beloved as a kind uncle or older brother perhaps, but not as a husband. The sideways stares of the Nazi guests seemed to press in on her like a wooden-toothed nutcracker. Josef waited with casual confidence. Had he always seen her this way? Was she so naive that she'd missed the indications?

The gemstones winked blood red in the candlelight.

Elsie dropped her hands to her lap. "It's too much," she said.

Josef forked the pig belly, piling stringy meat onto his plate. He took Elsie's plate and did the same. "I know. I shouldn't have asked tonight with so much going on, but I couldn't help myself." He laughed and kissed her cheek. "A superb Christmas feast!"

Elsie focused on the food before her and not the ring on her hand. But the pork was so lardy she needn't chew; the jelly rind slid down her throat; the potatoes were gray and mushy; the sausage mealy and under-cooked. She washed it all down with red wine and tasted again her First Communion host. Acid crept up her throat. Bread. She took a bite of the buttered brötchen, the taste and smell familiar and comforting.

She didn't speak the entire meal. At the end of the main course, the boy's musical performance also concluded. The orchestra, having had their break, returned to the stage in preparation for dessert and dancing. Elsie watched over the seated crowd as the SS guard marched her caged song-bird to the back of the hall and through a service door.

"That boy." She turned to Josef. "Does he have to go back?"

The silver candelabras reflected the empty cavity of the piglet's body and Nazi uniforms at every other chair.

Midair, Josef halted a last spoonful of potato spaetzle. "He's a Jew." He ladled the wormy noodles into his mouth before the waiter retrieved his empty plate.

Elsie tried to sound casual. "He's only half Jewish . . . and that voice." She shrugged. "Doesn't seem to belong with the rest."

"A Jew is a Jew." Josef took her hand, fingering the ring. "You are too softhearted. Forget those things. Tonight is a celebration."

From the candles, heat rose in wavy reflections. Elsie's temples pulsed. The pitchy squeal in her head crescendoed.

"Josef, would you excuse me." She pushed her chair back and stood.

"Is everything all right?"

"Please, don't let me interrupt. I need a minute to . . ."

"Oh." Josef nodded. "The WC is down the hall, to the right. Don't get lost or we'll have to send the Gestapo to find you." He laughed.

Elsie gulped and forced a feeble smile. She walked leisurely through the glittering banquet hall but quickened her pace alone in the shadowed corridor, past the sign marked *Toilette* until she reached the double doors leading to the back alley.

four

Reba's cell phone buzzed. "Excuse me." She read the text message: PROCESSIN VAN OF ILLEGALS. B HOME LATE. She sighed and tossed the phone back into her purse.

"Problem?" asked Jane.

"No, just more Rudy's Bar-B-Q takeout for me. I'm a regular."

"I hear that, honey." Jane tapped her fingers on the table. "Boyfriend?"

"Not exactly." Reba shuffled the items in her handbag, then zipped it.

"Oh, come on. It's just us girls." Jane made like she was locking her mouth with a key.

Reba paused. Again, Jane was toeing—no, *pushing* the line that separated the journalist from the subject. It wasn't professional to talk about her relationships. The job was to get interviewees to talk about theirs; then she'd write it up and the magazine printed it a thousand times over for public consumption. She was known for her feature profiles. She could wheedle out intimate stories from just about anybody her editor put in front of her; but *her* life was private, and she meant to keep it that way. She'd just met this woman. Jane was a total stranger. No, completely inappropriate.

But there was something about her, a calm intensity, that gave the illusion—correct or not—of trustworthiness. And the fact was, Reba didn't have many friends in the El Paso. She didn't trust most people. She'd been jaded by far too many who said one thing but did another. Lied, in essence. Not that she could point a finger. She lied too, every day, big and small, even to herself. She told herself she didn't need companionship. She was independent, self-sufficient, and free. Riki had been the only one she dared trust here, and only to a limited extent. But lately, even things with him were going sour. She felt a budding loneliness, and with it came the familiar emptiness that once threatened to swallow her whole. She missed her older sister, Deedee, and her momma, too. Family. The very people she'd traveled thousands of miles to leave behind.

On quiet El Paso nights when Riki was working late, the loneliness would sometimes consume her like it did in her childhood, and she'd pour a glass of wine, open the kitchen window, and let the desert breeze kick up the linen curtains. It made her think of her last August Sunday in Richmond. Deedee had come over with two bottles of Château Morrisette. They'd drunk barefoot on the fresh-cut lawn, green clippings stuck to their toes. By the second cork pop, wine wasn't the only thing being poured into the night. Tipsy on illusive dreams, they forgot all their girlhood tears, talking of quixotic futures until even the lightning bugs turned off their lights; and for once, they understood why their daddy drank bourbon like lemonade. It was nice to pretend the world was wonderful—to gulp away the fears, hush the memories, let your guard down and simply be content, if only for a few hours.

Reba rubbed the twitch in her forehead. "He's my fiancé," she relented.

"Really!" Jane leaned back in her chair. "Where's the ring?"

Reba reached for the chain at her neck and pulled the suspended solitaire from beneath her shirt.

"A sparkler," said Jane. "How come it ain't on your finger?"

"It makes it hard to type. Too tight, I think."

"You can get that resized, ya know."

Reba picked up the recorder and fiddled with the buttons.

"When's the wedding?" Jane kept on.

"We haven't set a date. We're both pretty busy."

"When did you get engaged?"

"Uh." Reba flipped her mental calendar. "August."

Jane nodded. "You best start planning. These days it takes a while to get all the doodads together. I can show you our wedding cake portfolio so you can get some ideas churning."

Reba regretted having said anything and immediately evoked a tried and true journalism tactic: the redirect.

"Are you married?"

Jane pulled the cleaning rag off her shoulder and waved it around like a gymnast's wand. "Ha. Not this old lady. I'm past my prime." She leaned forward, elbows on the table. "Never mind that nobody'd be good enough in Mom's eyes unless he had trim on his shoulders. 'Course she's never said nothing of the kind, but I always got the feeling she wanted me to marry a military man like my dad—US Army, the German Luftwaffe, or something. But I'm no soldier girl. All that ribbon and starch drives me batty. Don't get me wrong; I respect what they do. I appreciate their service and sacrifice for our country. It's an honorable profession, and each time Fort Bliss has a troop homecoming, I take all our breads and pastries over to the fort—no charge, mind you. But I *don't* want one in my bed, and I don't want to marry one." A silver strand fell over her eyes, and she pulled it hard behind her ear.

"I never even brought a boy home. Didn't see the point." She leaned back in her chair and cocked her head, looking hard at Reba. "But I got somebody. Been together for years. Since I was a skinny thing with freckles. Never asked to marry me. Now, that might not sound good but trust me, if you knew, you'd see it takes a lot for a person to be faithful when you can't put a label on it—can't say, this person is *mine*. Takes an awful lot."

Jane focused on the ring in the middle of Reba's chest.

Reba readjusted in her chair, trying to shake off her stare. She cleared her throat. "It sounds like we're the same suit in a pack of cards. I'm not racing to the altar either."

"It's a pretty ring," said Jane.

The bell on the door clinked, and a man in a gray army sweatshirt entered.

"Can I help you, sir?" asked Jane. She stood, picked up the lavender spray, and returned to the register.

"Yes." He frantically scanned the glass display case. "My wife wants me to order a cake. It's for my son's birthday. She tried to make one, but it kind of fell flat. His party's in a few hours, so I came here." He balled his fists and rubbed his knuckles together. The talon of a bald eagle tattoo stretched over his right wrist. "I'd appreciate anything you can do. She's from Germany, my wife. We moved to Bliss last month, and she doesn't know anyone. All her friends and family are back in Stuttgart. She said she couldn't find the right ingredients at Albertson's, and she threw out the frosted sheet cake I picked up this morning. She wants the cake to taste like home." He looked up at Jane, his blue eyes pleading. "I just want her to be happy. If you've got an extra German cake in the kitchen . . ."

Jane nodded. "Let me talk to my mom. She's got a knack for making things out of thin air." She went back through the curtained doorway.

Reba waited for a bang or a yell, but there was none.

Jane returned within a minute. "Can you give us a couple hours?"

He exhaled and relaxed his fists. "The party's at three."

"It'll be ready."

"Thank you so much. I really appreciate this," the man said. He turned to leave. Jane stopped him.

"What's your son's name?"

"Gabriel—Gabe."

"We'll put it on the cake."

"My wife would like that. Him too. Thank you again. You have no idea how much this means." He left, the wind banging the door behind.

"Now that's love." Jane laughed. "Man's all aflutter trying to help his missus pull off a nice party for their kid." She scribbled the name on a sheet of paper. "I've never been fooled by the romantic, grand gestures. Love is all about the little things, the everyday considerations, kindnesses, and pardons."

Reba had always imagined love as wild and untamed. True love was a passionate flame that burned bright until it was snuffed out. It didn't flicker and dim, weakened by the banalities of daily life. Reba thought about how she and Riki acted these days, every word so carefully chosen, so frustratingly polite, like actors with scripted lines. She tucked the necklace and ring back into her blouse.

"Now that we got this order, I'm not sure Mom's going to be able to talk today. Could you come back?"

When she'd walked through the door, Reba had the goal of getting all she needed in one trip, but now, after being there only an hour, she didn't mind returning. Actually, she thought it'd be kind of nice.

"Yes, of course. I'll bring my camera next time. The magazine will send a photographer, but I'd like to take some photos myself, if you wouldn't mind."

The neat stacks and colorful sweets in the display case would make a pretty shot. Her mouth watered.

"Can do! Here." Jane opened the back of the case. "You waited so long. Take something. Mom always says you're never lonely with a strudel." She picked up a slice oozing cream cheese icing.

"No, I can't," Reba said appreciatively. "I don't eat dairy."

Jane stopped. "Oh, you poor thing. Don't they have medication for that?" She realigned the slice in its row.

Reba shook her head. "I'm not lactose intolerant. I can eat dairy. I just don't. I was involved with PETA in college—animal rights, milk sucks, and all that."

Jane raised both eyebrows high. "Milk sucks?"

"It was a PETA campaign," explained Reba.

"Oh." Jane pursed her lips together. "Well then, how about lebkuchen? They're Mom's specialty. She uses almond oil. No butter. That's the family secret. You got to promise not to tell."

Jane obviously wouldn't let her leave without something, so Reba agreed. "I promise."

That night, Reba sat alone at her kitchen table nibbling on the edge of the lebkuchen. Decorated with almond slices fanned like flower petals, the squares were almost too pretty to eat; but it'd been a long day and she had no remaining self-restraint. The rich molasses and dry cinnamon stuck in her throat, so she poured a small tumbler of skim milk, froth bubbling on the surface and coating the glass pearly white.

When she'd first gotten home, she'd set the German bakery box on the kitchen counter, committed not to eat any, but she was unable to throw the cookies away. The sweet smell permeated the kitchen, the den, up the condo's stairs to their room where she sat in bed transcribing notes. Finally, after the sun melted into the desert and the autumn moon rose orange like a Nilla wafer, she gave in to the loneliness, came down, and found solace in the sugary snack.

She wondered if she ought to leave a cookie for Riki, but then he'd ask about her day and she hadn't the energy to explain how she'd talked to Jane for an hour without getting a word on record. Inevitably, he'd want to know what they'd talked about, and she refused to open Pandora's box. But she couldn't seem to get Jane and the bakery out of her mind, or mouth.

She dipped the last square in the milk, popped it in, and chewed. Out of sight, out of mind—wasn't that the mantra? She gulped the milk and rinsed the glass, leaving no evidence.

It all started as such a small lie: pretending she didn't eat dairy. Now, she'd been doing it so long, she didn't know how to stop.

It began in college. Reba's roommate, Sasha Rose, the daughter of expatriates in Singapore, was a petite girl, passionate about two things: veganism and Italian art. She didn't take part in the midnight pepperoni pizza binges or the all-you-can-eat chicken wing buffets. Instead, she nibbled dainty bowls of pebbled edamame and ruby organic figs while studying Botticelli and Titian.

On family weekend their freshman year, Sasha's parents had flown in from overseas. Her mother looked like her twin with silver-streaked hair and a distinctive British accent.

"How I've missed you, darling," she cooed, and she held Sasha so close and true that Reba had to look away. It pinched her chest.

Sasha's father, originally from Tallahassee, was tall and tanned with an infectious smile and a happy spirit. His charisma radiated like the Floridian sun. Sasha had flown from her mother's arms to his, and Reba had watched Mrs. Rose for the smallest flash of jealousy, fear, or resentment; but the reflection of Sasha in her father's embrace only seemed to make her glow.

"Reba, you're coming with us to dinner!" Mr. Rose had insisted; but when he put a gentle hand to Reba's back, she'd flinched so noticeably that he'd made the addendum, "Of course if you have other plans, we totally understand."

She hadn't, but the moment was marred by a discomfort she feared would persist throughout the meal.

"I have a test on Monday," she'd lied, and by the way his smile softened at the corners, he knew it.

Reba's momma and sister, Deedee, hadn't come that weekend—schedule conflicts. Momma had a Junior League reception. Deedee was busy with graduate courses. Initially, Reba had been thankful, but seeing Sasha with her perfect parents, she felt an aching desire for kin—for Momma, Deedee, even Daddy. It was a hopeless longing.

"Good luck studying," said Mr. Rose. With his girls on either arm, the trio had strolled out.

Closing the door behind them, Reba caught a glimpse of herself in the mirror nailed to the back. The image seemed in such stark juxtaposition to the pretty Roses that she immediately threw on a hooded sweatshirt and burrowed in the blankets of her dorm bunk like a rock vole.

She'd always been melancholic and unsatisfied with nearly everything about herself. Thick in places that should have been thin, flat chested and too tall, she'd never fit in with the high school cheerleaders and Glee Clubbers—the little sisters of her sister's friends. At sixteen, when her daddy died, she pulled away completely and spent her lunches and after-school hours in the journalism room over quiet newspaper spreads and silent photographs.

During Reba's first semester in college, Deedee suggested she take up a self-improvement activity: yoga, dance, swimming, art. Make a new beginning, she'd said. Reba profiled the university boxing club instead, lacing on a pair of gloves and sparring with a trainer. Everyone on campus knew her from the photographs in the *Daily Cavalier*: her lips bulging on the mouth guard; fuzzy, dark hair matted beneath the headgear; gloves up and ready. They thought she was an anomaly coming from the Adams family. Daughter of a commemorated Vietnam veteran and great-granddaughter to one of Richmond's largest ironworks owners. Deedee had been a celebrated debutante. Rosy-cheeked and always smiling, smart and witty, she was already in law school. While Reba . . . Reba was scribbling in her notebook and playing dress-up with the boys. She felt she was always letting her momma and sister down.

Thus, in a sudden strange twist of reason, she resolved to emulate Sasha, learn from her and hopefully channel her sophistication. First step: veganism. She did a quick library search on the lifestyle and diet. The basics were hard to swallow. No animal products. Period. Reba decided it might be worth it to be connected to a cause, to truly stand for something, but *all* of the animal kingdom seemed radical. So she chose cows. No yogurt or cheese, butter or beef. She'd save a cow with each declined bowl of ice cream—and did so for nearly three weeks.

Then Valentine's Day arrived, and Sasha reminded her that dairy cows were sucked of their mother's milk for the production of chocolate. Sasha and her boyfriend attended a PETA "Veggie Viagra" event, while Reba stayed home.

The sadness had returned stronger than ever that night, gnawing on her insides. The hungry wolf, her daddy had called it. In bleary binges, he'd described it to her and Deedee when they were girls: how it crept after him in the daylight shadows and shredded his nights to jagged fragments. Then he'd pour himself another amber glass, sip, smile, and playfully make them swear not to mention it to their momma. They'd agreed but kept their fingers crossed behind their backs. It didn't matter either way. Momma brushed it off, "Nothing but boogeyman tales. You know better than to take anything he says seriously when he's in one of his moods. Now go to bed and sweet dreams, my girls."

After Daddy's death, Reba discovered his medical records while helping to clean out his office. He'd had years of electroconvulsive treatments for severe depression, and up until the very week he died, he met each Thursday with a clinical psychiatrist at the Medical College of Virginia. Dr. Henry Friedel notated that predeployment, her daddy had suffered from chronic sadness, anxiety, and feelings of hopelessness; food binges followed by periods of no appetite; insomnia; inability to make decisions; unresolved guilt; extreme high-low mood swings; and an altered sense of reality. Reading his symptom list, she'd buckled: they could've been her own. Dr. Friedel further noted that all these preexisting symptoms were withheld from army recruiters and, thus, exacerbated by combat conditions.

Alongside the file was a volume of handwritten notes from her daddy's sessions. As she was lifting it into the brown packing box, a page came loose from the metal prongs and slipped to the ground. Though it was his private business, Reba's curiosity got the better of her and she'd read:

February 28, 1985

In addition to the patient's previous complaints and aforementioned clinical treatment, Mr. Adams continues to suffer from insomnia due to night terrors and waking flashbacks related to his active duty service in the Vietnam War. In discussion, he continues to focus on the Sơn Tịnh District woman and her teenage daughter whom he claims to have raped while under the influence of psychotropic agents, which he had obtained illegally from local Vietnamese. Mr. Adams states that he later stumbled upon a black wolf devouring the women's ravaged bodies. (I have still not established if the wolf is a factual experience or more likely, simply represents the manifestation of his subconscious guilt.) Particular patient attention is focused on the company insignia carved on the victims' naked chests. Mr. Adams cannot recall if these acts of mutilation were perpetrated by himself or his fellow soldiers, nor can he ascertain if he was instrumental in their deaths. However, the deliberation of this point remains the central focus of our discussions and fuels his anxiety, guilt, drastic mood swings, and resultant autophobia. He vacillates between rationalization and self-incrimination.

Today, Mr. Adams once again described in meticulous detail the order from his chain of command to attack and kill all Viet Cong within the small village. When asked how he felt about the assassination of civilian men, women, children, and elderly, Mr. Adams stated, "They said we had to wipe them out for good. We were following orders. I was trying to be a good soldier. I didn't want to be there. I wanted to be home with my family." When asked if rape was ordered by his chain of command, Mr. Adams became

*extremely emotional and erratic and required an IM dose of an anxiolytic. The
session concluded early. I have prescribed him lorazepam and scheduled an
additional consultation for Tuesday, March 5.*

Reba stuffed the page back in the volume and immediately wished she
could turn back time—snatch the page from the floor with closed eyes.
She didn't want to know her daddy's secrets. Her own memories were dark
enough. She'd packed the files down deep in the box and double-taped it shut
with duct tape, hoping to seal in the past and bury Daddy's wolf for good.

But alone in her dorm room that Valentine's, she could hear its lonesome howl reverberating through her skin, so she went to the neon-lit
campus minimart and bought a pint of milk and the biggest box of cherry
bonbons on the shelf. "He's a lucky guy," the student cashier had remarked.
Reba had nodded and smiled, "Yes, he is." She went home and ate the
whole box herself, comforted by row upon row of cherry chocolates and
the thought that the cashier imagined she had someone wonderful to share
them with. She drank the milk straight from the container. As a forbidden
fruit, it tasted even sweeter.

Later, when the jug began to sour in their trashcan, Sasha asked what
the smell was. "Soy milk," Reba replied. "I think it was a bad batch of beans."
Sasha had studied her for a moment, then shrugged, "I had that happen
once. Buy the organic kind next time. It's always good."

Just like that, it had begun. So trivial at first. Yet over a decade later, Reba
was still lying. The problem was that her lies didn't stay contained to a jug.
They cultivated like mold and grew on various parts of her life, rotting the
fruits of her labors.

But fabrication seemed the easiest path to reinvention. She could forget
about her family and childhood: her daddy's hysterical giddiness followed
by deep spells of despondency; the smell of whiskey on his breath during
nightly prayers; hiding in the closet, the lace of hems of church dresses
tickling her nose; Daddy limp on the floor, rope burns purpling his neck;
the sound of sirens and her momma's tears; the anger and guilt she felt
standing over his grave because he'd taken the easy road out, because he'd
left them all alone.

She needn't be that Reba. All it took was a story, and her family was as
perfect as her momma pretended them to be. Daddy was a Vietnam hero,
not the haunted man who put on a smile like a colorful tie until the knot
started to choke.

She never understood why her momma made up so many excuses for him. If she'd acknowledged his illness to her daughters, maybe they could've helped him, saved him from hurting himself. Maybe the three of them could've loved him enough to make him well. But whenever Reba tried to place blame, she remembered when Daddy's voice growled through the walls, her momma's soft cries, shattered glasses, and the smell of pecan pancakes in the morning. Momma always made pecan pancakes the morning after one of Daddy's bad nights. They covered up the stink of bourbon in the floorboards. Cloyingly sweet, she and Deedee would eat heaping piles, eager to please, as if they were their last meals. Momma pretended for the same reasons Reba did—it felt nice to believe the lies. The only thing Reba knew for certain was Momma loved Daddy, and love could make a person turn a blind eye to just about anything. It terrified Reba to be so handicapped.

As she grew older, the desire to flee her reality grew. Sometimes in airports or train stations or any other transient place where she'd never see the people again, Reba professed to be someone else entirely, and what frightened her most was that for those moments, she believed her own deceptions.

Once, on the train from Richmond to Washington, D.C., she struck up a conversation with the businessman beside her, introducing herself as an Olympic speed skater meeting her teammates in the capital. The businessman paid for her lunch—his pleasure to dine with an athlete of such caliber. When they parted, a sudden wave of guilt made Reba sick to her stomach. She threw up the New York strip steak in the restroom and prayed to God she wasn't certifiable—multiple personality, psychotic, or manic like her daddy.

Moving west was her solution, a clean slate. She could be anybody she wanted. She could be herself. But then, she wasn't quite sure who that was. Her first encounter with Riki had been out of character, another attempt to act the part: the brazen reporter who jumped in bed after a handful of dates and said she believed in love at first sight. In truth, she only wanted to believe. She'd hoped declaring love aloud might be the all-inclusive cure to her heartache. When it wasn't, she began to wonder if love was enough.

This was why she didn't wear the engagement ring. If she married Riki, she had two choices: become the lies forever or expose her true self and risk losing him. She wished he could simply know her without her having to explain her past. Before she could marry anybody, she had to decipher where the truth ended and her lies began.

Headlights spun round the kitchen and a minute later, the front door opened.

"Reba?" Riki called.

"I'm in here."

He came in and turned on the light. "Why are you sitting in the dark?"

The brightness burned Reba's corneas. "I wasn't in the dark. The stove light's on."

"Practically the dark." He pulled change and gum wrappers from his pocket and dumped them in the empty fruit bowl on the table. "Don't turn into a vampire on me." He kissed the top of her head, took off his border patrol jacket, and sat.

"Long day?" She knew the answer by the hollows beneath his eyes.

"We picked up a family living out of their four-door in a Walmart parking lot. Pretty sad. Processing them back to Mexico tomorrow. The youngest is an infant. He'd been sitting in dirty diapers for God knows how long." He scratched his cheek. "It gets under your skin. The father's just trying to give his family a better place—better life."

The daily barrage of illegal immigration stories had long ago callused Reba's compassion. While usually Riki was on the US side, lately he seemed to be championing the Mexican nationals more and more. She couldn't keep up with whom he wanted her to empathize, so she slouched on the higher fence of principle.

"Don't make yourself the bad guy," she said. "Like you always tell me, there are rules we have to follow. Otherwise, there are consequences." She swallowed a milk-mushy crumb that came loose from her molar. "You get dinner?" she asked, a change of subject. "I stopped off at Rudy's after my interview and have some leftovers if you're hungry."

"How'd that go?"

"Rudy's?" She didn't want to talk about the interview. "You know I love their smoked turkey." She got up and went to the refrigerator.

"No, the profile you're writing, Miss Sun City."

"It was fine. I have to go back though. You sure you don't want some?" She pulled the paper take-out bag from the shelf.

"I ate. You have to go back? Why? She blew you off in person, too?"

Reba shrugged. "I'll get what I want for the story. But right now, what I really want is . . ." She grabbed his hand and slid it around her waist. "To stop talking. I've been talk-talk-talking all day." She knew how to change the subject for good.

He got up and pulled her close. "Whatever you say, boss."

She breathed easy and led him upstairs. This was one thing that was always real, and she prayed Riki felt the whole truth in it.

five

*I*t had begun to snow. Thousands of iridescent spindles careened blindly down to earth. Elsie leaned back and let the spongy flakes pile on her face. The chill cleared her mind, and though she shivered, she remained in the alley's silence, watching the world transform into a fairy-tale masquerade. The dirty streets were powdered white. The dark trees, trimmed neatly in crystal. Parked cars were already being transfigured to mounds of sugar. She loved new snow. It changed everything.

The wind swept under her dress, numbed her legs, and shot goose bumps up her back. She hugged her arms to her breast. Josef's ring on her hand was ice cold. She pulled it off and rubbed the metal warm between her palms. It was a beautiful ring from a good man, but she felt little for a moment so big. She turned it round and round, rubies and diamonds, red and white. Why couldn't it simply be another Christmas present? Like the dress and champagne.

She began to put it back on her finger when she noticed something, a scratch? No, too precise and even. She turned the ring toward the window light. Worn to near nothing, an inscription: *Ani ledodi ve Dodi Li.* Hebrew.

A wave of heat flushed through her body, and her chest tightened under a varnish of flash-frozen sweat. She knew the Gestapo confiscated all

Jewish valuables, but she never considered what became of them. Like their owners, they simply vanished.

The snow picked up. The flakes were no longer light but beaded with icy hearts that pricked the skin. The wind stung her eyes. She blinked away the tears so she could clearly see the ring. It was someone else's wedding band, and she wondered if that unknown finger missed its weight.

Elsie steadied herself against a blanket-covered crate under the balcony and breathed the frosty air until her heart slowed its pounding.

"What are you doing out here?" Kremer pushed through the back entrance doors.

Elsie slid the ring on. "The heat inside—I guess I'm not very good with champagne. I'm fine now." She reached for the doorknob, but he stopped her.

"Look at you—you're shaking. How long have you been out here?" He rubbed her arm with rough fingers.

"I should go in," said Elsie.

"You need somebody to warm you up." Before she could pull away, Kremer yanked her into his coat. His breath reeked of red wine and sausage.

"Major Kremer, please." Elsie tried to free her arms, but her limbs were heavy and cold.

"You smell like a baker's daughter." He leaned in. "Do you taste like a baker's daughter?" He kissed her neck.

"Let go! Stop!" she yelled.

Kremer put a hand over her mouth. "Hush!" he commanded. "If you make another noise," he growled into her ear, then unbuttoned the holster of his gun. "Officers have been commended for shooting female spies in the act of seduction." Holding her tight with one hand, he quickly pushed her skirt up and slipped his other up her thigh.

"Disgusting pig! How dare you!" She kicked hard and pulled away. "I am not a spy!" She spit in his face.

He slapped her, spinning her around. "Such a pretty fräulein and with so much spirit." He thrust her forward against the crate, pinning both her arms overhead. "I don't want to hurt you." He fumbled with his belt buckle.

"You beast!" Elsie cried. "I'm going to tell Josef!"

Kremer smiled. "Do you think he'd still want you—after he finds out that you seduced me?" He pushed up her chiffon and undid his trousers. "And on such a holy night as this?"

"Please," Elsie panicked. "I've never . . ."

His thighs were hot and coarse; the friction of his stiff uniform against the beaded gown broke her skin beneath in small puncture wounds.

"Whose story do you think they'll believe, eh? An immoral concubine or an officer of the Third Reich."

"God, please!" she cried.

Kremer wrenched her arms tight and anchored his feet.

Suddenly, a high-pitched scream, a single note, cracked the air like a siren. And to her shock, Kremer let go. She fell to the ground. Delicate crystals dotted his muddy footprints.

The banshee's cry continued.

Kremer took out his gun and did up his pants. He aimed left and right before homing in on the source. The wooden crate behind them. He yanked off the covering.

The Jewish boy sat inside with a blanket draped over his head like a Nativity figurine. Sound emanated from the hooded face.

"Quiet!" Kremer ordered and cracked the metal butt of his gun against the wooden slats.

The boy's note did not waver.

"Jewish demon!" He cocked the pistol.

Elsie crawled to the banquet doors and met Josef's boots coming out.

"Elsie!" He lifted her to her feet. "What is going on?"

Kremer stood with outstretched arm; the polished barrel pointed at the boy's head.

Elsie buried her face in Josef's stiff shoulder.

"Günther, put the gun down!" Josef boomed.

The boy hushed.

"He's a Jew. Why waste time driving him back to the camp?" Kremer's finger moved for the trigger.

Josef slapped the gun from his hand, and the bullet zipped through the dark snowfall. "You do not have authority," roared Josef.

It was the first time Elsie had seen him angry. Her body trembled at his ferocity.

Josef picked up the gun from the powdered street and emptied the chamber. Bullets dropped soundlessly into the snowbank. He placed the barrel against Kremer's forehead. Neither spoke.

The wet chiffon grew stiff around Elsie's body, a gossamer cocoon of ice. She tasted iron. A finger to her mouth returned crimson. The inside of her lip was split, and she sucked the warm blood to make it stop.

The blanket over the boy fell away, exposing a pale skull and tear-streaked cheeks. His chin quivered and reminded Elsie of the only time she'd seen her nephew Julius. After he was born, they visited Hazel in Steinhöring. Julius cried for milk from the bassinette. So small and fragile; his tears seemed too large in comparison. The Jewish boy looked the same. Elsie wanted to reach out to hold him and rock them both.

"Josef. My friend," said Kremer.

Josef pressed the metal against his skin. "'And then she will call all those before her judgment seat, who today, in possession of power, trample *justice* and *law* underfoot . . .'" He pushed the gun harder and spoke steadily, a man entranced. "'Who have led our people into misery and ruin and amid the misfortune of the fatherland have valued their *own* ego above the life of the community.'" He pulled back. The barrel left a circular indent on Kremer's forehead.

Josef composed himself. "It would do you good to understand our purpose." He handed the empty gun back to Kremer, cleared his throat, and readjusted the cuffs of his uniform jacket so they aligned perfectly. "They are serving dessert." He took Elsie's arm and opened the door; the strains of festive violin spilled out to the alley. "Come, Günther."

Kremer obeyed and followed behind.

The boy in the cage was silent. Elsie wanted to look over her shoulder one last time but kept her eyes forward for fear of being turned to a pillar of salt.

six

ELSIE'S GERMAN BAKERY
2032 TRAWOOD DRIVE
EL PASO, TEXAS

NOVEMBER 10, 2007

A Friday wedding kept the bakery busy the rest of the week so Reba came back Saturday, determined to get her quotes and, perhaps, a few more lebkuchen.

When the bell over the door jingled, Jane turned from the shelf of hot loaves and rolls. "Well, lookie here. Good to see you." She came round the register and hugged Reba.

Shocked stiff at first, Reba quickly relaxed in her embrace. The scent of Jane's perfume—honeysuckle and sandalwood—reminded her of childhood summers at the beach. She and Deedee spent whole days snacking on sweet flower stems and building driftwood castles on the dunes.

"You too," she said and rocked back on her heels, eager to shake off the nostalgic ache.

She hadn't returned any of Deedee's calls since Riki's proposal. Each time Deedee rang, Reba convinced herself the timing wasn't right; she was too busy to chat; she'd call back later, then didn't. The weeks added up, and soon so much had happened that it seemed a daunting task to talk at all—too much to cover in a single conversation. I'll e-mail Deedee tomorrow, she promised herself.

"You've been busy?" she asked Jane.

"Yep, a little gal we've known since she was in diapers hitched up with a feller in Cruces. We do wonderful wedding cakes." Jane winked. "Give us the date of yours and we'll have it ready."

"It'd be stale by the time I got around to it," said Reba.

"We'll double the fondant. Locks it up airtight. The inside keeps light as a feather. Honestly. One of our brides kept a piece in her refrigerator—not even the freezer—until her third anniversary and said it tasted as good as the day she married! And that's no bull."

A laugh popped up Reba's throat, and she liked the sound of it. "I bet they had wicked stomachaches that night."

"Maybe so, but they sure as heck didn't go to sleep empty." Jane turned to the kitchen. "Mom! Reba from *Sun City* is here for the interview."

A Mexican man sat at a café table with a gooey chocolate twist and a cream coffee.

"This is Sergio," introduced Jane. "He's a regular."

Sergio nodded.

"You need any more sugar, suga'?" she asked.

"I got all the sweetness I can handle." His heavy Spanish accent made the sentence musical.

Reba felt a sudden undercurrent in the room like when she rubbed her socked feet along the carpets in the winter. "How long has he been coming?" she asked Jane and took a seat.

"Hmm—how long have you been eating my rolls, Serg?"

"Since you started counting your mama's nickels and dimes." He dipped his pastry in the coffee.

Jane laughed. "That was a test, and he did a good job slipping the noose."

Reba's muscles tensed slightly at the idiom.

"Since I was nineteen," Jane continued. "I remember the first time he walked in—didn't speak a lick of English, never mind German. He pointed at a roll and handed me change, half of which was in pesos." She slapped her thigh.

"That's a long time. I've never known anybody outside my family that long," Reba said.

"Time sneaks up on you. You're still young, you'll see." Her gaze drifted to Sergio, then quickly back to Reba. "Mom will be out in a minute."

On Jane's way to the kitchen, she stopped to hand him a napkin. Though he hadn't asked for one, he took it with a smile and wiped melted chocolate from his lips.

Reba set the table. Steno pad, pen, recorder. While she waited, she tried to imagine the young girl from the photograph over sixty years later.

Then, through the door frame came Elsie. Her snowy hair was bobbed short, the sides pinned back with brown bobby pins. She was cozy plump through the hips but narrow in the waist and wore a contemporary pair of khaki pants with a cream blouse rolled up at the sleeves. Even at seventy-nine, she was stylish and determined in her gait. She carried a plate with two slices of cinnamon raisin bread and set it in the middle of the table.

"Hallo." She stuck out her hand. "I am Elsie Meriwether."

Reba shook. "Reba Adams."

Elsie's grip was firm but warm. "Nice to meet you. I apologize for not being able to speak the last time you visited." She spoke clearly despite the German clip.

Elsie sat and nudged the plate closer to Reba. "Jane says you do not eat milk, so I made this without. It is good."

Reba didn't want to start the interview on the wrong foot. "Thank you." She picked up a slice and ate. "Yes," she mumbled. "It's very tasty." And she wasn't lying.

"Gut," said Elsie. She broke off a piece and popped it in her mouth. "So you would like to talk to me about being old."

Reba swallowed too fast and choked a little. "No, no. I'm doing a Christmas story." She composed herself. "A cultural profile on holiday celebrations around town."

"Germans celebrate like everyone else. Christmas Eve we eat and drink. Christmas Day we do it again. I think this is how the Mexicans and Americans do as well, correct?" Elsie arched her eyebrow at Reba, challenging her.

Reba tapped her pen on the steno. It wasn't exactly a quotable statement. At least not for the angle she wanted. "Do you mind if I turn this on?" she asked and thumbed the recorder button.

Elsie shrugged. "As long as you promise not to put it on the Internet. I'm not so old that I have not seen the horse manure they put there. Nothing but naked bosoms and foul language. I was looking for sticky buns, and you would not believe what came onto my computer screen."

Reba coughed.

"In all my years, I have *never* seen such a thing."

"Mom," said Jane from behind the register. "Reba doesn't want to hear about that."

"I won't mention what happened when I tried to find a chocolate jelly-roll recipe."

Reba turned her face to the steno pad to hide her smile.

"Mom!"

"I'm just telling Missus Adams, I don't want anything to do with such things."

Reba cleared her throat. "I promise. No Internet. And, please, call me Reba."

Reba pushed the button on the recorder. It was time to get answers. "So you're from Garmisch, Germany, correct? Jane talked to me a little about that photograph over there." Reba pointed across the room. "The one of you on Christmas Eve."

Elsie broke off a raisin-laden corner of the bread. "That old thing. I'm surprised the sun has not faded it to nothing. Probably best if so. That was a lifetime ago. I left Germany soon after."

"Did you ever go back?" asked Reba. "Didn't you miss home?"

Elsie met her gaze and held it. "People often miss things that don't exist—miss things that *were* but are not anymore. So there or here, I'd still miss home because my home is gone."

"Do you consider the United States your new home?"

"Doch! Texas is where I am, where my daughter is and my husband is buried, but it is not home. I won't find home again—not on this earth. That is the truth."

Reba inhaled deep and licked her lips. She needed a new approach. This was not coming easily. "Could you tell me about a typical Christmas in Germany?" She decided to be direct, cut and dry, get the information.

"I could not." Elsie popped another piece and chewed. "I grew up during the wars, so there were never typical Christmases."

"Okay." Reba drew a circle on her pad—a bull's-eye she needed to hit. "How about that Christmas." She nodded to the photo. "Can you just tell me about that one?"

Elsie's gaze moved past Reba to the wall and the photograph hanging slightly askew on its nail.

seven

*B*ack at the banquet table, Elsie trembled beside Josef.

"Here, eat something hot. It will help," he offered.

Though they served her favorite cinnamon *reisbrei,* she could barely swallow the steamy spoonfuls. They burned her tongue tasteless and left her chest stone cold.

Josef didn't ask her about Kremer in the alley, and she was glad. She couldn't have spoken of it, even though she wanted to—wanted to stand, point her finger, and scream out his offense. But he was an admired Gestapo officer, and she, a baker's daughter. With Hazel in the Lebensborn Program and her family's resources dependent on Nazi patronage, she had responsibilities beyond her honor. Her silence protected them all. For now.

The waiters cleared the dessert plates. The musicians played a jazzy number, and couples rose from their seats to take the dance floor.

"Please, I'd like to go home," Elsie whispered. She collected her gloves from the back of her chair and slid them over her newly ringed finger. The diamond and rubies bulged the once perfect silhouette.

Josef pulled her chin gently toward him and inspected her face. She averted her eyes. He took her hand and kissed her knuckles. "Of course, Fräulein Schmidt."

Minutes later, he escorted her out of the banquet hall, down the silver corridor, and into the black car, humming warm and waiting. A short drive across town and they parked outside the bäckerei. A light flickered in the upper window. Mutti waiting up, no doubt.

Elsie and Josef hadn't spoken since leaving the table. Made paranoid by Kremer's slander and still in shock, she worried Josef might be angry with her or blame her for the disgraceful incident with his colleague. She played with the buttons on her gloves, loose on their threads.

"I'm sorry to have made you leave early." It was all she could say without her panic mounting. She had to remain calm. Exhibiting too much emotion might cause him to suspect Kremer's espionage accusations to be true.

"I'm not one for late parties anyhow," Josef said and looked away from her, out the window. "I apologize for what happened. I hope you were not hurt."

Elsie fingered her lip. It had stopped bleeding but had begun to swell. "Nein." She swallowed hard.

Josef exhaled, but his attention remained fixed in the opposite direction. "Kremer is a good officer. He had too much to drink tonight. Unacceptable behavior." He cleared his throat. "His marriage is one of convenience, not love. So sometimes he goes searching for it in places he oughtn't."

Elsie nodded, her body rigid as a nutcracker soldier.

He drew in a long breath before facing her. "You never gave me an answer, Elsie."

Then it was she who looked away, to the bakery front door; she wished she were already safe inside with the yeast rolls sleepily rising. She had to tell him how she felt. She wasn't Mutti. It wasn't enough for her to simply be a good wife, and she bristled at the thought of Kremer's "marriage of convenience." She wanted much more. She wanted the effervescence she felt when Myrna Loy asked William Powell to marry her in *Libeled Lady*. "To the moon," Powell had said right before he kissed Loy. That's what Elsie wanted—the moon.

Emptied, the snow clouds hung low, shrouding Zugspitze Mountain and the stars above and ensconcing the valley in a globe of endless winter.

"I—" She forced herself to meet Josef's gaze. "I can't," she began, but Josef interrupted.

"I understand. Your first Nazi party, Christmas Eve, an engagement proposal and . . ." He stroked his thumb over her hand. "So much in one night."

His hand was warm against hers, and she wished it were enough to heat her whole body, melt her into liquid sugar. He unlatched the door, and a chill swept through the inner cabin. "I'll come to wish your family a Happy Christmas."

She shivered. He was right; there was enough heartache this evening. On Christmas they all deserved a little peace. She'd make him understand later. She nodded good night and stepped out.

Josef pulled her back. "Elsie?"

She turned slowly, afraid of the question she imagined to follow. Instead, Josef kissed her. Unlike Kremer's wet mouth and sharp teeth at her neck, Josef's lips were soft and precise, like a *springerle* mold on cookie dough. She dared not breathe for fear the imprint would be ruined.

"I'll see you tomorrow."

"Tomorrow," Elsie whispered.

She left the car, worn T-straps slipping on new snow. The door handle was frozen and took a good push and pull before turning. In the dark car window, Josef's shadow watched and waited until she was inside before driving on.

Elsie shut the door. After the sharp click of metal, all was quiet. No violins or Jewish songbird, no gust of wind or screams, nothing but the peaceful cadence of the cuckoo's pendulum. She put down her purse and slipped out of Mutti's shoes, the cold tile floor warmer than her toes.

"Elsie," Mutti's small voice called. "Is that you?"

Elsie wrapped her cloak tight around her body and went to the base of the staircase. At the top, Mutti stood in her nightgown holding a waxy chamberstick. The candle flickered light and shadows down the steps.

"Your papa is asleep, but I couldn't. Was it a nice ball?" she asked, sprightly for the late hour.

Elsie longed to collapse at Mutti's feet and cry herself to hiccupping, but she was no longer a child and the gravity of adulthood weighted her to the spot.

"Did you do as I said? Were you good and proper? Was Josef pleased?" She waited with bated breath for Elsie's response.

"Ja." The lump in Elsie's throat grew harder. She swallowed, but it stuck.

Mutti smiled down at her. "You are lucky, Elsie. Josef is a handsome man."

Elsie nodded. "Please, go back to bed. It's late. You'll catch your death."

"Ja, good night. Happy Christmas, dear."

The light of Mutti's candle grew dim and finally disappeared. Elsie went to the kitchen, lit the stove, and put on a kettle of water. Lebkuchen gingerbread hearts lay on the floured wooden table, their icing hardening into neat curlicues and dots. Papa made five: Max, Luana, Hazel, Elsie, and Julius. Per tradition, he'd rise before them all to hang the hearts on the strongest branches of the Christmas tree.

The kettle steamed. She undid the buttons of her gloves and began to take them off. The ring snagged the satin. She pulled the material free, then examined the hole and loose thread. Not even Mutti could fix that. The ring glinted in the light of the stove's flame. She took it off and searched the underbelly for the Hebrew letters. Though she couldn't see them, she knew they were there. She set the ring on the table and rubbed the tight indention on her finger. She'd think about that tomorrow. The night was already too long. Her head throbbed, her eyes burned; all she wanted was something hot to drink and the eiderdown of her bed.

In the dark, the kettle steam rose like an angry ghost. Elsie took it off the heat and picked chamomile from Mutti's collection of hanging herbs. A frigid gust swept under her. The back door was chained but left open. A carp, no bigger than her outstretched hand, lay in a tub of ice beside it. Families traditionally kept their carp outside on Christmas Eve. Some said it was for the blessing of Saint Nikolaus; others claimed it was to flavor the fish with Alpine air. In the last few years, the practice had ceased. People were desperate. A scrap of bacon fat left out for a dog was snatched by hungry hands. Elsie guessed Papa had bargained a great deal of their bread on the black market to acquire this small fish. Mutti's attempt to keep tradition by leaving the door ajar seemed a frivolous relic of happier times, but Elsie couldn't reproach Mutti for something she did in her own ways every day. Burning pine lingered in the night air. She inhaled deeply.

Needle-thin icicles had formed on the metal links of the door chain. She broke them off and tossed the blades out onto the backstreet. Just as they darted the snow, something shifted in the dark. Elsie stopped. Her breath caught.

"Who's there?"

The snow fell. The wind crackled the stiff trees.

It was the snow playing tricks on her, she decided. She hadn't eaten much that night and had her first champagne; it was a wonder she didn't see purple polar bears. She touched the back of her hand to her cheek. Without having drunk the chamomile, she was hot—feverish. Straight to bed, that's what she'd do.

"Please." A thin, pale face appeared at the bottom of the door.

Elsie jumped, knocking the chamomile buds to the floor.

"Please," it said again and reached a hand through. "Help me."

Elsie scrambled away, crunching on dried blooms underfoot. "Go on," she hissed. "You—you ghost. Get out of here." She lifted the simmering kettle.

The hand retracted. "I followed your car."

"What?" Elsie's heart beat fast. Her arm, raised high, trembled with the weight of the water.

"They're going to kill me." He leaned into the crack and turned his eyes up to her.

And then she recognized him, the singing boy, the Jew. "What are you doing here?"

"He broke the cage open, so I ran," he said.

"You ran away?" She set the kettle down. "Oh, God." She rubbed the growing ache in her temples. "If they find you here, they'll arrest us all. Go on!" She shooed him from the door. "Get out of here!"

"I helped you. Please, help me." He stayed pressed against the frame. His breath came in short spurts; his skin was tinged blue from the frost.

He was just a boy, nearly the same age as Julius and as dangerous and evil as any—Jew or German. He'd die out there, by nature's will or man's force. She could save him, if she unlocked the chain.

The wind blew across his face. Fat snowflakes stuck to his eyelashes.

She thought of Kremer's allegations. Obviously people were talking about her and her family. If the boy stayed, died on their doorstep, the Gestapo would surely think she had a role in his escape. She closed her eyes. Her head pounded. He was only a child. Nothing of importance or threat. She could turn him out tomorrow; take him to the wooded Eckbauer trail and let him loose like Hansel and Gretel. What did it matter? One boy. One Jew. She wished he would simply vanish.

Outside, voices carried down the quiet street, ice crunched, dogs yipped. They were coming. Elsie moved forward, undid the chain, and pulled the icy child into the kitchen. She closed the door behind. He was smaller than he looked on the Nazi stage, his wrists as thick as petite almond rounds, his fingers like vanilla beans.

"Quickly," she said. "You've got to hide."

The voices became shouts. The dogs barked.

Elsie searched the kitchen. There was no secret place here. The only one she had was upstairs, the crawl space in her bedroom wall, but they'd never reach it in time. There was but one option. Elsie opened the oven, still warm from the day's baking. She lifted the boy, his whole body as heavy as a double batch of pretzel dough.

"You'll be safe," she told him.

His bony fingers gripped her arms.

A light flashed through the narrow kitchen window. They had to hurry.

She locked eyes with him. "Like you said, you helped me earlier, so trust me now."

He let go and scooted deeper into the sooty, brick mouth.

"Here." Elsie took off her wool cape. "Cover yourself."

He took the cape and did as she commanded.

Elsie closed the oven with clammy hands. Sweat beaded on her upper lip. The cuckoo clock sang out midnight as two wooden figures emerged from their doors, danced round and return. A steady beam shone through the front windows, followed by a bang on the door. It was Christmas Day.

eight

"*That*," said Elsie, "was a crappy Christmas."

Reba tapped her pen. "How come?"

"Miserably cold. I got sick. Probably pneumonia, but who could say. There was no legitimate medicine available. We were at war. People were dying—that raisin bread is good." She finished her slice, cinnamon crumbs sprinkled her blouse. "I will put it on our menu." She turned to the kitchen. "Jane, make more of that bread. Reba's Bread, we call it." She turned back. "You like, ja?"

Reba nodded quickly and continued, determined to keep Elsie on track. "But in the photo, you're all dressed up. Where were you going?"

Elsie picked at a raisin skin from between her teeth.

Reba listened to the tape gears churn.

"A Nazi party," Elsie finally replied.

Reba's hand lifted off the page. This was more interesting than expected. She tried to keep a neutral tone. "Were you a Nazi?"

"I was German," replied Elsie.

"So you supported the Nazis?"

"I was German," Elsie repeated. "Being a Nazi is a political position, not an ethnicity. I am not a Nazi because I am German."

"But you were going to a Nazi party?"

"I was invited to a Weihnachten—a Christmas Eve party by an officer. So I went."

Reba nodded and gave her best pensive look.

The oven buzzer went off. Jane went back to the kitchen.

"It's no different than here," Elsie went on. "You can love and support your sons, brothers, husbands, fathers—your soldiers—without supporting the political agenda behind war. I see it each day at Fort Bliss." She leaned back in the chair.

Reba cleared her throat. "You can hardly compare the Nazi regime to Americans in Iraq. It's totally different."

Elsie's stare didn't flicker. "Do we know *everything* that's going on over there? No. This was the same then. We knew things were not right, but we were afraid to change what we knew and even more afraid to find out what we did not. It was our home, our men, our Germany. We supported the nation. Of course, now, it is easy for outsiders to look back and make judgments." She lifted her hands. "So, yes, I went to a Nazi party with a Nazi officer. They weren't all monsters. Not everyone was Hitler or Dr. Mengele. Some were plain men—some even good men." She sighed. "We were trying to live. That was hard enough."

"Did you ever witness any—any Jewish abuse or violence?" Reba stumbled over her words. How did you phrase a question like that?

Elsie narrowed her eyes. "Yes and no. What is the difference? You would never know the truth. If I say no, does that make me a good person? Innocent of everything you understand about the Holocaust and Nazi Germany? But what if I say yes? Does that make me bad—does it spoil my whole life?" She shrugged, brushed a crumb off the table to the floor. "We all tell little lies about ourselves, our pasts, our presents. We think some of them are minuscule, unimportant, and others, large and incriminating. But they are the same. Only God has enough of the story to judge our souls." Her olive eyes penetrated. "So I've told you one of my secrets. It's your turn now."

Reba's heart sped up. "My turn?" She gave a nervous laugh. "No, no. I'm interviewing you."

"That doesn't seem fair." Elsie crossed her arms. "I won't say another word for your tape recorder if you don't answer my questions."

Reba weighed her options. She'd never had an interviewee who didn't get the traditional process. Journalists questioned; interviewees answered. Done. There was no role reversal. However, her deadline was fast approaching. No time to play hard to get.

"Okay. What do you want to know?" she relented.

"Jane says you are engaged. What is your fiancé's name?"

Reba sighed. "Riki."

"Is he a good man?"

"As good as they come."

"What does he do for work—his occupation?"

"He's a US Border Patrol agent."

"Border Patrol!" Elsie laughed. "Then he is a busy man here."

Sergio finished the last of his coffee. "Have a good day, ladies." He handed his empty plate and cup to Jane behind the till, and it seemed their hands lingered a moment past casual.

"See you mañana," said Jane.

On his way out, he rubbed his belly affectionately. "Your crullers might put me in my grave, Missus Meriwether."

"This you have been saying for years," replied Elsie.

Jane laughed. "At least you'll go down with a smile and a belly full of sugar!"

He nodded to her as if tipping an imaginary hat. The door chimed behind him.

"He seems like a good customer," said Reba.

"As good as they come," she countered. "So please explain. Why have you not set a wedding date with this Riki?"

Reba turned to Jane and scowled.

Jane shrugged. "Sorry, you never said it was a secret."

Reba squared her shoulders. "I'm simply not ready."

"Not ready! Do you love him?" Elsie asked.

The directness caught Reba off guard. She fumbled her pen. "Of course. I wouldn't have said yes if I didn't, right?"

Elsie leaned forward. "Then take advice from me; it is not often fate gives you a good man to love. Fact. All those movies and television shows with people saying, 'I am in love!,' the bachelors and bachelorettes picking people like different kinds of cookies in a jar—pshaw! Nonsense. This is not love. This is nothing but sweat and spit mixed up. Good love . . ." She shook her head. "It does not come often. I hear on the news last night: fifty percent of marriages end in divorce and the newsman says, 'Oh, that is awful. Can you believe it?' and I say, ja, I can, because those people lied to themselves and to each other—all sugar hearts and giggles. The truth is, everyone has a dark side. If you can see and forgive his dark side and he can see and forgive yours, then you have something." She gestured to the necklace dangling in the middle of Reba's chest. "Wear that ring or give it back. This is my advice."

The bakery was empty. It was the quiet hour between the breakfast and lunch crowds.

"Can I interrupt?" Jane came to the table with a bowl of icing. "Mom, taste this. The buttercream's got a funny tang."

Elsie stuck a finger in the frosting and sucked. "Throw it out," she said. "Bad egg whites."

"They looked fine in the bowl." Jane stomped a booted foot. "Damn it, I got an anniversary cake to frost by this afternoon."

"No one is at fault. Sometimes you cannot tell until you try," said Elsie.

nine

*U*pstairs, Mutti and Papa stirred. Elsie brushed the fallen chamomile leaves out of sight under the table. What little was left, she put into a mug and poured hot water over, her hand surprisingly steady. Josef's ring lay on the floured board.

Outside, shouts followed another bang.

"What's going on?" Papa's voice carried down the steps. He turned on the electric light. "I'm coming, I'm coming."

Elsie snatched the ring into her palm just as Mutti pattered into the kitchen. "Elsie, what is it?"

"I don't know. I was having chamomile and then . . ." She turned her back to Mutti, dropped the ring in the teacup, and tried to keep her eyes from the oven.

Four Gestapo entered with guns. Two flanked Papa.

"Search what you want," he said. "We have nothing to hide. It's the middle of the night and Christmas Eve for heaven's sake!"

"My apologies, Herr Schmidt, but we have orders," said a stocky soldier with an oak leaf on either collar.

"What's happened?" asked Mutti. Bare feet against the tiles, she shivered.

"A Jew escaped," replied the man.

"There are no Jews here, Standartenführer," said Papa. He patted the oven. "Only pastries and bread."

A chill ran through Elsie. The hairs on her arms stood on end.

"Where were you?" A trooper motioned to Elsie fully dressed beside her night-capped parents.

"She's come from *your* party," replied Papa. "With Lieutenant Colonel Josef Hub."

"It was an excellent evening until now," she said flatly.

"I'm sorry to disturb you. This shouldn't take long," said the standartenführer. "May we?" He pointed up with his truncheon.

"Yes, of course, go—search what you want," said Papa.

Two went up, their boots clomping the aged floorboards. The other two stayed in the kitchen.

Mutti gave a huff. "I left my girdle out," she whispered.

Elsie rolled her eyes. From Hazel's description of the lace garter belts her SS companions sent her as gifts, she guessed men like these had seen far more prurient novelties.

"I doubt they'll mind your old underwear, Mutti."

"Hush," commanded Papa.

Elsie pushed the teacup away from the ledge and crossed her arms over her chest. Mutti clutched her nightgown under her chin. One of the soldiers cleared his throat and went to search the front.

The remaining guard walked around the kitchen, stopped beside the oven, then turned to Papa. "Your lebkuchen are my favorite. Are you making more?"

"We're closed on Christmas."

The soldier nodded. "But it's warm?" He put a hand to the metal.

Elsie's heart beat like a juggernaut in her chest; her muscles locked tight.

"Doch, brick ovens don't turn to ice overnight." Papa yawned and scratched his neck.

The soldier caught the yawn, took off his cap, and wiped his brow. In the lamplight, Elsie saw how young he was. No more than fifteen.

"Here." Papa went to a tray and uncovered a handful of distorted gingerbread. "Take as many as you want. These are the misshapen ones. Just as tasty."

His hesitation lasted a fraction of a second. "Thank you, Herr Schmidt." He came to Papa's side and stuffed cookies into the front pocket of his uniform. He stopped as soon as his comrades returned.

"Clear," said the standartenführer. "Let's go to the next. Gute nacht."

The soldiers filed out, but the boy-soldier lingered. "Happy Christmas," he said. His eyes twinkled with youth and sleepiness.

"A blessed Christmas to you and your family," said Papa.

He gave an awkward grin, then ran after his unit.

Papa bolted the front door after the men.

"Can you believe it?" Mutti tapped her fingernails on the wooden baker's board. "An escaped Jew! On the eve of our Savior's birth. Unbelievable."

Elsie's head began to pound. The room went topsy-turvy. She took a gulp of the weak tea, lukewarm and slightly bitter. Gold flickered back at her from the bottom. She set it down beside a bowl of *Christstollen* dough, fat and leavened under its cloth. Papa would bake it for breakfast. She had to get her parents upstairs and the child out.

"I left this open." Mutti quietly slipped her hand up the closed back door to the loose chain. "For the carp." She turned to Elsie, head cocked.

"Let's get back to bed," called Papa from the stairs.

Elsie's fingers and toes went numb. "I was cold."

Papa's footsteps thudded up, up, up.

They held each other's gazes for a long moment. Sweat trickled between Elsie's breasts.

"I'm sorry." She tried to make her voice casual.

Mutti rechained the door, cracked it open, then scanned the kitchen. "You are tired," she finally said. An icy breeze fluttered her nightgown, and she hugged her arms across her chest. "Finish your tea and go straight to bed." At the bottom of the staircase, she stopped to look around once more before slowly ascending.

It was only then that Elsie's hands began to shake. She poured the tea out and collected the ring. Not knowing where else to put it, she slid it back on her finger. The house quieted, and she wished it could stay that way, wished there was nothing inside the oven but coals and ash. She wanted to crawl under her eiderdown and pretend this night was all a terrible nightmare.

An old woman, haggard and white, reflected in the small kitchen window. Elsie looked over her shoulder. The woman did too. And then she recognized herself, sighed, and ran a hand through her hair. What was she doing? She should put the boy out in the snow. The Gestapo would find him soon, and he'd go back to where he belonged. Elsie cringed imagining him in a work camp, so thin and frail; but if they found him in the bakery, her family could lose everything. Her head whirled, and she grasped the oven latch to keep from falling. She regretted her earlier actions. She should have shut the door and been done with the Jew. But she hadn't. So what now?

Carefully, she opened the oven. Blackness, then a pale face emerged like the moon from behind a cumulous cloud.

"What's your name?" she asked.

"Tobias," he whispered.

"Come." She extended her arms.

ten

*S*econd Lieutenant Josef Hub stood on the doorstep with a holstered gun and a heavy sledgehammer. The three comrades in his charge eagerly awaited his command to carry out Gestapo orders; but the twenty-three-year-old lieutenant paused, unsure of himself and the power of his hand against this door. The yellow star gave no counsel. To use the brass knocker, stained and marred by the painted "u" of Juden, seemed inappropriate for the occasion.

"Should we break the windows first?" asked Peter Abend, a nineteen-year-old graduate of the Hitler Youth. The ranks were full of soldiers like Peter, boys just out of lederhosen shorts who converged in the cities from the German countryside, determined to demonstrate absolute devotion to the Reich. Naive stories of war glories filled their heads; rifles, their hands; and their lives were suddenly imprinted with a new purpose that transcended hayseeds and pig corrals. None of them had studied at the university. All were students of one school of thinking and one course of action.

"Nein," said Josef. He pounded the sledgehammer on the door. "Open!"
Nothing.
"Open or we must come by force."
Silence.

It was time. His orders were clear. He wore the uniform, trained in the ranks, fell in line and step at the grand parade for Führer Hitler. It was time to act the part, despite all reservations and all personal convictions. "The individual should finally come to realize that his own ego is of no importance in comparison with the existence of the nation." Those were Hitler's words. The unity of the nation. Pure Germany.

He reluctantly blew his whistle, and the three young *sturmabteilung* charged the familiar door. The oak held at first but then cracked and split the frame. A woman yelped inside.

"We are here by order of the Third Reich for Herr Hochschild," said Josef.

The family huddled in the dark hallway. Frau Hochschild stood strong at her husband's side, four children behind them. The three girls cried "Papa," and the youngest, a four-year-old boy, valiantly held his father's hand.

Herr Hochschild stepped forward. "I have committed no crime."

"You are a Jew. Your very nature is offensive," said Peter.

"Quiet," said Josef.

Peter hushed, but he cocked his gun audibly. The two soldiers at his side followed suit.

Josef moved in front of their barrels. "Herr Hochschild, please come with us and there will be no harm to your family. On my word."

He could carry out these orders without barbaric measures. He was an officer of the Third Reich and had read *Mein Kampf*. He understood that one could influence the individual and group by way of rhetoric more than any other force on the planet. These soldier-boys at his command knew nothing but target practice and military games.

"Make this easy on your children, Herr. Come," He gestured to the doorway.

Herr Hochschild stepped closer, out of the shadows. "Josef?" he asked. "Is that you?"

Josef angled his head so that the lip of his cap darkened his brow.

"It is. Josef, you know me."

And he did. Herr Hochschild had been his literature professor. He had taught courses at the University of Munich where Josef had studied for a semester. That was before the Jewish professors were dismissed, and the SS had recruited him.

Those years ago, he'd come to this very home for supper and been welcomed by Frau Hochschild, an almond-eyed, cheerful woman who said she always wore emeralds to complement her dark hair. She wore none now. All Jewish jewelry had been impounded to finance the New Order. Though some, he knew, bobbed on the ears of his commanders' wives.

The girls had been young the last he saw them; babies cared for by a stern Austrian nurse who disapproved of children eating sweets. Josef had learned that quickly when he presented sacks of rainbow gummi bears to the rambunctious brood, and she promptly seized them. Huddled in the hallway, they stared at him now with hollow cheeks.

The house had been different then too, effulgently lit by electric lamps that made the wallpaper flowers seem to grow right off the boards. It had reminded him of his mother's herb garden in summer. Now, the paper blooms were torn and singed around electric wires. The hallway smelled of mold and smoke. This had been a joyful place, and he couldn't help but wince at the familiarity of Herr Hochschild's voice. The same voice that discussed Goethe and Brecht with him and read Novalis and Karl May over plummy wine by the fire. For a moment, he wished he could close his eyes and return the world to that simpler time.

"I can't leave my family," Hochschild pleaded. He reached out to Josef.

"Don't come any closer," Peter warned.

"You must do as I say," said Josef.

"Please, don't do this," begged Frau Hochschild.

"We have orders."

The two men came to either side of Hochschild, their guns aimed at his back.

"We were your friends!" cried Frau Hochschild. "You—you traitor!" She raced forward to slap Josef.

Peter fired. So close, the bullet cracked Frau Hochschild's sternum and thrust her back into her children's arms. Her final gaze met Josef's.

"A curse on you!" Herr Hochschild yelled to them. He extended a hand to his wife's cheek but was forced to the ground before reaching it. His children's faces froze in mute screams as the soldiers dragged him from the house.

When they had gone, Josef turned to Peter, took a deep breath, exhaled, then smashed the sledgehammer down on his hand. The gun skittered across the wood floor. Peter fell to his knees clasping splintered bones that poked through the flesh of his palm. Josef grabbed him by the throat.

"They're . . . just . . . Jews," wheezed Peter.

Josef squeezed harder, his leather gloves groaned against the strain. Before the two sturmabteilung returned to stop him, Peter was dead. The children watched it all, covered in their mother's blood, silent to the sound of shattering glass, shouts, and gunshots in the street.

Josef let go. His fingers trembled and ached.

"Traitor." The boy whispered his mother's last word.

Josef stepped over Peter's broken body, swallowing the impulse to vomit as he left. The frosty November night helped to ease his nausea. Inside the police wagon, Herr Hochschild wailed.

"What about the children?" asked one of the troopers.

"Leave them," said Josef.

"Where's Peter?"

"The next house. Go," Josef commanded and handed the young man his sledgehammer. "There can be only one people, one empire, one leader."

eleven

US CUSTOMS AND BORDER PROTECTION
8935 MONTANA AVENUE
EL PASO, TEXAS

NOVEMBER 10, 2007

"I tried to call you on the radio," said Agent Bert Mosley. He picked his teeth with a wooden toothpick.

Riki tossed the remnants of his Taco Cabana breakfast burrito in the trash. "Sorry, must've been off on the way in. What's up?"

"We received a call from a resident. Says she's seen a couple Mexican kids on the trail behind her house. Real young ones. A couple junkers are parked nearby. She thinks the parents have set up camp in them. Lady doesn't speak no Spanish so she wanted somebody to come check. Figured since you were already out," Bert explained. He handed Riki the address.

"I'm not out now, though." Riki took the paper and read. "Westside?"

Bert nodded.

"All right, but you owe me." He picked up his car keys. "Mind sprucing up the detainment room while I'm gone. That fellow from Tolentino looked pretty sick when I handed him to the Chihuahua police."

"Old man had some kind of Mexican plague. Did you see the sores on his arms? He's crazy to think we'd let him walk into our country—infect everybody with Ebola or something."

"It was shingles," said Riki.

"Sorry, I didn't realize I was talking to *Doctor* Chavez," Bert scoffed.

"The point is, he was sick. We should air out the room."

"Call me Martha Stewart. I'll be sure to iron the linens and arrange the tulips."

"Don't be a lazy Anglo," Riki joked to lighten the mood. After working together for three years, their inside jokes and quips could be reduced to a handful of ringing statements.

"Fat and ignorant's my gig. Laziness is all yours. We got to stick to our roles, otherwise—*what* will become of things." Bert laughed. Riki grinned.

On the drive, a Shakira song came on the radio. It reminded Riki of Reba. He always said she looked like a dark-haired version of the singer, especially in the mornings when her hair lay uncombed and wavy on the pillow. He'd just left her that way, messy and beautiful. Sometimes it took all the strength he had not to climb into bed beside her and bury his face in her hair and skin and sleepy smells. But he knew the moment he did, she'd wake and push him away. He couldn't have both the Reba he saw and the Reba who saw him. They were different women, and he supposed he'd rather have one than neither.

He turned off the music and checked the address. The area was vaguely familiar. A new development of Easter-egg-colored homes strung along streets with providential names like Via Del Estrella and Via Del Oro. Behind the large neighborhood was an agriculture canal, and beyond that the river, smudge sodden and rusty as a penny. A concrete jogger's trail whimsically snaked along beside, heat rising from it in clear currents. A realty sign boasted the subdivision as LUXURY LIVING ALONG THE RIO GRANDE! A couple years ago, you couldn't have paid someone to live there. Nothing but scrub grass, dirt, and gopher burrows as far as the eye could see. Now, big windows and manicured yards glistened under the desert sun. Unnatural yet beautiful. He pulled up to the resident's home, a two-story, pink palace with iron balconies lacing the upper levels like a tiered *Quinceañera* birthday cake.

Before he'd had a chance to turn off the truck engine, a petite woman came to the front door in pressed khakis. He got out.

"They've been there for over a week," she immediately began. "My husband said to let them be, and I would have—I really would have—but there are *children* involved, and it's simply unhealthy for them to be living out of a car and bathing in that muddy river like animals! So I told my husband I was calling you guys for their own good—the children that is. They need proper care. Their mother should be ashamed." She ran a hand through her bobbed hair. Diamond-drop earrings shimmered against her neck. "She's out there, too. Every morning, washing dishes—dishes!—in that muck. You'd think if she was going to hop the border like this, then she'd at least try to be more inconspicuous. I mean, seriously. Every day, I look outside and there they are, acting like it's the 1800s." She gestured for Riki to follow her into the house. "Then yesterday, there was a little girl—a toddler—crawling in the dirt with no adult supervision and I said to myself, what if a snake or a coyote came along? I wouldn't be able to live with myself if I had a dead child in my backyard and did nothing to prevent it."

Inside, a miniature schnauzer yipped at Riki's heels. The house smelled like new paint and vanilla candles, like the ones Reba lit when she took long baths.

"Hush it, Teeny." The woman moved the dog away with a foot. "Hope you aren't afraid of dogs."

"No, ma'am."

"I'm Linda Calhoun, by the way." She stuck out her hand.

"Agent Riki Chavez." Her fingers seemed to slip right through his clasp, soft and slick with oils.

"We're from North Carolina. My husband's with Union Pacific—the railroad. We moved here a couple months ago. I'm still getting used to . . . everything." She waved a hand round like she was swatting flies, then led Riki to the back door. "The cars are over there." She pointed to the riverbank but stayed inside her refrigerated air.

Down the Rio, a weathered, four-door Dodge parked off the concrete trail. He couldn't see the second vehicle.

"Are they there now?"

"I guess," said Linda. "I don't know where else they'd be."

"I'll go talk to these folks." He slipped on his cap and went out around the stone fence separating the Calhouns' green turf and the sandy West Texas dirt.

A quarter of a mile down, the new development of adobe homes and green sod abruptly ended with a half acre of horse pasture between it and a scattering of trailers on cinder blocks. Reaching the car, he noticed a second set of thick tire tracks leading up to a trailer with a padlocked front door and plasterboard over the windows. He pulled out his handheld receiver.

"El Paso, do you copy?"

There was a crackle and pitchy squeal. "10-4."

"Bert, I'm at the location," said Riki. He surveyed the trailer once more, then turned to the Dodge before him. Its windows were covered with blankets and dark shirts cinched up by the window glass. The ends stuck out, fluttering in the breeze.

"What's your 10-20?" asked Bert.

"Off Doniphan, on the Rio canal about a mile from the tracks. There's a horse farm and some trailer homes. Underpass behind me."

Riki knelt down to the baked mud and put a finger in the second tire tread. It was deeper than a four door. It had to be a van.

"Hey, Bert, are there geophone sensors in the brush out this way?"

"Should be. Why?"

He followed the tracks up the embankment to the double-wide and scrub brush desert stretching all the way to the horizon. "Just want to make sure we're watching this location. Looks suspicious. Could be a safe house."

"Copy. Need backup?"

"10-23. The trailer appears empty now. If the tip-off says she's seen kids around for a week, then I got a good feeling they were left behind. Just send a tow for the vehicle and do a 10-29. Maybe it's tagged to the smuggler."

The radio squawked and fuzzed.

"10-4. Be careful, Rik. Don't try to be a hero."

"Copy that. No hero."

Riki undid the holster of his gun. Bert was right. He couldn't take any chances. Last month, a patrol agent received third-degree burns and a stint in the critical care unit after an illegal alien threw a balled T-shirt at him, soaked in kerosene and aflame. The immigrant left the agent to burn in the chaparral and ran. He was probably halfway to New York City by now while the agent was undergoing his second round of skin grafts on his arms, chest, and face. His wife put on a brave face in the hospital room when her five-year-old shied away from a man he didn't recognize. Alone later, she wept in the hallway.

Riki knocked on the driver's window, then stood aside from the glass. "Hello? Anybody there?" He tried the handle. Locked. Near the front tire was a doll wrapped in a colorful *rebozo*. Small footprints matted the dust.

Linda Calhoun had described a mother and children. He knocked again. "Señora?" There was soft movement of the window blanket. "I'm not here to make trouble. I want to help. Open up," he said firmly, then again in Spanish.

Slowly, the lock to the door clicked and opened. A tanned Mexican woman stared hard at him, tears ebbing. "Por favor," she begged. "Mis niños." Two small heads peeked out from the backseat.

"Do you have papers? Citizenship or visa?"

"No—no visa."

"You can't stay here if you aren't a US citizen. Where are you from?"

"Para mis niños," she repeated.

"You're an illegal alien. I know you understand that. Are you alone or did you come with a group—a leader?"

She covered her face and sobbed.

He sighed. The woman had probably given every peso she had for a smuggling organization to transport them over the border. Once across, her paid leader had either abandoned them or brought them to this car and told them to wait inside. In either case, she'd most likely been through hell the past couple weeks, living in desert heat and dirt, hunger and fear. And now she was watching her dreams shatter for herself and her children. She'd rather stay in that car and possibly die on American soil than be sent back to her homeland. He'd seen it a hundred times over: desperation justifying the implausible.

"Señora," Riki comforted. "This"—he pointed to the car—"is not a good life for your children. There's a way, and this isn't it." He opened the door wide. "Come on now."

She took his hand in both hers. "No deportación. Por favor, señor."

He gulped down the knot in this throat. It came every time. "I'm sorry, but it's the law, and you're breaking it."

Riki was born in El Paso, an instantaneous American. His father and mother, born less than a mile away in Juárez, Mexico, waited two years for a visa and another seven for citizenship. It was a broken system that only benefited the very wealthy or very patient. His parents had been the latter. He understood this woman's trepidation, but he also understood duty and justice. His family obeyed the laws of their new land, and, like it or not, he thought everyone else should too. Riki believed that the only way to appreciate what life gave was to respect and honor the rules that governed it. Subvert those and you might as well steal from your neighbor and piss on the Bible. Still, the greater law of compassion made him uneasy carting a woman and her children off like criminals.

In the distance, Linda Calhoun watched from her doorway holding her dog. Her diamond earrings sparkled like bonfire licks.

Riki radioed Bert at the station while the woman collected her things.

"I'm bringing in a woman and two kids. Pretty sure they're Mexican nationals. Haven't seen anybody else."

"10-4."

A toddler in shorts and flip-flops sat on his rusted tricycle in the yard of a nearby home. He did not watch them. His eyes were fixed on the padlocked trailer next door.

"Headed back to the station," Riki said and slid the handheld back into his front pocket clip. He kicked a wad of mud from his boot.

The Mexican woman instructed her children to gather their things. The older boy shoved a worn shirt and a pair of jeans into a duffel bag. The girl climbed between the driver and passenger seats and over her mother's lap. She sat by the front tire, clasping her doll to her chest and sucking her thumb. Beautiful black eyes watched Riki, never blinking. He wondered if this is what his daughter would look like, only with Reba's strong nose and fair skin.

The boy on his tricycle turned to them. "Bye!" he called out and waved. "Bye-bye!"

His mother stuck her head out of her open trailer doorway. "¡Vete aquí! Lunch."

Smiling wide, the boy threw his tricycle to the side and obeyed. The woman glowered at Riki before closing the door. All the while, the little girl at his feet hugged her knees and continued to stare up at him. The outline of his CBP baseball cap reflected in her dark gaze.

twelve

SCHMIDT BÄCKEREI
56 LUDWIGSTRASSE
GARMISCH, GERMANY

DECEMBER 25, 1944

Happy Christmas, Hazel. I write to you with cold feet and a mustard rub on my chest. I slept poorly last night. The Gestapo came to our house past midnight searching the town for a runaway Jew. They made Mutti and Papa stand in the kitchen wearing only their nightgowns—on Christmas Eve! What horrible times we live in.

Mutti said I've caught a fever. Perhaps I should have eaten more at the banquet. They had suckling pig, potato cream, white sausage, and reisbrei for dessert, but none of it tasted the way it should. I didn't care for the champagne, either. The bubbles made the food feel wrong in my mouth. Mealy, like it'd already been chewed. My stomach was soured. As for the dress I spoke of in my last letter, chiffon might be lovely to look at, but it's not much good against the cold. It's ruined anyhow. The skirt is stained, and the crystals hang from their stitches.

We tried to enjoy Christmas Day as best we could, but everyone was in poor spirits. Mutti fixed a little carp. Papa made a bit of Christstollen. I ate by the fire until the heat made Oma's wooden bird ornaments take flight. Then I came back to bed. My nose is raw and swollen, my eyes red and cheeks pale as a boiled fish. I look and feel like the plague. Josef came by a few minutes ago. I told Mutti to send him away. I must confess to you. So much has happened--.-.-. Josef gave me an engagement ring. I put it under the mattress for the time being. I haven't decided what to do. Hazel, I don't love him, but he's a better man than any I know. He protects us and is good to Mutti and Papa. They say it's an excellent match for the family. Mutti says you don't need love to be a wife, just a good brötchen recipe and a strong back. But you were in love with Peter, right?

Oh, Hazel, there's so much more I want to tell you, but don't have the strength or courage to write. Are you ever coming home? I miss you. You always knew the right things to do. I wish I were more like you. Please write soon and give my Christmas greetings to Julius. Heil Hitler.

Your loving sister,
Elsie

P.S. Does the Program inspect incoming letters?

LEBENSBORN PROGRAM
STEINHÖRING, GERMANY

DECEMBER 27, 1944

Dear Elsie,

Today, I received your December 21 letter and laughed out loud at the story of Frau Rattelmüller. She's always been odd. But we must remember her history. If my husband and children were burned in a house fire, I would go crazy too. I was only a small child but still recall how she wailed by their graves. They say each coffin held a scoop of ashes. Four whole people reduced to a few scoops, can you imagine? I wish Mutti and Papa hadn't taken me to the funeral. I hate remembering. Sometimes I wish I could erase memories—erase the past.

I'm sorry Julius and I couldn't come home again this year. With the fighting in the Ardennes, the Program banned all women and children from travel. How I miss you, Mutti, and Papa. You're right. It's been too long since we visited. Garmisch is full of old ghosts for me, but I promise to bring Julius for my birthday in the spring if all goes well with the war effort.

As I wrote in my last letter, we honored the winter solstice with a wonderful Julfest banquet yesterday. Many more officers attended than expected, which pleased us greatly! One named Günther asked specifically for me. It caused quite a stir among the girls since he has only been partner to a privileged select. His Aryan ancestry is among the highest in all of Germany. And it showed. His mother hails from the Stern family—of Stern-bier. He was quite interested in our family's bäckerei and asked all kinds of questions. There are many similarities between the fermentation of wheat and that of bread. We had a lovely time. I hope he comes back again.

More good news. I finally received an honorary card! All my fears about the twins were for naught. The Program only gives these cards to the *best* girls, so they must be pleased with the children's development. The girl is quite hearty and fearless. She wailed through the entire SS christening, and when they held the dagger over, she reached for the blade! Everyone says she has a true Viking spirit. The boy is somewhat deficient, but so was I at first.

With my honorary card, I am allowed to pay lower rent and have special shopping privileges. I haven't been able to buy extra dirndl notions—satin ribbon, lace, and pewter buttons—in a year. Everything must go to the greater good of our nation, of course. But I must admit, my toes curl up with excitement knowing I can buy the finest fabric, threads, and hooks should I choose. It's like Christmas all over again.

I saw Julius on Christmas Eve. The children sang "Weihnachtslieder." It was beautiful. I swear I could hear Julius's voice high and pure above the others. I know that's a shamefully maternal notion. Our boys' choir is much better than Vienna's, so they say. We hope to produce some of the best vocalists in the world, but we all admit there's still work to be done. The natural aptitude is present, but the spark is missing. Perhaps Hans Hotter could come and provide lessons.

After the performance, we were given an hour with the children. Father Christmas served thick slices of sugar-dusted <u>Weihnachtsstollen,</u> and the young ones ran around with it stuck to their lips and hands, leaving white fingerprints on our arms and skirts and faces. I haven't felt that dizzy with happiness for months. Julius seems to be doing well. He said he loves his classes and has learned to click his boot heels in true party fashion. He's quite the expert at it and gets a good laugh from the popping sound of leather. Then he strikes up his hand and yells, "Heil Hitler!" I'm amazed at how fast he's become a little soldier.

He asked again about his father. I still don't have the heart to tell him, so I said he's driving a Luftwaffe truck somewhere in Yugoslavia and can't find a postman to deliver letters. He was pleased to hear this news and immediately asked for a toy truck. I offered him another piece of stollen instead, but took none for myself. I'm trying to lose the weight I gained from the twins.

So you attended your first SS party? My little sister, all grown up. I'm sure you loved it. My first Hitler Youth ball with Peter was a dream. By the way, is Josef single? I can't recall if you said he was married or not. I hope not, for your sake. But if he is, do not be disappointed. Perhaps they'll ask you to join the Lebensborn Program. I'd certainly love your company. It can be lonesome here. Sentimental folly, I'm well aware. However, I miss the sound of sleep; the rhythm of someone else's breathing. I guess I spent too many years sharing a room with you.

I don't sleep much these days. I try to imagine Julius across the compound in his tidy bunk bed and the sound of his steady in and out. It helps. I'm confident he will be a better man, a better German, because of my sacrifice. It is not too long before you could be a wife and mother too. You will see.

I think of you often, Elsie, and send my love.

Heil Hitler.

Hazel

thirteen

*R*eba was disappointed with the interview that day. She'd come home and transcribed the recording with the hope that her steno notes had missed some illuminating statement. But there hadn't been one happy word about Germany or the yuletide. Reba hadn't a clue how she'd rig together a feel-good article out of what she had, and her deadline was less than a week away. Her *Sun City* editor had already left two messages on her voice mail.

Reading through the transcription, Reba grumbled. Elsie's comments had been so sporadic, but Reba couldn't blame her entirely. She hadn't been as professional as usual. Talk of weddings, fiancés, and love. Good Lord, what was she thinking? It was the Nazi thing. It threw her for a loop, and she never quite recovered. She'd forgotten all about writing a festive Christmas story; instead, she'd jumped into a World War II crime drama, dreaming of Elsie's secret SS life. Now she reaped the consequences.

She turned the tape recorder on. "You, Reba Adams, are seriously screwed." She clicked it off and flung it into her purse.

Frustrated and tired, she powered off her laptop. A nice, hot bath. That's what she needed. She turned the tap as far to the right as possible, filling the tub up with steaming hot water, then she lit some candles. Something about the smell of matchsticks blown out reminded her of home, of summer campfires in the backyard and s'mores that tasted of a touch of pine.

When Daddy was on a happy high, the world was perfect—a "once upon a time" place that eventually showed itself equally fictitious. Summer had been his favorite season, hers too. She seemed as light as the long day hours, and all her memories dripped with honey and sunshine. On the first chill of fall, when she'd wake to find her momma had put an extra blanket over her bed during the night, she'd shudder and feel her heart go as cold and dormant as the Virginia maples.

"The trees are playing dead," her daddy had once said while carrying her piggyback through the snowy woods behind their house. "Maybe if we tickle them, we could get them to give up the game." With chapped fingers, he'd scratched the bark, put an ear to the trunk, and sighed. "Not a giggle. Quiet as a church."

He never knew the hours Reba later stood outside, tickling the trees and hoping to hear something.

There was maybe one icy night a year in El Paso. Riki joked that the city had three seasons: spring, summer, and hell. It was the hard truth. She preferred that to the alternative. Reba's hell wasn't boiling; it was frozen.

She threw on her hooded college sweatshirt while she waited for the bathtub to fill. On the way home, she'd grabbed a McDonald's salad and still tasted the Ranch dressing in the back of her throat. Wine would help clean her palate. She went downstairs and found an open bottle of chardonnay, poured it, and tried not to notice the stale pungency. It was late and the moon had risen round and full over the Franklin Mountains. She liked drinking in the moonlight. It made wine look magical, even in a tall water tumbler. Riki wasn't home yet, not that that was unusual. But tonight, she felt like talking. She wanted to tell someone about Elsie and the Nazi Christmas party and watch their reaction.

To cut the wine's bite, she searched the cupboard for something sweet. A can of tuna, a box of penne, a half-eaten bag of vinegar potato chips, Raisin Bran with less than two scoops within. There wasn't much. A pastel bag of Whoppers Robin Eggs lingered in the back. She took a handful. She couldn't remember the last time she'd grocery shopped or the last time she'd been compelled to. She and Riki never ate together, and maybe that was part of the problem.

Reba had grown up in a roomy, southern-style kitchen as the heartbeat of her home. It was a safe place away from the wet bar in the den and the darkness of the bedrooms. Over cheese omelets and buttermilk biscuits, her momma welcomed the mornings in robe and slippers. In the afternoons, she drank peppermint tea year-round. It was her momma's domain, a stable comfort, that Reba found herself drawn to despite herself.

Only on his good nights could you find Reba's daddy there. Then, he'd call his girls to the fridge to nibble leftover fried chicken and cold grits before bed. Her momma didn't believe in eating after eight o'clock, and she pretended not to hear their laughter or see the bare bones in the garbage the next morning. Reba thought of her childhood like a coin, two sided and easily flipped: happy Daddy, sad Daddy.

She was nine years old the summer Deedee left for boarding school, and it seemed overnight a shroud had been wrapped around her home. Reba stayed in bed for days, heartsick, and not falling for any of her momma's attempts to paint the situation in Technicolor cheer. Finally, it was a sharp cry one evening that pulled her toward the lamplight of her momma's bathroom. There, Reba found her blotting a bloody nose.

"What happened?"

"Nothing," said her momma. "I ran into the door."

It was well past 11:00 p.m., and her daddy was nowhere to be found.

Momma balled the spotty tissue into her palm and quickly put a fresh one to her face. "Daddy's gone for a walk. I want you to go back to bed and stay there. He's in a mood tonight." When she'd attempted to smile, the tissue hanging out of her nose hid it. All Reba saw were her eyes and the fear.

She'd done as her momma commanded and gone back to her room where she lay in bed cracking her knuckles over and over, waiting to hear the click of the back door. When it finally did open, she held her breath as step by step her daddy moved up the stairs and into his bedroom. After half an hour of quiet, Reba finally allowed herself to sleep, but it was the kind that jumped at every creak and wind whistle.

The next morning, Reba's momma, already wearing day makeup, woke her. "Rise and shine," she'd said. "We're having pecan pancakes and how about a matinee movie later? It's a girls' Saturday. Daddy's sleeping in." Purple shadowed her eyes despite the cakey foundation. "I can smell the toasted pecans! Better get those out of the oven before they burn," she'd exclaimed, and off she'd gone without another word.

When Deedee came home for Columbus Day weekend, Reba pulled her into their old hiding place on the closet floor and tearfully explained what happened the weeks prior. It was the first time Daddy had ever hit Momma, and though he'd never laid a hand on them, it made Reba question if he might. After she'd finished the story, Deedee's eyes had shifted down to the floor.

"Sometimes I have trouble sleeping," Deedee had said. "I dream there's a snake in my bed, but I just say, 'Stop, you old snake, go away, I don't believe in you, you aren't real' and away it goes. Try that next time, okay?"

It broke Reba's heart that her older sister hadn't immediately taken up arms in her momma's defense, in her defense, too.

"He *hit* her," Reba insisted, but the tightness of her voice made her sound unsure.

It'd been late at night, and how often had she dreamed things that felt so real she could've sworn to heaven they were?

Deedee had simply nodded. "Try the dream trick. If it doesn't work then we'll . . ." Instead of finishing, she'd kissed Reba's cheek and left her amid a pile of patent leathers, Mary Janes, and Keds.

For years, Reba wondered "then we'll *what*?" But she never again brought up that night, not even after their daddy died; and despite their close relationship, she'd since censored every word to her sister. She never told Deedee about their daddy's medical file or the transcription she'd read; part of her was afraid to receive a similarly dubious response.

Reba crunched a malted milk ball. Maybe she'd surprise Riki and make Momma's southern-fried chicken, she thought. She popped another Whopper. But then, she didn't know if Riki liked southern-fried chicken, and she hadn't a clue what went into the recipe besides the obvious— chicken. She was pretty sure you couldn't microwave it either. Reba took a sip of wine, closed the cupboard. No, preparing a bad meal would merely make matters worse.

She went upstairs, peeled off her clothes, and slipped into the bath. The piping hot water dissolved the pink and blue sugar dye from her palms. Her breasts bobbed and looked bigger in the clear water, but so did her thighs and stomach. She considered it a fair trade-off. She set her tumbler on the tub ledge and dipped down deeper until she was eye level with the pirouettes of steam rising off the water like dancing phantoms. The chain around her neck glistened below the surface. She held the silver band up and swung it back and forth like a hypnotist pendulum.

"Don't sit under the apple tree," she hummed to herself.

She thought of Elsie all dressed up to spend Christmas with the Nazis. She said some were "even good." *Good* Nazis? Wasn't that an oxymoron?

"Sounds like someone's had a good day," said Riki. He leaned against the bathroom door.

Reba dropped the ring with a plunk and brought her knees to her chest. "I didn't hear you come in."

He sat on the tub's edge. "It's nice to see you . . ."

"Of course it is. All guys like naked chicks." She wrapped her arms around her shins. A wave of hair stuck to her cheek.

Riki pulled it behind her ear. "Well, that's true, but I was going to say *happy*. It's nice to see you happy."

He had brought the metallic coolness of November in with him. Her skin goose-bumped. She let go of her legs and stretched them out long to the spout side where the water was piping hot. Her toes tingled.

She offered her tumbler to him. "Got old chard on tap."

"I'll pass. It's been a long one." He yawned. "We have a young mother and her two kids in detention. Found them over on the Westside. A resident called—some lady from North Carolina."

"God, I miss their pork. Have you ever had Carolina barbecue? It's nothing like Texan. More sauce, less smoke," said Reba, trying to head the conversation off at the pass. Every day, Riki walked in the door with another heartbreaking story; she didn't want to be weighed down by any more sadness tonight.

"The kids were so scared," Riki continued. "I know it took that woman all she had to get across." He shook his head. "This is one family I wish to God I didn't have to send back."

Reba toed the spout. "It's your job. It's for the good of our country." She repeated what he'd said to her a hundred times before.

"I know but lately . . ." He thumbed a twitch between his eyes. "It isn't the same as it was a couple years ago—groups of men sneaking over to make some money and then go back home. Now it's families. Women and children. They're all really no different from you or me, only they were born on the wrong side of a river."

"You *are* different." She sat up too fast, and water sloshed over the side of the tub. "You're an American with a college education. They're illegals breaking the law. You can't categorize yourself the same. You've got to . . . I don't know, emotionally distance yourself. It's like me with my interviewees. I can't get my job done if I make it personal." Her nipples grew hard from the cool air, so she slid back down in the bath.

The faucet *drip-dropped*. She sipped the wine.

She'd done her research on immigration legislation. That was how she'd met Riki, after all; and hadn't he been the one to go on record that the law could not be bent for anyone? He was a man who saw the world in black and white, and she'd always found security in that. Suddenly shifting to gray scale was discomforting.

"You've got to step away. You can't get all touchy-feely with people," she went on. "*You're* the one who ends up hurt in the end—or at least that's been my experience." She squeezed liquid soap into a pink sponge. "Get my back for me?"

He took the sponge. "That's a bit naive, never mind insensitive, don't you think?"

She pushed a barge of bubbles to the side. "It's the truth."

"Is it?" He scrubbed her shoulders in circles. "Sounds more like fear. If you put up fences around yourself, you're doing more harm than good. Everybody needs somebody, Reba."

"Very John Wayne of you," she said and turned completely around so her back was to him. "Sure, everybody needs somebody, but it doesn't mean *you* have to be their hero." She swallowed hard.

Part of her wished it could be that simple—to ride off into the sunset without fear of disappointment—but she'd learned a long time ago that trust was made of fragile stuff. The heroes galloping across the horizon appeared tarnished and mediocre at best in the lamplight of their living rooms.

"Maybe I want to." Riki dipped the sponge in the water and squeezed it down her spine.

"Then you're in the wrong line of work." Reba blew out all the air inside her chest, then took the sponge from his hand. She didn't want to get into this tonight. She hadn't the energy. "That German lady I interviewed today at the bakery." She changed the subject and scrubbed her ankles. "She told me she was involved with a Nazi during the war."

Riki sat back. "She's a Nazi?"

"Is? I don't think so. *Was?* I'm not sure."

"Either you're a racist supremacist or you aren't. There's no in between."

Here was the Riki she knew. "There isn't?" She'd said it as a statement, but it came out more like a question.

Riki turned her to face him. "No," he said firmly.

"Right, I totally agree." She nodded. Her head was fuzzy warm. "But doesn't everyone kind of hold their own above the others?" She swam her hand through the suds.

"We're all human, Reba. We're all people."

"People betray each other."

The diamond solitaire glinted in the bathwater. Riki hooked his finger through the chain. "It'd look better on your finger, you know."

She pulled away, and it fell back into the soapy water. "I don't want to get into this again."

"I'm just saying—"

"I *know* what you're saying." She washed her legs, the stubble snagging the loofah sponge.

"I think I've been pretty understanding, Reba." He stood. "But there comes a time when we all have to make a choice, like you said."

She kicked the water. "I made my choice. Look! I'm here. Why do you keep pushing?"

She scrubbed hard until a pink rash bloomed on her kneecaps; her breath came fast.

"It's been almost four months and we haven't set a date, haven't even talked about setting a date. Shoot, I don't even think you've told your family."

She ignored him and continued. The water splashed up the sides of the tub.

"Talk to me, Reba."

She stopped. What could she say? She loved him, but this wasn't the life she wanted. He said not to put up fences, but that was exactly what he'd done *to* her. He'd anchored her to this border town, trapped her inside his barbed-wire perimeter. From the moment she'd accepted his proposal, she'd felt the urge to leave, to run as fast as she could. She might've abandoned the old Reba in Virginia, but this new Reba didn't feel right either. It was like Jane said: she was stuck between. Her mind bounced from east to west, from who she was to who she wanted to be. The only thing stopping her crossing was Riki and that ring roped round her neck.

"I need a Motrin," she said instead and rubbed her temples.

Riki sighed. "You need to make a decision. We can't go on like this."

Reba counted the popping bubbles on the water surface, feeling as heavy as a stone.

fourteen

LEBENSBORN PROGRAM
STEINHÖRING, GERMANY

JANUARY 1, 1945

Dear Elsie,

A proposal from an officer! Of course you'll accept. Elsie, I am so proud. And jealous, I'll admit. I know it's all for the good of the nation, but I don't think it's disloyal to wish I'd meet a man (whatever age) looking for a wife. We're making Germans not love, so they keep reminding me. But I do miss the latter and often wonder how different my life might be if Peter were alive. I would have been like you, an SS bride. Of course, if I had known then that I was pregnant with Julius, I would have insisted we marry before he left for Munich. But that kind of thinking does me no good. He is gone. No use fighting fate's will. Everything happens for a reason. Isn't that what the minister used to say?

I haven't been to church in some time. The Program doesn't approve of religious sentimentalities, but I still wear my pewter cross. The ones Papa gave us that Easter when Herr Weiss accidentally threw his mother-in-law's table in the <u>Osterfeuer</u> bonfire. Though we all know he did it out of spite because she wouldn't let him smoke his pipe in the house! I laugh still remembering her face.

That's when I met Peter, too—at the spring festival. He was so handsome in his Hitler Youth uniform and so eager to show all the girls his medal for best class marksman. What a wolf in sheep's clothing! In Gymnasium, he was the quiet boy who always smelled of his mother's breakfast oranges. Then he went off to the Hitler Youth and came back . . . changed. A man, ready to conquer the world. It's odd how you can be with someone day in and day out and never notice until lightning seems to strike their face. Then you see what you never saw before, and no matter how hard you try, you can't go back to seeing nothing again. Listen to me. I'm rambling. Yes, I loved Peter, but there's so much more to it than that. At least that's been my experience. It's nice that Josef and Papa are friends. Mutti is right. This is a good match, Elsie.

Today, I bought beautiful fabric for a new dirndl. My friend Ovidia works at the merchant shop, and she says it's handwoven from Italian lamb's wool. I've sent a portion of it to Mutti to make the skirt. She's so good at embroidering. I haven't decided which I'd like, red poppies or white edelweiss. Which do you think? Perhaps Mutti should choose, though she's always said red is my best color. For my part, I'm sewing a brown bodice to match either. I hope to have it done in time for our spring visit. Mutti may be able to sew a dirndl in a week, but I never had her dexterity or your aptitude in the trades. As well, my body is still swollen from the twins, and I want the dress to fit properly. The Program suggests I begin weaning them early, so hopefully that will help.

The girl is doing wonderfully, rosy and round as a cherub. The boy, however, has not turned out as hoped. He's physically substandard but good-natured. He never cries or fusses like his sister. The nurses say he lies in his crib all day without a sound, and sometimes they forget he's there at all. During feedings, the girl gobbles up nearly all I have to give, but the boy only sleeps at my breast. They are such opposites. It's hard to believe they shared the same womb. The doctors are concerned about the boy. While I know he is not mine but a child of the Fatherland, I can't help wanting to protect him. I feel every bone in his body when I hold him. I named him Friedhelm until he is well enough for the Program to christen him with a new one.

I'm sorry to hear that a Jew spoiled your Christmas. I wonder why they had him come at all. Why not a German youth? We have many boys here who can sing like larks. But I suppose they didn't want to risk transportation at such a time.

Word from the Ardennes reached us with more news of lost Program fathers. They have closed down many of the other Lebensborn homes and brought the children here. I now share a room with a mother from Luxembourg named Cata and one from Stuttgart named Brigette. Though Cata is new to Steinhöring, Brigette has been here since the Program's inception.

Awarded the Silver Mother's Cross last year for her abundant fertility, she's a favorite companion for many admired SS officers. She's had seven perfect children and calls them by number rather than name. I'm uncertain if that is because their christened names pain her or if she is so wholly committed to the nation that the names do not matter. Brigette used to have the largest private room on the compound, but it has since been turned into a nursery for incoming children.

We are not friends. Our relations were strained after Julfest when Major Günther chose my companionship over hers. He was one of her regulars, apparently. So I am making the best of this difficult time. I try to stay out of Brigette's way and make Cata as comfortable as possible in her new surroundings. She has a skittish personality, speaking her thoughts when she oughtn't. Brigette says she's as pestering as a magpie. But if Cata is a magpie, then Brigette is a griffon vulture.

I'm hoping for a swift victory of our fighting men so the New Order of Germany can soon begin.

Then maybe I could come home for good, find a respectable officer to marry, and raise our Volk children together. This is what I dream, Elsie.

Give my love to Mutti and Papa and Happy 1945 Silvester to you all. Heil Hitler.

Hazel

P.S. There is a random inspection of all incoming post to the Program, but none of your letter seals have ever been broken. I mail my letters directly through the Steinhöring Post Office or give them to my friend Ovidia to do so. Our words are safe between us, sister.

SCHMIDT BÄCKEREI
56 LUDWIGSTRASSE
GARMISCH, GERMANY

JANUARY 2, 1945

Dear Hazel,

It's been weeks without word from you. With the fighting so near, I understand that the mail cannot run at its usual timeliness. I'm trying to be patient, but it is difficult. Mutti worries about you and Julius. Our enemies are closer than ever. I pray for your safety. I miss you so terribly.

I'm still recovering from the sickness I wrote about in my last letter. Despite Mutti's best efforts, the mustard rubs didn't do much good. Finally, Papa called for Doktor Joachim who gave me a spoonful of Dover's powder and instructed Mutti to make me anise tea. He had no medicine to spare—all the drugs going to our fighting men. Thank heaven it wasn't the influenza! I've heard rumors that the illness has taken many lives in the cities, Hamburg and Berlin. I pray it is not there in Steinhöring!

Seven bitter cups of tea later, I awoke with a full bedpan, but my coughs had subsided. I had an angel watching over. By the last day of 1944, my constitution was weak, but I was finally able to rest. I missed Silvester, sleeping into the new year. It's an odd feeling to lose important moments such as this, like something valuable was stolen, but there's no thief to blame. Perhaps that is why 1945 feels especially strange.

On Silvester eve, Frau Rattelmüller stopped by to do the annual bleigiessen fortune. Did you do bleigiessen at the Program? If so, what shape did your future make? Papa's lead made into the shape of a feather—change in his household. He attributed it to the coming victory of the Fatherland and business improving. Mutti's took the shape of a cow—a cure for sickness. She's had me drinking different herbal brews ever since. They dropped the molten lead into the water on my behalf. It formed a ring. Mutti, of course, interpreted it as a forecast of my marriage to Josef, but Frau Rattelmüller reminded her that a ring shape is also a warning of forthcoming escapades. It would be like the frau to give me a bad prediction. Perhaps the old witch has put a curse on me for badgering her about the brötchen.

Last night, I dreamed that Josef was tied like a suckling pig and put into our oven with the broggenbrot. I tried to save him but couldn't open the latch and woke drenched in sweat. In another, you stood on the back stoop with a gun and told me to run. I asked where, but you wouldn't say. You simply said "run" and so I did, through the empty streets and up Kramer Mountain until I reached St. Martin's Hütte. There, I stopped and looked down over Garmisch, which wasn't there at all, just one black hole in the valley. You used to tell me that dreams had meaning. Do you still believe that? If so, what does this mean? I'd rather forget the nightmares altogether—too horrible to think about. Demons, Mutti claims, and so I dust off my bible and pray, pray, pray.

I accepted Josef's proposal. Mutti and Papa are delighted, and seeing their happiness brings me courage, but still I wonder if this is enough.

I hope that you are able to visit in the spring. Your opinion means everything. Having you with us during these difficult times would make everything so much easier. I must tell you, Hazel, I have a secret. I haven't the bravery to write it down, but can tell only you— and the sooner the better. I'm so consumed by it that my mind has no peace. I worry I've made a grave mistake. I pray that if I have been wrong, the consequences will not affect you, Mutti, or Papa. Please write soon, Hazel. The days between letters have been so long.

Heil Hitler.

Your loving sister,
Elsie

Mutti's footsteps creaked across the floorboards. Elsie glanced at the loose wallboard to ensure it was secured.

"You must feel better?" Mutti asked as she entered with a tray of parsnip onion soup. "It's good to see you awake."

Elsie pointed to the letter on the side table. "I was writing Hazel."

Mutti set the tray down beside. "Shall I mail it for you?"

Elsie scooped it up. "It's not urgent."

While Mutti hadn't the prying nature, Elsie couldn't chance it. "I'll take it to the post office as soon as I'm well. It helps to talk to her like she's close." She fingered the papery corner. "I miss her."

Mutti pulled the covers high up on Elsie's chest. "I'm glad she writes to you. Papa and I haven't received a letter in over a month." She straightened the spoon on the tray. "She's busy and with the war as it is . . ." She placed a palm on Elsie's forehead. "Good. No fever. I'm sure Josef is anxious to see you." Mutti patted Elsie's hand. The rubies gleamed in the dim light. "We need you fully recovered. Thank God this wasn't an infection. Doktor Joachim says there's not an ounce of medicine—not even on the black market." She wrung her hands. "I pray they have better supplies in Steinhöring."

Elsie put a hand over her mother's. "Hazel said to give you and Papa her love. She sounds as though she's faring the best of any of us."

She didn't want Mutti to worry.

Mutti massaged the tips of Elsie's fingers to circulate the blood. "Gut. That brings me comfort. Be sure to send her our love when you write again." She let go. "I must get back to your papa. There was a lull so I brought your lunch. Eat while the soup is warm." She stood and headed for the door.

"Mutti." Elsie stopped her. "Is there a spare roll or two I might have?"

Mutti nodded. "Appetite. An excellent sign."

Elsie listened to the creaky stairs' diminuendo then crescendo, and the door reopened.

"Two straight from Papa's oven. And a pat of the butter I've been hiding in the icebox." Mutti set the plate on the tray. "I told your papa we need to bake extra batches of brötchen in the mornings. Frau Rattelmüller bought a dozen before we even opened!"

"She's been doing that for months," said Elsie. "I told you she's lost her mind."

"As long as she pays with hard coin." Mutti winked and closed the door behind her.

Elsie sipped her soup. The rising aromatic steam made her chest feel balmy and full. Mutti's soup with Papa's bread—there was nothing better in the world. She held the bowl as close as possible without burning herself.

Downstairs, Mutti's voice carried through the pine planks, greeting customers and taking orders.

Elsie checked the door and listened for footsteps before pulling herself from the feather comforter with key in hand. The floor was warmer than the air, and her feet welcomed the heat. Once the lock had been turned, she whispered, "Tobias?"

The wide board in the far wall pushed out.

"Parsnip soup," said Elsie.

Out of the crawl space squirmed Tobias wearing a thick, cable sweater that looked more like a dress. Papa's midsection had long outgrown the item, and it lay unused at the bottom of his cedar trunk. He'd never notice its absence. In the cold of the upper rooms, Elsie couldn't risk Tobias catching a cold and sneezing himself to discovery.

She moved the bread off the plate and ladled on parsnips and onions, carrots and cabbage, then split a roll and placed the butter inside. "Here."

"For you?" whispered Tobias.

Elsie shook her head. "For you."

His eyes sparkled.

Up until that day, Elsie hadn't been able to stomach much more than tea, broth, and pretzels that she sucked until the pieces turned mushy in her mouth; so Tobias had eaten the same. While Elsie grew thinner from the diet, Tobias had surprisingly managed to gain plumpness in his cheeks and through his middle, making him less apparition and more boy. Though he rarely spoke, Elsie had become somewhat attached to his company, like the imaginary elves of childhood that lived in garden sheds and wooden armoires.

"Go back and eat where it's safe," she instructed.

Tobias nodded and tiptoed to the wall, shimmied through the plank, and pulled the plate inside.

This had been their routine since Christmas. Initially, Elsie panicked each time her parents came to take her temperature; her heart beat fast, and she broke out in a sweat from head to toe, making her symptoms appear worse than they were. When Doktor Joachim arrived, she nearly fainted with fear. But Tobias seemed divinely cloaked. Even Elsie forgot he was there until a cough gripped her chest and her breath came shallow. Then he'd appear, bringing water to her lips and a hum to ease the pain. She tried to forget he was a Jew. It was easier that way. She had yet to think past concealing him.

In a fever pitch, she'd dreamed she called the Gestapo and said she'd discovered a boy hiding in the woodpile—saving herself and her family and being championed by the authorities. She awoke to Tobias's gentle hum at her side and winced at the macabre thoughts. She couldn't cast him off. Not anymore. Things had changed. He was someone to her now.

At every meal, she broke half her bread with him, and she'd shown him the secret items she'd collected in the hollow wall. His favorite was the advertisement for Texas baked beans, which featured an illustration of an American cowboy riding through a field of sunflowers. Tobias would run his fingers over the man's smiling face, drawing up and down the sharp letters U-S-A. She also had an Edelweiss pin; movie stills of Jean Harlow, Myrna Loy, and William Powell; a copy of *A Boy's Will* with the covers torn off; a jar of pebbles from the coast of Yugoslavia; a small vial of rose shampoo; and a bar of Ritter Sport Schokolade still in the wrapper. For fear Tobias might be greedy, she warned that if he ate the chocolate, they'd surely find him, the smell too distinct and familiar to a baker's senses. But after a week of scraps, she learned he hadn't the gluttonous nature.

Minutes after he'd moved back into the hiding place, the plate slid out. Elsie pulled back the covers and took up the plate. Under the lamplight, Josef's engagement ring shimmered red droplets against the wall. She still wasn't used to its ruby glare. The decision to accept his proposal had come suddenly.

The day after Christmas, the Gestapo had returned. With Tobias still missing, the units were ordered to do a final community search in daylight. Their boots woke Elsie from her delirium.

"She's ill!" Papa had yelled.

They entered her bedroom with guns slung round their chests. The room seemed too bright to Elsie's burning eyes, every corner and secret exposed. She'd pulled the covers over her thin nightgown and whimpered with fear and delirium.

A soldier stomped the corner boards and knocked the wall with the butt of his gun. Another looked under her bed and then through her cedar wardrobe, pulling dirndls and sweaters to the floor.

"Please, stop," Mutti had begged.

"We must check everywhere," replied the trooper. He went to the back wall.

"No!" Elsie's chest had tightened to cough, but she pushed out the words. "I am the fiancée of Lieutenant Colonel Josef Hub. If you don't leave this minute, he will make sure you are adequately disciplined for disrespecting our family." Her breath wheezed and sputtered into a hacking fit.

The men looked to their standartenführer leader, who gave the signal and they filed out. Mutti and Papa stared speechless. Papa said, "Fiancée?" And thus, a decision was made.

The gems glittering round the gold impressed her parents. They owned nothing that could compare. Mutti guessed Josef bought it from a Parisian jeweler, but Elsie knew better.

Now, she knelt by the wall. "Tobias?"

The board opened a crack.

"Can you read Hebrew?" She pulled the ring from her finger. "What does this say?"

A hand came through. He took the gold band and held it so the dusty light shone on the inner etching, then he gave it back.

"Well?" she asked.

Silence.

"Is it too worn?"

"I am my beloved's and my beloved is mine." His voice was clear and songlike. "It is from the Torah."

fifteen

*C*aptain Josef Hub obtained a Saturday pass and took the early train to Garmisch Bahnhof. He'd befriended a chatty secretary at the Nazi archive with a terrible sweet tooth and rosacea to show for it. After months of flirtation over sugar-dusted kreppels and carefully chosen innuendos, he convinced her to pull Peter's file from the Hitler Youth archive. In it was the Abends' street number.

The city map stretched across the train platform wall, and he searched the colored lines. He'd stood in the exact spot four years earlier at the 1936 Winter Olympic games. Then, the station had been filled with people waving vibrant country flags, extolling the virtues of Hitler's new stadium and rushing to catch glimpses of their favorite athletes. Now, except for a handful of passengers, it was empty.

The train gears moaned and popped like arthritic joints. He was glad to be off and fingered the paper address: Herr and Frau Abend. They rented a handful of rooms above their home to visiting skiers and couples on holiday. Small-scale innkeepers, Peter's file stated. Simple, hardworking countrymen. They had two children, Peter and Trudi. Peter was the elder.

"Any bags, Officer?" asked the porter.

"Nein." Josef slipped the address into his pocket. "What time does the last train return to Munich?"

"Nine o'clock."

That gave him nearly twelve hours, though he didn't plan to stay as long. "Which way to Schnitzschulstrasse?"

"Down the road." The man pointed. "Do you need me to call a ride?"

Josef adjusted his cap. "A walk will do me good."

The porter shrugged and gave directions.

What Josef truly wanted was a little more time. Preparation. He'd longed and feared this day for over a year; but now that it was here, it didn't have the proportion he'd imagined. The morning was too tepid and sunny for January. He'd expected bitter cold and lonesome streets to match his mood. Instead, the town bustled with Saturday commerce, smells of baked bread and stoked fires. Children chased each other across the cobblestones; shop bells chimed as lady patrons in heels and feather-trimmed hats exited and entered. Two young women smiled at him and giggled as they passed. A butcher dumped a bucket of pink water into the gutter. "Guten morgen, Hauptsturmführer."

"Guten morgen." Josef paused and checked the street signs.

"Can I be of service?" asked the butcher.

"I'm looking for Schnitzschulstrasse—the Abend innkeeper."

"Around that corner. Frau Abend makes a wonderful lamb soup for her guests. The meat comes from my shop. It is always the best. I promise you will not be dissatisfied."

Josef nodded, knowing full well he wouldn't be dining.

It had been an act of impulsive rage that November night. He was embarrassed at his lack of forethought and restraint. Peter was correct. They were just Jews. But despite all he read and heard and preached, despite the party's belief that they were an execrated race, the Hochschilds had been his friends and his teachers and gracious beyond measure. He couldn't deny that experience any more than he could deny the murder of Peter Abend. They were equally true, but he'd never profess as much. He was now a captain in the army of the Third Reich and up for early promotion. Peter had disobeyed authority. Discipline and faith, those were the central tenets by which they stood.

But no matter how he rationalized his actions, his mind was not at ease. He'd developed migraines over the last year. Searing pain made his vision shake and shrink to cylindrical tunnels of darkness. He'd lay for hours, catatonic and breathless, wondering if that was how Peter felt in his grip and Frau Hochschild in her grave. He prayed for God to take him in the night, but then he would rise at dawn, put on his uniform, and report for duty. His superior noticed his gaunt figure and sickly complexion and ordered him to the Waffen-SS physician who prescribed methamphetamine injections and told him to come in whenever he felt tired, anxious, or worried. The migraines stopped, but the drug did nothing for his insomnia. He stayed awake pacing the floor and reading *Mein Kampf* over and over until the doctor gave him sleeping pills as well. The injection-pill combination seemed to do the trick and he was back to good—no, he felt better than ever. Except for the nightmares. In them, he heard Herr Hochschild's son's whispers and felt again the slowing pulse of Peter's heart in his hand. He'd awake wet with sweat, shaken by the knowledge that the dream was reality.

He hoped to hush the specter's murmurs and lift the weight of Peter's death by going to the Abends'. His guilt drew him, moth to the flame.

He knocked on the door.

"Ja," answered a teenage girl. Trudi, Josef reckoned.

"I'm looking for Herr Abend?"

"Are you here to ski?" She put a hand on her waist and cocked her bony hip in a manner of maturity beyond her years.

"Nein."

She looked over his uniform. "My father is not at home, but my mother can rent you a room."

"May I speak to her?"

Trudi swung the door wide. "Come."

Josef followed. In the narrow hallway, one photograph hung from a fat nail: a girl with pigtail bows and Peter in uniform posed by their parents' side.

"Mamma, we have a guest." Trudi led Josef to the parlor room where a gray-haired Frau Abend sat darning.

Seeing him, she slid the basket of threads under the couch. "A guest? Sit." She beckoned. "We charge per night and include dinner and breakfast. I'll give you a discount since you're an officer. My son was an officer."

Josef sat. "Nein—I'm not here for a room. I came to speak with you and your husband."

Trudi turned. "But you said—"

"Hush," Frau Abend commanded. Trudi quieted and picked at her fingernails. "Herr Abend will not be home for some time. What do you wish to speak to us about, Captain . . ."

"Hub," said Josef. "Josef Hub—Josef." He swallowed hard. "I knew your son."

"Peter?" said Trudi.

Frau Abend gave her a look, and she went back to her nails.

"Ja, what about my son?"

"I was his command." Josef's eye flickered with an initial throb. "The night he died. I was there." He paused. He'd come for exculpation, but he was unsure of how much to disclose. "I knew him. He was a dedicated soldier." The heat of the Abend parlor made him sweat. His uniform collar constricted. "I was by his side when he was killed. So I came to tell you— that is, I came to say . . ."

Frau Abend's chin dropped to her chest. On the table sat an empty tea-cup, a warped orange peel limp at the bottom. "My Peter," she whispered. Her lips trembled. "My only son."

Though Josef made sure to receive an injection before leaving Munich, the room began to quake, the corners shadowed. He took a deep breath. If a migraine began, he'd have no retreat.

"He was an excellent soldier." Josef cleared his throat. "His death was a great loss. A tragedy."

Frau Abend sniffed and steeled herself. "Thank you." The starkness of her tone snapped the air. "None of his friends ever came. We got a tele-gram. There was no body. They said—" She stopped.

"Burned," whispered Trudi.

Josef recalled the torches the Hitler Youth troopers haphazardly threw into the buildings and the subsequent blaze that swept through the street.

"We had a nice funeral to honor him. We buried a few of his things in our family plot at St. Sebastian's."

Josef nodded.

"Were you in the Reich Youth? You must know his fiancée, Hazel," chimed Trudi.

Josef frowned. "Engaged?"

"He has a son, too," she went on.

"Trudi, go do the breakfast dishes and give the bread crusts to the dog," Frau Abend commanded. After the girl had gone, she continued, "Peter was engaged to Hazel Schmidt, daughter of Max Schmidt, the baker. A nice fräulein." She sighed. "Since their child wasn't legitimate by marriage but of good German descent, it went to the Reich program at Steinhöring. It's the most proper place for him."

"I had no idea," said Josef.

A pine log crackled in the fireplace. The heat of the room seemed sud-denly unbearable.

"Well." He stood. "I must catch the train back to Munich."

She nodded. "If you ever return, we have good rates. There was so much business during the Olympics, but not anymore." She walked him to the door.

He winced at the daylight, but the cool mountain air calmed the mounting ache.

"I'll pray for your safekeeping, Captain Hub," said Frau Abend. She shut the door before he could thank her.

A man passed with a large, round loaf wrapped in paper. Josef's stomach growled. He hadn't eaten that day, and the smell gnawed at his gut as fiercely as the migraine to his head. He went in the direction the man had come, past an alleyway where two boys stick-fought amid pigeons picking crumbs. A fur-trimmed woman stepped out onto the street carrying a pastry box. Above her hung the sign: Schmidt Bäckerei.

There was a line. A man wearing thin, wire glasses waited behind a wizened frau leaning on her cane.

"I need a good, solid bread. Nothing full of sweet air. It rots the teeth," said the frau.

The young woman behind the register pulled a studded, brown loaf from the shelf.

The frau looked it over, then nodded. "That'll do well enough." She took her bread bag, dropped her coins on the counter, and hobbled out quickly. A bell over the door clanged with her departure.

"You are welcome, Frau Rattelmüller," called the girl behind the register. She huffed and itched her head, pushing askew the blue scarf she wore.

Was this the baker's daughter, Josef wondered, Peter's Hazel? She looked far too girlish: her skin flushed and glossy; her neck and arms twiggy like a fledgling. Could she really have borne Peter's child? The older he got, the younger everyone else seemed. He'd pegged the Nazi archive secretary for a mature thirty and was shocked to discover she was a decade younger.

The man in glasses ordered neatly braided poppy seed rolls and paid with SS ration coupons. The young woman reached inside the bread bin and wisps of wheat blond hair fell over her eyes. She pushed the strands back into the messy braid beneath her scarf. Pretty.

"May I help you?" Wide, pine-colored eyes met him.

He had yet to look at the menu or the bread rack. "What's fresh?"

"Everything," she answered confidently.

"Everything?" He smiled. "Really?"

"Things don't sit around long enough to get stale. People are hungry. We're at war. Or hadn't you noticed?" She rolled her eyes at his uniform.

He cleared his throat to keep from laughing. She was feisty in a way markedly different from the pubescent Trudi Abend. There was a fearless intelligence in this girl that he quite admired.

"Well then, I shall have brötchen and butter to eat here. If it is not too much trouble."

She shrugged and turned to the bread bin. "You get fed. We get money. I don't see how that could be trouble." She spoke with her back to him.

Her waist was slim and bent easily without the bulge of full womanhood. He could have fit one hand around.

She returned with a roll and a pat of butter. "The butter costs extra. 30 Reichspfennig or the equivalent in ration coupons."

Hub set coins on the counter, but he halted her hand before she took them. "Hazel?"

The girl frowned then and swept the coins into her palm.

"My name is Captain Hub. I was a soldier with Peter Abend," he explained and waited for her reaction.

She gave none. Cool and steady, she deposited the coins in the till and closed it with a shove. "I am Elsie. Hazel's sister."

He nodded. Yes, of course. If Hazel shared this fair skin and light hair, it was no surprise they took her into the Lebensborn Program. Even the bones of Elsie's cheeks and nose showed classic signs of Nordic descent. He'd spent hours researching the scientific legitimacy of Aryan supremacy, hoping to further validate his actions and the hooked cross he wore.

He took the plate. "I've come from the Abend home and paying my respects to his family. They said Peter was engaged to Hazel."

Elsie moved sticky cinnamon-swirled buns from a metal tray to a glass cakestand. "Is that why you've come?" she challenged.

"Why I've come?" He looked down at the brötchen, the cracked top split into four quarters by a baker's cross.

She finished arranging the cakes and wiped away a dribble of icing with her finger. "Ja, they were engaged. He died, and she went to Steinhöring with Julius, their son." Elsie sucked her finger clean, pursed her lips, and ran her eyes from his collar insignias to his boots. "If you want to ask questions, you will have to speak to my father. It is not my place to discuss our family matters with a strange man. Nazi officer or Winston Churchill, I do not know you." She flipped the fishtail of her braid over her shoulder and took the tray back to the kitchen.

She was bold, a trait both championed and admonished by the statutes of the Bund Deutscher Mädel. Right or wrong, Josef found it refreshing.

"Doch, I came for breakfast," said Josef with a shrug. His headache was receding.

He sat at one of the two small café tables and tore the roll apart with his fingers, exposing tender, white flesh, slightly gummy in the center.

A woman and her son entered the shop arguing over a sugar roll versus a cheese pretzel. The woman told the boy he'd grow fat as a cow if he ate nothing but sweets, while she herself was round and soft as a baked apple. Exasperated by the cold walk and prolonged argument, she wheezed through her mouth and yanked the boy to the counter.

"Pick something healthy," she instructed. "How about a bialy?"

The boy pressed his nose against the display case, leaving a greasy smudge.

His mother crooked her head toward the back kitchen. "Elsie!" she called. "Max—Luana! Did you decide to take a holiday?"

The boy stuck out his tongue at her while her attention was deviated.

Josef crunched his crust, amused by the child's disdain and eager to see Elsie again.

She returned clapping flour from her hands. "We are here, Frau Reimers."

An older man with a ruddy complexion and hair the color of sea salt followed close behind. "Grüs Gott, Jana! And Herr Ahren. How are my best customers?"

"Gut," said Frau Reimers curtly. "I need a loaf of bauernbrot and Ahren will have—" She looked down at the boy. "Well? Tell Herr Schmidt what you want?"

"A cinnamon roll," he said flatly.

The woman sighed and adjusted her hat. "Of course you pick the most expensive thing. Fine, but remember, the Hitler Youth doesn't take fat boys."

"I don't want to go to Hitler Youth," he spat back.

The mother smacked his cheek. "Stupid. Look—" She turned to Josef and pointed. "All good Germans want to be officers. But you've got to fit the uniform."

Josef continued to chew without acknowledgment. The boy was far too young to worry about joining the military ranks or the consequences of a sweet bun.

"Oh, Jana. Let the boy be. Look at me! I grew up on sugar bread and pastries and the doctor says I'm fit as a fiddle."

"One cinnamon roll?" asked Elsie.

The woman shrugged her shoulders. "I suppose. But Max, at these prices . . ."

"Sugar is hard to find. Supplies aren't what they used to be."

"And wouldn't it be God's punishment to give me a child who eats nothing but sugar and butter!"

Elsie bagged the bread and boxed the pastry while her father changed the discussion to that of the cold weather's effect on his dill plant by the windowsill.

"Here you go, Ahren," Elsie whispered to the boy. "I like these, too." She winked.

He gave a quick smile.

"Wunderbar!" Frau Reimers peered into the bag. "Max, you are the best baker in the Fatherland." She pulled shiny coins from a velvet change purse and clinked them on the counter. "Now come, Ahren."

The boy followed her out. In the absence of the woman's loud breathing, the bakery seemed too quiet. Herr Schmidt's footsteps thudded the tiled floor as he approached.

"Hello, Officer," he said. "My daughter says you have some questions about my eldest, Hazel, and Peter Abend, God rest his soul."

Josef respectfully stood and wiped crumbs from his lips. "That is partially true—I came to see the Abends and stopped here for breakfast."

"Ack, ja. And we are happy you did." Herr Schmidt extended his hand for a firm shake. "The Abends are good Volk. Losing Peter was terrible for us all." He took a seat at Josef's table and gestured for him to do the same. "Elsie, bring us black tea."

"All we have is chicory root," she replied.

"Then brew the chicory," instructed Herr Schmidt.

"But, Papa, we don't have much left and—"

"Do what I say, child," he firmly commanded. "It is not every day we have an officer and a friend of the family as a customer."

Elsie obeyed and left the room.

"She misses her sister," explained Herr Schmidt. "She's young and doesn't fully understand politics, war, patriotism . . . But we are very proud of our Hazel."

Josef swallowed a last bit of brötchen caught in his cheek.

"Sag mal, where are you from?" asked Herr Schmidt.

"Munich," replied Josef.

Herr Schmidt leaned back in his chair. "Ah, the capital of the movement."

Josef nodded with a smile and pushed away his plate, a lump of the sweet butter left unused.

sixteen

EL PASO BORDER PATROL STATION
8935 MONTANA AVENUE
EL PASO, TEXAS

NOVEMBER 11, 2007

"Carol's making spaghetti with meatballs for dinner, Rik. You sure you don't want some?" asked Bert, pulling on his coat.

"Thanks, but I picked up Taco Cabana." Riki pointed to the large take-out bag on the minifridge. "Figured the kids would like it, too."

"I don't know how you do it!" said Bert. "I tried your Taco Cabana diet and gained six pounds in a week. That's almost a pound a day!"

"Must be genetics." Riki flexed an arm. "A body knows the food of its heritage."

Bert laughed. "Or more likely, when I have a meal with Carol and the kids, I only get to eat half of my plate. There's always too much going on." He shrugged with a smile and rapped the schedule board with his knuckles. "Tomorrow, you're taking them over?"

"Bright and early."

Bert cleared his throat and fished his keys from his pocket. "Have you talked to Reba?"

Riki propped his feet up on the desk. "I'll probably call later."

"'Cause I could drive by for you. Check, since she's by herself." He scratched his stubbly jaw with a large, square-headed key.

It was a considerate gesture, but Bert didn't know the Reba he did. "That's how she likes it."

"Right." Bert paused. "You don't have to stay here, you know. Carol and I can put you up until you find a new place."

"Thanks, Bert. I appreciate the offer."

Bert mimed a tip of his cap and left.

A handful of officers milled in and out, but the station was still too quiet. Riki turned on his desk radio. A catchy pop tune bounced over the airwaves. He hummed along while surfing Internet destinations. It was his kind of travel. He visited the vineyards of Northern California, the bayous of Louisiana, lobster boats in Maine, the White House and Lincoln Memorial, the rolling Blue Ridge Mountains, and the oceans on either end; moving from place to place in the click of a button without his body leaving the comfort of his chair.

Riki was a homesteader by nature and had only been north as far as Santa Fe and east to San Antonio. That was partly what drew him to Reba. She was from "beyond." She'd walked into his life with the world on her shoulders, and through her, he'd hoped he could see everything he ever wanted without stepping outside his door. It wasn't that he was afraid of leaving so much as it seemed more natural to stay where he felt he belonged—with the people he belonged to.

His parents had imbued this sense in him. While brave in their endeavors to cross the Rio Grande and become US citizens, they never let Riki forget exactly who he was: the son of Mexican immigrants, set apart by culture and tradition, race and religion.

Even in Riki's father's final days when tuberculosis crippled his body and tired his spirit, he'd turn on CNN and watch as broadcasters, politicians, and common men debated immigration laws.

"They're stealing American jobs from *real* Americans," one protester said to the camera.

"Stay on your side!" yelled another.

"See, mi hijo, see," his father said before his breath would turn to coughing. "You must be cautious. Only trust your own people."

It pained Riki that on his deathbed, his father still regarded himself and his family as aliens in a foreign land. Riki had been determined to prove him wrong when he'd applied for a CBP job. He'd show his father how American he was by working to protect his fellow citizens; then no man could call into question his national allegiance, no matter his racial profile or ancestral line. He was a devoted countryman of the United States of America, a loyal resident of El Paso, Texas, and he was content to stay right where he was, or so he'd thought. But coming up on his third full year as a CBP officer, he'd seen enough to know that behind the glitzy carnival show were callused men pulling puppet strings. These were more than borderlines, sides of the fence, American versus Mexican. These were people, closer to him in Mexico than any of the politicians dictating edicts from the US Capitol thousands of miles away.

He pulled up the tourism pages for Washington, D.C., and its sister suburbs in Virginia. Nothing but names. Reba never spoke of where she came from except in isolated uncensored moments. Once when a rare storm swept over the city in waves of angry rain, she'd stared out the window, briefly transported across the miles, and said, "Virginia's weather was like this. Sunny and clear one day, thunder and lightning the next. I used to cry when it rained." She'd hugged her arms tight to her chest, and he could clearly imagine what she'd looked like as a child.

"It's just one storm," he'd comforted.

"Yes, but it reminds me that they'll still come."

That was the first time he felt it—that sense of secret insecurity and distance. It worried him. He loved her. So in an effort to prove his fidelity and her sanctuary with him, he'd proposed. But the impending union only seemed to make the distance between them expand, filling up their house like a balloon ready to burst and leaving little room for him. He wanted to be with Reba for the rest of his life, but what should have been devotion manifested as resentment on both their parts. He imagined her again in the steamy tub, cheeks and nipples flushed, drinking wine like she'd won the lottery, and his ring, dangling in the suds.

A smiling blond family in a garden of tulips stared back at him from the computer screen with the tagline: *Virginia Is for Lovers.* He sucked his teeth.

"Señor," a woman's voice called from the detainment room. A series of knocks followed.

"Yes." Riki got up and opened the door. "What can I do for you?"

"Puedo tener una manta mas para mi hija?" said the woman.

He'd moved a small TV into the detainment room. The children watched an episode of *The Simpsons.* The girl, cuddled beside her brother, sat up at Riki's voice and pulled the green blanket from the boy's back. He groaned and yanked hard, whipping the blanket completely from her. She said nothing but gave a swift kick to his spine.

"Ay! Mamá," cried the boy. "Ella me pateó."

The woman shushed the children. "Lo siento, señor."

"They're fine," said Riki. "I'll get an extra one."

He went to the storage room and dug through the stacks until he found a soft, pink flannel. When he returned, the children were chasing each other round the room. The girl ran, dragging the green blanket behind as her brother followed, growling and snarling like a wild pig. He soon caught her, turned her over, and snouted her stomach to squeals and laughter. The woman sat quietly on the cot; her face furrowed with silent trouble.

"Here you go." Riki set the pink blanket beside her.

She ran her hand over. "Gracias."

The girl asked her brother to be a pig again and away they went.

"Niños paren," the woman instructed.

"No, they can play," said Riki.

He was glad to see their spirits lifted from earlier. They'd remained mute and shamed for much of their stay, but they were children, not criminals.

He took a seat beside the woman; the cot springs bowing low under his weight. "Where are you from? Qué pueblo?"

"Barreales, Juárez," she replied, keeping her gaze to the floor.

Riki nodded. He knew it. A poor neighborhood at the far east of Juárez. "You have familia there?"

"Están muertos." She shifted uneasily.

"I'm sorry." He scratched his neck. "My family's gone, too."

With each breath, her body rose and fell heavily like a woman ten times her age. "Usted tiene niños?" she asked and lifted her face to him, eyes wide as cups of coffee.

"No." He couldn't even get Reba to wear his ring, never mind bear his children. "I'm not married." The words singed the tip of his tongue.

In a bout of giggles, the girl ran to the woman and buried her face in her lap. The boy snarled and snouted, then quieted when he saw Riki.

Bart Simpson cried "¡Ay, caramba!" from the television.

"Are you hungry?" asked Riki.

The boy leaned against his mother's shoulder and narrowed his eyes.

They'd devoured their prepackaged lunches: turkey and American cheese sandwiches on white bread; Doritos and chocolate chip cookies. The American brownbag special. Not a crumb was left behind. But it was dinnertime now, and he knew they could use something warm.

"I got Taco Cabana." It might not be homemade, but it was the best he could offer. "Tacos?" he said to the children.

The boy shrugged.

"Follow me." Riki stood and gestured for them to come through the open door, but the trio remained behind invisible bars.

They hadn't left the detainment room since arriving. With a clean bathroom, bedding, and a television, it was the Ritz-Carlton compared to the rusty Dodge. No amenities could compensate for freedom, though. Riki had seen enough men and women locked in that room to understand the truth. It pained him to deport these people—his people—like cattle, herding them back to the ghettos of Juárez with no hope or prospects. But these were the rules, and Riki believed in the rules. Keep your head down, do what you're supposed to, don't ask questions, and you'll eventually be rewarded: that was the code by which even his father had ascribed. In the recesses of his mind, however, he wondered at what point human compassion trumped blind obedience.

"Venga," he encouraged.

The boy held his sister back by the shoulders, his face set hard with suspicion.

"I promise you won't get in trouble," said Riki, but the boy's grip on the girl only tightened. Reluctantly, Riki started toward the office. He'd have to bring the food to them. "Jesus, kid, you've got to trust somebody sometime," he sighed.

"Why should I?" the boy snapped.

Riki whipped around. "You speak English?"

He wrapped his forearm protectively around his sister's chest. Her head bobbled back and forward, from her brother to Riki. "Yeah."

"So you understand," said Riki. "This isn't a trick or a test. You can come out. It's safe. I have hot food for your family, if you want it."

His mother chimed in, "Qué? Qué él dijo?" But her son ignored her.

"My papi warned me about you. He said the troopers would tell you to trust them, to follow them. They'd give you food and then they'd lock you up with the rats y los serpientes."

Riki gestured to the fluorescent, air-conditioned room. "Have you seen any rats or snakes?" He pretended to look around.

The boy gnawed on his top lip, then shook his head.

"Okay. So why don't you trust what I say to be true and not what you know isn't?"

The little girl fidgeted under her brother's hold. The mother crossed her arms; her brow knit with worry and confusion at being on the outside of the dialogue.

After a moment's contemplation, the boy ceased biting his lip. "If you really got any, what kind of tacos?"

Riki suppressed the urge to laugh. "Two soft beef tacos, three chicken flautas, two steak fajitas, and a side of rice and beans."

The boy's eyebrows rose. "Really?"

Riki nodded. "Right in there." He gestured to the patrol room.

Slowly, the boy's arm fell away from his sister. Having understood the words "tacos," "flautas," and "fajitas," she raced through the door with no more incentive.

"Must be her favorite," said Riki. "Mine too."

The mother kissed her son on his crown and followed her daughter; but before the boy would step across, he dug in his pant pocket and produced a tarnished penny.

"Gracias."

"No," Riki waved a hand. "It's on me, kid."

The boy persisted, holding the penny out further until Riki opened his palm. "We had to pay the other man too," he said.

"Other man?"

"Carlos." The boy wiped his nose with his wrist. His eyes no longer glinted with suspicion but anger. "He made my mama cry." His lower lip trembled. He sucked it in and squared his shoulders. "He put us in the car because we didn't have any more money to give. Then he left us."

"Carlos," Riki repeated.

The boy nodded.

"How many people were in the group?"

The boy shrugged. "A lot."

"Do you know where they are now?"

In the patrol room, the little girl squealed with delight.

"Espera," cautioned the mother.

The boy hovered at the line of the doorway. "The United States," he said, then stepped over.

Riki waited until he was down the hall before pulling his cell phone off his belt. In his palm remained the worn penny. He sighed. To catch Carlos, he'd have to round up all the people in his keep: men, women, children, young and old, from Mexico, El Salvador, Colombia; simple, hardworking people paying crooks and criminals to get them over the US border, sacrificing so much and enduring abuses of every kind for a chance—not even a guarantee—at prosperity. He hated this business of dredging dreams, but he had a job to do.

He slid the coin into his pocket and dialed Bert. "Sorry to interrupt dinner, but we got a lead on a smuggler."

seventeen

LEBENSBORN PROGRAM
STEINHÖRING, GERMANY

JANUARY 4, 1945

Dear Papa and Mutti,

Heil Hitler and Grüs Gott. This is a difficult letter to write. As you know, the goal of the Program is to produce fine Germans for our nation. I came here to do my duty, honoring both our family and the memory of Peter, and I believe I have served our Fatherland well.

A couple months ago, I sent you word of the twins born to the Program. The girl is perfect. However, her brother is continually sick and weak. The Lebensborn directors have decided that, despite our efforts, he will never be of quality. Therefore, they request that I sign paperwork to relinquish him from the Program. I have asked to contact you so that our family might care for the child, but they refuse to confirm their intentions. I am deeply troubled for his well-being. Though he has been determined inadequate, he has the Schmidt nose, light hair, and a slight bow to the lips like Mutti's. They will not permit me to see him—afraid I may become emotional and upset the daily routine. But shouldn't the routine be upset for something like this? I curse these doctors and nurses for having such little consideration for the children of Germany. Remember when I was young and sickly during my infancy, but look at me now! If only they would wait. If only they would see his spirit. It is strong. I know. I felt it in my womb. Oh, Papa, Mutti, how I ache for him—if not to save him then to say good-bye. It is a similar aching to when my beloved Peter left so unexpectedly. Peter calls to me in my dreams, and I fear my new son will haunt me in similar fashion. I know this is nothing but my own weakness. There are no spirits in this world. The sun rises and sets, seasons come and go, life begins and ends. It is nature's way, as the führer says. But sometimes I think there may be more. Sometimes I know there must be.

I have been committed to the Fatherland in every measure, even personal sacrifice, but this is too much for me to bear. I wish you were here to comfort me.

Heil Hitler.

Hazel

P.S. A woman who works in the market has mailed this letter on my behalf and at much personal risk. She understands my pain. After giving birth to a Mongoloid last spring, she was released from the Program. The child was taken by the SS-Gefolge not a minute after reaching the world, and to this day she does not know of its placement. Her name is Ovidia. She is my friend. I pray this reaches you.

LEBENSBORN PROGRAM
STEINHÖRING, GERMANY

JANUARY 6, 1945

Dear Elsie,

They removed Friedhelm from the Program yesterday. I couldn't sleep last night but had to feign it and keep my tears quiet or chance exposing my true feelings to my roommates, Cata and Brigette. As I suspected, they are vulgar Lutzelfraus! Brigette has whispered my every word and action to the Oberführer. Spying on me as though I were a traitor when I have given no cause. All I admit to is loving my babies! The Program does not approve of its mothers claiming maternal ownership over the children of the Fatherland, but I cannot help what I feel. They were inside my belly for nine months, not the führer's. Friedhelm is flesh of my flesh and bone of my bone. How could I be expected to cast him off with such little care? It's like asking the seasons to stop because the führer demands. Impossible! Don't they see they are asking me to change the very basics of nature? After yesterday, I question my duties here. My faith in our purpose has been broken. I want to know where my son is! I cannot go on as if he never was. What kind of mother would I be if I could? What kind of woman? Pray for me, Elsie. The world has never looked so dark and hopeless as it does now. The only way to do what they command and subvert my maternal instincts is for my heart to stop beating. I prayed for that through the night but saw the sunrise nonetheless. I don't blame God for not listening to me. I shut him out when Peter died and I joined the Program. I don't deserve his mercy now.

I understand this is treasonous talk and should this letter fall into the hands of the authorities, they will send me to the camps with the other enemies of the Reich or shoot me on the spot. But I cannot keep silent. The weight of this sadness is too great. I can only write my true feelings to you, Elsie. I know you will not betray me.

Since my roommates watch my every turn, I'm giving this letter to Ovidia. Hopefully it will reach you. After you've read it, please, tear it up and burn it in Papa's oven. Not for my sake, but for your own and the safety of our family.

Love,
Hazel

LEBENSBORN PROGRAM
STEINHÖRING, GERMANY

JANUARY 8, 1945

Elsie, today I write to you with a spirit burdened by anger and despair beyond all hope of redemption. I'm living with demons so I must already be in hell. My roommate Cata, having recently borne a healthy son to the Program, was permitted into the newborn nursery to wean. There, she saw my daughter, round and blond as an angel, but she overheard the nurses discussing Friedhelm. One of the nurses said that Doktor Ebner was disappointed to learn of the twin Friedhelm's failure given the Program's fertility drugs and proscribed prenatal vitamin regimen. To that, one of the nurses claimed that if the mother had a hidden deficiency, then it would surely be passed on to one, if not all, of her offspring. Therefore, Cata said, they have begun testing my daughter to ensure she does not carry some mutation or derivation of our Aryan race. Unthinkable! As to my son, Brigette claims that after too much wine, a Gruppenführer confided to her in bed that they poisoned the Program's unwanted newborns and threw them in the fire, burying their bones alongside the exterminated Jews in the camps! Oh, Elsie! If the stories are true, then they are damned to hell and I along with them. I pray for the Americans and Russians to come. I welcome them and hope we all are burned to ash for the sins committed here. I do not think I will ever find rest again. It is near dawn now and I must get this letter to Ovidia before the Monday market opens. I love you most dearly, Elsie. Please know that—whatever comes.

Hazel

Dear Hazel,

The last letter I received from you was postmarked the 27th of December. I asked Postmaster Hoflehner if the mail had stopped due to the fighting in the north. He assured me that it had not and that Reich Postal Ministry is working at the highest standards of German efficiency, albeit at a slightly protracted punctuality. Then he handed me a letter from Herr Meyer to Papa as evidence. I told him one swallow does not make a spring. Herr Meyer lives in Partenkirchen. I could ride my bicycle there and back faster than it took this letter to arrive at the Garmisch Post Office.

I cannot help worrying. I've awoken many nights with you in my dreams. A notion that refuses to leave the mind is a sign, so Mutti has said. A sign of what, she's never articulated. I try not to tell her anything that will cause her concern. She's so easily troubled and doesn't understand our times. The world is not as it was when she was our age. So I keep my night-mares and thoughts to myself. You were the only one I could talk to, Hazel. I understand now that we must be prudent in every written word. Perhaps in my earlier letters, I made the mistake of impertinence. I pray they did not fall into the wrong hands and that is the reason for your silence! I was not thinking of the danger to you—only of myself and my longing to tell you so much. Please, forgive me and consider it the frivolous scribbling of a silly girl. Is it possible to be nearly seventeen yet feel one hundred years old?

Remember the story Mutti told us of Frau Grunwald whose hair went from red as summer strawberries to winter white after finding her three sons hung in the stables by the French at the end of the first war? To this day, Herr Grunwald's ancient mother appears younger than his wife. I thought nothing could be as tragic as that. But now I believe I understand. I feel the weight of this war pressing down on me. I see it in Mutti's and Papa's faces. We are all growing older too quickly. I barely recognize any of us. Sometimes I forget your face and it frightens me so that I take your photograph and stare hard until I'm sure it's burned into my mind's eye.

I wish you were home, Hazel. I miss my sister. If only you were here. If only, if only, if only. I pray for your safety and health, and the same for all your children.

Heil Hitler.

Your loving sister,
Elsie

LEBENSBORN PROGRAM
STEINHÖRING, GERMANY

JANUARY 13, 1945

Elsie, promise me you'll take care of Julius. He is all that is left of the happy life I dreamed for. Knowing what I do now, I cannot bear another day here. Elsie, I hope you can understand why I did what I felt I must. I love my children—all of them. But I am not the mother they deserve—flawed in my love for them. I pray there is truly a God and he is forgiving. Try to make Mutti and Papa see. I love you all and will miss you, my dear sister, most.

Yours eternally,
Hazel

eighteen

SCHMIDT BÄCKEREI
56 LUDWIGSTRASSE
GARMISCH, GERMANY

JANUARY 19, 1945

*E*lsie nearly dropped her tray of sweet *honigkuchen* squares when Josef came through the bäckerei doors midmorning. He'd been called away from Garmisch on business for three weeks. This was the first she'd seen him since Christmas Eve. It was one thing to use her affianced status to save her family from the Gestapo, but quite another to take on the responsibility of being the wife to a man she didn't love. She wore the ring, though each glimpse of it shamed her. The truth must be made known, or she risked living the lie forever. But keeping Josef close was her only guarantee that she and her family were protected. With Tobias hidden upstairs, she couldn't jeopardize them now by revealing her true feelings.

"You're back!" she welcomed.

"Just yesterevening." He nodded and kissed her hand.

"Papa, Josef is here," Elsie called over her shoulder. She pulled the handkerchief off her head and smoothed her hair. "It is very good to see you, Josef, but what brings you to us at this hour?" He had never come in before noon before.

"Your papa sent a telegram this morning." His face was tense.

Elsie's palms grew moist. A telegram was serious. The fact that she hadn't known about it made it even more significant.

Josef glanced at the ruby ring on her hand. She gave him a shaky grin.

Their time apart had made her nervous and unsure of where their relationship and alliances stood.

They know about Tobias, she thought, and she wondered if Josef's undisclosed business away from Garmisch had something to do with her. She tried to imagine how someone might've seen Tobias through her bedroom window. He was so small, and she'd made certain to keep her bedroom door locked, the rouladen shutters closed tightly at an upward angle. Only the birds and clouds could've caught a glimpse. Perhaps the Luftwaffe flew over and surveyed her room. She heard they had such technology. Mutti and Papa never went upstairs during the day, and Tobias had been instructed to be as silent as a ghost or risk discovery and death.

Her imagination swelled and with it, her pulse. "Papa?" she called. Though her fever had long passed, her cheeks blazed hot.

Papa came out wiping his hands clean. "Josef, my future son-in-law, it is good to see you. Thank you for coming so quickly." He patted him on the back and matched Josef's somber expression.

Elsie cursed herself for putting her family in jeopardy. She'd surely pay the price. Her head spun.

Papa motioned for them to take a seat in the far corner. Pulling her along by the elbow, he whispered, "I don't want your mutti to know of this yet."

She sat heavily in the wooden café chair and gripped the table ledge to keep her arms steady. Josef sat close beside. Checking over his shoulder one last time, Papa pulled a letter from his apron pocket.

Unspoken anxiety swayed the room like a ship's deck. Elsie wondered if the Gestapo had intercepted her letters to Hazel and she was being charged for some flippant remark made therein. She tried to recall everything written but couldn't. Her mind scrambled back and forth from her pen to her room to the Hebrew ring on her finger and the starched cotton of Josef's uniform against her arm.

Whatever it was, she'd take responsibility. She'd tell the authorities that her parents had no knowledge of her letters' contents or Tobias. It was all her.

Suddenly, Mutti leaned her head through the doorway. "You want me to make the pumpernickel, Max?" She lifted her hands, gooey with dough.

"Ja, ja, pumpernickel." He waited until she'd returned to the kitchen before unfolding the letter.

Elsie immediately recognized Hazel's script.

"I received this yesterday, and thank God I was the one to get the mail and not Luana." Papa placed weighted palms on it as if he could knead the words smooth like piecrusts. "Hazel is in trouble. She is not—of her right mind." His rough fingers, stained with spices, lay in stark contrast to the ivory page. "You must understand, Hazel is a faithful daughter of the Reich despite the things she says here. Please, Josef, I trust that what I share with you will stay between us?" His breath quickened, and he continued before Josef answered. "She is one of Germany's finest. This is a difficult time for her. If we could find a way to get to Steinhöring, we could help her return to her good nature."

It was only then that he allowed them to read.

Elsie's chest tightened. Papa was right. Hazel was in great danger. In all her life, Elsie had never heard her sister speak with such hopelessness, such anger, and with such scorn for authority. If the Gestapo found this letter, Hazel would be arrested or worse. And what of the baby boy? Could it be true that they intended to give away her flesh and blood?

Elsie balled her fists on the table, the selfish fear from minutes before changed to panic. "Papa, it can't be true. They wouldn't do such a thing— take a child from its mother." She looked to Josef, but his gaze remained steadfast on the letter.

Her anger flared, and before she could stop herself, she blurted out, "It's barbaric!"

Josef's head jerked high like a puppet by a string.

Elsie covered her mouth, but her eyes burned on.

A customer came in; the snap of the door hinge cracked the air. "Hallo!" the unfamiliar woman called, rapping her mittens on the glass display when no one greeted her.

From the kitchen, Mutti yelled, "Elsie! My hands are kneading! We have a customer."

Papa stood slightly and bowed to the woman. "I'm sorry, frau, I'll be with you in a moment."

The woman sniffled against the cold and perused the tray of marzipans. "Fine."

Josef cleared his throat. "Night travel is nearly impossible. If you want to get to Steinhöring, you'd have to leave early and you'd need an escort."

Papa nodded firmly.

Josef leaned back in his chair, scratched his chin. "It won't be an easy trip. I warn you. You won't be able to stay away long. It would cause suspicion. But . . ." He turned to Elsie and his face softened. "Hazel means a great deal to us."

Elsie nodded. Her eyes welled.

"Tomorrow at dawn," he told Papa.

"Ja, dawn."

The woman at the counter clucked her tongue. "I'm ready."

"Elsie, go," said Papa.

Though she loathed leaving the conversation, this was not the time for disobedience. So she rose and went to the baskets of bread.

"What would you like?"

"The bauernbrot." The woman pointed to the farmer's bread.

Reaching for the loaf, Elsie strained to hear what Papa and Josef were discussing at the table—something to do with their departure route. She was glad she hadn't refused Josef's proposal yet. She would use whatever she could to help Hazel. Whatever the cost.

The woman paid with ration coupons and left. Papa called Mutti from the kitchen.

"Ja, ja, what is it now?" she asked, her hands powdery with the SS flour that mixed like concrete and hardened just as fast.

"Luana." Papa sighed. "We must go to Steinhöring."

Mutti brought her fists to her chest. Silty flecks of gray dough fell to the floor. "What's happened? Is it Hazel? Julius?"

Papa took her by the shoulders. "Wash up and pack our bags. Hazel is . . ."

Mutti's lower lip trembled.

"She's ill," he said.

"Ill?" asked Mutti. Her floured fists left balled imprints on her dirndl. "Is there a fever epidemic?" she asked Josef. He looked away. "The blei-giessen cow," she murmured. "Dover's powder and tea is the cure." She blinked back tears. "What about the bäckerei?"

"Elsie will have to run things while we are gone," explained Papa.

"But the roads aren't safe. The reports say—"

Papa put a hand on Mutti's cheek. "Hazel needs us."

"I'll be escorting you, Frau Schmidt," said Josef. "You'll be safe with me."

nineteen

ST. SEBASTIAN CHAPEL
CEMETERY
GARMISCH, GERMANY

MAY 23, 1942

Josef had come to the cemetery late in the day. Wild poppies sprung up between slate and granite crosses. The setting sun cast long shadows, giving the flowers height and life. They moved with each passing breeze, reaching their rainbow of petals to some unseen spirit high above.

He was on his way back from an afternoon of Watten cards and raisin kuchen with Herr Schmidt when he saw the sign for St. Sebastian Chapel. Peter's death still haunted his waking and dreaming, but he'd grown accustomed to the ghostly presence, an aching in his vision that rarely abated. The methamphetamines and weekend holidays to Garmisch helped. The town had become as familiar as his own, but he'd never ventured here before. It seemed illogical when he knew Peter's ashes had been swept up by the western wind and probably settled in Munich's *Hofgarten*'s hemlock and clover. He imagined park visitors walking through the grassy topsoil not knowing their toes gripped the mud of men, not knowing Peter Abend.

That afternoon, he wasn't sure what drew him to the church. Nonetheless, there he stood above the small marker: PETER KLAUS ABEND, BELOVED. 1919–1938.

A dried daisy chain encircled the dates, and Josef wondered who placed it there—Peter's sister, Trudi, perhaps. Josef hadn't any siblings. His father had been hit by an automobile when Josef was too young to remember.

Embittered by her loss, his mother had been a strict disciplinarian who believed hard work and diligence might help them find happiness again. She encouraged his participation in the Memmingen branch of the Greater German Youth Movement and lived long enough to see him join the official military ranks. Two years after he moved east to Munich, she passed away in her sleep. A neighbor friend found her, stiff as a log, and stained from neck to navel in blood. The doctors diagnosed it as acute tuberculosis. It'd been so long since he'd returned home, and so infrequently did they speak that he couldn't recall if she'd even had a cough. Since his mother was a needlewoman known for her meticulous floral embroidery, he'd paid handsomely that her casket be sheathed with every bloom imaginable. That would've pleased her, he thought.

A scarlet poppy fluttered against Peter's slate. Josef wondered who would mourn when he died. He hadn't sisters to make daisy chain remembrances, nor brothers to carry on the family name. He was well liked by many friends, but his absence would not touch any of them so deeply. Standing in the waning light over Peter's grave, he tried to imagine his own funeral assembly. The landlady in Munich would surely come out of respect and duty. Perhaps a girl or two he once courted. Frau Baumann would cry for him but not dare show her face—a renowned prostitute at any man's funeral was inappropriate. It comforted him, however, to know she'd feel loss, probably more than any other. And then the Schmidts, he hoped. He'd become close to Herr and Frau Schmidt and watched as Elsie blossomed from a gangly girl to a young woman. They were genuine people. True to each other and those around. Yes, they'd be there too. He pictured Elsie clutching a bouquet of cornflowers and drying her eyes with a handkerchief. Lovely, even in sorrow.

"You were smarter than I gave you credit for," he said aloud, then shook his head and laughed, embarrassed to be talking to a dead man—and worse, a dead man who wasn't even there. But he meant it.

From all he heard, Hazel Schmidt was even more charming than her sister, her beauty only matched by her reputation as a generous lover. He attempted to visit the Lebensborn Program at Steinhöring, not as a companion but with the hope of helping Hazel and Peter's son in some capacity. His application was rejected on the grounds of inferior health records. The names of the Lebensborn women were so greatly protected that not even a hundred kreppels could convince his archive secretary to pull Hazel's file. So he stopped trying to reach her directly. His migraines continued, and his shots increased.

He stayed up nights tallying all the pain he'd caused: a widow before a wife, two families' heartache, a daughter's banishment, a fatherless son; and he continued to struggle with the part of him that remembered the Hochschilds fondly. However, this in no way interfered with his staunch commitment to the Reich. He turned the Kristallnacht scene over and over in his mind, rationalizing every action, and concluding that while the Hochschilds were Jews, Peter acted recklessly. Josef did not regret his anger, but rather his lack of control. The one thing he couldn't excuse or deny was that Peter's death was wrong. "Good care should be taken not to deny things that just happen to be true"—so it was written in *Mein Kampf.*

But even after visiting Frau Abend two years prior, Josef was unable to shake the heavy guilt he carried. He tried to call on the Abends once again, but Trudi claimed no one home and ignored her mother's calls from the parlor. He took it as a not-so-subtle indication that his presence caused more grief than consolation. But from whom could he request atonement? On that second visit, he went again to the bäckerei, distressed by the Abends' rebuff. The Schmidts greeted him as a son returned. They were his only connection to Peter's life, and through them, he wanted to make right.

He bent down to the headstone and picked the flower. The smell reminded him of poppy seed rolls.

twenty

Reba entered the bakery at quarter till closing. Overhead, the tinny doorbell jingled, familiar and welcoming. Hearing it, Jane peeked through the kitchen curtains.

"Well, hello there, gal." She greeted Reba with another hug.

Reba's muscles tensed only slightly. She even hugged back a little and was pleased by how pleasant the reciprocation felt.

"How are you?" asked Jane.

"Living," said Reba.

"Oh now, that's no kind of answer. Mold on bread is *living*. I hope you're doing more than that," she teased. "If you need Mom, she's gone this afternoon—had a doctor's appointment. A slap-n-pap."

"A what?" asked Reba.

Jane laughed. "It's our nickname for gynecological exams. We treat dough better than they do our lady parts. They slap your boob on the machine like it don't feel nothing, then add insult to injury with the stirrups and paper nightie. I've been on Mom for nearly four years to get a checkup. She hates the docs—even though my daddy was one." She scratched her head. "Well, maybe it's only the gyn-ohs. But I finally convinced her to go. You wouldn't know yet, but when you hit a certain age, lumps and bumps and all kinds of things grow everywhere. You go to sleep and wake up with a grapefruit attached to your derriere. It's scary." She threw a dishtowel over her shoulder. "Never mind all that. What can I do you for?"

Reba didn't know exactly why she'd come. She left the condo convinced she needed to get more information on German Christmas traditions, but she could've looked that up on the Internet just as easily. On the drive, she told herself she wanted to take a few more snapshots of the bakery in case the assigned photographer didn't get enough, but then she'd forgotten her camera. In the parking lot, she realized she'd only eaten a couple microwaved Jimmy Dean patties for breakfast, so maybe her stomach led her, subconsciously. But now, with the question posed, she wasn't quite sure at all.

"I—I . . ." Reba pinched the bridge of her nose and took a deep breath.

Riki had officially moved out the week prior. He said he was giving her space to decide what she really wanted. For a couple days, she was relieved, even grateful for the freedom, but all too soon the old sadness moved into Riki's vacant closet and drawers.

She rang her editor to talk word counts, headlines, and layouts; it made things better for an hour, but afterward the emptiness seemed larger than before. Riki called late Sunday while she was at the grocery store picking up a deli-made dinner. He left a message saying he was checking in. Children laughed in the background, and she wondered where he was. She played the message ten times over while scraping creamy chicken salad from its plastic container, still hungry when it was all gone.

Maybe he was staying with Bert, she thought. Riki hadn't any family left in the city. His parents were dead, both buried back across the border in Juárez. He'd asked her to come with him to their graves during the Día de Los Muertos celebrations, but she'd said she was working a story and hid in the magazine's editorial room while everyone else paraded about with sugar skulls and masks. She feared a day dedicated to the dead. It seemed ghoulish, unnatural, and far too intimate to hover over the bones of loved ones. Reba had never returned to her own daddy's grave, and she didn't want to. Riki said the dead came back to visit the living on Día de los Muertos, a religious superstition she prayed was *entirely* mythical. Because if she ever saw her daddy again, she knew she wouldn't be able to contain the simmering grief within. She'd tell him he was a damn coward for leaving them the way he did, for not loving them enough to fight for himself and their family; for not being a better man. She'd tell him she'd never let anybody hurt her the way he had, never let anybody get close enough to try.

Jane watched her. "Are you here about the article or . . ."

Reba bit the inside of her cheek. It was exhausting to be on guard every minute. Maybe Riki was right. Maybe she did need someone to help share her burden a little.

"I'm." Reba sighed. "Hungry."

"Wunderbar!" Jane went behind the display. "Let's see what we got. Mom just finished making *schaumkussen* earlier." She pulled out a tray of neatly lined chocolate balls.

"Truffles?" Reba's mouth watered.

Reba's momma made white-cherry truffles every Christmas. It was a recipe passed down from her granny, who had won first prize in the Virginia State Fair baked goods, candy truffles division. The framed blue ribbon hung in the kitchen. As the story went, Granny never entered another cooking competition, claiming it was unfair to the amateur cooks. Reba's momma passed on the recipe to both her daughters, but when Reba took a stand for cows, she gave up the family tradition. Like everything else, she snuck one or two while everybody was distracted. Hidden in the pantry, she savored the chocolate cherry mouthfuls, though they were never as good alone.

"No—not so fancy. Foam kisses. They're like a Mallomar," explained Jane. "Only Mom makes them with a springerle cookie base and a foamy meringue center, then she dunks the whole shebang in milk chocolate. Lord-dee-day!" She slapped her thigh. "They're my favorites, but we only make them in the cooler months 'cause this desert heat melts the meringue and chocolate."

"Can I try one?" asked Reba. She rummaged in her purse for a dollar.

"Oh, honey, I wouldn't take a dime from you, but . . ." She tilted her head and pursed her lips. "They got *milk* chocolate. Ain't that against your rules?"

Reba tapped the display glass with her fingernail. She didn't want to do it anymore. Couldn't she just be? Standing before the array of colorful confections, she took stock of all the butter and cheese and cream sweets she'd publicly rejected, only to eat later with a guilty conscience. Her reflection in the glass stared back at her. She was tall and sturdy with a strong, peachy pale face despite the arid sun. Her hair fell in dark, orderly waves down her back. It never did that in Virginia's humidity. She wasn't the overlooked, college tomboy anymore or the scared little girl in lopsided pigtails. She'd grown up and become someone. Reba Adams. When was she going to stop pretending to be what she wasn't?

"I've changed my mind." She shrugged.

"Just like that!" Jane snapped her fingers. "Well, congratulations. I was wondering when you'd come to your senses. God gave us the creatures of the earth for a purpose. I don't believe in all that Hindu stuff—reincarnation and washing your face in cow piss." She wiped her hands on her apron. "Mom will be so happy. Now you can try all of her pudding-filled kreppels, butter breads, Black Forest cake, and . . . oh, gracious! The world's opened up."

Reba winced a moment, feeling the lie exposed, even if nobody knew it. But then Jane gave her a foam kiss and took one herself.

"The way to eat it is to not pop it in all at once like some factory Milk Dud. These are special. You take a little bite in the side." She bit slowly. "And . . . you see . . . the chocolate sticks to your teeth and the middle gushes out." Her mouth was full, but she kept on talking. "And lastly is that cookie crunch." She closed her eyes and swallowed. "Hmm . . . sweet Jesus."

Reba did as instructed, biting into the rich chocolate foam and satisfying crunch. "Oh my, that's good."

"Now, are you ready to eat these like a true German?" Jane winked, then ripped open the side of a brötchen, pulled out the soft middle, smooshed a kiss within and cut it in two. "We call it a *matschbrötchen*—a mud bread roll."

They clinked halves as if they held champagne glasses and bit into the warm, sticky rolls at the same time. Reba couldn't remember the last time she tasted something so real.

The bakery was busier than usual the next day. Sergio sat at his regular lunch place. Two women chatted over slices of cherry bundt cake; their three children played with dolls and racecars beneath the neighboring table. In the ordering line, an elderly gentleman squinted to read the pastry labels while a teenage girl wearing a LATINAS DO IT BETTER T-shirt texted on her cell phone.

"Mom, Reba's back!" Jane called to the kitchen. "Perfect timing! Mom's just put the loaves in the oven. For the next hour, she has no excuses. I wish I could visit, but like you see, we got us a full house."

"No problem. I don't have much new to tell," said Reba.

She'd spent three hours at the bakery the night before, staying long after Jane had turned over the Closed sign and returning home so intoxicated with laughter and sugar that she barely noticed Riki's absence. For the first time in a long while, she felt energized and worked late revising her résumé and cover letter to send to a handful of magazines in California. By the time she lay down, the darkness was a friend not a foe. She wondered if this was how most people felt every day and night, and if so, she was envious.

"Do you have Mozart balls?" asked the old man in line. "I had the most delicious pistachio Mozart balls in Salzburg—you ladies from there?"

"Sorry, sir," said Jane. "My mom is from Germany, not Austria. We don't make *Mozartkugel,* but I think you can buy them online."

"All right, I guess I'll have a pretzel," he conceded. "But you gals really should think about making Mozart balls. There's big money in them."

"I'll pass your advice along to the head baker." Jane pinched a pretzel with her tongs and placed it in a paper bag.

"Dank-a sh-ay-n," said the man halfway out the door.

Reba grinned. "I'm sure Mozart would be thrilled to know he's German."

"Most folks don't know the difference anyhow. I tell you—we Americans are something to behold." She laughed. "I saw this little girl on the TV— a celebrity, Kelly-something-or-another—she didn't know that France was a country. Can you imagine! Child should have had her nose tied to a globe."

Miss Latinas Do It Better put away her cell phone and stepped up to order.

"If they know Germany's in Europe, they get an A for effort. Can I help you, hon?" Jane asked the girl.

"Uh, yeah, I'd like some cheese bread." She popped her gum. "To go, please."

"Easy does it." Jane swiveled her tongs like a six-shooter.

Reba went to a free table across from Sergio. She felt the inkling to say hello but sat with her back to him instead, precluding any awkward contact.

"Here again you are." Elsie's voice boomed through the bakery. Even the three children beneath the table paused in their make-believe to look up, then resumed running over their dollies with speedsters.

Elsie wore a brown, fringed skirt with a cobalt V-neck; her hair was swept back in a matching striped handkerchief. A flattering color, Reba thought.

"Jane said you came here yesterday." She took a seat. Her freshly washed hands were dewy and smelled of floral soap. "I was at the doctor's—nothing of importance."

"The slap-n-pap?" Reba's cheeks flushed hot as soon as the last syllable left her lips.

Elsie laughed. "You have it! Jane told you our little code, I suppose."

Reba looked round to make sure neither the children nor their mothers heard. The ladies continued to move their hands in casual conversation; the children slid across the tiles on their kneecaps.

"But you are not here to talk about all the cookies you and Jane wolfed down either, correct?" Elsie lifted an eyebrow.

"They were awfully good." Reba smiled. "I came about the story."

Reba's deadline was past, and her editor had insisted that the article be on her desk by morning; otherwise, the local publishing press wouldn't have time to run it in the holiday issue. Reba had a mission to complete; as long as her mind was focused on that goal, she could forget about Riki and everything else. She needed one good quote pertaining to Christmas in Germany and could already hear what she wanted said: *Christmas is a wonderful time; we have many German traditions that we continue wherever we are.* BAM—that'd be it. One unambiguous statement that did not involve Nazis. She took out her steno and pen.

"You see, I didn't do my job last time," Reba explained. "What I mean is, I didn't ask the questions I need for the article. I need to know about Christmas, about the holidays, about how you celebrated with family and friends."

Elsie tipped her chin up and squinted at Reba.

The two mothers beside them discussed hyperactivity, debating if it was a symptom of attention deficit disorder or the effects of chocolate and Coca-Cola.

Reba tapped her pen and waited for an answer.

"To tell you honestly, I cannot remember what we did before the wars. I was very young when the führer came to power and by the time he was gone, it was a new Germany. We had to reinvent ourselves, our traditions, our families. It was not the same. As I've told you, those years were . . . traumatic." Elsie shrugged. "Even the happy moments are clouded by pain. So you see, I cannot tell you about celebrating with family and friends without betraying."

Reba shook her head. "Betraying whom?"

"Myself. It would be a lie—a made-up story of what I thought you wanted to hear. Oh, we danced and sang to oompah music, toasted with beer steins, marked the birth of Christ, and waited for Saint Nikolaus to come to our snowy Alpine lodges. Is this what you want me to say?"

Yes, yes, it was. Reba pinched the bridge of her nose.

Elsie shrugged. "I am sorry. Those are not my memories."

"Then what are your memories? Give me the truth," begged Reba.

Elsie sucked her top lip then began, "In Germany, I remember

Christmases without a lot of food, my father trying to run our bakery on a cup of sugar a week. Cold Christmases. So cold a person could freeze to death. Drunk soldiers in wool uniforms. Dirty boot prints in the snow. Families unable to see each other and secrets that had nothing to do with Saint Nikolaus or reindeer or magic . . ."

twenty-one

SCHMIDT BÄCKEREI
56 LUDWIGSTRASSE
GARMISCH, GERMANY

JANUARY 24, 1945

"Wake up, Tobias, wake up." Elsie tapped the wallboard lightly but with urgency.

Tobias pushed the plank open, crawled out with a yawn, and extended his legs long on her bedroom floor. The wall cavity was just large enough for a small boy to sit and lie comfortably with bent knees, but she knew there was nothing so freeing as stretching your fingers and toes as far as they could reach. She tried to give him the opportunity to do so as often as was prudent and possible.

Her parents had left for Steinhöring five days before, and Elsie was grateful for their short absence. It gave her reprieve from worrying over every bump and creak. That past Sunday, she'd even been so bold as to put Tobias to work in the early morning hours. He was surprisingly skilled at pretzel making, knowing exactly how to roll and twist the dough for perfect knots.

Elsie huffed and puffed against the cold while Tobias slipped into an old pair of wool stockings that came up midthigh. He pulled a slouchy knitted nightcap over his head and reminded her of the costumed *Fastnacht* parades of her childhood. She couldn't help but smile despite the sunrise headache in her temples.

"Come on, little one." She patted him on his cap. "I've already lit the oven. We're out of brötchen. There aren't even any stale ones to bulk up the bin, so I have to bake an extra batch this morning, which leaves you in charge of the pretzels," she explained.

Being the youngest in the family, she'd never been given an exorbitant amount of responsibility in the actual baking process—until now. With the business and Tobias in her keep, she felt older and wiser, and she liked it.

"I know it's *ungodly* early, but that's the life of a baker and those who live with them." She sighed. "Maybe when you grow up, you could be a singing baker." She winked at him. "I bet you'd bring in double what we do for sweet rolls and a song."

Tobias smiled. "I'd make *babka* with heaps of cinnamon."

"Excellent," said Elsie. "Tobias, the great, singing babka baker. That will be your title."

She turned to make sure Tobias was safely hunched in her shadow before opening her bedroom door and making her way down the steps. Though she rolled the blinds each night, she still feared Gestapo surveillance, so she had designed a system for their morning kitchen routine. She stationed Tobias on the floured wooden table, underneath which they stored the giant iron pot Mutti used for soups. Whenever Elsie perceived any hint of danger, she'd whistle and Tobias slipped into the pot and closed the lid. This was only during the morning preparations. Half an hour before opening, she made sure he was locked safely in her room again.

Rumor had spread that her parents were personally escorted to Steinhöring. No one dared ask what the business was about. Too many had left town already with unknown destinations, and people liked it that way: unknown. So they ordered their usual, ignoring her parents' absence, and took their bread home where they could eat and whisper among themselves.

Elsie had taken to closing at lunch, something her papa never did. When she locked the door from noon to half past one, she received no complaints. This allowed her ample time to punch down the risen dough batches and check on Tobias.

While he'd been hiding in her room for a month, it was only in the last few days that Elsie finally felt at liberty to speak openly with him. The first time she heard him say more than a handful of words was over a bratwurst the night before.

"It's forbidden," he told her and turned away from the plate.

But it was all Elsie had to give. Lamb, beef, chicken, and fish were non-existent. It was winter and wartime. Had he forgotten he was a Jew hiding in her home? This wasn't the Romantik Hotel. She would have taken the sausage back and eaten it herself if it hadn't been for Tobias's elbows. No matter what he put over them, they stuck out like bird wings, reminding her that while parts of him had plumped since Christmas, he was still painfully frail.

In the last week, he had developed a slight wheeze, no louder than a mouse's chirp. When it paused, Elsie worried the chill had finally crept under his thin skin and frozen him solid. He needed hardiness. A diet of bread and winter vegetables wasn't doing the job. She grew up with Jews in the community so she understood the gravity of her offering, but it still frustrated and outright annoyed her that even now, in the midst of bloodshed and death, their customs took priority over his life.

"Eat. In times like this, God can't be so hardheaded," she told him.

He crossed his arms, tiny elbows bowing out.

"Please," she begged.

"I cannot," he insisted.

She'd huffed with frustration and momentarily contemplated physical force to get the meat down his throat, but she couldn't bear the thought of hurting him.

"Tobias, if you don't eat something more than a turnip, you're going to . . ."—she rubbed the thudding in her temples, then faced him—"die. And I don't want you to die." Elsie pressed, "You're my friend. I care what happens to you. So please eat. If not for yourself, then for my sake."

Tobias gulped and tucked his chin to his chest.

Elsie held out a piece of the sausage staked on the tines of her fork. "Please."

He whispered a prayer to himself in Hebrew. The cadence of his voice as lyrical as when she read the poetry of Robert Frost.

"God will fill me up," he said.

Perhaps, Elsie thought, but the human body was made of corporal stuff—flawed and sure to betray even our most earnest desires for immortality. From what Elsie had experienced of God, she knew he was more forgiving than any religion and more loving than any laws. She wished she could convince Tobias of it.

He considered the divided link on the plate. "My mother cut herself at dinner once while slicing my Chorissa," he began. "Her finger bled and left a scar. Right here." He rubbed his index finger. "I always felt badly for it, but she said the marks on our lives are like music notes on the page—they sing a song."

Elsie put the fork down. It was the most she'd ever heard him say, and suddenly, he was not merely Tobias the boy anymore. He had people, a mother, somewhere. While Josef had told her about his parents, they didn't seem real, just as Tobias hadn't seemed real until he was.

"Where is your family?" asked Elsie.

He'd shrugged. "I don't know where my parents are, but my sister is at the camp."

She thought of Hazel, and a sharp pang threaded her chest. "What is your sister's name?"

"Cecile," said Tobias.

"Older or younger?" Elsie asked.

"Younger. She is five and likes blue ribbons. She cried when they took them from her." He picked a rough fuzz ball on his wool stocking.

"Who took them?"

"The soldiers." His eyes went flat as dusty silver coins. "When we were getting off the train. They tore them from her hair. She cried. A soldier hit her, and she fell onto the tracks." His hands balled into fragile bird nests trembling in his lap. "I tried to stop them. I tried to pick her up, but I couldn't. There were too many people pushing and yelling and the train whistle was so loud. She couldn't hear me calling."

"Tobias, I'm sorry." A lump formed in Elsie's throat.

He turned to her and his expression lightened. "A lady carried her into the camp. She's there. I saw her once when I was singing. She does buttons in the sewing room. But she really likes ribbons." He gave a wan smile. "One day I'm going to buy her new ones."

Elsie imagined a child with bouncing brown curls held back by robin's-egg-blue ribbons like the ones she and Hazel wore as girls. "I'm sure she'd like that very much." Her breath caught. She swallowed hard. "I have a sister, too. Hazel. She's older than me and has three children. One is your age. His name is Julius."

His eyes widened with interest.

"You and he are alike," she continued. "You both love to sing."

He looked away and ran willowy fingers over his shorn head, sprouts growing back in dark patches. "I shouldn't sing anymore," he whispered. "When I sing, people get hurt."

Elsie remembered what Josef had said about Tobias singing for the camp detainees.

"You sang for me, and you saved me," she reminded him.

Tobias didn't lift his gaze.

She took his hand in hers; skin, thin as baked pastry. "One day, you'll sing for a great crowd. They'll stand with applause and throw roses at your feet."

Tobias looked up, eyes soft and hopeful in the bedroom lamplight. "Promise me, you will?"

"But how can I promise what I do not know will be?" he asked.

"I have faith in you. If you say it, you will do it," she said.

He needed to believe in something. She needed to believe too.

He seemed to dream on that a moment. Then he turned to her with great resolve and said, "I promise."

Without giving herself time for thought or fear, she leaned forward and kissed his forehead. "Thank you."

Afterward, she'd gone down to the kitchen and carefully removed every fleck of mold from the Quark. Papa's favorite, Mutti had been rationing the cheese for his breakfasts, but they were gone and Elsie didn't know for certain when they would return. So she scraped it up and spread it thick in a brötchen for Tobias. Then she ate the cold sausage. It sat uneasily in her stomach, and she felt it still this morning, heavy like a river stone in her gut.

A morning woodlark trilled in the distance. Tobias helped her empty risen batter onto the wooden board.

"Let's make two batches," she said. "Tomorrow we'll sprinkle water over the extras and heat them in the oven. Nobody will know the difference. I'll start the brötchen."

She went to the semmel dough and sunk her hands deep into the velvet bloom. The paste stuck to her fingers and between the gems of the diamond-ruby ring. Mutti's smooth gold band had no such crevices. It was a ring fit for a baker. Elsie's was not. It was made for someone else—for a songstress or a banker's wife. Someone with manicured hands and Yardley Lavender on her wrists. Elsie's hands were dry and cracked, and since the Grüns' store closed, she smelled of yeast and sweat. How she missed their floral soaps, French eau de toilettes, and citrus colognes. The vial of rose shampoo in her hiding place was too precious to waste on an arbitrary washing; instead, she'd place the open bottle below her nose and imagine its scent surrounding her.

The kitchen temperature increased. The wood burned musky in the oven, and Elsie fell into the comforting rhythm of rolling palm-size brötchen. By the time she'd completed a dozen, the bleary blue of coming dawn had crept into the shadowy kitchen. It was then that she noticed the oven woodpile: two thin logs deep. She'd forgotten to restock. The wood outside was wet with snow and would need time to dry in the kitchen before burning. If she didn't bring it in now, they'd never keep the oven aflame. Her hands were covered with gobs of dough. Tobias had set the pretzels' baking powder bathwater on the stove to boil and was rolling up his sweater sleeves in preparation. The wood was just outside the back door. He could snatch an armful or two. Daylight had yet to break. No one in town would be up and out at this hour.

"Tobias, we need firewood." She lifted a hand to the door.

He stared at her a long moment.

She smiled reassuringly. "Crack the door and check first."

He nodded, opened the door an inch, and peeked through. "No one," he whispered.

Elsie's heart sped up. "Slip into my boots and be quick." She infused her voice with confidence to make up for her lack of it.

He pulled the boots on and carefully unlatched the chain, pausing a second longer than Elsie thought he should.

"Hurry!"

His breath plumed in the frosty air and then he was gone, a white mist in his wake.

Elsie squeezed too hard on the dough ball, flattening it to a disc. She counted the balls on the sheet: one, two, three . . . six, seven, eight . . . ten, eleven, twelve. She checked the door. It didn't take her but ten seconds to fetch an armful of kindle. She tried to continue but lost track of which she'd counted and which she hadn't, so she slid them all into the oven. The coals blazed bright orange. She evenly spaced the rolls inside and latched the door. Her cheeks and forehead burned. Tobias still hadn't returned.

"I should have gone myself," she muttered. Gummy bits of excess flour clung to her fingers. She didn't bother washing, moving fast to the back entrance.

Tobias greeted her at the threshold. "Is this enough?" His elbows trembled with the weight of five logs.

Elsie ushered him in, and he put the wood beside the oven. She sighed away her worry. When suddenly, there was a rapping sound. Frau Rattelmüller was at the back with the door wide open.

twenty-two

*H*alf a dozen CBP and El Paso PD vehicles rumbled down the concrete path meant for joggers, bicyclists, and El Pasoans taking their children for twilight strolls along the Rio Grande. It was empty now, and at the sound of the convoy's approach, the ducks waded to the underpass's shady banks; a white crane flapped its way to a secret nest in the river thicket.

They'd gotten a tip-off from a neighbor: the padlocked trailer had new occupants. Smugglers typically kept illegal aliens in safe houses for one to three days before transporting them into the desert where they were dropped off at dusk to walk miles through the wilderness; thereby, circumventing highway checkpoints in the dark. On the other side, the smuggler would pick up the survivors and continue north.

Time was limited. The CBP had to do a roundup now or risk missing the group entirely. The El Paso Police Department helped assist in the arrests.

Riki and Bert led the motorcade. In the passenger seat of the truck, Bert checked his pistol magazine—the standard issued H&K P2000, a German semi. He holstered it at his waist.

Riki shifted in his seat. It was standard operational procedure, but loaded guns had always made him ill at ease. He'd seen one too many men get twitchy and draw their weapons prematurely, channeling Wyatt Earp, no doubt. Only the people in their sight weren't gunslingers and outlaws but farmers and masons.

"Are we ever going to get those rubber bullets?" asked Riki. The ammunition stunned the victims, giving them a solid punch without penetrating. These weren't menacing criminals. The CBP's duty was to prohibit their entry into the United States, not kill them.

"What's the point?" Bert shrugged. "Guy's coming at me, I'm stopping him dead in his tracks. Damned if I'm going wait till he throws a fireball in my face." He cinched the sides of his bulletproof vest. "Carol's rather fond of it." He grinned. "And I've gotten used to it myself."

Riki kept one hand on the wheel and scratched the base of his five o'clock shadow with the other. "A lot of women and kids these days though. Guns scare them more than they help."

Bert gave a caustic laugh. "That's the point! Scare them so bad they won't break the law twice! Don't go soft on me, Rik. Americans today are a bunch of bleeding hearts. Oh, human rights, human rights, they whine. What about the rights of the law-abiding people of our country? What about them, huh? So easy to sit around talking all philosophical-like when you're eating a cream cheese bagel in New Hampshire, but out here—shit." He sat up quick.

A Hispanic man stood on the path directly across from the division of trailer homes Riki had scouted two weeks prior. Bert flicked on the truck's police lights. The guy took off in a sprint down the trail. Riki slowed the truck near the targeted double-wide, and Bert opened the passenger door.

"Looks like we got a runner." He swung himself out. A sandy mushroom rose from the braked tires. "10-33!" He said into the handheld. "Going south along the Rio. Should be easy to spot. Hispanic male in a green jacket."

"10-4, this is Chief Garza. Sending one of our cars to rope him in."

A police car whizzed by in pursuit.

"Copy," said Bert. "Let's get in the house and see what we got."

Reluctantly, Riki drew his pistol from its holster.

A gray, windowless van parked outside. The trailer was still padlocked, but now the boards had been removed from two small windows.

"Nice find, Rik." Bert pulled his cap lower on his forehead and extended his steel baton. "Bet we got us a real rat's nest here."

The men in the following CBP and El Paso PD cars joined them, then quickly dispersed around the trailer.

"Van's empty," called an agent.

Bert and Riki headed to the front door with a handful of armed men at their heels.

Riki pounded with his fist. "Open up! Abierto!"

Without waiting for an answer, Bert smashed the padlock with his baton butt, and it broke free from the rusty aluminum. Chief Garza jammed a metal comb into the door frame and cracked it open. Within a minute, they had infiltrated the house.

Inside, people lined the walls and huddled next to one another in the corners.

"Abajo, abajo!" commanded Riki, pointing to the dirty mattresses on the ground.

The immigrants did as instructed, instinctively lying like canned sardines, facedown.

"Put your hands up!" Bert thwacked his truncheon against the wall. "Up, goddamnit!"

"Ponga sus manos," interpreted Riki.

The women flung their hands in the air superman-style; the men laced them behind their heads.

Agents and officers raced through the rooms, herding people into the main living space.

"Any more?" asked Bert.

"I think this is all," said Chief Garza.

"How many?" Riki assessed the space, so full of bodies that the room's temperature had risen considerably. He was drenched with sweat; his uniform clung to his back like sheets of hot wax.

"Twenty-five. Thirty, maybe. Not sure," said Bert. "A shit ton." He collapsed his baton and tucked it in his belt. "Don't know how these people can stand it." He wiped the perspiration from his nose. "One crapper, no food, cockroaches, and black widow nests everywhere you turn. It can't be worth it. We're just going to send them back where they come from and that has to be better than this." He picked up his handheld. "El Paso, do you copy? We're going to need a damn bus."

A young man in a Timberland T-shirt dared to lift his head from the mattress.

"You—do you speak English?" Riki asked him.

"Yes," he replied.

"Where are you from?"

"Mexico," he answered quickly.

Riki nodded. Guatemalan, Honduran, they could be Chinese, but they'd all claim Mexico, hoping to only be deported a mile across the border and not any farther. Riki understood the game.

"How old are you?"

"Seventeen."

"Where's your family?"

He shrugged.

The girl to his right started to cry, and Riki noticed her eye was split and swollen.

He knelt to her. "What happened, señorita?"

She whimpered and turned her face away.

"Bert," Riki said over his shoulder. "We need to get the medic kit from the truck. Looks like this girl—"

Suddenly, the seventeen-year-old sprang to his feet, waving a Buck knife. He kicked Riki square across the jaw, slashed the bulletproof vest of the CBP agent to his right, then made a dash for the door.

The room spun sideways and split open wet as Riki fell back against the trailer's corrugated metal siding. A childhood memory returned afresh: eating warm watermelon in the back of his father's pickup. Initially, his parents had been day croppers, reaping fields in Canutillo and selling the produce on I-10. For their work, the local farmer gave them lodging on his land and a percentage of the earnings. Now again, Riki tasted the melon's sweetness on his tongue, the steely truck bed beneath his back. He spat. The seeds suspended before him, floating black spots in a sea of pink.

The room erupted in shouts.

"Get down!" Bert yelled at the boy. "Drop the knife or I'll shoot!"

The girl screamed.

A gunshot ripped the air.

Boots thudded the floor.

Bert's face appeared overhead, hovering among the seeds. "Rik? You okay? Nod if you can hear me."

Riki nodded. He blinked hard. The pink cleared, and he realized he was lying on his back staring up at the pockmarked ceiling.

"The ambulance is on the way," someone said.

"I . . . I don't need . . . an ambulance," said Riki. He tried to lift himself but couldn't gain balance; the room was still rolling like a melon down a hill.

"It'll be here in five," said the voice.

"I said"—Riki reached up and grabbed Bert by the sleeve—"I'm fine."

Bert patted his hand, and Riki felt a tremor in it. "I know you are, Rik, but he ain't."

The girl cried. "Lo siento. Tuvimos que hacerlo para nuestra familia. Mi hermano. Por favor. Señor, señor, señor," she called and reached feebly out to Riki.

A CBP agent crooked her arm behind her back, forced her to a stand and escorted her away.

"Kid had 300 grams of cocaine in his pants." Bert cleared his throat. "Guess he figured he was screwed either way. Might as well . . ." He wiped the sweat trickling down his neck. "I got him in the leg—just to stop him. Paramedics are on the way."

Riki's hand to his face returned bloody. Bert helped him sit upright.

"The kid kicked your face." Bert's Adam's apple wobbled.

Riki took a sharp breath. "Hurts like hell." A fiery throbbing commenced between his eye sockets and the back of his skull.

Agents and police officers ushered people out. "Agent Mosley," called Chief Garza. "Looks like the boy and his sister are a couple of drug mules. Smuggler says he didn't know. When he found out, he gave her the eye."

"They caught him?" asked Riki.

"Yup," said Garza. "Name's Carl Bauer. Funny thing is, he's not even Hispanic. He's from Nebraska. Prior record. Figured he'd come down to Mexico and make a killing bringing people over. One of the immigrants says everybody in here paid $4,000 a pop."

"Same guy on the Rio?" asked Bert.

"Naw," said Garza. "That was a local. He checked out. Legal."

"Shit." Bert shook his head. "Guy looked as Mexican as they come. Why'd he run?"

"'Cause we were chasing him," said Riki.

"Carl was hiding in the trailer next door. Came in and told the lady and her kid he'd give them ten thousand if they kept quiet. Scared the kid so bad he pissed his pants. Mom dialed 911 when he wasn't looking," explained Garza.

"Dumb fellow," said Bert. "He didn't know it was the same lady who tipped us off in the first place."

Riki recalled the woman's scowling face from weeks prior, her little boy on the tricycle: "Bye! Bye-Bye!" She had to be of Mexican descent too. Maybe she thought the same way he did: that rules were there for a reason, even if the reasons didn't exactly add up. Better to be on the side of authority than against it.

Still, as the paramedics arrived and flashed penlights over his eyes, Riki couldn't help but think there had to be a better way than this—useless suffering, unwarranted loss. There had to be a way for him to be loyal to his country and his personal convictions.

"You got a nasty cut and a concussion." The paramedic had a thick Spanish accent made even more distinct by the wad of bubblegum he chewed. "You're lucky. They say that guy almost broke your neck. Lights out." He handed Riki two Tylenol. "Rest, and don't bang your head for a week. You got someone to take care of you at home?"

Riki didn't answer. Instead, he swallowed the pills dry. They scoured the back of his throat as they went down.

He'd accused Reba of being the one with the problem, but maybe deep down, it was him. How could he demand decisions from others when he hadn't made them? Before he could be true to her, he had to be true to himself.

twenty-three

"*T*his is a surprise." Frau Rattelmüller gave a hacking cough into the sleeve of her coat.

A chilly wind swept round the kitchen.

"I saw the chimney smoke." She banged her cane against timber door frame. "Your oven was lit early, so I thought I'd get my brötchen."

Elsie swallowed hard and stepped in front of Tobias, shielding him with her skirt. "Six o'clock. You know we don't open until then. With my parents away, I haven't the time for special purchases. I'm sorry, but you'll have to wait like the rest."

Frau Rattelmüller craned her neck around Elsie. "Seems you have a helper." She pointed with the shepherd's hook of her staff. "A little elf."

Elsie stiffened. "I must ask you to go." She moved toward the door, aching to lock the chain, usher Tobias up to his hiding space, and pretend it was all a bad dream. The consequence of this moment was more than she could bear. Even Josef wouldn't be able to save her now.

Tobias cowered by the oven, its kindle burning and hissing within.

"Is he a Jew?" Frau Rattelmüller asked, unyielding.

Elsie's knees buckled. She couldn't throw the old woman out now or she'd go straight to the Gestapo. "A Jew?" She forced an awkward laugh. "Nein, this is—"

"Because he seems to fit the description of the Jew child the Gestapo searched for on Christmas Eve." She stepped inside the kitchen and closed the door behind her. "They came to my house, too, and scared my old Matilda into a hairball fit."

Frau took a seat on the nearby stool and leaned her wrinkled chin on the wooden cane handle, inspecting them.

"You are mistaken," said Elsie. Her cheeks were as hot as the oven's coals. A pitchy note rang shrill in her ears. She tried to sip in air.

"Come here, boy," said Frau Rattelmüller.

Elsie held him by the hand. "This is my nephew Julius. Hazel's son."

Frau Rattelmüller narrowed her eyes on Tobias. "Tell me then, when did they start marking the German boys like the Jews in the camps?"

Tobias's sleeves were folded up to the bend of his elbows. A centipede of inked numbers scrawled down his left arm. He covered them.

Frau Rattelmüller huffed and thudded her staff against the tiled floor. "Don't lie to me, child. I know your family too well. It isn't in your blood— the art of deception." She grinned with yellowed teeth that reminded Elsie of a children's recording her papa bought them long ago: *Peter and the Wolf.* The wolf's French horns and Peter's pitched violins played in her mind.

Though the sun climbed in the sky, the room grew darker and blurred at the edges. Elsie steadied herself, dug her fingernails into her palms. She had to think clearly, to find an explanation, but all she could hear was the squeals and moans of the logs in the oven.

"You've been hiding this child for what—a month now? I'm impressed. Are your parents involved?"

There was no way out, but Elsie would not drag her family into her mess. "No," she said.

"Gut." Frau Rattelmüller nodded. "Then may I make a suggestion?" She stood and came within whisper distance. "Get him out of here. You don't know what you're doing. And if they find him, your whole family will pay. Herr Hub, too."

An ache shot through Elsie's chest, then thudded about like Peter's duck trapped in the wolf's stomach. Her mouth went dry, her fingers numb. Tobias stepped away from them both. His body shook.

Frau Rattelmüller's expression softened. "Don't be afraid, boy." She reached out a shriveled hand.

He cringed and hid his face against the table ledge.

Elsie put her arms around his shoulders and drew him to her. "If they find him, they'll kill him."

"Ja, that is certain," said Frau Rattelmüller.

Elsie closed her eyes a moment to think. Better him than her family, right? In the darkness of her mind, she thought perhaps. She couldn't keep Tobias hidden in her wall forever. But if she turned him in, his blood was on her hands. Could she live with that?

"There are others." Frau's voice was soft as the crackle of breadcrumbs underfoot.

"Others?" Elsie matched her whisper.

"Why do you think I buy so much brötchen in the mornings?" Her eyes were clear and true. She shrugged. "One cat and an old woman don't eat that much."

Elsie felt a sudden release inside, like the snapping of a twig, the noose come undone. She took a full breath and tasted the toasting rolls in the oven.

"I have friends in Switzerland. I am trying to get them there—out of Germany." Frau Rattelmüller turned to Tobias. "What is his name?"

Elsie held his hand firmly in hers. She didn't know whom to trust anymore. "He's a gifted musician, like his mother and father, and a skillful pretzel maker. His name is Tobias."

First, she'd test Frau with keeping this secret.

Tobias looked to Elsie, ingenuous and grateful, and an overwhelming guilt swelled up deep within her. In a world where everything seemed an illusion and nothing was what it should be, the thought came to her with chilling clarity: Tobias was her responsibility now, and she had to save him.

twenty-four

The December holiday issue of *Sun City* magazine arrived in the afternoon mail. Reba sat at the kitchen table examining the layout of her article. She'd sent her editor an altogether different story from her assigned topic. Plucking the American heartstrings at Christmas beat out hard news and educational commentaries. Her editor loved the piece and even made a last-minute cover swap. Reba's story headlined the copy. She smoothed her hand over the slick photo. A young soldier in desert fatigues with a red bow on his rifle held a weathered photograph of his great-grandfather in World War II uniform. The banner read: "Wartime Christmas Carols." Reba came up with that.

The story virtually wrote itself after one phone call to the Fort Bliss USO and all her visits with Elsie. She was proud of the article's honesty. No saccharine sentimentality to cut the bite. Men and women were away from their families, alone and afraid, the same as they'd been sixty years before. Across cultures and generations, they shared a bittersweet reality: Santa and his reindeer didn't always make it to your rooftop, and war stole even the hope that they might.

Reba and Riki had been playing phone tag for three weeks. They hadn't actually spoken to each other since the night he moved out. He came by the condo with a U-Haul when she was at work and left a handwritten note:

Reba, I got my stuff. I'm renting a one-bedroom downtown. Call me if you need anything.

    —Riki

The magazine's office was on Stanton Street across from the Downtown Plaza. When she went in to work, she purposely parked near the Plaza Theater and walked the full length of the historic district, wondering if he might look out his window somewhere and catch a glimpse of her. Not that it would change anything if he did, but she liked imagining. She still wore his ring on the chain around her neck.

The day before, Jane asked why she didn't take it off. Reba came to the bakery often. She genuinely liked Jane and Elsie's company. They felt more like family than her own mother and sister these days.

"I don't know." She'd shrugged and smoothed the band between her fingers.

"Because he means more than you thought," Elsie had chimed in from behind the register.

Reba couldn't agree or deny, so she dipped a lebkuchen in hot cocoa and stuffed her mouth.

In the centerfold, the magazine ran a couple photos of Elsie posed with trays of Christmas stollen, nut bars, and lebkuchen hearts. "During times of war, Christmas may mean fewer gifts under the tree but more gifts from the heart." That was her all-star quote. Reba had pushed hard to get it.

Reba wondered if Riki had seen the magazine yet—in a checkout line, a dentist's waiting room, a local restaurant lounge, somewhere. She picked up the phone and instinctually dialed Riki's cell phone. She got all the way to the last digit before her stomach dropped, and she hung up. The phone in her hand seemed radioactive. She put it down, but her fingertips continued to burn. Did he think of her? And had he ever dialed her number and then hung up? The clock in the kitchen ticked quarter to five. No, probably not. He was busy with work.

She decided to call Jane and let her know the magazine was out, but at near closing time, Reba doubted anybody would answer. Elsie avoided last-minute cake orders by ignoring the existence of any communication technology after 4:00 p.m. Reba thought it better to go by tomorrow. Then she could bring a copy. She put the phone back on the charger stand. Just as she did, it lit up and sang "Jingle Bells."

In an attempt to be merry, Reba had changed the ring tone on the first of December. Caller ID: *Deedee Adams.*

Reba had sent Deedee a handful of one-liner e-mails and left voice messages when she knew she was at work, thereby avoiding a lengthy phone call but still alleviating her guilty conscience. An attorney by trade, her older sister shared her talent at ferreting out others' secrets, while not giving up any of her own. It was different talking to Jane and Elsie. They chose when and how to divulge their secrets. It was a common factor in their friendship: acceptance without forced confession. But family was different. Reba's momma had a notorious habit of seeing the elephant in the dining room and asking for someone to pass the gravy. She avoided family confrontation and encouraged her daughters to do the same. Perhaps that was why Deedee went into the vocation she had—unearthing others' truths to make up for years lived in personal denial.

The phone's "jingle all the way" echoed through the empty house. Reba bit her cuticles. She couldn't ignore Deedee forever. She was her sister, and underneath all the hurt, Reba loved her more than anybody on earth.

On the last ring before the answering machine responded, she picked up. "Hello."

"Well, hello, my prodigal sis!" Deedee's voice was as warm and bubbly as apple cider in a Dutch oven.

"Hey, Deedee." Reba sat down at the table with the magazine open to her article.

"Momma! Reba's on the phone," Deedee yelled into the background chatter. "Yes, right now! On my cell! Momma says you better call her. She'd be on the line right now if we weren't over at Uncle Vance's birthday party, and she didn't have a mouthful of smoked salmon. Do you still eat salmon? It's not an endangered fish or anything right?"

Reba sighed. "Yes, I do; and no, it's not."

"That's what I thought. How about pork? Uncle Vance bought himself this new gadget that roasts a pig in less than two hours. So we're all waiting to eat some fancy barbecue. Personally"—Deedee's voice quieted—"I could give two nickels about his silly roaster. He bought it off eBay, for Christ's sake. You'd think he reinvented the wheel the way he's peacocking around. And just so you know, it's already been two hours and that thing is still pink as a baby's hiney. Thank God for Aunt Gwen's toddies— delicious as always. They've saved the day for everyone. You better believe Uncle Vance is already four mint juleps deep and singing 'Happy Birthday' to himself. You know how Momma is—the drink makes her nervous—so she's pushing hors d'oeuvres in her mouth and laughing like we're at the circus, which of course, we are in a sense." She gave a strained titter. Reba knew it well. "Wish you were here with me. I asked Momma if she'd heard from you recently. Said she hadn't. Come to think of it, *nobody* had. So I picked up my phone and dialed. Honestly, I was expecting to leave another message but—here you are!" She paused and Reba couldn't tell if it was to catch her breath or take a sip.

Mud Slide Slim and the Blue Horizon played in the background. It was the same CD her momma put on for every family gathering—good "ambiance music," she claimed. A pang of homesickness ran through Reba, and she clasped the ring dangling in the middle of her chest.

"You really can't go this long without calling. I know work and the time zones make it hard, but, honey, you've got people who worry about you," said Deedee.

"I know. I'm sorry."

"I miss my little sister."

"I miss you, too." Reba leaned back in her chair and tried to keep her voice steady. She could feel something inside rising to a pitch, but she couldn't break. Not now.

"How are you?"

"Doing good, doing good."

"Yeah, you sound like you're jumping for joy."

"I'm tired."

"Take a vacation! Come home early. That's the real reason I called. I wanted to know when you're coming for Christmas."

"I—well—" She swallowed hard.

Last Christmas, she hadn't gone home, claiming the new job as her excuse, but in reality, she simply couldn't face another Christmas with Daddy's stocking hung next to theirs and Momma trying to be as holly-jolly as ever. At the time, she was newly dating Riki and excited by the prospect of a romantic Christmas Eve with just the two of them. No traditions or expectations to uphold. A clean slate. Momma and Deedee had accepted the explanation with disappointment, but she doubted it would work again this year.

"Don't even start to tell me you *aren't* coming home. I swear to Mary and Joseph I'll throw a fit!"

"Deedee, please." Reba fingered her engagement ring, rolling it round her thumb.

"Don't Deedee me. I don't want to hear it." She huffed. "I can't *force* you on a plane."

Reba relaxed a little. That's right, she couldn't.

"So I guess I'll have to come to El Paso."

"What?" Reba stood up and knocked the magazine to the floor.

"I suspected you might pull another MIA routine, so I already bought a ticket. I'm coming the week between Christmas and New Year's."

"This is crazy. I've got work and you've got work and . . ."

"What're you going to do—lock me out of the house? I'm coming, Reba and that's all there is to it. So unbunch your panties and get used to the idea."

twenty-five

SCHMIDT BÄCKEREI
56 LUDWIGSTRASSE
GARMISCH, GERMANY

FEBRUARY 2, 1945

*E*lsie celebrated her seventeenth birthday with a midnight picnic on the floor of her bedroom. Tobias had sprinkled some of Mutti's sweet aniseed into the rye dough and braided it into the shape of a crown. It'd baked off dark and fragrant as candied licorice. They placed a blackout candle in the center. Though small and lacking in the feasts and family of previous birthday celebrations, she had great hope for her seventeenth year and was grateful for Tobias's company in welcoming it. When the cuckoo chimed twelve o'clock, she blew out the flame, and the room snuffed into darkness.

Three days later, Papa, Mutti, and Josef returned with a boy Elsie would never have recognized if he hadn't entered the bakery and immediately announced, "I'm Julius. I don't belong here."

So unlike his mother and father was he in both appearance and disposition, she'd almost agreed with him.

Instead, she'd replied, "I'm happy to meet you. I feel as if I should know you better. I'm your *tante*."

"Doch! I know," he'd said and wriggled up his nose like a piglet. "What's that stink?"

She'd just finished a batch of onion rolls and ignored her nephew's disparagement. "Where's Hazel?" she asked.

Papa handed Mutti his suitcase. "Take these up, Luana." He turned to Josef. "Thank you again for all that you have done for us."

The men exchanged heavy nods that spoke beyond words.

"What?" Elsie asked one, then the other. "What?"

Papa held up a commanding hand. "Later. It has been a long day, Elsie." He gently took Julius by the shoulder. "Come. Let's find something to eat before bed." He led him to the kitchen.

Alone, Josef turned to her.

"You must tell me," she begged.

He placed his cap on snugly. "Hazel left the Program."

"Left? And went where? She would be here, ja?"

"Your parents will explain. It's not my place."

She understood when to stop asking questions. The week before, the Gestapo shot Achim Thalberg, the orchard farmer. His crime: he announced to the *biergarten* news of German retreat in Slovenia. A handful of Gestapo sat at a nearby table. With a quick exchange of words, they pulled their pistols and in less than a minute, poor Achim lay dead, his beer stein frothy and cold on the table.

Frau Rattelmüller continued to purchase her morning brötchen and had filled her in on the details. Elsie didn't fully trust the frau yet, but with each passing day, she proved herself a faithful confidante. In her parents' absence, Elsie had given the frau extra rolls and honey buns with her usual order. Nothing that would be noticed when her papa returned. Tobias was still painfully thin, but she suspected it was the nature of everyone these days. Her own dresses hung loose on her frame. They had no more meat, and there wasn't so much as a scrawny rabbit to be found on the black market. The forests had been stripped of every animal aboveground. She hid the handfuls of root vegetables they still owned in a burlap sack behind the kitchen kindle pile and prayed for an early spring. If there wasn't, she was sure they'd all waste away to skeletons.

She fidgeted with the baggy cuff of her sleeve. Josef took her hand and ran his thumb over the ring he'd given her. Elsie continued to wear it as a kind of talisman. Something was happening. She'd felt it for days, fear rolling closer like an ominous storm.

"I'm sorry, I cannot stay," said Josef. "I received immediate orders to report to Dachau."

"You're leaving? For how long?"

"Until our forces have pushed back the Allied forces."

A wave of nausea swept through her. Who would protect them now?

Rumors swirled that the Red Army was a greater power than anticipated, and it wouldn't be long before they marched directly into the heart of Berlin. As fearful as she was of the enemy, the thought of what her own countrymen would do to her made her chest seize up with nettled panic. The Grün family disappeared in the night, but as proven by Achim Thalberg, the soldiers were becoming more brazen and eager to make examples of anyone who crossed them. Josef was her ally, but now he was leaving, Hazel had disappeared, Julius was in their care, Tobias was hidden in her bedroom, and Germany was losing the war. All of it swept over her, and her hands went clammy despite the sheen of sweat on her face.

Josef misread her expression as concern for his well-being. "I'll be fine," he reassured. "You'll see. All will be well." Then he leaned in to kiss her.

Instinctively, Elsie turned her cheek and saw the hurt and disappointment in Josef's eyes. Kind Josef who wanted nothing more than to protect and keep her safe; and yet, she did not love him.

He cleared his throat. "I'll write to you."

She nodded and didn't turn to watch him go. They were on their own now.

Elsie went up to Mutti's closed bedroom door and knocked. "Mutti?"

"Come in, dear."

Inside, Mutti unpacked the suitcases, placing items into the cedar wardrobe; her face pin-straight.

"Did Julius get supper? The ham we bought wasn't to his liking. Slightly rancid, I suppose, but what could we do? I made your papa eat it. Spoiled or not, it was something. He must keep up his strength. He's not the young man he used to be," she prattled on, folding one of Papa's sweaters over and over. She looked up briefly at Elsie, the hollows beneath her eyes deeper than ever Elsie could remember. "We left in such a hurry," she went on. "But like your papa keeps reminding me, you girls are all grown up. You can take care of yourselves. I've showed you how to make goulash a dozen times. At your ages, I can't be worrying over feeding you or what clothes you wear or where you go." She took a quick breath. "You aren't children anymore and I haven't the time with the bakery and customers and keeping up this drafty house, and now there is Julius who needs looking after. Of course, he isn't an infant like the twins . . ." She fingered the fat cable knit of the sweater. "But he needs a mother. So, you see, you'll need to help your papa more downstairs. I can't be in the kitchen as often now that Julius is here and—"

"Mutti, please," Elsie put a hand over Papa's sweater. "Where's Hazel?"

Mutti's fingers slipped to her sides. "Hazel?" She blinked hard. "We don't know. They only told us she is gone."

"Who told you?"

"The Program administrators. Her roommates. They say she went to the market and never came home. She simply left."

Mutti bit her bottom lip, fearful and confused. The story didn't make sense to her, either. It wasn't in Hazel's nature to run away, but if she had, she'd have sent word to them. She'd have written Elsie first. Though Postmaster Hoflehner had assured Elsie that the mail was running routinely, they had not received anything from outside the Garmisch-Partenkirchen valley in weeks. Hazel's January 4 letter to Papa was the last to arrive. What if Hazel had written and the letters had been intercepted? Perhaps she was hidden in someone's safe house, like Tobias in hers, and could not contact them; but then she'd left Julius behind. Hazel would never have left her children without a significant reason—unless she had no alternative. Elsie's scalp burned, as if her hair had been plaited too tight.

"Where are the twins?"

A furrow deepened between Mutti's eyes. "They belong to the Fatherland."

"So did Julius, but they gave him to us."

"Julius is the son of Hazel and Peter."

"And the others—aren't they the blood of your daughter? Doesn't that count for something!" Her voice pitched.

"Quiet," Mutti hissed.

The tone chilled Elsie to the bone. She had never heard her mother speak in such a manner.

"You must always remember your place. We are women." She locked eyes with Elsie. "We must be wise in our words and action. Do you understand?" Mutti pulled a crumpled blouse from the suitcase and smoothed it on the bed. "Josef was very helpful in getting Julius out. We almost had to leave him behind. Josef knows a woman who works inside the Nazi offices. He says she's good at providing information. We'll find Hazel. We'll find my grandchildren." She swallowed hard and nodded to the open suitcase. "Would you mind putting my brush and pins back in their place, dear?"

Elsie took the needle-thin hairpins and bristle brush and set them side by side on the dressing table.

"Flesh of our flesh. Blood of our blood," whispered Mutti.

"What was that?" Elsie asked.

"That's what the führer said in Nuremburg—it's biblical—and we can't forget. Before us is Germany, in us is Germany, and after us is Germany." She lifted the gauzy blouse into the air.

Elsie watched the lace neckline flutter through the vanity mirror. "Germany has changed," she whispered.

In the dim of the candlelight, Mutti sighed; a single tear eked out the side and she flicked it away with a finger. "Go help Papa lock up for the night," she said and hung the blouse, her expression hidden by the shadow of the wardrobe.

twenty-six

T he interior of the bakery was decorated from top to bottom with plastic garlands, silver tinsel, colorful nativity scenes, and fake snow sprayed foamy white along the edges of the glass windows.

"Merry Christmas week!" called Jane from behind a long line of customers. Despite the holiday having passed, she wore a Santa cap with a puffball dangling at the end. It bobbed up and down with each order request.

"Merry Christmas week," Reba replied.

The bakery was packed. Schools were out on holiday; cherry-cheeked youngsters stood in line chatting and pointing at the chocolate and sugar-glazed sweets under the display case. Christmas carols jingled overhead and patrons hummed along absentmindedly, giving the store an altogether whimsical feel. Even the entry bell seemed jolly.

Reba was glad for the hustle and bustle. Deedee had arrived the day before and after nearly twenty-four hours together in the small condo, Reba craved external distractions. She wanted to avoid any circumstance that would provoke her sister into interrogation mode. She'd already had one close call that morning.

In a rarely used kitchen drawer, Deedee found a photograph of Riki and Reba in Mundy's Gap on the Franklin Mountains. "Who's the guy you're with?" Deedee had asked.

Reba hadn't lied. "Riki Chavez. He works for the Border Patrol."

Deedee had nodded, slid the photo back in, and gone on hunting for coffee filters; but the whole thing put Reba on edge. She wasn't ready to talk about Riki. She knew her sister would fly into a rage over the concealed engagement—even if it was off. As Riki had said, they were taking a break to come to decisions. She still had the ring. It was all far too complex to discuss at the moment. She could barely think about it without inciting a headache.

When Deedee searched the bathrooms for extra toilet paper, the suspense became too much. There was bound to be something of Riki's hidden in the nether regions of the bathroom drawers: a wayward men's razor blade, Old Spice deodorant, a condom.

"You want to get lunch?" Reba had called up the stairs, straining to keep her voice casual. "There's this German bakery. My friends own it. They have the best bread in town for sandwiches."

Deedee eagerly agreed after a breakfast of stale Froot Loops. It was the only thing left in the cupboard that didn't require a can opener. Reba had cleaned out all the expired junk food before Deedee's arrival but forgot to replenish it with typical staples. To add insult to injury, Deedee had to crunch the cereal sans milk. Reba had drunk it all before she had arrived.

"Who's that?" asked Deedee, nodding to Jane at the register.

"Jane. Her mother, Elsie, owns the place. Sharp as a whistle. Seventy-nine years old and still working every day."

Deedee widened her eyes and shook her head. "Lord, that's impressive."

They took a seat and set paper-wrapped packages of deli-sliced turkey and Swiss on the table.

"When I'm seventy-nine," said Deedee, "I want to sleep till noon and eat nothing but Krispy Kreme doughnuts in my silk pajamas. I won't give a fig about my figure or fashion. I'll be that crazy old lady and love every minute."

Reba laughed. Despite everything, she adored her sister. She kept things in perspective.

"Every loaf is baked fresh in the mornings," said Reba. "They have really good pastries, too. We should ask Jane for a dessert recommendation."

"She looks busy."

"It'll slow down." Reba checked her wristwatch. "This is the lunch crowd."

"You must come a lot."

Reba shrugged. "A couple times a week. Jane and Elsie—they've become my minifamily."

"Really?" Deedee raised an eyebrow high. "You've never mentioned them, but with the infrequency of your calls and e-mails, I'm not surprised. I know you're a big girl, but Momma worries."

"I've been *super* busy. Work, work, work." Reba waved a hand. "Besides, how much trouble can I get into—I hang out in a German bakery with women two and three times my age. Come on, Deedee!" She laughed too loud.

Deedee gave an unconvinced grin, then turned to the bread bins. "Do they make pumpernickel? I haven't had good pumpernickel in years. The store-bought kind tastes like cardboard."

Reba breathed deep. Relief.

They decided on a small loaf of pumpernickel but waited for the line to diminish before stepping up to order.

"Hey you, lady!" said Jane. "Sorry, I haven't had a minute. Is this Miss Deedee?"

Deedee smiled and extended her hand. "Sure is."

Jane shook it enthusiastically. "Glad to meet you. Reba's been talking about your visit for a couple weeks now. I like to see what kind of people my friends come from. Says a lot." She gestured to the back kitchen. "But I don't know what my people say about me!" She laughed and her Santa pom-pom bounced up and down. "So what can I get you?"

"We brought meat and cheese to make sandwiches. Thought maybe we could put them on pumpernickel."

Jane turned to the bread bin and pulled a fat, sable loaf from the shelf. "Always a good choice. Mom made this today. Let me run back and slice it up pretty."

She left the front. "Walking in a Winter Wonderland" came on.

"Hey, it's your favorite," said Deedee. She elbowed Reba and hummed. ". . . say are you married, hmm-hmm, no man . . ."

It *was* Reba's favorite, but in that moment, it only made her cringe and wonder if Adams family ESP was at work.

Jane returned with the sliced bread. "So you're from Virginia too, right?"

"Sure am. Just about everybody in our family's been there forever. Reba's one of the few to pack up and leave the state." Deedee tilted her cheek to Reba. "We miss her."

"I can imagine." Jane handed Reba the loaf. "Mom left her people in Germany. My oma and opa passed away when I was in diapers, but I think I still got some cousins over there. I understand why Mom moved to the

States, but sometimes I wish I'd had a chance to know my kin. I'm sure they missed her."

"Cry me a lake," said Elsie from the kitchen door. She clapped her hands together and sent up a flour cloud.

"River, Mom," corrected Jane.

Elsie paid no mind. "Do not be telling sentimentals about my life. We have enough of those on that foolish Lifetime Channel. You watch this? Nothing but crying and dying and pregnant fifteen-year-old girls." She huffed and threw up a hand. "And they call that entertainment these days!"

Deedee cleared her throat to quell a giggle.

"In my time, we had Bogart and Hayworth and movies that meant something more than a snotty handkerchief. You must be Reba's sister, Deedee."

"You must be Reba's friend, Elsie," said Deedee.

"*Old* friend." Elsie gestured to the loaf in Reba's hand. "This is my papa's recipe. He made it often during the wars. Rye was easier to come by than white flour. You know what pumpernickel means in English?"

"Mom—" Jane started.

"The devil's fart," said Elsie.

Deedee laughed, a kind of rolling giggle that grew thicker as it went. Reba felt her own laughter awakened by it.

Jane rolled her eyes. "I'm sorry—the things that come out of her mouth."

"Do not apologize for me," said Elsie. "I doubt any family of Reba's would be so easily offended."

"Not at all!" Deedee assured. "I understand why Reba likes spending time with you."

"Correct. It has nothing to do with my baking. She comes for my vulgar company." Elsie winked at Reba.

"That's exactly it. You've got me figured out," said Reba. She motioned to the waiting table. "Have you ladies had lunch yet? We brought extra."

"Thanks, but I grabbed something earlier," explained Jane. The next customer stepped up. "What can I help you to?"

Elsie came between Deedee and Reba, taking each by the crook of the arm. "There are twenty minutes before my brötchen is done. What kind of cheese you have?"

"Swiss," replied Deedee.

"Ack, ja!" said Elsie. "I have good Swiss friends. Very gut."

The trio took a seat and made sandwiches. Reba laid open the bread slices while Deedee doled out the turkey and Elsie the cheese.

"Oops," said Deedee looking down at the three piles. "No cheese for Reba." She reached to take the slice away, but Elsie stopped her.

"Nonsense! The girl has finally come to her senses. Besides, you've got to have cheese with pumpernickel. It sweetens the bitter bite."

Deedee cocked her head.

Reba gave staccato nods and flipped the tops on. "Sandwiches are ready!" She passed them out.

"She's—how you say—a dairy dee-va these days." Elsie took her sandwich and squished it hard so the meat and cheese held together.

Deedee crossed her arms. "Really?"

"I'm starving!" Reba shoved the sandwich into her mouth.

Elsie nodded. "Powerful stuff—dairy. They say it changes the hormones. I saw on a health science television show." She took a bite and continued talking. "A medical study found that women with the premenstrual syndrome had less emotional outbursts, depression, mood swings, and general bad temperament after eating more dairy. The doctors. They have documented." She gulped. "And I believe in science. Reba is a case in point. She began eating dairy and her head cleared so she could finally make a decision about that fiancé."

Reba closed her eyes tight.

"Um Gottes willen! It was about time." Elsie crunched her pumpernickel.

"I don't believe I had to hear about my baby sister's engagement from a seventy-nine-year-old German lady I met less than ten minutes before! Unbelievable!" Deedee paced Reba's kitchen.

Reba sat at the table, watching the moon outside climb steadily over the mountain ridge and wishing she were up there with it.

"That's the guy, isn't it?" Deedee pointed to the kitchen drawer. "Why didn't you tell me he's your fiancé?"

"Ex," clarified Reba.

"Whatever. You agreed to marry someone and you didn't bother telling your family—telling me!" She slapped her chest dramatically. "Your sister!"

Reba picked at the dark rind beneath her thumbnail—pumpernickel.

Deedee inhaled. "Are you pregnant?"

Reba snapped her head up. "God no. Deedee, this isn't *Jerry Springer.*"

"Well, I'm trying to rationalize why you'd do a thing like this." She put a hand on each temple, pushing the pressure points and pulling her eyes into slits.

"I knew you wouldn't understand," grumbled Reba. "That's why I don't tell you things."

Deedee took a seat beside her, leaning her cheek onto her fist. "What is there to understand? All you have to say is that you fell in love and I'll get it. But you haven't said a word!" She looked hopefully at Reba. "Do you love this guy?"

Reba cupped her hands over her nose. They smelled like Swiss cheese. She didn't know how to answer. It was complicated. She loved Riki, but maybe not enough. It was like cheesecake. She thought she loved it, but maybe that was only because she'd sworn it off. Now that she could have it openly, shouldn't she want to taste all she'd been missing: cheddar rolls and crème-filled pastries, hamburgers and beef satay, buttermilk pancakes with corn beef hash, and whipped cream on everything? The world was at her palate. So how could she go back to nibbling old cheesecake, even if she craved it, even if it was her favorite thing in the world? And how could she make Deedee understand?

She moved her fingers to cover her face and whispered through tented palms, "He's cheesecake."

"Huh—what? Cheesecake?" Deedee huffed. "And that's another thing. I thought you didn't eat that stuff. You made me adopt a cow, for God's sake!"

Reba groaned. She couldn't take it all at once. She buried her head in folded arms like she used to do during first-grade rest time.

"Talk to me, Reba." Deedee put a familiar hand on her back.

It was quiet inside the shelter of Reba's arms. Her steady breathing, the only sound. "I eat dairy now." She had to start somewhere.

"All right. Momma will be happy. It broke her heart that you wouldn't eat her cheese fritters. You know she's got a handful of recipes she considers prize-worthy, and all of them include cream, cheese, or a hunk of beef." Deedee's voice softened. "So how did you meet Riki?"

Reba raised her chin to her forearm. "I did a story on immigration in the borderland. I interviewed him at the station where he works. He was so different from the guys back home. He wore cowboy boots and a Stetson and not because it was in the latest J.Crew catalogue. There was real mud and horseshit on them."

Deedee laughed and so did Reba.

"And he treated me like I was . . . *refined* coming from the East Coast and having traveled places. He couldn't believe we could drive two hours and be at the water whenever we wanted. He was fascinated by my photos of Sandbridge Beach, and hardly anybody's impressed by the geriatric prominence of Sandbridge! But he's been here all his life. Landlocked in the desert. He's never seen the ocean. Can you imagine?"

Deedee shook her head.

"And most of all, he seemed to love me so much. I've never been loved like that. So hard, you know?"

"I don't. I won't even go into how many nightmare men I've dated. In case you didn't know, there are a lot of screwballs out there looking for a pretty face and a frolic." Deedee seemed to sigh out all the angry air. "To tell the truth, I'm jealous."

Reba sat up. "Don't be jealous! It's downright terrifying."

"Too bad. I'm already green-eyed. I saw the photo. The guy's hot." Deedee smirked. "So I can't wrap my brain around why you didn't mention he asked to marry you. Were you embarrassed?"

"No, not embarrassed." Reba stared hard at the full moon now high above the craggy mountaintop. "Unsure. I didn't want to tell anyone until I felt it back. Felt that kind of *big* love."

Reba pulled the necklace from its hiding place under her shirt and dangled the ring.

"It's beautiful," said Deedee.

"I never wore it."

"Why the hell not? If I had a diamond like that, I'd bling-bling it around town."

"It never felt right," explained Reba.

Deedee nodded. "Is that why you called it off?"

"I guess. We never technically called it off. We had a fight and he moved out. I haven't heard from him in over a month." Something in her throat caught. Her eyes stung.

"That makes it easier, right?" said Deedee.

Reba turned away to hide the welling tears. She couldn't stop them.

"Ever try calling him?"

Reba shrugged. How many times had she dialed all but the last digit? She prayed he'd call her, but he didn't so she didn't, and the days turned into silent weeks. She missed him, much more than she'd ever anticipated.

Deedee took Reba's hand and traced the bones fanning from her wrist to her fingertips. "You remember what Momma used to tell us when we were little. If you truly love somebody, you follow them to the ends of the earth; you give up everything you have, even your life—now that doesn't mean you slit your wrists for some jack-about-town just because he makes your heart flutter." She paused.

Reba knew they were both thinking the same thing: that was exactly what their momma had done. Not in the literal sense, of course, but their entire lives, they'd watched her bleed herself, die a little each day, to keep up the family reputation on the outside and the pretense of normalcy within. Momma tried to hide the unsavory truths from everybody, even herself, but *they* knew. They always knew.

"What I mean is, when it comes to the person you marry, you've got to know what you're getting into."

Here it was: that old splinter come to the surface. Reba was tired of its sting. She wanted it out, for better or worse.

"Do you think Momma knew what she was getting into with Daddy?" she asked.

Deedee blinked once. Twice. The right side of her mouth twitched. It was a subject that smarted them both.

"Daddy had too tender a heart. The war tore it up and nobody, not us or Momma, could put him back together." She sighed. "I guess you have to be ready even for that—for the person you love to leave you, in spirit or in body. Death comes in all kinds of disguises."

"A hungry wolf," whispered Reba.

Deedee ran a hand through her bangs, then continued, "I never doubted for a minute that Momma loved him. Whatever else might've been going on, they weren't faking that."

Reba wasn't debating the relationship between her momma and daddy. She remembered what they'd had. She remembered her daddy's good days. Him and Momma strolling through the woods behind their house: Momma fanning herself with a maple leaf as big as a bear claw; Daddy's arm around her waist. The way Momma looked at him across the dinner table like his laughter was music. Momma's smile when he brought home bright bouquets of sunflowers. When Reba first moved to El Paso, it struck her as ironic that sunflowers grew wild, clinging to the edges of alfalfa fields. Weeds. It made her wonder if in other parts of the world, roses might live the same double life.

"Maybe not, but there was a hell of a lot of other acting going on. Momma deserved an Oscar." Reba bit her bottom lip to keep it steady.

"I think about us as kids, and I don't know what's real and what's not. It makes a person feel like her mind's warped. Makes me understand how Daddy must've felt."

Deedee readjusted in her chair. "Daddy . . . had a rough time of it."

"A rough time?" Reba laughed. "God, Deedee, you make it sound like it was a bad day!" All the years of resentment piled inside her like kindling, and Deedee had just lit a match. "You always did that. When you left for boarding school, you pretended everything was peachy keen at home—well, it wasn't. Far from it. Daddy was seriously depressed. I found his medical files. He had ECT treatments. Do you know what those are?" She put a sharp finger to her temple. "Bolts of electricity to the brain. I don't know what you classify as a rough time, but I'd say that's *more* than a rough time. And he did things in Vietnam, Deedee. Horrible things. I read one of his therapy notes. There was a whole other person in there we never knew." Her mind raced faster than her lips could form words. "Remember—remember when I told you about him hitting momma. You told me it was a *dream*. A dream! You were the one dreaming! Pretending our house was fine when Daddy was clearly in need of help that didn't come from a whiskey bottle. But no, everybody was content to either pretend it away or leave. I'm happy for you. Happy you got out of there—got to live the Miss Prissy Perfect life at school, but things weren't going well at home, and it didn't take a rocket scientist to figure that out. You knew. I know you did!" Her face was hot. "He killed himself, Deedee!" She choked down her sobs. "Momma'd already cut down the rope when I came home from school. She was on the phone with the police. You weren't there. You didn't see it. And the worst part was, he didn't even look dead. He looked like he'd just passed out after a spell." She'd never spoken of that night. It made her feel like a bonfire out of control, flaming to the sky. "When the ambulance came, and they said he was dead"—she covered her eyes with her hand—"I was *relieved*. Relieved, Deedee! I loved him so much, but I was afraid of him too. How can that be—you can't love what you're afraid of, right?"

Tears coursed down Deedee's cheeks, but Reba couldn't cry. The burning inside was too great.

"We never talked about any of it," Reba went on. "It scares me still because I feel so much of Daddy inside me."

"Oh, Reba." Deedee took both of Reba's hands in hers. "I'm sorry."

Sister to sister, their gazes met. Reba's pulse steadied from a boil to a simmer.

"I didn't want to leave you." Deedee bit her bottom lip. "But I *had* to get out of there. I wanted to be free of all that sadness. I was so scared and hopeless."

Comprehension fluttered in Reba's chest. "Why didn't you talk to me?"

"You were a little girl." Deedee sniffed. "I thought I was helping by keeping it from you. Whenever Daddy went on and on about his fears, his demons, it upset you so. I didn't want you to worry any more than you already did. I wanted you to think everything was okay, but then, it all got to be too much. I had to get away—for my own sanity. I wanted to protect you from my pain, too."

"What about Momma? He was hurting her."

"Momma understood Daddy far better than either of us." Deedee cleaned away her runny mascara, smudging it between her fingers. "The law has taught me that despite all the facts we think we know, the truth can be an awfully hard thing to get a hold on. It's muddled by time and humanity and how each of us experiences those."

"Truth is truth," Reba whispered.

"It is and it isn't," said Deedee. "Every day, I walk into the courtroom with my truth in hand and it never ceases to amaze me that the other attorney is doing the same. Who's right?" She shrugged. "I'm thankful I'm not a judge."

"So are you saying we accept anarchy? We throw up our hands and live in delusions, never facing reality? Look how much good that did Daddy."

"No," said Deedee. "It means we let God be the judge. It's too big a job for you or me. We have to stop being afraid of the shadows and realize that the world is made up of shades of gray, light *and* darkness. Can't have one without the other." She squeezed Reba's hands. "Daddy went wrong by judging his own past with an iron fist and allowing those judgments to condemn his present. There was nothing any of us could've done for him except love him as best we knew how. You can't make someone else believe your truth, nor can you force forgiveness. We can only be responsible for ourselves." Deedee pulled Reba against her shoulder. "I'm sorry I wasn't there when you needed me. I'm sorry it's taken us so long to talk about Daddy's death."

Reba leaned into her. "I'm sorry too." And for the first time in what seemed like forever, there were no pretenses between them. With that came a peace Reba had longed for all her life.

"Deedee." She let the weight of her head rest wholly against her sister. "I don't want to be like Daddy."

Deedee leaned her own heavy head atop Reba's. "His biggest mistake was he couldn't see how big our love was for him."

Reba thought of Riki, and the center of her chest began to ache. "Riki's the most genuine man I've ever met . . . and I do love cheesecake."

"Ah," Deedee whispered. "Cheesecake." She nodded. "Well, maybe he's not cheesecake. Maybe he's the milkman."

They quietly giggled in each other's embrace.

"I never understood your whole dairy-free phase. It just didn't fit you." Deedee kissed Reba's forehead.

"I was trying to be what I wasn't," said Reba, and she smiled, feeling the lie lift. The truth as buoyant as air.

twenty-seven

SCHMIDT BÄCKEREI
56 LUDWIGSTRASSE
GARMISCH, GERMANY

MARCH 23, 1945

The sunlight was as weak as the dandelion tea Mutti made from the premature blooms she picked that morning. A storm at dawn had left their heads limp and bowed over like dejected schoolchildren. Now, the breeze was raw and wet and carried with it the scent of earthworms writhing beneath the hibernating strawberry vines. The mineral chill stuck to the back of Elsie's neck no matter how many scarves she wore or how quickly she worked. The usual crowd had already formed a line, their stomachs and voices grumbling at the workday ahead, the smell of bread, and the whispers of German defeat.

Elsie tossed stale rolls and loaves into cloth sacks and paper wraps, trading trinkets, coins, and promissory words alike. They were already running low. The brötchen bin was near empty, and Frau Rattelmüller hadn't come for her customary purchase.

"I paid for three," said a man in a stiff fedora. "You gave me two." He pointed a hard finger at the rolls in brown paper.

"I'm sorry." Elsie handed him another, and he left in a huff, mumbling under his breath and wrapping his scarf tight around his throat.

The next customer ordered, but Elsie failed to hear. Frau Rattelmüller's absence had unsettled her routine. She was uneasy; her mind drifted past the carousel of morning customers and down the lane to the frau's door. She wondered what had kept her.

A shifting of seasons was in the air, and it was more than spring. The Gestapo patrolled the streets night and day with rifles slung over their shoulders; news trickled in that Allied forces were at the Rhine and certain to cross over any day; the Volksempfänger said the Americans, Brits, and Russians were coming to rape and murder them, but Elsie wondered how much worse they could be than their own soldiers. Since Achim Thalberg's murder many more people had been quarantined, arrested, or simply shot. Having Tobias under her roof was grounds for immediate termination, for herself and her family; and with Julius constantly underfoot, keeping Tobias's presence a secret had become a daily labor.

Initially, Mutti proposed that Julius share a room with Elsie. The mere suggestion had precipitated the first of Julius's fits, which they soon learned were habitual. He refused to sleep anywhere near the opposite sex and bristled at all displays of affection between Mutti and Papa, be it a held hand or a kiss to the cheek. It was baffling considering Hazel's loving nature. Mutti made excuses, saying, "He's been raised with the highest morals of the Reich. Perhaps we all need a lesson in propriety." Papa had nodded but frowned.

In an attempt to appease Julius, Mutti fashioned a mattress out of old tablecloths and straw and cleared the kitchen pantry closet of its few remaining items. This was to be his bedroom. He wasn't thrilled but accepted it as the only extra space available. Sullen and ill-tempered in his new surroundings, he spent a majority of his days therein lining his toy soldiers in the grooves and divots of the wooden floorboards. Like curdled milk, he seemed soured with a great sadness no one could alleviate.

Elsie didn't blame him entirely. He didn't know them. Hazel moved to Steinhöring while still pregnant, and they'd only visited him as a newborn. His family was the Program. He talked incessantly of his instructors, of Nazi customs, and how much he hated foreigners. All of which no one dared debate, but such harsh words from a seven-year-old made them uncomfortable. Julius knew everything about authority and discipline and nothing of family and compassion.

Though they were of similar age and shared a fairness of eye, Julius and Tobias were as different as night and day. Julius remained stony and emotionless, even when Mutti showed him photographs of his mother, Hazel, and smoothed his cheek with the back of her hand. It produced not a flicker of reciprocated affection or appreciation. He refused to wear the sweaters Mutti knitted, declaring the wool smelled of sheep's dung as did the mattress on which he slept. It seemed the only pleasure he gleaned was in food, though he had a word of criticism for all they offered, balking at the vegetables and griping that the spaetzle tasted like shoestrings—a product of his own beloved SS flour and powdered eggs. Nothing was right. Nothing was good enough.

Mutti doted on him regardless, but Papa was reserved. Elsie knew him well. He didn't approve of the boy thinking himself so far above their station as bakers. After all, this was his daughter's son, his blood. So in the first week, he put the boy to work. Julius whined and complained through each batch of brötchen and pastries. He brought a bitterness to the kitchen that they all feared would bake into the bread. After a week, Mutti asked Papa to let him be, and he spent the rest of his days playing war games in the kitchen pantry.

Before daybreak, while Papa heated the oven and Mutti catered to Julius, Elsie often had the whole upstairs to herself, allowing her time to tend to Tobias before joining Papa in the kitchen.

After all her earlier descriptions of Julius, Tobias was curious about her nephew's arrival. Still, it came as a surprise when he whispered one morning, "I've been listening for his music."

Elsie was in a rush to give him the wool socks Mutti had knitted for Julius, and Julius had subsequently thrown to the floor for their itchiness. He would never wear them, and Mutti would be wounded once again for a gift rejected. Elsie figured it worked out well to put the items to Tobias's good use.

"I put my ear to the floor, but all I heard was the pots and pans and customers," Tobias continued as Elsie pulled the socks up to his knees. "What songs does he sing for you?"

"Sing? Who?"

"Julius. You said he sings. Since I can't anymore, I thought I might listen to him." His eyelashes fluttered.

Elsie handed him the breakfast Mutti had brought her: a deformed pretzel wrapped in a muslin napkin.

"He hasn't had a chance yet," she said and tugged his nightcap down over his ears so he wouldn't catch cold. "Now eat."

Tobias nodded. "I haven't sung in a long time either—not really. The officers made me sing, but their songs are not so beautiful. Not like the ones my father wrote and my mother, sister, and I sang together." He cradled the napkin in his lap. "Sometimes I worry that I'll forget them. Sometimes I think I've already forgotten my voice."

Elsie winced and ran her hand over his head. "I'll never forget your voice," she comforted. "And you haven't forgotten either. It's still inside you and always will be. Trust me."

He nodded and scooted back into the nest of blankets and items in the crawl space. *A Boy's Will* lay open to "The Trial by Existence."

"That's a good one," said Elsie. "'And the mind whirls and the heart sings, and a shout greets the daring one,'" she recited from memory.

"'But always God speaks at the end,'" Tobias whispered back as Elsie secured the board closed again.

Papa had been pleased with Elsie's success while they were in Steinhöring and entrusted her with many more of the family recipes. Elsie enjoyed her new responsibilities in the kitchen and had grown accustomed to greeting Frau Rattelmüller at the back door prior to opening. She'd been doing it for so long now, Mutti and Papa thought nothing of it. Her daily order became a kind of unspoken code. A dozen brötchen meant all was well. Her absence today signified trouble.

The customer line had shortened. Elsie was grateful. Papa's sourdough loaves wouldn't be out of the oven for another thirty minutes.

Julius came from the pantry room with his face freshly washed and hair still holding comb tracks. Mutti had pressed his pants and shirt for him, just as they had in the Program.

"You look very nice," said Mutti. She took his hand and gave his arm a jiggle. "Say good morning to Tante Elsie."

His stare shot straight through her. "I would like lebkuchen for breakfast."

"Come now, you shouldn't have sweets for breakfast. They didn't let you have that for breakfast in Steinhöring, did they?"

"Nein." Julius rolled his eyes. "We had soft-boiled eggs and sausage, white bread with fresh butter, apricot jam, and fruit from every corner of the German empire. But I don't see that here." He pulled his hand free from her and crossed his arms over his chest.

Mutti nodded. "Doch, you don't." She wrung her hands together. "Elsie, give Julius a lebkuchen—and a glass of milk."

Elsie had no time to cater to her spoiled nephew. She picked up the last gingerbread, a large witch house hung ornamentally from the bread bin since Christmas, broke it in half and handed it to Mutti.

"Elsie!" snapped Mutti.

"Pumpernickel raisin?" asked the next customer while balancing a bundled child on her hip. The child slept, cheek against the woman's breastbone, mouth hung open.

"No raisins. Only pumpernickel," replied Elsie.

The woman dug in her pocket and extended a gold christening cross. "It's all I have?"

Elsie paused long enough to notice the young mother's sharp cheekbones and ashen lips. "Keep it." She patted her hand and reached for the dark loaf.

The woman's eyes glazed tearful, and she kissed her sleeping babe. "Thank you so very much."

"Elsie, the milk?" asked Mutti.

Elsie huffed. "I'm sorry, but you'll have to get it yourself, Mutti. I'm busy."

Julius's icy glare pricked the back of her neck. Mutti led him away, presumably to get milk, but Elsie knew they would find none. They hadn't had milk for weeks. Papa had made do by watering down cream and bartering with the cheese maker for the leftover whey.

"Next?" Elsie called, and a new customer stepped up.

"A word with you?"

Elsie didn't recognize the figure at first, wearing an ankle-length trench coat and a black lace-trimmed hat. Frau Rattelmüller lifted the edge of her veil, revealing a terse expression and sunken eyes. The patrons behind groaned impatiently.

"Give me two minutes, and I'll meet you by the back woodpile," whispered Elsie. She wrapped a thin slice of stollen in brown paper and handed it over the counter. "Thank you."

Frau Rattelmüller left with the parcel.

"Mutti," Elsie called. "Would you mind taking the front for a minute? I forgot to get firewood." It wasn't entirely untrue. The pile was low.

Mutti came from the back and nodded to the next customer. "Grüs Gott, Herr Baumhauer."

Elsie retreated to the kitchen, past Papa kneading dark *schwartzbrot* and Julius lazily munching his bewitched and brittle lebkuchen on the stool. She stepped into her boots, threw a shawl round her shoulders, and went out into the drizzly March day.

Frau Rattelmüller waited on the far side of the pile. Elsie had to keep her legs steady, her gait unencumbered, in case she was being watched. If the frau was finally turning her in, she wanted to at least appear innocent; maybe they'd allow a poor baker's daughter reprieve. But if it was Frau Rattelmüller who had been discovered, then this very meeting indicted her as an accomplice. She slowed to a stop on the opposite side of the neatly crosshatched wood.

"Ja?" she asked, colder than was her nature. "What do you wish to speak to me about?"

Frau Rattelmüller sensed the hostility. "I come alone and with no ill intentions," she promised. "I would not be here if I had any alternative." She leaned heavily on her cane. "I know some people on the inside of the Dachau camp. They say that the Nazis are planning a Jewish expulsion. The Russians and Americans are close. Soon, they plan to move the Jews to Tegernsee on foot."

"Now?" The March rain had turned to sharp ice needles, pelting her forehead and nose. "They'll freeze to death."

"I'm sure that's part of the plan. Save the bullets for the soldiers in Berlin."

"But Josef"—Elsie's heart beat fast—"he's at Dachau."

"Ja." Frau Rattelmüller's face turned away under the veil. "He's one of the officers in charge."

"In charge of this death march?"

Josef had never discussed his business with her. She always assumed it had something to do with the mountain brigade, not Jewish camps. The rumors of Dachau's violence and mass graves had circulated for years. Too horrific, most chose not to believe. These were their countrymen. Elsie was not prepared to imagine Josef leading such brutality. The piercing rain stung her cheeks.

Frau Rattelmüller leaned in closer. "I know a man who can bribe the guard to turn a blind eye while the Jewish women move between the workhouses and the sleeping quarters. There are two girls—family members of my . . ." A tree cracked. She turned quickly. A sparrow fledgling flew from a branch. She continued in a whisper, "Once I have them, they will leave at once for Switzerland where trusted friends wait."

"Are you leaving too?"

"I am too old. I'd only slow them down." The frau swallowed hard. "I've come because I need your help—with the bribe. I've given all I can, but it isn't enough."

Elsie stepped back. Here was the crux of it. The old woman wanted money. Was this how she bought her daily bread—with coins stolen under the premise of charity? Elsie took a good look at Frau Rattelmüller. Her veil was tattered about the edges; the hem of her dress hung round her heels; her feet were stockingless despite the weather; and her hands, bone thin, were chafed an angry red. This wasn't a woman who gorged on rolls and sweets.

But Elsie had nothing to give. The bäckerei till held a meager amount, enough to be noticed if missing. She rubbed her forehead, trying to heat her skin against the throbbing frost, and then she saw it: red glints beneath the melted ice. How easily she'd forgotten her promise to Josef, gone with no written word as he had promised.

"Here." She slipped it from her finger. "This should be enough."

"Your engagement ring?" Frau Rattelmüller took it but frowned under the dark veil. "What will you tell Josef and your family when they ask?"

Elsie rubbed her fingers, suddenly warmer than they'd been. "I'll tell them I gave it to save the Fatherland."

The frau nodded. "Your sister, Hazel, had courage, but Elsie—you have the heart of the prophet Daniel."

Elsie winced at the mention of Hazel in the past tense. She looked away and shook her head. "The ring was never truly mine."

Frau Rattelmüller grasped Elsie's hand. "There are still people who remember that God's law is above all mankind." Her voice caught. "These men will not lead us down the path of destruction. I learned early in my life that the dead cannot save the living. Only we can do that. While there is life, there is hope." She turned to leave.

Elsie stopped her. This was her chance. "I ask a favor of you in return."

Elsie took a deep breath; the glacial air choked the flesh of her throat. The branches crackled under the sleet. Every whisper was a danger, every move suspected, but Tobias had become too important to Elsie. Each hour he spent in her bedroom was an hour closer to revelation and ruin. If this was a chance to save him, she had to take it.

"When you first discovered Tobias in our kitchen, you offered to take him with the others. Will you do so now—will you get him out of Germany?" she asked.

Frau Rattelmüller gripped the crooked handle with both hands and lowered her voice to barely a murmur, "Elsie, it is too dangerous now. Moving him from the bakery to my home could put us all in our graves."

The wind swirled gusts of budding flurries.

"And in this weather—he is so small and weak." The frau shook her head.

Elsie pictured Tobias's knobby elbows and knees, his tiny earlobes beneath the stocking cap. His health was poor. She was right. There was a good chance he would not survive the elements.

"I'm sorry," said Frau Rattelmüller. "Please believe me, if there was a way to safely transport him, I would do it. The Gestapo patrols your bakery day and night. Perhaps it is under Josef's order of protection; nonetheless, they are there . . . watching. I must think of my friends first."

Elsie nodded. She'd seen the headlights of the cars rolling by late at night but assumed every street in Garmisch was being carefully guarded. The news that it was just hers made her knees go slack.

"I will help you in every way I can," Frau Rattelmüller continued, "but I cannot do this."

Elsie couldn't fault the old woman for prudence. Every measure of caution had to be taken. Acting impulsively cost lives. So for now, Tobias would stay hidden in her bedroom.

Then Elsie remembered: "He has a sister in the camp. Her name is Cecile. She works with the seamstresses. Could you get her out with the others?"

This was one thing she could do for Tobias.

"Ja." Frau Rattelmüller thumped her cane on the icy cobblestone. "If she is still there, we will take her to Switzerland."

Elsie nodded. "Tell her that her brother is well and speaks of her with great love. Tell her he promises to see her again." She sighed out a plume of white. "He'll be the one waiting with blue ribbons."

"Blue ribbons?" asked Frau Rattelmüller.

Elsie nodded. "She will know the meaning."

A dog barked, and both women jumped.

"Go." The frau turned and hobbled down the slippery lane.

Shaken, Elsie scooped up an armful of logs, splinters pricking her arms. Inside, Julius had finished the lebkuchen and moved on to brötchen with the last bit of the family's butter and jam. Elsie dumped the wood beneath the stove and coughed to clear her throat of any residual sentiment. Knowing Julius's nature, she couldn't take the risk of exposing her true emotions.

"Has your oma eaten?" she asked.

The boy crunched the side of his roll and shook his head.

"Well, perhaps you should take her some before you eat it all yourself." Papa turned from the mounds of spongy schwartzbrot bread.

Julius continued chewing.

"Did you hear Tante Elsie, son?" asked Papa.

Julius swallowed hard. "I am not your son."

Papa gripped the wooden roller with white knuckles. "Elsie." His voice boomed through the kitchen, reverberating against the pots and pans. "Take Mutti breakfast. I need to speak with my grandson."

Mutti had opened the last jar of her cherry jam for Julius. Elsie scooped a teaspoonful onto a plate, grabbed a hot brötchen from the rack, and went to the front, glad that her nephew would finally receive true discipline—the kind only a father could give.

The breakfast rush had ebbed. Mutti stood arranging a tray of cookies end to end so that their paucity was less conspicuous.

"Ach ja, how nice that looks," she said softly to herself.

Elsie held the plate before her. "I brought you something to eat."

Mutti waved it away. "Throw it in the bin with the others. We need the extra money. I'm not hungry."

Elsie set the plate beside the register. "Eat, Mutti. It does us no good if you become ill and bedridden."

Mutti cupped the roll but did not break its crust.

"Cherries. Your favorite." Elsie held out the jam knife. Mutti had taken to eating little since she returning from Steinhöring. It worried Elsie.

Mutti studied the jellied-jeweled spoonful. "Whenever I taste these, I think of that cherry tree in your oma's garden."

"I remember it well. Hazel and I spent many summer days pretending it was a fairy castle with magical fruits. We used to play a game. Every cherry we ate, we got to make a wish. I really believed I'd get all my wishes. Some of them did come true. Once, Hazel wished for a bottle of lavender perfume, and I wanted rose shampoo, and when we came to visit Oma the next week, there they were." Elsie smiled and conjured the smell of her secret rose vial.

"Oma was a good mother," said Mutti. "I miss her very much in these times." She wiped the corner of her eye. "What a fool I am. An old woman talking like a child."

"Nein," said Elsie. "A woman talking like a daughter."

Mutti smoothed Elsie's cheek with her thumb. "You've grown to be so fine. Beautiful and wise. Those are gifts from God, dear."

Elsie put her hand atop her mother's and felt a blossoming in her chest. Mutti had never complimented her so.

"You've got to eat something." Elsie held out the plate again. "Please?"

Mutti took her hand from beneath Elsie's and split the brötchen. "Oma always said the best bread was broken together." She spread the cherries inside. "You need to eat as well."

It was true. Elsie had given her pretzel to Tobias. Her middle knotted with hunger.

Mutti passed her the half roll and licked the knife clean. Elsie ate and thought of all the magical fruits she had shared with her sister, her oma, her mutti. All the dreams they still shared. Though little, it was the best meal she'd had in months, filling much more than her empty stomach.

twenty-eight

3168 FRANKLIN RIDGE DRIVE
EL PASO, TEXAS

——-Original Message——-
From: Leigh.goldman@sanfranmonthly.com
Sent: January 3, 2008 8:52 AM
To: reba.adams@hotmail.com
Subject: San Francisco Monthly—Editor position

Dear Ms. Adams:

The publisher and I have reviewed your résumé and publication samples. We were particularly impressed with your recent story entitled "Wartime Christmas Carols." Our current Local Scene editor is moving to New York City in February, leaving an editorial position to be filled. Therefore, we would like to offer the position and schedule a phone interview with you for next week. Should you join our publication staff, I'd be happy to help you make an easy and quick transition to the San Francisco Bay Area. Please feel free to contact me by e-mail or phone as soon as possible. I look forward to hearing from you.

Best regards,
Leigh Goldman

Editor in Chief
San Francisco Monthly
122 Vallejo Street
San Francisco, CA 94111

✿

——Original Message——
From: reba.adams@hotmail.com
Sent: January 3, 2008 7:08 P.M.
To: deedee.adams@gmail.com
Subject: FW: San Francisco Monthly—Editor position

Deedee,

See the forward below. Today, I heard from Leigh Goldman. Note: *The* Leigh Goldman of the award-winning *San Francisco Monthly*. Yes, I know, I nearly passed out when I opened the e-mail. They want me, Deedee. Can you believe it? San Francisco, California!

Remember when we were little and would play Daddy's old 45 records, dress up in Momma's long silk nightgowns, and sing, "San Francisco (Be Sure to Wear Flowers in Your Hair)"? It always made him so happy. I'm humming it now.

I feel really good about this, D. It's the opportunity I've been waiting for since I left home. I can't pass it up.

I still haven't heard from Riki. It's been so long now and with this offer on the table, I'm not sure what I'd say even if I called him: "Hi, I'm leaving." I miss him, but I'm taking this job as a sign. I've got to move forward.

Love you, Reba

✿

——Original Message——
From: deedee.adams@gmail.com
Sent: January 4, 2008 11:11 A.M.
To: reba.adams@hotmail.com
Subject: FW: San Francisco Monthly—Editor position

Congratulations, Reba! This is the best news I've heard in months. Send me the contract before you sign anything. I'll take a gander.

I laughed out loud remembering our musical exhibitions. What a riot. It was a surefire way to make Daddy smile. Be happy, Reba. Promise me you'll let yourself. I'm thrilled for you. I can't wait to tell Momma. She'll be so proud.

Speaking of Momma: I've given it a lot of thought, and I believe we should talk to her about what you found in Daddy's medical records and about his death. We need to discuss everything as a family. It's been over a decade since he died. Things have changed. We're not little girls anymore. The past can't hurt us. Daddy's wolf is nothing but a sad old hound dog that's lost all his teeth. Momma misses you. I do too. Think about coming home soon for a visit.

I'm glad to hear you're moving on, but make sure that what you think is forward isn't propelled by fear. Then it's running away made up to look pretty. Trust me, I know. If the "milkman" doesn't contact you, perhaps there's some California cheese you're meant to try. I hear their cheddar is delish.

Love you back, Deedee

twenty-nine

SCHMIDT BÄCKEREI
56 LUDWIGSTRASSE
GARMISCH, GERMANY

APRIL 29, 1945

*I*t was eerily quiet in the streets. Birds perched in pairs along the roof shingles chirped back and forth of a season that felt hollow and muted. Their squawks echoed off the cobblestones and timbered house frames.

The Gestapo had stopped bringing baking supplies upon Josef's departure, and little by little, they'd used up the reserves. By the first week of April, the sugar was gone. Elsie had resorted to melting marzipans. It had worked for a while, but now there was nothing—not even a spoonful of honey or molasses to spare. The flour bag was down to its last flaxen cupfuls. The mills had stopped churning. Papa tasked Julius to collecting filberts and chestnuts from the forest floor, which he did reluctantly after being baited with Elsie's hidden Ritter Sport Schokolade. Papa ground the nuts into substitutionary meal for brötchen. His hands were callused and stained brown; yet each morning, he lit the oven anew and somehow managed to make bread as golden and rich as any other day.

But they couldn't go on much longer this way. They'd have to close soon. The till was empty anyhow. They'd been bartering with customers for weeks.

When Elsie went to the butcher looking for scraps in exchange for brötchen, he'd replied, "My family eats boiled rats and rotten turnips. We aren't kings of a bakery like you."

Kings of a bakery? The very suggestion was laughable. How easy it was to assume that elsewhere was infinitely better than where you stood. Sometimes at night, she dreamed of the *TEXAS, U.S.A.* magazine advertisement, envisioning a land with row upon row of fat loaves laden with jeweled fruits; bread cubes sodden with thick lamb stew; sugar-dusted sweet breads, ginger-spiced cookies, and fat wedges of chocolate cake soaked in Kirschwasser. She'd awake with cold drool down her chin.

Regardless of the family's lack of resources, one of Papa's famous Black Forest cakes had miraculously prevailed. Dressed in a layer of bittersweet chocolate shavings and liquored cherries, it was too expensive for anyone to purchase. So while all the other sweets were parceled out, it stood perfect and untouched beneath the display. Elsie caught herself staring at it with a kind of craving that transcended hunger. She knew every cherry dimple, every beautiful chocolate curl. For her, the cake was a reminder of all that had been and a pledge of all that she'd have again. Somewhere in the world, there was real butter and sugar, flour and eggs, and smiling people with shiny coins in their pockets. Papa would soon take a knife to the cake, cut it up for hungry customers and their family.

A slice of late-April sunlight came through the front windows making the cherries' cheeks glossy and bright. Yes, Elsie thought, the sun still shines.

Mutti and Papa came from the kitchen, Sunday hats and gloves in hand.

"Julius isn't coming," announced Papa.

They were on their way to the Lutheran Church. Elsie had feigned a headache and said she feared a trip out might exacerbate a coming illness. God forgave white lies if they worked for the good of another, she figured.

She wanted to stay home alone with Tobias. His hair had grown out to a short crop, and she'd promised to wash it for him with heated water.

"*Real* hot water?" Tobias had asked.

He'd never had a warm bath. They'd bathed with rainwater in the Jewish Quarter and by hose in the camp. It pained her to hear of Dachau, both because of Tobias's poor treatment and her knowledge of Josef's hand in it.

A tepid bath seemed a small offering. If she could make a pot of tea, she could certainly heat water to wash the hair and neck of a little boy. She should've thought of it sooner, and she planned on using the last of her rose shampoo to compensate for so much denied him.

Elsie hadn't told Tobias about Frau Rattelmüller or Cecile and didn't intend to. Since she couldn't be certain of the frau's success, she decided it best to keep it to herself. She was acutely aware that the cruelest pain was false hope. Sometimes she thought it would be a relief to discover

Hazel dead instead of agonizing over whether she was or wasn't. Such thoughts shamed her so severely she'd developed headaches that left her inconsolable.

"He's not feeling well either. Hawthorne berry and meadowsweet tea. I'll make a pot when I get home," said Mutti.

Julius had been to church a handful of times since his arrival. During his first visit, he complained the entire service of the chill in the chapel and swore the attendance would put him in the grave like his father . . . and mother. A bitter remark meant to sting them, and it did until Papa said, "Rather to die in righteousness than live in soullessness. That is your mother's belief. It is what the people's community was based upon."

To that, Julius shut his mouth. He knew better than to disagree with Nazi dogma, and he was learning fast not to challenge Papa, either. He never again used Hazel vengefully, but church was an uphill battle. Mutti stopped insisting he attend a few weeks prior when Julius demanded to wear his Pimpfen uniform, though it was still cold out and the short leder-hosen completely inappropriate. He'd gotten his way then and stayed home to play toy soldier in his closet.

This Sunday, Elsie hoped Papa would step in, force the boy to wear practical leather trousers and accompany them. No such luck.

"But Papa," began Elsie.

He lifted his palm to her. "I need more nuts for the week. I want Julius to collect at least two dozen by the time we return."

"If he's in poor health, he shouldn't be outside," said Mutti.

Papa huffed and put on his Trenker hat. "Best be off, Luana. We don't want to be late.

"Keep the windows and doors shut," called Papa over his shoulder. "There's a storm cloud to the west."

Elsie assessed the sky. The sun shone bold and clear. She went back to the kitchen to prompt Julius in his chore. She hoped to give Tobias the promised bath during his absence.

Julius lay sprawled on the floor, his tin men in neat lines before him. "Ja," he said without looking up.

"Didn't Opa ask you to get nuts?"

"He did."

"It could rain. You should go now," said Elsie.

Julius noted the sunshine through kitchen window and rolled onto his back.

"We need nuts for the week's bread," she pressed.

He yawned. "Nobody comes in anymore, so what does it matter?"

Elsie stomped her foot, knocking over a row of toys. "Do *you* want to eat?"

He met her gaze. "I'll go when I feel like it, and I don't right now, so get out of my room." He kicked the pantry door closed, and it battered against Elsie's forehead.

That was it. She'd had enough. He'd been with them three months, and she was tired of everyone treating him with kid gloves when he showed no concern for them or his absent mother. On impulse, she lunged through the door, picked up Julius by the collar, and brought him Schmidt nose to Schmidt nose.

"You listen to me, child," she growled. "Your mother, my sister, would *never* allow such pigheadedness! And your papa, God rest his soul, would have taken you to the woodshed with a heavy belt by now. Trust me, I knew him well. He was not a man who tolerated insolence. And as for your precious Program." She shook her head. "Look outside your little closet! Have you heard of the bombings in Vienna, in Berlin? You silly boy. The Third Reich is falling. It will fall absolutely, and all your comrades and teachers will be shot through the gut by the Russians."

His eyes grew round as eggs.

"It. Is. Over. The Program is over, and I am tired of being hungry. I'm tired of watching Mutti and Papa suffer. I'm tired of good Germans humiliated because why?" She gave him a good shake. "Because their birthrights aren't pristine enough! Well, *you* are the son of a common baker's daughter with as much right to a good life as—as Isaac Grün!"

As much right as Tobias. She felt her insides coming loose at the seams. Her fists trembled with his weight.

"I'm tired of all the hate and fear and ugliness, and most of all, I'm tired of ignorant boys who are too selfish to see that the people around them are dying for them and *because* of them! I am *tired*!"

Julius's lower lip began to quiver; his neck grew red where the linen shirt pulled hard against his skin.

She let go. He buckled at her feet. She clenched her hands together and placed them against her throbbing head.

Julius whimpered, and when she looked down, she saw not the spiteful child but her sister, Hazel. How she missed her. With no letters for months, Elsie could only imagine the worst. Julius was Hazel's son, her kin and a frightened little boy. She reached out and ran her fingers over his soft, blond crown.

"Forgive me, Julius."

He wrenched away, angry tears streaking his cheeks. "I hate you!" He screamed. "I hate you all!" He grabbed his brown Pimpfen-patched jacket and ran out the back.

Elsie's hands went numb; her vision trembled around the circumference. The throbbing sharpened. She stumbled out of the kitchen and up the stairs. She had to get to her bed or collapse where she stood.

She gave a soft cry when her temple hit the pillow.

"Elsie?" Tobias whispered behind the wall. "Elsie, what has happened?"

The room went spotty, smoldering black and gray polka dots.

"I'm unwell," she moaned. It took all she had to form the words.

The board scraped open and feet pattered across the room. As with the fever at Christmas, Tobias climbed into the bed beside her and hummed in her ear. The dulcet melody eased the stabbing. He smelled sweetly of lamb's wool and pretzel dough.

"Thank you, Tobias." She rested her cheek against him. For a moment she wanted to forget everyone: Julius, Hazel, Peter, Frau Rattelmüller, Cecile, Josef, Mutti and Papa, even herself. She wanted nothing to exist but Tobias and his beautiful voice in the darkness.

"I knew you were a traitor!"

Elsie awoke to the thunder of boots. She hadn't been asleep very long, but enough that her perception was bleary and her mind disoriented. Before her eyes had time to focus, someone had her by her hair; he dragged her out of bed and downstairs to the company of armed Gestapo.

"Traitor!" boomed the voice behind her.

Overhead, boots stomped, a lamp crashed, furniture overturned with great thuds that shook the dust from the floorboards aloft.

Tobias, she thought. *They have Tobias!* Her heart flapped like a hawk in a snare. She couldn't catch her breath between palpitations.

The guard holding her by the head swiveled her to face her accuser.

"Kremer!" she gasped.

"Fräulein." He grinned smugly.

The Gestapo released her, and she fell to her hands and knees at Kremer's boots.

"Josef will be so disappointed that his little baker turned out to be a

Judas." He shrugged. "But I knew. I knew." He pulled off his leather gloves, finger by finger, and tossed them on the wooden baker's table.

A guard aimed his rifle at Elsie's head, so close she could see the soot ringing the barrel.

Kremer stroked his mustache sprout. "We have the authority to dispose of traitors in private, but I'm a firm believer in the power of spectacle. Don't you agree? Those who betray their country must be made examples, so what shall it be, hmm? Bullet or rope? As a German, I'll give you the choice."

For herself, she cared not. She hated this man and if her blood was on his hands, she prayed for all God's vengeance with it. But what had they done with Tobias? She couldn't bear to think of his torture.

"He's just a boy!" she cried.

"That doesn't change your treason," said Kremer. "It's a shame. Herr Schmidt makes the best lebkuchen in Bavaria."

Papa and Mutti? No, she wouldn't let them be sacrificed for her actions.

A small bowl of filberts sat on the table with a nutcracker. Kremer pinched a nut, placed it between the metal levers, and squeezed. Shell fragments fell to the ground exposing the sweet kernel. He popped in his mouth.

"Please, spare my family. They are innocent." She gathered her skirt in her palms. "I'll give you anything you want. *Anything.*"

He scoffed and spat the hazelnut back in the bowl. "Wormy."

From upstairs came a shout and the armed man at her side turned sharply.

Kremer nodded up. "Go." He unclipped his pistol from the holster sling and pointed it at Elsie. "Just you and me, fräulein."

The guard obeyed and left them alone in the kitchen.

"Please, Major Kremer," begged Elsie. "It's one Jew. What does it matter now?" Her voice broke.

It was almost the end of the war. Everyone knew it. Hitler was holed up in a Berlin bunker awaiting surrender. Why more bloodshed? Even a man like this had a conscience capable of recognizing unnecessary savagery. Heaven and hell saw no race or creed. Death would come for him as surely as it would come for her and Tobias. But it was the choice he made now that determined which gate he walked through.

Kremer turned to her, his eyes two ghoulish lights. "Jew?"

"If you believe in God, please."

"Bring the boy here!" Kremer yelled over his shoulder, then knelt down to Elsie.

"'Peoples that *bastardize* themselves, or let themselves be bastardized, sin against the will of eternal Providence.' So says our führer." He winked at her. "That's the only God I believe in."

"Let me go! I *told* you what she said—she's the traitor!" Julius squirmed and pitched against the Gestapo's grip.

Kremer studied him, then gave a horsy snort. "Amazing. It's so hard to tell sometimes. He doesn't even look rodent." He cocked his head. "Maybe in the teeth. The shiftiness of the eyes, perhaps."

"Me? I'm not a Jew!" screamed Julius.

Kremer raised his pistol. The soldier moved out of the way.

"Nein!" Elsie stood and shielded Julius. "He is the son of my sister, Hazel, and your comrade Peter Abend. He's pure Aryan—born and raised at the Lebensborn Program."

Kremer held the gun straight ahead with his right hand. "I'm not the one who called him a Jew. You did." With his left pinky, he picked a nut skin from behind his incisor.

"Liar!" Julius fisted Elsie in the small of her back. "Traitor!"

She winced and bowed to the side.

Kremer chuckled. "I believe you, boy. Too much vigor in you to be inferior."

The Gestapo who'd ransacked her room came down to report: "Nothing, sir."

Elsie looked up. Tobias was safe? Lowering her gaze, her eyes locked tight with Kremer.

He looked to the ceiling and clucked his tongue. "I do believe there is something." He smiled at Elsie. "A mouse in the attic?"

Elsie's heart stammered, stopped, and started again. She shook her head.

The two soldiers turned to go back upstairs, but Kremer halted them. "Stop!" He pointed to Elsie. "*You* will bring the Jew to us."

Elsie swallowed hard. "There's no one here except my nephew and me. My parents are at the church."

"A traitor and a liar, indeed," said Kremer. He pushed her to the floor and clapped Julius about the face, his hand over the boy's mouth and the barrel of the pistol pressed hard at his temple.

"He's German!" Elsie cried.

The Gestapo in the kitchen shifted uneasily.

"Come, come, come," he baited. "This is the bastard son of a whore. A good whore albeit. I rather liked her myself, but truly our race has no use for such depravity. It may be more humane to put this child out of his misery rather than allow him to grow up in a family of deviants like this—traitors and harlots." He shrugged.

Julius's eyes, ringed red from crying, bulged under the pressure and panic; his arms went stiff by his side; the suede front of his pants grew dark and wet.

Kremer scoffed at him. "No son of the Fatherland. He's not even toilet trained." He leaned in to Julius's ear. "Retarded, perhaps. You know what the Program does with the retarded—cyanide in the breakfast milk or"—he pressed the gun—"a quick bullet to the brain. This was the case for your brother."

Julius's tears spilled down.

Elsie gripped the cold ground, steadying herself. Her vision tunneled as if the universe were imploding.

"I'll tell you what I'll do." Kremer released Julius and thrust him down beside Elsie. "You bring me the Jew, and I'll let the whoreson live. Of course, I can't offer the same to you, fräulein, but I will promise to make your sentence quick."

Julius lay heavy against Elsie's side, a soggy, catatonic rag doll. Was his life worth Tobias's? Was hers? Tobias had done nothing but trust and love her. He didn't deserve to be handed over like currency in some immoral purchase. But surrendering her family? She couldn't live or die with that kind of guilt. She believed in the afterlife and had no wish to meet God with either burden.

Elsie closed her eyes; starbursts flamed behind her lids. The nightmare was so close to ending. The Americans and Russians were said to be camped in the pastureland outside town. Better to die by their hands than to make this choice.

"What's it to be?" asked Kremer.

Thoughts seesawed, cutting her mind in two. She couldn't think her way to a solution. Logic had no power here. She could only hope for divine guidance and pray it was enough to absolve her. Slowly, she stood.

"I'll bring him to you." Her voice warbled like a sickly finch. "But you must let me go alone. He won't come out if I'm not alone."

The guards looked to Kremer.

He sucked his teeth. "You have five minutes, and then I'll shoot your nephew, find the Jew myself, and shoot him, too. I'll shoot you last, so you can watch the rest bleed."

thirty

Josef Hub was a shadow of the officer he'd been. The march from Dachau to Tegernsee had not gone well for the prisoners or the SS. He saw things in the daylight that shook his soul, and his migraines worsened. Sometime during the three-day journey, he'd stopped sleeping and eating; instead, he injected himself with methamphetamines as often as possible. Near Percha, he took a wool coat off the back of an elderly German sheepherder. It hung over his bones like a great bearskin, and he felt as beastly as he looked. He hadn't shaved or bathed in weeks. His reddish-blond beard concealed his features. Swollen eyes and tremors made most turn away, and he found an anonymous freedom in his degradation.

The handful of travelers he encountered moved to the opposite side of the road on his approach. *As well they should,* he thought to himself, *if they knew what I've done.* Most of the pilgrims were Aryan families, women carrying babies, children in wool socks with cheesecloth sacks on the end of sticks, fathers armed with rakes and scythes for protection. Was this what Germany had come to: a land of wanderers?

No matter where these people ventured, they would always be German. He would always be German. So where did you go when your home was no longer safe—when the world stopped making sense? At what point was the decision made to go or to stay?

For Josef, it came when he watched a young Jewish prisoner drag her dead mother for over a mile. The old woman's legs, blue and frozen stiff, left a trail like ski tracks in the mud. When a guard commanded the daughter to drop the body, she refused, and he shot her where she stood; her blood splattered thick against her mother's rimy cheeks.

Then, Josef had turned his horse around, abandoning the Jews and his post, and dared anyone to shoot him in the back as he went. Galloping away, he prayed someone actually would. His horse succumbed to exhaustion halfway to Garmisch. He left it spent and dying on the side of the road and began to walk, still hearing the trailing footsteps of Jewish prisoners behind him. When he walked faster, the cadence increased. He broke into a run but they caught up. "Murderer, traitor!" They beat against his back. He fell then, tripping over the picked carcass of a vulture; its skinny head screwed sideways in the mud. Pulling his gun from beneath the bearskin, he fired a shot straight up.

"Go away!" he shouted.

But when he looked, there was no one. The long road stretched empty to the horizon. The only sound was the bitter wind whistling past his ears. A finch flittered against it, then caught the current up into the brindled sky. The pain of his head anchored him to the ground. He lay beside the dead animal, watching the maggots gorge themselves on its innards, smelling the rot of flesh, and seeing again the mass graves at KZ Dachau.

In all his years as an SS officer, he'd never personally taken the life of anyone after Peter Abend, but he'd been there. He'd seen death all around and ordered it into action under the guise of duty. He was steeped in their blood, more guilty than the simple soldier with a bullet. He closed his eyes, but the assembly of corpses only sharpened in his mind.

He was convinced the vengeful ghosts would stay on German ground. If only he could leave, he could be free of them and all the horrors of this war. Günther Kremer and his Garmisch comrades had an escape route. A ship bound for Venezuela awaited them in Brunsbüttel. He had to get there. But he needed payment—gold and jewels stockpiled and hidden in his Garmisch apartment. He'd collect those and Elsie. They could start anew in South America. She would help him find happiness. Faithful and true, she would help absolve him.

With that in mind, he gritted his teeth and peeled himself up from the dirt. In the distance, the chimney stacks of Garmisch plumed gray ash. He knew one of them was the Schmidt Bäckerei.

thirty-one

*E*lsie took the stairs one at the time, each step an insurmountable climb. She imagined this was how the road to Calvary felt. She prayed for some kind of salvation, but unlike Christ, she wasn't endowed with supernatural powers over hell. Three days dead, and she'd smell like worm rot.

She didn't need to turn around; Kremer's stare burned into her back.

The bedroom door was ajar, something rammed behind it. Her overturned nightstand barred the way. She pushed through and went to the wall, smoothing her palm along the long plank.

"Tobias," she called.

Though there was not the slightest flutter, she could sense the warmth of his breath like a single flame in a church cloister.

She leaned her cheek to the coarse wood. "You must come out." She knew he was leaning back against her—a finger width between them.

The plank scraped open half an inch. "Are they gone?"

The warmth evaporated into the upturned room, and a chill settled in Elsie. Her bones seemed to rattle against it, and she wrapped her arms about herself.

Tobias crawled from his refuge. "What did they want?"

Elsie pulled him to her breast. "Hear me, Tobias," she whispered. "There are men waiting to take you." He flinched. "I'm sorry." Her knees shook, and she swayed unsteadily.

Tobias tightened his grip, holding her back. "Don't be sad," he comforted. "I'll get to see my family."

"Forgive me," begged Elsie. "Please, forgive me."

She pulled his stocking cap off and kissed the top of his head. Before she could place it back, the door slammed open; the nightstand splintered; boots pounded into the room. She closed her eyes and didn't open them as Tobias was silently yanked from her arms.

"'And so the choice must be again, but the last choice is still the same,'" she recited. Her palms remained warm from him. She clasped them together tight and hugged them to her chest. "'And God has taken a flower of gold and broken it.'" She leaned her forehead to the wall, moored to Tobias's hiding place.

The stomps retreated down the steps and out.

"We'll deal with the Jew," said Kremer behind her. "You and your family are under house arrest."

She turned then, "But you said."

Julius stood under Kremer's grip, his cherub face bloated red.

"There's never one rat in a nest." Kremer came close and pushed a disheveled lock back into her braid. "Besides, I'm not sure I'm ready to kill you. Your sister was more beautiful and quite skillful in her trade, but you—you've got a healthy German spirit. We were interrupted on Christmas Eve." He grabbed the back of her neck and jerked her onto the bed. "And I always finish what I start."

Julius bleated softly and shrunk down in the corner.

Kremer's hand was thick and hot around Elsie's throat. She stared at the cotton sheets, each thread distinctly linked to the next. Her body was as numb as the stiff pines against the windowpanes. The hem of her dress fluttered over her ears, Mutti's stitching so neat and even. Kremer's skin pressed coarse against her thighs. What came next was separate from her. Her spirit hovered at the threshold. No tears. Those were too much of the living. Only darkness.

Then, a shot rang out. Two more followed by the *rat-tat-tat* of machine guns.

"Major!" A soldier burst into the room. "He got away!"

Kremer's nostrils flared. "What?!" he seethed, and in one fluid motion, he slapped the soldier and did up his trousers. "How could a child get away from four SiPo?"

The guard tucked his chin, his jaw rosy. He flushed at the sight of Elsie prostrate on the bed. "He bit Lieutenant Loringhoven and ran." He kept his eyes to the floor as he spoke. "We went after, but then I thought I saw—I couldn't say for certain, but it looked as though—he vanished, sir."

"Vanished?"

"Ja." The young guard was visibly shaken both by the slap and all he'd witnessed. "A sudden fog came, a storm, and then there was a sound unlike any I've heard in my life and . . . he vanished." His breath caught. "A poltergeist," he whispered.

"I heard nothing. Which way did he go?" Kremer cocked his pistol.

"East. Toward the forest of Kramer Mountain."

"Fools! Done in by the Brothers Grimm!" He raced down the stairs with the guard at his heels.

Minutes passed; street shouting trickled in through the windowpanes; Julius sniffled in the corner; a train whistle blew somewhere far; rain started to fall then stopped; the world outside pressed on.

There was a sharp pain in Elsie's legs, and she realized the metal edging of her bed had grated both her knees. Her sheets were stained with smears of blood.

"Elsie! Julius!" called Papa and Mutti from below.

Julius stood and ran to them.

Papa and Mutti gasped when they entered.

"Oh, Elsie . . . Elsie!" Mutti sobbed. "What have they done to you, child?" She held her palms above the bloody sheets like a priest above the sacrament. "Not my daughter."

Papa turned away with Julius. Mutti swaddled Elsie in her arms and rocked her.

"It's my fault. I betrayed us all," said Elsie. She remained in Mutti's steadfast clutch and felt like a child again, safe and protected.

"Shh—I'm here." She rocked and smoothed the sweat from Elsie's forehead. "We came home as soon as we heard the news," explained Mutti. "Everyone is leaving the city."

Papa picked up the broken ledge of the nightstand, turned the splintered wood over, then set it down again. Julius hid in the hemline of his coat, covering his face and moaning.

"It's the end of the world," said Mutti. "The Americans have taken Dachau. They could be here any hour."

Josef, Elsie thought, then curled herself into the buttery smell of her mother's embrace.

"Every SS soldier has been ordered to evacuate and meet the enemy en route," Papa continued.

"They're abandoning us," said Mutti.

Only then did Elsie's eyes sting hot.

"Don't cry, dear," Mutti soothed.

"Thank you, God," whispered Elsie.

Mutti stopped rocking.

"We're saved!" said Elsie, unable to contain her tears any longer. "All of us! It's over."

Papa studied her sternly. "God is not responsible for the end of the Fatherland. That is man's doing." His eyes were sorrowful dark.

"'Whatsoever man soweth, that shall he reap,'" quoted Elsie.

Papa lifted his chin to her.

"She's in shock, Max," Mutti reminded.

"Who did this to you?" demanded Papa.

Nazi countrymen; an officer friend of Josef; men capable of atrocities she could not say in front of her papa—because she concealed a Jewish child, because she didn't believe in the man Papa quoted, because she didn't agree with this land anymore. Elsie wasn't sure how to begin or if it was wise to at all. She tucked her knees to her chest and turned away from him.

"Are we to leave, too?" Mutti asked.

Papa gave a heavy exhale. "This is our bakery, our home. I won't leave it to be looted and destroyed. We'll lock the doors and pray for God's mercy."

Mutti squeezed Elsie's hand in short, nervous bursts. "I best bring in a bucket of water. We need to tend to your wounds as soon as possible." She turned to Papa. "The stove is cold. Light a fire, Max."

"Come, Julius," said Papa.

Julius looked up then, tracing over Elsie and Mutti to the bloody bed-sheets. His pants were still damp with urine, his eyes shot red as cordial cherries. His shoulders bowed inward with shame. Papa put his arm around him and ushered him out quietly.

Perhaps he would tell her secret, but not today. Today, he finally saw that the world was not contained in the delusion of his perfect reflection. Today, he bore witness to the end of his childhood.

❁

A hard rain fell through the night and next day, washing the cobblestone streets as clean as the stream floors. By the first of May, the whole town smelled of thawed dirt and wet pine needles swept down the valley from the melting mountain peaks.

Though Elsie had searched the alleyways and roads around the bakery, there was no sign of Tobias. It was as the soldier had claimed: he'd simply vanished. In the haze of morning when mist rose from the streets like awakening ghosts, she almost convinced herself he had done exactly that—been spirited to heaven on horses of fire like the biblical Elijah.

From the bakery storefront, she watched the American tanks roll into the city. Brandishing flags of colorful stars and candy cane stripes, it looked almost like a holiday parade if not for the gigantic chain-link wheels that grumbled and screeched over rubble and cars and anything else that got in the way. Helpless to stop them or find Tobias, she could do no more than pray—not for peace and understanding, though. Such things she knew would only be found in the afterlife. She prayed simply for a reprieve.

Hitler was dead. It took less than a day for word to spread from one corner of the German Empire to the other. Shot through the head with a Walther pistol. With defeat undeniable and Nazi authority extinguished, public reaction was divided. Half the town cried for him and thought his end noble. The other half called him a coward and deserter. After all, they'd stayed to face his adversaries; and though the Americans entered with pointed guns and grim expressions, Elsie quickly discovered they were far less terrifying than Nazi propaganda portrayed, far less terrifying than her own Gestapo.

The day before, a handful of American soldiers stormed the bäckerei and cleared the shelves. Mutti locked herself in the bedroom with Julius, but it took more than a gun or a foreign accent to scare Elsie anymore. She insisted on facing the enemy. Indeed, the men were not as Nazi propaganda had described. Their banter had the happy, songlike quality she remembered from the movies she'd idolized as a child.

One young soldier let a smile slip over his lips when he discovered Papa's Black Forest cake, stale and sagging in the display case. Despite its age and crumbling sides, his face lit up, exposing hidden dimples on either cheek. She couldn't help smiling back. And that's when it happened: his comrades saw them smiling and smiled too; then they said something to another soldier who laughed, and the cheer seemed to spread like butter on a hot bun. Soon, all the men in the unit were carrying on like Christmas morning, cutting and wrapping dense cake wedges in paper. Elsie liked it. It'd been too long since she felt that kind of contagious satisfaction, even for the briefest moment, and part of her was pleased to see the cake go in such a manner.

Papa remained stern and indignant throughout the invasion. "I hope it rots their stomachs," he mumbled under his breath. It was his cake, his bread, his domain, being stolen by enemy soldiers. Mutti buried her wedding band in the window dill plant for fear of confiscation. However, besides the cake, the men left with relatively no damage done or family goods seized. On his way out the door, the soldier who first discovered the cake nodded and said, "Danke schön." Elsie had naturally replied, "Bitte schön."

Papa gave her an earful once they'd gone. These were foreigners who would as soon as rape and murder as share a sweet taste or smile, he said. But she'd already seen her countrymen do such things. She'd stood at death's doorway with wickedness at her back. She'd experienced what her papa could never have imagined and would never have believed. The stranger's smile held little malice in comparison. Papa was of an old and withering generation. Hitler was gone, the Nazi government was in ruins, and Germany was under Allied control. If they were to survive, Elsie understood that they'd have to befriend these new faces—these foreigners. And she'd be the only one in their family to do it.

Today, the bäckerei was empty and quiet. Papa had enough nut meal and powdered rations to make brötchen, but no one came. The townspeople remained locked in their homes, afraid of the tanks and men and the uncertainty of their futures.

"What will they do with us?" Mutti asked everyone and no one in particular.

The four of them assembled together in the empty bakery, staring out the storefront window at the unrecognizable streets littered with building debris and trash and alien faces. It reminded Elsie of ancient Fasching carnivals, a pageantry of merriment. Only now, they were inhibited observers, not participants.

"Max?" Mutti sought an answer.

Papa read Möller's *Das brüderliche Jahr.* "I don't think they know." He didn't lift his attention from the page.

Mutti murmured a prayer and sipped cold chamomile tea. Julius hid behind the dill plant and marked each head that passed with finger pistols. Elsie stood by the door, unable to look away from the chaotic street scene.

American soldiers gathered by the small public fountain pump. They threw a pack of cigarettes around. Their voices siphoned through the beveled glass windows, bubbly and buoyant. A raven-haired soldier tapped the pack against his wrist, then flipped a cigarette to his lips in a single motion. His stature reminded Elsie of William Powell, and that's exactly how it felt—like watching actors on film. Completely captivating.

The soldier caught her glance and held it. A fever swelled up from her chest and swirled into her cheeks. She turned her back to him. That never happened with Powell.

Outside, the soldier laughed. "We got ourselves an audience!"

Elsie kept her eyes to the ground so Mutti and Papa wouldn't see her blush. At her feet, shuffled under the front door frame, was a small, white paper, dirty and unnoticeable except for its shape; the edges were too purposefully square to be litter. She picked it up and unfolded it, immediately recognizing Josef's handwriting.

"What's that?" asked Mutti.

"Nothing. Street trash blown under the door." Elsie crumbled the paper in her palm. "If no one else is going to eat our bread, I might as well have a bite. Papa?"

He grunted over his book as she passed to the kitchen.

In the back corner by the oven, she smoothed the note open.

Elsie,

We have friends who welcome us to warmer climates. Do not fear. We'll make a new life together. I know it will be hard to leave your family, but they have no connections to the party. They will be safe. As for us, we must leave Germany as soon as possible. I wait for you at the bahnhof, six o'clock. Bring only what you must. We have a long journey ahead.

Your husband, Josef

Your husband? She clenched her left hand. Indeed. She hardly knew him. Lieutenant Colonel Josef Hub working at the Dachau camp. How many men had he killed? How many women and children? Elsie wondered if he ordered the Gestapo search for Tobias on Christmas Eve, if he sanctioned Kremer's brutal tactics. A sour taste crept up her throat. She tore the note to bits and threw them in the oven ashes. No, she would not meet Josef at the bahnhof. She would stay. Despite everything her parents had seen and not done, despite her nephew's callused upbringing and her sister's sacrifice, they were her family. Josef was not. Though she had worn his ring, her heart had never committed to him. She hung her head, ashamed of all the lies, big and small, she'd fostered. She was tired of pretending to believe what she didn't and be what she wasn't.

On the rack, half a dozen crusts cooled nutty brown and shiny. Elsie split one open and ate the sweet, steaming center. Tomorrow, she'd help her papa find real milk, flour, and eggs. Then they'd light the oven and bake bread.

thirty-two

Reba was surprised to see JANE MERIWETHER flash across her cell phone display. She'd given Jane her number months before, but this was the first time she'd ever called.

Reba muted the television. It was 8:15 p.m. Anthony Bourdain was about to eat roasted pig rectum in Namibia. She'd been watching various reality TV shows all night in an attempt to keep her mind preoccupied. She'd spoken to Leigh that morning in a forty-five-minute interview. It went well, Reba thought, until Leigh said she was considering one other candidate. The unknown competitor made Reba paranoid. Leigh promised to e-mail within twenty-four hours with her final decision. The anticipation had Reba as twitchy as a puppy begging for a Milk-Bone.

"Jane!" she answered, grateful for a new distraction.

"Reba, I'm sorry to bother you so late." Jane's voice pulled tight. "There's trouble. I thought you might be able to help."

Reba sat up on the couch. "Is it Elsie?" Her heart sped up.

"No, Mom's fine. I don't want her to know about this. It's Sergio." Her voice cracked. "They've arrested him."

"Arrested? For what?" Reba couldn't imagine Sergio doing anything to upset anybody, except perhaps buttering his buns too slow.

"He's an illegal. He had a visa, but it expired years ago and he never got it renewed—didn't have the money. They're shipping him over the border, and he won't be allowed back for ten years!"

The line went silent. Reba wondered if they'd lost the connection, but just as she was about to speak, Jane continued: "He's the one I told you about. The man I've been with. He loves me and could've asked me to marry him anytime to make himself a citizen, but he didn't. He knew how it'd come off—so many people marrying for green cards. He respected that I was happy like we were. But I was a dang old fool. I should've done it for him," her voice broke. "Reba, I can't live without Sergio."

Reba bit at her cuticles, unsure of what to say or do. "Where is he?"

"That's the thing—they got him detained at the station."

Reba bit too deep. Her nail bed welled a pinprick of blood.

"I remembered you said your ex was a Border Patrol guy. I thought, maybe . . ."

"I can try." Reba sucked the blood and swallowed the taste of iron. "You just hold tight."

She hung up. On the television screen, Anthony Bourdain's face puckered with nausea. Reba felt similarly. She dialed Riki's number.

He answered on the second ring. "Hello?"

His voice took her breath away.

"Hello?" he repeated. "Reba?"

"Yeah. It's me. Hi—sorry." She pulled herself together. Right now, she had to forget about her feelings and give him the facts. "Riki, I have a friend who's in trouble. His name is Sergio Rodriguez. He got picked up by the CBP. He's an illegal, but he's been here for decades."

There was a long pause. Reba tucked the phone close to her chin, listening to his breath whisper over the line. God, she missed him.

"We have him in detainment," Riki finally said.

"Is there any way to release him? He just needs a new visa." Her fingers shook, so she knit them together. "We can't let them throw him out of the country for good."

"Reba, we have a process, and you know better than anyone that I can't bend the law. Not even for you. I—" he began, but faltered. He cleared his throat.

As hard as it was for Reba to hear his voice, she realized it was equally hard for him to hear hers.

"Riki, I wouldn't have called, but you're the only one I trust. I hoped you could help."

"What's so special about this guy? What makes him different from all the rest?"

His bitter tone grated her bones, and her confidence floundered. "My friend Jane loves him." Again, she sucked the blood from her finger. It stung.

"I could get in a real mess of trouble for this." He sighed. "But we've had paperwork oversights in the past. It'll only buy him a few days."

"Anything," said Reba.

"Give me an hour. He'll be in front of the station."

Reba leaned her cheek into the heat of the phone, willing him close to her through the wires and signals. "Thank you."

Another empty silence.

"Well, I better—" Riki began.

"I miss you." Reba didn't know where it came from. She covered her mouth and listened to the snaps of static.

"Yeah," he said curtly.

"I was wrong." Reba gulped. "About a lot of things. I was . . . scared."

Something clicked in the background. A pen, she guessed.

"I was wrong too." Riki exhaled. "I was asking for things I wasn't offering. I need to change."

Reba's chest seemed to draw in all the air it could hold, then burst with joy and relief and love.

A tourism commercial flickered across the television: *California. Find yourself there.*

Early the next morning, Reba stood beside Jane, Sergio, and Riki in the El Paso County Clerk's Office. They needed two eyewitnesses. Reba was an obvious choice, but the second was hard to come by on such short notice. Jane refused to call Elsie. Explaining all this at sunrise was not a good introduction to her new son-in-law. Reba agreed, so she dialed Riki once more. He consented to come, saying it would serve to verify Sergio's status. Reba hoped it was more than that.

Jane wore a gauzy, white shirt and a flowing skirt dotted with bluebonnets. Her hair was pulled back in a neat twist that accentuated her blond and minimized her gray. She glowed and bore a striking resemblance to the young Elsie in the black-and-white photograph.

For forty-two dollars, the county clerk conducted a concise but earnest ceremony and handed them a certificate. "I pronounce you man and wife."

Reba swallowed hard. Beside her, heated tension rose palpably from Riki.

"Well, I never thought the day would come." Jane kissed Sergio.

"Congratulations," said Reba.

"I want to thank you very, very much for everything you've done." Sergio shook her hand and then Riki's with such sincerity that Reba blushed. All she'd done was make a phone call. Riki, alone, warranted the thanks.

"Time for the reception!" proclaimed Jane. "I'm going to cut me off a fat wedge of cake and lick up every last chocolate crumb." She stopped suddenly and rubbed her forehead. "That is, after I tell Mom. Lord help us."

Sergio put an arm round her shoulder.

"She's just going to have to face the facts." Jane leaned into him. "Reba, Riki, you're coming, right?"

"I best get back to the station. Otherwise, Bert's going to kill somebody for letting Sergio slip. Need to straighten things up," said Riki.

Reba shifted uneasily. It'd been so long since she'd seen him, and it felt so nice standing that close. She didn't want him to leave.

"Please," Jane interceded. "Come have some Black Forest cake on the house. I insist. I got to thank you for all you did for us. You know, I keep reminding myself that we've just met, but it sure does feel like I've known you awhile—probably because Reba's talked about you so much."

Reba caught Riki's eye.

"I guess I can spare a few." He rubbed his stomach. "I haven't had breakfast, and I hear you make the best pastries in town."

Jane winked. "Sure shootin', I do."

Pulling into the bakery parking lot, they knew there was trouble. At quarter after nine, the Closed sign still hung over the door though the lights inside were on.

A patron battled the wind back to his car. "Not open today," he yelled to them.

Jane jingled her keys in the front lock and entered. "Mom!"

"*Where* have you been?" Elsie's voice came from behind the curtained kitchen.

All four gave a collective sigh.

"I am not young anymore. I cannot be mixing, baking, icing, *and* helping customers. At one point in my life, ja, but not now." A pan banged. "I wake this morning and you are disappeared. I think you have come early for the pretzels, so I drive over myself, but in the kitchen is no one. The dough is bloomed to hell!" Another bang. "Customers knocking on the door all morning. I hurry but . . . Damn old hands! Damn new ovens! Gas does not cook like a good wood fire." She emerged from the kitchen carrying two loaves, her face as pale as her floured palms. "Oh, you have been out with friends. How considerate." She tossed the loaves on the shelf and pushed thin, white strands behind her ears.

"Mom, it was an emergency," explained Jane.

"An emergency? Uh-huh. So *emergent* you could not wake your mutti to let her know?" Suddenly her face twisted up, and she covered her mouth.

"Mom, I'm sorry." Jane went to her side and pulled her close. "I'm here now."

For the first time since Reba had met her, Elsie looked her age, worn hard by days and nights, weeks and years. Reba had to look away, down at the floor, at her shoes, at Riki's. She thought of her own mother and all she had been through.

Elsie recovered fast, shook off angry ghosts, and lifted her chin. "Excuse me. This morning has been difficult. You will explain later." She cleared her throat and proceeded with business. "Mach schnell! Reba, please would you flip the sign. We are open. Jane, bring Sergio his usual and . . ." She turned to Riki. "I don't believe we have met."

"Riki Chavez." He extended his hand.

Elsie raised an eyebrow. "Reba's Riki?"

Riki adjusted his stance.

"Yes," said Reba.

He looked to her, as though he was about to ask a question, but then returned to Elsie and nodded.

"A pleasure to finally meet. Excuse my hands. I've been in the dough rolling." Elsie wiped her palms on her apron and smoothed back her hair. "Your first time here, you need something special—how about a lebkuchen? This is gingerbread. Baked this morning."

Riki nodded. "Sounds delicious, but Jane mentioned something about celebration cake."

"Celebration cake? It is your birthday?"

Reba winced.

"No, uh . . ." Riki looked to Reba, then Jane.

"It has to do with what I was talking about," said Jane. "The emergency, Mom." She balled her fists and stood tall. "Sergio and I were married this morning. He got picked up yesterday for not renewing his visa, and Reba and Riki helped get him out. We've been seeing each other—romantically—for years, and I figured it was high time I stopped taking things for granted. I'm a forty-five-year-old woman, after all." She reached a hand out to Sergio and inhaled deep, her breath spent.

Elsie stood completely still. Reba worried for her health.

"Missus Meriwether." Sergio caught them all off guard. He stepped forward. "I know I am not what you hoped for your daughter, but I respect you very much. You have been kind to me since my first piece of bread, and I would be honored to call you my family. I love Jane. Please, we ask for your blessing."

Jane bit her bottom lip. Reba gulped. There was an awkward pause that nobody dared interrupt. They waited for Elsie. Slowly, she lowered her head to her chest and sniffled.

"Mom," Jane whispered.

Elsie looked up with a wide smile. "Thank Jesus! I thought you were lesbian."

"What!" Jane put her fists on her hips.

Elsie dabbed away tears of joy. "Like you said, you are a forty-five-year-old, unmarried woman, always playing with the boys. Never took to the feminine side and then Miss Reba came."

"Huh?" said Reba. "Me?"

Elsie continued, "She is so strong-minded and not deciding about . . . well, you know. I'm no dummkopf—that kind of thing has been going on for years. Look at Marlene Dietrich." She put her hands on either side of Sergio's face. "Bless you, bless you." She kissed his cheeks.

"Ha!" Riki popped.

Jane frowned. "Mom, are you serious? All these years, I've been looking for the perfect man for *you*."

"He is dead and gone." She shrugged and threw up her hands. "If you were into women, it was none of my business as long as you were happy. But you did not seem happy—and I would like grandchildren!"

"Oh, Lord-dee-day." Jane's complexion broke out splotchy red.

"Don't worry about your age, either. On the computer, I read about a woman having a baby at sixty years old. You are—what do they call it—a *spring chicken* compared to her." Elsie bent down and pulled a tall black-and-white cake from the display case. "Ack ja, a celebration!" With a serrated knife, she cut through the vanilla icing swirls and chocolate shavings, perfectly partitioning each slice with its own cherry. "Come eat." She placed the wedges on a stack of nearby tea saucers.

"A lesbian—really, Mom, you need to get off the Internet," huffed Jane.

"And you have needed to get your head out of the dirt for years, but did I say anything?"

"Sand, Mom," corrected Jane.

"Sand what?"

"It's 'head out of the sand.'"

"Exactly!" Elsie nodded. "I always thought you and Sergio would make a nice couple. It was the way he smiled at you." She patted Jane's cheek.

Jane gave an exasperated grin, then took her piece of cake and sat beside Sergio, feeding him with her fingers.

"One for you." Elsie handed Riki a slice and started to cut another. Reba stopped her.

"I'll share with Riki." She turned to him. "I eat dairy now."

"Really?" he said. "What else about you has changed since I've been away?"

"A lot of things needed to," she said.

He took a fork from Elsie and gestured to a café table. "Care to tell?"

After their last bite of cake, Jane put Sergio on the till while she and Elsie worked double time in the kitchen. Riki and Reba sat at the table a long while, sharing their slice down to the last chocolate morsel as one by one the day's patrons filtered in.

thirty-three

The 6:00 p.m. train came and went with neither Elsie nor Josef on it. Josef worried that Elsie hadn't received the message he'd slipped under the door, so he trudged back to the bäckerei, keeping to the alleys. He tapped on the back entrance. No one answered. Voices echoed around the building, and he followed them to the front where a handful of enemy Amis lounged. He hid in the shadows, the setting sun slowly expanding the dark perimeters.

"Mighty kind of you, miss," said a portly soldier with a fat bullet embedded in his helmet. "We've been living on hardtack, cigarettes, and chocolate for weeks. Good to get something fresh." He shoved a roll in his mouth, pulled it apart with his teeth, and chewed. "You should meet our cook. Teach him a thing or two," he muttered, then gulped. "Hey, Robby!"

A dark-haired man with a burning cigarette dangling from his lip turned.

"You need to learn to bake these—make some decent food for a change."

"Give me ingredients and maybe I will," Robby quipped.

"You got a pretty little town here," said a slim, soft-spoken Ami who looked as Aryan as they came. "Climate reminds me of home. I'm from Gaylord, Michigan—you ever heard of it. North of Detroit?"

"Shut up, Sam. We ain't supposed to be fraternizin' or talkin' to these people. Not countin' she don't understand a word you're sayin'," said another.

Josef craned his head around the corner to see to whom they were referring. There stood Elsie, a basket set on her cocked hip.

"Lady gave us food that don't come out of a cold can. She deserves at least a thank you," Sam mumbled and readjusted his rifle on his back. "Besides, everybody's heard of Detroit."

"Not if you're German and don't know the difference between hello and good-bye, never mind New York and Hollywood." The portly trooper picked his teeth with a dirty thumbnail, then took another bite.

"Hollywood," said Elsie. "Jean Harlow?" She put a hand on her waist, cocked her chin up, and recited in near perfect English, "'You don't know the tenth of it. You wouldn't believe the things I've stood for. The first night I met the guy he stood me up for two hours. For what? A woman in Jer-zee had quad-ruplets, and it's been that way ever since.'"

The group went silent then burst into laughter.

Josef leaned back against the cold building. A searing pain cleaved his skull. What was Elsie doing giving them bread? Talking to them—in a foreign tongue! He questioned whether it was another hallucination.

"Looks like you're wrong, Potter," said Robby. He stubbed his cigarette out on the cobblestone and tucked the nub behind his ear. "She knows more than you think. That's right, Jean Harlow." He nodded. "But personally, I'd peg you for Lana Turner."

Somebody whistled. Potter puffed up his chest and batted his eyelashes. The men laughed. Elsie laughed. Josef gripped the stone against his back, trying to keep the pounding in his head from knocking him over.

"*Libeled Lady*?" said Elsie.

"You sure are." Robby winked.

Elsie smiled and handed him a roll.

He took it. "I could get written up as a Benedict Arnold for saying this to you but—to hell with it. Thank you. Danke schön."

"Bitte schön," she replied.

"Sure is an eager beaver. Ain't like most of these German girls," said Potter.

"Ee-ager bea-ver?" repeated Elsie.

"Ha!" Potter slapped Sam on the back, knocking his bread from his hand. "Fast learner."

Sam picked it up and cleaned away the dirt on his sleeve. "Maybe we should give her something. Pay her for the meal?"

"Good thinking." Robby dug in his side satchel and pulled out a rectangular bar. "Being a baker, she's gotta like chocolate." He handed it to Elsie.

She turned the bar round, then tore back the paper in strips. Her eyes lit up. "Schokolade!" She took a bite of the side. "Ist gut!"

"Now we're talking," said Robby. "What else you boys got?"

"Pack of cigs," said Sam.

Robby took the pack and offered her one. "Smoke?"

She selected one of the thin fingers. Somebody threw Robby a lighter, and he lit the end for her. She sucked and blew out a curl of smoke with the ease and sophistication of a movie star.

Josef couldn't believe his eyes. Elsie was a completely different woman. Even the way she stood, so confident and bold. Not at all the dainty girl who clung to him at the Weihnachten ball.

Suddenly, she set to mouse coughs, and the men came round the sputtering Elsie.

"You okay?" asked Sam.

Elsie took deep breaths. "O-key, o-key?" she repeated like a squawking blue jay, then handed the cigarette to Robby. "Nein." She took another bite of the chocolate bar, then wrapped it back in the package and slipped it into her basket. "Thank you."

Again, the men broke into laughter.

"She's a trouper." Potter scratched his belly and readjusted his gun over his shoulder.

"Wie ist your name?" asked Robby.

"Elsie Schmidt," said Elsie. "Und sie?"

"Sergeant Robby Lee." He bowed.

"Cook extraordinaire," added Potter. "I'll admit, given the time and rations, this boy can make a mean pork barbecue."

"North Carolina, born and raised." He took a drag from Elsie's cigarette. "It's in the blood. My momma ate nothing but barbecue the whole time she was pregnant with me. My baking is a little rusty, though."

Elsie held a roll up high. "Brötchen."

The two locked eyes, and even from the alley shadows, Josef felt the electricity between them. An ache shot through him. There was no ring on her hand. After everything he had done for her, how could she have so quickly abandoned him and their country? *Traitor,* he thought, and suddenly the voice that cut his mind in two was not his own but Herr Hochschild's son. His muscles tightened from head to toe; his breath stopped. He closed his eyes, unable to fight the spasms and the tunneling of his vision.

thirty-four

"*A*dd Kirschwasser to cream," instructed Elsie in English. "Stir to stiff."
Robby nodded. "Gotcha." He whisked.

"More oomph!" She motioned with her arm for him to do it harder.

He picked up the pace. Beneath his olive-drab undershirt, his biceps
moved in rhythm with the sweet filling, round and round the bowl. Elsie
tried not to notice, not to imagine the familiar flesh beneath. So she focused on shaving chocolate with a carrot peeler.

She'd made *schwarzwälder kirschtorte* a thousand times, but never before had sifting flour and pitting cherries seemed so provocative. It was ir-
rational and absurd—this was a normal kitchen with an oven and pots and
pans. Nothing alluring or risqué about it, except that it was an American
kitchen with Robby Lee in it.

"How's that?" Robby held the whisk right side up. The cream remained
a perfect whorl.

Elsie swiped a finger through the twist's top curl and licked. "Gut. Taste."

Instead of sampling the filling, he put a hand behind Elsie's neck and
kissed her sticky lips.

"Sure is," he said.

Elsie elbowed him back to his bowl. "We have to bake a cake," she told him in German.

"Ein kuchen. Jawohl, fräulein." Robby laughed and saluted.

Elsie had been coming to the Armed Forces R&R Center since it opened. Within a week of occupation, the Americans turned the Nazi compound across town where she'd attended the Weihnachten ball into a G.I. playground. Soldiers across Europe came on vacation passes to ski, hike, play cards, and eat food that didn't come in a C-ration. The town was swarmed with smiling men wanting a day or two out of the trenches.

When the war ended, her family all hoped to hear from Hazel. Elsie expected her to walk through the bakery doors any hour, but she didn't; and with each passing day, their hearts grew more certain of what their minds refused to imagine. Rumors swirled of men, women, even whole families killed by foreign bullets or their own hand. The Lebensborn Program and all its members had disappeared overnight. Even those who spoke of it with high regard months prior now shook their heads and shrugged their shoulders. It infuriated Elsie, who saw it as another act of betrayal. She bit her tongue whenever Papa brought up Josef.

"What's the news? Did you check the mail?" he'd ask daily, as if nothing had changed and the post was running routinely. "Josef might've sent word."

She hadn't heard from Josef since his scribbled note and imagined him on the shores of Argentina or Brazil, someplace far from Germany. He would not make good on his promise to find Hazel. He had no remaining authority. There was no German authority. Berlin had been obliterated. Whatever archives might've been were piles of dust.

She hadn't heard from Frau Rattelmüller either since that icy day by the woodpile, before the Allied troops invaded. The Americans confiscated the frau's home and made it into a makeshift officer's quarters. At first, Elsie had feared for the old woman's life and the lives of her hidden boarders, but the house had not been ransacked by the Gestapo as they had the bakery. Elsie had gone to check, peering through the open windows. There was not one crumb on the floor. Not one cat hair. The pillows on the parlor couch sat comfortably in their usual places; the Hummel figurines aligned just so. The house had been purposely abandoned.

Elsie hoped Frau Rattelmüller had joined her Jewish friends after all, and it brought her great peace to imagine Cecile might be in the care of such kindness. It would have brought Tobias solace, too, she thought. She missed him profoundly. Her room felt as if its heart had been extracted, void of the quiet beating that had become a natural rhythm. Her consolation was that despite the thorough searches of the town and forests, the Americans had not reported the body of a small boy. He got away. She had no doubt of that and only hoped that one day she might hear from him again.

Julius never spoke of Tobias or Kremer's attack. He never spoke of those grim April days at all. Something in him had changed. He was still a brooding boy, but the affectation of his former self had greatly diminished. He did as he was told without argument and seemed to have a natural aptitude with numbers. He helped Mutti count the money in the till and was excellent at gauging the dough segments to make an exact baker's dozen. They were all glad to see his interests expanding; his toy soldiers were piled in a milk pail, abandoned.

In an attempt to usher in normalcy, Mutti enrolled Julius in Grundschule as soon as the local elementary reopened; but it was nothing like his Lebensborn education. He sulked for two days because the teacher sat him next to a girl with a strawberry birthmark across her forearm. Papa explained that skin colorations had nothing to do with a person's character. It was a lesson lost when two black Amis came into the bäckerei and Papa refused to serve them.

Elsie thought it foolish to turn away any coin. A full till meant full stomachs for the patrons and themselves. Without Nazi patronage, the bakery's accounts suffered. Weeks after the American occupation began, neither old nor new customers had come through their doors consistently. Though Papa never said a word, Elsie could tell by his gruff demeanor that something had to give. Since no one else was amenable, she took it upon herself and asked Robby if they could use a practiced baker in the R&R Center's kitchen.

Military regulations were strict, however, and German citizens were suspect. Robby's commander said he couldn't run the risk of underground agents infiltrating the kitchen and conspiring a mass poisoning; but Robby convinced him she was harmless and might even make the men's recreation a bit more *recreational*. A seventeen-year-old who looked like a pinup girl was an easy sell, though his superior warned him not to get too chummy. Military nonfraternization laws had been established. Any soldier found engaged in unprofessional socialization with a German was threatened with sedition charges. Luckily, the US War Department was an ocean away. Robby gave his commander a wink and a nod, and three days later received an authorized, semiofficial work permit for Elsie to be hired as a waitress.

She worked the dinner shift, but told Mutti and Papa that she got a job washing dishes at the Von Steuben restaurant. Papa grumbled at that. The Von Steuben had earned a fast reputation for catering to rowdy American soldiers who stumbled in for steins of dark ale, bratwurst, and oompah music. It was distasteful to think of Elsie among the patrons, but he soon relented, considering the pay and the fact that she was only a dishwasher. The truth would be harder for him to accept, and she simply didn't have the energy to argue over it right now. They needed the money, and this provided it. She'd tell him eventually. Meantime, she hoped he never questioned why her hands weren't raw and sore or why she consistently smelled of molasses, onion, and tomatoes. Robby's barbecue was the center's weekly special.

She didn't like taking orders and carrying trays of hamburgers, fried potatoes, mac and cheese, and other dishes labeled "Home Favorites," but she did enjoy the time in the kitchen. After hours, Robby taught her more English than all the lines of *Libeled Lady,* and how to cook American food. In exchange, she taught him German recipes.

Robby's first lesson was American apple pie, which was basically Papa's *versunkener apfelkuchen,* give or take an ingredient. She showed him how to make *bienenstich,* bee sting honey cake. He said he'd never tasted anything like it, and Elsie was glad for that. Next, Toll House cookies. Robby argued that they weren't the same because they used military-issued chocolate instead of his favorite Nestlé chocolate. The cookies weren't anything special, in Elsie's opinion. Sugar dough with chocolate bits thrown in haphazardly. Too sweet for her palate.

So the days went: early mornings in the bakery and long nights in the R&R kitchen. She liked spending time with Robby, and it hadn't taken long for their butter and sugar to come together outside the mixing bowl.

The chocolate cakes were baked and cooled. Elsie cut each through the diameter. "Kirschwasser." She dosed the four moons with cherry liquor.

"This stuff might as well be German holy water." Robby put his arms around her waist and kissed the back of her neck. Her arms and knees went weak, and she let the bottle glug into the soft center.

Before the wars, the Lutheran Church proclaimed sex outside of marriage as sin. Virgins were championed in life and fables; girls of lesser reputation were shamed and ridiculed; children born out of wedlock were shunned as bastards. But all that had changed. Hazel was regarded as a Nazi broodmare; commended, revered, and now, simply ignored as an unsightly artifact of war. Sure, everyone in Germany had regrets; acts no man could right or cleric forgive. Piety was out of fashion, and Elsie had quickly learned that her youth and beauty would either be put to others' devices or her own. Never again would she be powerless. What she did with Robby had nothing to do with him and everything to do with herself.

She set down the Kirschwasser bottle. "You will ruin the kuchen," she warned, then grabbed Robby by the shoulders and yanked him closer.

"What's the next step?" he whispered under her grip.

"Fill layers mit creme," Elsie commanded and nodded to the bowl of whipped white.

"And then?" He ran his fingers across her collarbone.

Her cheeks were hot, her dress too tight. "Icing."

"And then?" He undid the buttons of her bodice.

She could breathe so much better with the front of the dress open, the cool air on her bare skin. The heat of her cheeks rushed down her center like molten chocolate, satisfying her hunger without restraint.

"Schokolade und . . ." He kissed the ridge above her breasts. Her skin goose-bumped. "Cherries."

She shoved the bowl and cakes aside as Robby lifted her onto the counter.

thirty-five

"Happy birthday, dear Elsie. Happy birthday to you," they sang.

Elsie sat at the café table, face aglow in the candlelight of the largest cake Jane could manage to bake secretly.

Reba and Riki came together. They'd reconciled since Jane's wedding day but had decided to take things slow. He stayed in his apartment downtown, but Reba no longer had to guess in which building he lived. She went there often, bringing dishes she'd cooked at home, and they finally ate together.

Jane and Elsie were giving her a crash course in Baking 101. Her cinnamon sugar kreppels were a hit. Riki said they reminded him of *churros* his father used to buy him from street vendors in Juárez. Reba's farmer's bread was less successful. The yeast hadn't bloomed, and it came out as hard and flat as cardboard. Riki commended her effort and said they could pretend it was a large, rectangular tortilla. They'd laughed and eaten the bread with homemade salsa and *queso fresco*. Reba hadn't felt so light in all her life.

Elsie blew out her candles and the room went dark. "I'm happy to have made it this far!"

Sergio flicked on the lights while Jane cut the cake in thick squares.

"I made one of your favorites, Mom—spiced crumb cake."

"Spiced crumb cake?" asked Reba. "My granny used to make this. Is it German?"

"No." Elsie passed them all forks. "I learned the recipe from a friend, a chef from North Carolina. He was stationed in Garmisch after the war."

"You never told me that," said Jane. "I figured it was an adaptation of a German cake." She took a bite.

"Proof—even at my age, I still have secrets." Elsie scooped a heap of caramelized topping into her mouth. She chewed thoughtfully and swallowed. "Delicious. I could not have made it better." She winked at Jane and took another forkful.

Jane smiled. Sergio kissed her cheek.

"So you bake German and American recipes—ever considered learning Mexican? You'd make a profit round these parts," said Riki.

Sergio nodded in agreement.

Jane wagged a finger. "You can get flan or *tres leches* on every corner of town, but ain't nobody's got authentic German bread. That's what makes us unique. We've cornered the market."

"Actually, I would like to learn," said Elsie.

Jane's cake crumbled off her fork.

Elsie shrugged. "Why not? You are never too old for learning a new trick. It will not be as good as my neighbor Maria Sanchez, but I don't expect to open a Mexican bakery." She turned to Riki. "Do you know how to bake?"

Riki swallowed hard. "Not really. My recipe repertoire consists of one: *pan de muertos*. The bread of the dead. I used to help my mom make it for el Día de Los Muertos."

"The bread of the dead." Elsie enunciated each word. "How appropriate!" She laughed alone.

"Don't be morbid," said Jane.

"Ach was! It is my eightieth birthday. I've lived long enough to know you can't take your own mortality so seriously. We have a saying in Germany: Alles grau in grau malen. Don't paint everything black. We have no right to when others have had it far worse."

Reba gave Jane a consoling smile.

"The bread is actually a reaffirmation of life," explained Riki. "Mexicans see death entirely different than folks in Western culture. We celebrate death and life as a continuum, a coexistence of sorts. We even eulogize it as an elegant woman."

"Catrina—Lady of the Dead," said Sergio. "A beautiful, fleshless woman with a flowered hat." He grinned; cinnamon sugar stuck to his lower lip.

Jane brushed it away with her thumb. "Isn't that uplifting."

Elsie ignored her. "I love flowered hats. After the war ended, I went to a *strassenfest* in Munich and wore a hat with red geraniums. I've not thought about that summer in many years." She patted Riki's arm. "This Lady of the Dead sounds like my kind of woman. You'll show me how to make the dead bread. That can be your birthday gift. Jane and Reba will learn too."

"Us?" Jane looked to Reba.

Elsie nodded. "You must teach your children their culture. German and Mexican. Same for you, Reba."

Reba choked on her mouthful of spongy spice.

Riki smiled. "Deal."

"Prost!" Elsie lifted her glass of *apfelsaftschorle,* half apple juice and half mineral water. "To new friends and family! And, God willing, another year in this crazy world."

A slow tune came on the car radio. Reba and Riki parked in front of Reba's condo on Franklin Ridge. She couldn't put off telling him about San Francisco any longer.

Leigh had called and left a message while Reba was at the bakery celebrating Jane and Sergio's nuptials. The job was hers. She'd gone numb when she heard the news. Too much happiness packed into one day: seeing Riki, Jane and Sergio's marriage, and then her dream job. It was everything she'd wanted. So why did she still feel like the sun had been eclipsed? She remembered Deedee's words, *Be happy, Reba. Promise me you'll let yourself.*

Reba returned Leigh's call, accepted the job, and asked for the latest possible start date. Leigh hadn't budged much. "First Monday in February," she'd said. Reba gave the *Sun City* editorial staff notice and put the condo on the market with a local realtor. She boxed up what she could and offered the rest to her neighbors, paid the utilities through the month, canceled her subscription to *El Paso Times,* and emptied the cupboards. She'd told almost everyone about her impending departure except Riki. Things had been going so well. She didn't want to burst the bubble.

Writing the date atop Elsie's birthday card, she realized she'd have to start the drive to California by the weekend. Elsie's birthday party wasn't the appropriate moment to break the news to him; however, now didn't feel right either. This was her chance at big-time journalism. She had to make him understand and had just gotten up the nerve to speak when he turned down the radio.

"Can you imagine being eighty years old?" He scratched his five o'clock shadow. "She's seen so much."

Reba nodded, deciphering how she could segue to San Francisco. "A real adventurer. Not afraid of the unknown." It was the best she could come up with.

Riki nodded.

"What I mean is—all her life, she went for it, whatever that 'it' was."

He cocked his head.

She was spiraling and needed to get to a definitive point. "It's inspirational. Makes you want to—to take the bull by the horns, you know?"

The radio played a low jingle through the pause in conversation.

Finally, Reba blurted out, "Riki, *San Francisco Monthly* offered me an editorial position. It's a top-notch magazine. A dream job! I start right away."

She stared hard at the neon lights of the radio station: 93.1. The car idled loudly. She didn't dare face him.

"You're going?" he asked.

"It's what I've always wanted."

"Uh-huh." The car heater whizzed and popped. "San Francisco. You'll be on the water."

Reba nodded. "The bay. You could come." It was a weak offer, but she wanted him to know she'd considered.

He breathed in deep and held it. "My life is here. I can't pick up and leave." He blew out the air. "I'm happy for you, Reba. Really I am." He put his hand on hers.

She turned and saw that he meant it. His eyes were soft and painfully earnest, and instead of feeling relief, the sadness within welled up.

thirty-six

"*T*hey got pretzels with mustard over there!" Robby yelled above the oompah band. He bobbed and weaved through the crowd, pulling Elsie along by the hand. Sam and Potter trailed behind with tall pints of frothy pilsner.

Elsie tasted bile at the thought of spicy mustard. She'd been feeling poorly for a couple weeks. At the end of her night shifts, she barely had the strength to wave to Robby from the kitchen galley and bicycle home. She was exhausted from sunup to sundown, and her lack of appetite wasn't helping. The butcher received a new shipment of pork, thanks to the Americans, and Mutti was able to buy long links of sage sausage—Elsie's old favorite—but the smell of grease from the kitchen made her nauseated, and she hadn't craved a single bite. Mutti brushed it off as "working too hard," which they all were; but after so many months of paucity, it was strange to now have no hunger for the very foods she once desired most.

A day off, that's what she needed. The R&R kitchen was closed that Saturday so a leaky water pipe could be replaced. Elsie asked Papa if she could take the day off from the bäckerei, too. Robby and a couple friends were catching the train to Munich for a summer street carnival. Since the Nazis forbade celebrations unconnected to the party, no town had been able to host their traditional events in years. Deep down, Papa missed the old ways as much as everyone. He consented for her to go with a friend from the Von Steuben, though no such friend existed.

The morning of the festival, she'd slept longer than usual and it helped. She awoke energized and seemingly restored, even eating a plate of boiled ham for breakfast, though it tasted off.

Mutti surprised her with a new dirndl beautifully embroidered with delicate poppies and trimmed in matching red. It was the material Hazel had sent.

"You need something new to wear to the festival," Mutti had said and smoothed the dirndl's seams between her fingers. "I know red was your sister's favorite, but she would want you to have it. With your eyes, you can wear any color and look beautiful."

It was the first time Mutti had ever praised Elsie's beauty over Hazel's, and Elsie understood all too well: Mutti didn't believe Hazel was ever coming home.

"Here, dear." Mutti handed over the dress. "Take this before I ruin it with flour," she said, though she had yet to begin baking. "Promise to show me how it looks on before you leave." Mutti shut the bedroom door behind her.

Elsie laid the dress on the bed so that the brown skirt spread wide like a peacock tail. Hazel would've been lovely in it. A striking garment, it was as if Mutti had threaded the fabric of her heart onto each sleeve and hem. Elsie hadn't worn anything so fine since Josef's gown on Christmas Eve. This, however, was more precious than all the chiffon of Paris, all the silk of Shanghai, all the wool of Castile, because of everything it had survived— everything they had survived. She slipped out of her muslin robe and undid the dress's waistline. Snaps of electricity arced between her gauzy slip and the copper buttons.

In the mirror, she admired herself, astonished that the dress made for Hazel's measurements fit her to a T. Her figure had blossomed over the past few months. Even with her recent lack of appetite, her chest and hips were rounder and fuller than ever before. She buttoned the dirndl, dotted her wrists with rose shampoo, grabbed a matching hat from the closet, and gave herself one last inspection. She was ready. Almost.

The outfit needed something. Pizzazz, like the American poster girls in the R&R Center. A flash of red fluttered in the outdoor window box. Red geraniums against the summer breeze. She pinched the largest cluster at the base and stuck it in the brim.

Now, someone in the carnival crowd knocked her hat askew. The bloom fell and was smashed by clogged feet. Elsie readjusted once they reached the Johanns' bäckerei booth. The artfully arranged pretzels looked like they'd spent too little time in the soda ash bath and too much in the sun, in her opinion.

"Two." Robby made a peace sign with his fingers.

"Nein," Elsie protested.

"You've got to eat something." Robby frowned. "Are you bent on getting pie-eyed?"

She'd drunk an entire beer stein alone. The malt magically settled her stomach. She craved another, but knew it unwise. Her head already felt a blissful airiness. Papa told her that dark lager, like dark chocolate, had that effect.

"They've got fried kreppels. How about one of those?" pressed Robby.

Petite sugar dumplings floated on tufts of brown paper, leaving slick shadows beneath.

Her mouth watered. "Ja."

Robby ordered one pretzel and one kreppel. Sam and Potter were content with their beers and distracted by two busty girls wearing frilly, low-cut dirndls.

The kreppel was warm in Elsie's palm. She bit expectantly only to find the sweetness cloying. Gulping down the morsel, she handed the remaining portion to Robby. "Take." She screwed up her nose and waved it away.

"Not up to Schmidt quality?" he teased.

"Schmidt?" interrupted a woman in line behind them. She was round in the belly with a similarly pregnant pustule on the tip of her nose. "Hazel Schmidt?"

Elsie tried to focus past the blemish. "My sister," she clarified.

"Oh! Then you must be familiar with Josef Hub?"

The kreppel nearly came back up. She tried to walk away, but the woman followed.

"He was looking for your sister. Did he ever find her? He was the commander of her fiancé's unit in Munich. Peter Abend?"

Elsie turned so that Robby was to her back. The woman did the same and continued.

"I used to be a Naz—an archive secretary in Munich. Never forget a name." She rubbed her belly. "Josef and I were acquaintances before I met my husband." She pointed over her shoulder to a corpulent man waiting in line. "Josef asked me to pull the file on Hazel Schmidt, which of course I never would have done. That was classified information then."

She straightened her shoulders defensively. "We lost touch. I wondered if he ever found her."

"When was this?" Elsie's heart fluttered, hope alive.

"Hmm . . ." She tapped her fingers on her belly bulge. "1941–42. I can't remember. It seems like a lifetime ago, doesn't it?"

It did. Elsie recalled the first time Josef strolled through the bäckerei doors in his starched uniform, tall and dignified; it was like a scene in a dark movie theater, out of focus around the corners.

"So much chaos when the Reich fell. I haven't heard from Josef in months," said Elsie.

"So you *did* know him. A good man." She cleared her throat. "Such a shame."

The summer sun blazed hot despite Elsie's hat.

"A shame?"

"You've heard the news?"

She shook her head. Her ears burned.

The woman looked to her husband, then leaned in close. "They found him and a group of SS officers on a docked boat in Brunsbüttel. Mass suicide."

Elsie blinked hard. Her vision tunneled.

"Everyone had been shot—a bloody mess. But not Josef. His was lethal injection, so they say," she whispered.

Elsie sipped in the air, but it did no good. Acid rumbled up her throat and before she could turn away, she vomited on the woman's wooden clogs.

Robby rushed to her side. "Elsie?"

She knelt to the ground and gripped the blades of grass to steady herself.

"I'm sorry. It's the drink," Robby explained to the woman. "She's been sick all week. Hasn't been able to stomach much."

The woman stamped the pottage of fried dough from her toe. "It's fine. Reminds me of myself not too long ago—terrible pregnancy sickness with this child."

Elsie focused on a bright dandelion, its yellow bud wide open. Her head still spun, but the din of the crowd quieted. She put a hand to her stomach. Impossible.

thirty-seven

EL PASO BORDER PATROL STATION
8935 MONTANA AVENUE

EL PASO, TEXAS

———-Original Message———-
From: reba.adams@hotmail.com
Sent: February 14, 2008 6:52 P.M.
To: ricardo.m.chavez@cbp.dhs.gov
Subject: Thinking of you

February 14, 2008

Happy Valentine's Day, Riki!

I tried your cell but you must be finishing up at the station. I'm sorry I wasn't there to watch the sun turn the sky all our favorite sherbet flavors. How many did we count that one time— thirty-three different sky scoops? That's two more than Baskin-Robbins. My favorite will always be passion fruit pineapple marshmallow cream. That scoop right above Sunland Park, New Mexico. So if you see it tonight, give it a little taste for me.

It's a different kind of sunset here on the bay. A little watered down in my opinion. But the apartment is beautiful. My editor, Leigh, helped me get the place—fully furnished, too. There was a long waiting list at this apartment complex, but one word from her and they bumped me to the top. You'd like it. You can see the water from my balcony. Leigh's a real ballbuster in the office. Kind of reminds me of Elsie with an organic, Napa wine, locavore twist. Hoping this is just hell week and things ease up after I've been initiated.

My first story assignment is on the new trend in nightclub-restaurant hybrids. Interesting.

Leigh says she wants me to get my feet wet in the city scene, but the majority of my work will be in the editing room, not the beat. I'm wondering what exactly that means.

San Fran is a lot bigger than El Paso, that's for sure. A lot bigger than Richmond, too. I went walking downtown yesterday. I thought I'd see a couple city staples—the Fisherman's Wharf, the Ghirardelli Chocolate Factory, the Boudin Bakery. I bought a bread roll in the shape of a turtle. Seriously, it was the spitting image, and it tasted about the same. Bland as pond water. You'll have to tell Elsie that nothing compares to her brötchen—not even the famous big-city bakeries.

Have you been by the bakery lately? I've called a few times, but (no surprise) got the answering machine. Elsie should really open an e-mail account. The spam filter siphons out all the porn and Viagra ads. You tell her that.

Miss you.
Love, Reba

thirty-eight

SCHMIDT BÄCKEREI
56 LUDWIGSTRASSE
GARMISCH, GERMANY

AUGUST 2, 1945

*E*lsie made her way upstairs to change for the night shift. The American R&R Center was preparing for a crowd, a bomb squadron on weeklong leave. The whole unit was busing in from Fritzlar, Germany. Robby asked Elsie to help in the kitchen in addition to her waitstaff duties; she'd reluctantly agreed. She dreaded the busy night ahead. It'd already been a long day in the bäckerei. Papa had gone to Partenkirchen where a flour mill had reopened, leaving Elsie as head baker for the day. She was thoroughly exhausted with only an hour to change clothing and bicycle over to the R&R Center.

She'd sat down with a calendar immediately following the strassenfest. A pregnancy was possible. She hadn't menstruated in months; a product of being on her feet too much and eating too little, she'd reasoned. Her cycle had stopped often during the war and this, she thought, was no different. There wasn't time to be pregnant, she told herself, as Monday and another week began. During the day, her mind and hands were busy mixing, rolling, and taking orders. But at night, her fear of carrying a bastard child kept her awake.

Her sleeplessness and physical fatigue made even climbing the stairs to her room a daunting task. Now, she stopped midway and leaned against the wall, fighting the urge to give in to gravity and let the weight of her body pull her back. She steadied herself with arms bridged to either side, then continued to the top.

In her room, she lay fully dressed on her bed—just for a moment, to pretend sleep and perhaps trick her body into rejuvenation, but the pillow was hot. Her ear burned from the friction. She sat up, rubbed her forehead, and prayed for strength she was certain she didn't deserve.

"You don't look well." Mutti stood in the doorway. "Not keeping much down." She nodded to the basin.

Elsie had been careful to clean it immediately after each bout of nausea and assumed Mutti was too busy and preoccupied with Julius to notice.

"I've got something," she explained.

"Ja." Mutti stepped into the room and closed the door behind her. "So you do."

The hairs on Elsie's arms pricked upright. "Is Julius back from school?" She changed the subject.

"He asked to go to his school friend's house. Rory Schneider. Bitsy Schneider's eldest son."

Elsie remembered them well. Bitsy and Hazel had been friends in school. From a poorer family, Bitsy married the blacksmith Henri Schneider, a friend of her father's and twenty years her senior. They'd all pitied Bitsy at the time: her husband was too old to come to the Hitler Youth parties or join the SS forces. Now, three children later, with a fourth on the way and a husband safe at home, more than a few envied her flourishing marriage.

Elsie's feet were icy numb in her shoes. "It is good he is making friends."

"Ja, I gave him ginger and rose hips to take to Bitsy. She says the baby kicks her ribs all night. I told her it's a sign of a strong boy. A blessing to have in these hard times."

Elsie nodded quickly.

Mutti sat down beside her. "I'm sorry it's going so badly for you. That's normal at the beginning."

Elsie arms and legs went weak. "I don't know what you mean, Mutti. I ate bad cheese."

Mutti laid her palm on Elsie's abdomen. "I fear it is a great deal more than that."

Elsie couldn't stand or move or speak.

"You are with child."

The bluntness of Mutti's words turned her to stone. Though she had thought it for weeks, hearing it said aloud made it real. But no, how could it be? She couldn't have a child; she didn't want one, not now, not like this. Her shoulders slumped forward, followed by her chest until her whole body lay puddled on the ground. She was too tired to cry. She hadn't the stamina to produce tears or wail or beat her breast. All she could do was be still.

"God, help me," she whispered.

Mutti knelt to the floor and put her arm around Elsie. "Do you want this?"

Elsie closed her eyes. "I'm sorry, Mutti."

She knew it was a sin against God to not want her child, a sin against everything natural and sacred. She thought of Hazel: the pride she'd gleaned from her children; the ragged heartache in her last few letters. They had arrived the week before. Ovidia had been unable to mail them until recently. Elsie read what she could make out through the dirt and water stains, muffling her cries in the dark of night and wondering where Hazel could possibly have gone. She wouldn't allow herself to consider that she was dead—couldn't. The totality of her grief was too severe and fresh as an open wound. If she continued to let herself bleed with sorrow, she feared she'd lose herself completely to it. She wouldn't show the letters to Mutti and Papa. It was the one promise she could keep to Hazel when in the end it seemed she'd failed her—failed Tobias, too, and now, failed her own child.

"Shh. It's not your fault." Mutti smoothed the tears from Elsie's cheek. "Dead or run off, Josef's gone. He left you unprotected against . . ." She cleared her throat. "You're too young to have your life ruined."

Elsie's chin fell to her chest. She knew she should tell Mutti about Robby, but she'd never been able to talk to her about such things.

Mutti stared straight. "It is probably three months along. We caught it in time to stop it."

Elsie had heard of women who nearly died from inserting ice picks, razors attached to cigarette holders, and knitting needles into their wombs. She winced.

"I have a special tea." Mutti's eyes remained wide and fixed. "Brewed pennyroyal and cohosh. Six cups a day for five days. On the sixth day, the bleeding starts. As normal as every month."

Elsie swallowed hard. A tea? It seemed so pedestrian and benign. "Have you used it?"

Mutti pursed her lips. "Like I told your sister before you. Men and war don't change. Things happen that are out of our control. It doesn't mean we have no control. Your father was not the first man I was with." She bit her bottom lip. "What happened to you happened to me, too. During the first war, Russian soldiers came to the house." She twisted the apron of her skirt. "I had never been with a man, and they took that from me. There was nothing to be done. I never told your papa. Only you and Hazel. When Peter died and Hazel found herself pregnant with Julius, she had a choice. Her baby was made of love. But yours and mine . . ." Her voice broke. "If only I had come sooner. I should have protected you better. I swore my children would never know that kind of suffering."

Elsie's whole body throbbed. Almost thirty years later, and Mutti's guilt remained. Might the same fate be true for her?

"You did the best you could," Elsie reassured her, then crossed her arms over her belly.

Mutti sniffed back tears and blotted her eyes with the apron. "It's summer. Pennyroyal is in bloom." She kissed the crown of Elsie's head. "We won't speak of it again. No one need know. We'll go on and pray for God's mercy. That's all we can do."

Elsie leaned against Mutti's arm. She smelled sweetly of dried herbs and honey milk. Elsie wished it would wash over and through her. Slowly, she nodded.

thirty-nine

*R*iki arrived early to the station with baggy eyes from sleepless nights. Dreams. The kind that left him anxious and uncomfortable despite the soft nightfall and fleecy sheets. The apartment didn't feel like home. He couldn't remember exactly what he'd dreamed. As soon as he awoke, the visions vanished into the stucco walls.

His mother used to tell him that dreams were the spirit world's communication with the living. He'd believed that as a child until one day he dreamed that his mother died in a plane crash. He decided there could only be three rationales: (1) the spirit world was full of liars, (2) it was nonexistent, or (3) dreams were complete fabrications of the subconscious. The last was most practical considering his mother had never been on a plane. She died a decade later of TB, followed by his father. Upon their deaths, he wished he still believed. He would've liked to see them again, if only in his dreams.

Even more, he wished Reba were there now. He wasn't the sort to lie to himself. He missed her. Her sleeping body and tangle of hair had once been a comfort, and for as long as he'd slept next to her, his nights had been deep and dreamless. He'd tried to imagine her next to him and perhaps conjure serenity, but the bedside was empty and bitterly cold.

Riki had purposely not returned most of Reba's calls and e-mails. He'd hoped that the weeks after Jane's wedding were a new beginning, but it was abundantly clear that Reba didn't see her future with him. He wouldn't force her—shouldn't have to. But his mind and his heart were at odds. Work gave him something to do, but even that had become an alienating duty.

At 5:00 a.m., he got up, ate a bowl of Corn Pops, showered, shaved, and headed to the station.

Bert was already at his desk with a large cup of coffee.

"You got the report?" Bert asked.

Riki dropped down in his chair, his bones too heavy and energy too little.

"Report?" He clicked on his computer and had to look away from the flashing start-up icon. His eyes burned.

"Yeah." Bert slurped his cup. "I got the call at eleven last night. Didn't you?"

Riki's cell phone was off. He'd been charging the battery overnight and had forgotten to turn it back on when he woke.

"Nope. Phone was charging."

Bert reached over to the fax on the stand. "Seriously, man, you've got to keep the phone and radios on 24/7. Technically, they're government property. I understand you have to charge but . . ." He huffed and tossed a handful of faxed pages onto Riki's desk.

"What is it?" Riki rubbed his eyes.

"Juárez kid got shot," said Bert.

On the top page was a news report.

"*El Paso Times* wanted a quote for the morning paper," explained Bert. "Damned reporters. They smell blood in the water—I guess it'd be blood in the Rio, right?" He yawned and scratched his neck. "I told them 'no comment' until we get more info from the Chihuahua side. They're latching on to something about the kid and his family being deported by our station back in November. Sure as shit they're going to spin it like we're as guilty as the guy who pulled the trigger." He took a container of antacid tablets from his desk drawer and tapped out two. "Damned liberal media. Don't they know what the word 'illegal' means? It's simple English. They got no respect for the people trying to protect them." He popped the chalky disks.

Riki picked up the newspaper copy:

EL PASO, Texas—Residents on both sides mourn the loss of innocence today. A 9-year-old boy was caught in the crossfire between Customs and Border Patrol agents and a group of Mexican nationals crossing illegally into the United States, administrators stated.

Monday evening at 7 p.m. near the Paso del Norte Bridge, CBP agents on bikes were assaulted by rock-throwing members of a group attempting to enter the U.S. through a gap in the border fence, said Special Operation Supervisor Adrian Rodriguez.

"They threw rocks at United States agents," said Rodriguez. "We train our men to respond in self-defense."

A CBP agent fired his gun several times. While the bullets missed their intended victims and halted the group of Mexican nationals, a stray bullet made its way across the divide, killing 9-year-old Victor Garcia who stood watching the scene on the Mexican side of the bridge's embankment.

"We use gunfire as a scare tactic," explained Special Agent Marsha Jenkins, spokeswoman for the FBI in El Paso. "This is a most unfortunate accident."

The Border Patrol did not identify the agent who fired. He has been placed on paid leave, Rodriguez said.

The Mexican Secretary of State today condemned the death. Mexican officials said they want the U.S. to conduct a full investigation into the events that prompted the shooting.

The use of firearms in response to a rock attack is a "disproportionate use of force," stated Mexican officials.

Deported in November 2007, Garcia's mother, Carmen, a resident of the Barreales District, was unreachable for comment. His father, Felipe, is currently incarcerated at Juárez County jail on drug-related charges.

The Customs and Border Protection Agency reported 398 border deaths for 2007. Garcia's marks another distressing count in this year's fatality sum as the border wars continue.

Riki ran his finger over the facts: Carmen and Victor Garcia; Barreales District. His heart quickened. He got on the computer, flipped through the deportation files to November, and there they were. Carmen, Victor, and Olivia Garcia deported November 12, 2007. His head reeled. He felt sick and tried to stand to get to the restroom. His knees gave way.

"You okay, Rik?" asked Bert.

He shook his head. If only he'd done things differently, he thought. If only. Unlike the raid, there was no one to blame. No offense or defense. No right or wrong, good or bad. The facts stared back at him in black and white: Victor was dead, and he had been the one to put the boy in harm's way. Unthinkable; unbelievable; it couldn't be true. He dropped his face into his hands. It wasn't his fault, but somehow, it was.

forty

EL CAMINO VILLAGE
APARTMENTS
2048 EL CAMINO REAL

SAN FRANCISCO, CA

———-Original Message———-
From: reba.adams@hotmail.com
Sent: April 12, 2008 12:18 P.M.
To: deedee.adams@gmail.com
Subject: It's raining here . . . AGAIN

Deedee,

When we skipped around to the Mamas and the Papas, I never imagined the flowers in my hair would be *drowned* by the rain. Obviously, they were smoking something floral because this place is not the promised summer love-in.

I already wrote you about work. It is what it is. The stories make me yawn. You can only read so many essays on the week's newest Bordeaux before you want to crack a bottle over your head. B.O.R.I.N.G. At the very least, you'd think they'd send the magazine some samples. Maybe the reporters are drinking it all before it gets to me. Being an editor is a completely different animal from feature writing. You should see my desk—it's a paper monsoon! It matches the weather and my mood.

And no, I haven't forgotten. I'm checking my calendar for a weekend to fly home, but it isn't looking good. I have next-to-no vacation allowance, and it takes almost a full day's travel to get to the East Coast. I'm trying to find a long weekend when I can dovetail my vacation onto the end of a magazine holiday, but I've already been tasked with being the editor on call for the

Memorial Day events. Maybe I could fly home for the 4th of July, but didn't you say Momma's going up to see the Capitol fireworks with the Junior League? Let me know so I don't waste energy planning.

Riki's doing fine, I guess. I called him last week, but he was in the middle of something at the station. He sounded preoccupied. I don't know what's been going on with him or us this past month. All I know is that he feels . . . distant. Did I make the wrong decision, D? I ask myself that at least three times a day, like meals.

That's the cruddy view from the Pacific coast this week. How's the world facing the Atlantic? Miss you.

Love, Reba

At dusk, Reba watched a ship come into harbor. The raging nimbus clouds had abated and the temperature was mild enough to sit outside on her balcony; however, a ghoulish fog rose from underfoot, climbing higher and higher until it blocked the sun and moon entirely.

Reba hadn't gone with so little sunshine since Virginia, where she'd felt the urge to cry every January to April. In college, Sasha had asked if she had SAD, seasonal affective disorder. Reba thought it some kind of gibe until she took Psychology 101 and her professor devoted a whole lecture day to its symptoms and treatment. Too closely resembling her daddy's depression, she'd denied any association and kept her tears at bay when Sasha was around. With an average of 302 sunny days a year, El Paso had been unknowingly therapeutic.

Now, she felt the familiar ache times ten. Her lips trembled; her eyes burned to expel the weighty sadness that filled her like the rain in her balcony's empty flowerpots. She couldn't blame the weather entirely. The feeling remained even when the California sun twinkled on the bay and the sky above Crissy Field was painted true blue. Then, it seemed even worse, and a tear or two would make its way out.

In the harbor below, the ship seemed no bigger than a toy boat, a winding streak of charcoal-colored waves in its wake. A man stood on the empty deck, a miniature tin soldier with a splinter of wood between him and the deep ocean. His small size made Reba feel small too.

The magazine was bigger than she'd expected—so many bylines, deadlines, and word counts, she barely saw the same people twice in the coffee room. Unlike at *Sun City, San Francisco Monthly* expected her to work exclusively from the office, never at home. She spent many long nights eating kung pao shrimp at her cubicle desk, the sour smell of garlic the only thing permeating the gray fabric walls. She didn't know which was worse: alone in her office or alone in her apartment. Sitting at home watching *Sex and the City* reruns was a blatant reminder that there was no sex in her city, no glamorous life of martinis and columnist fame. The tragedy was that she didn't particularly long for it. Instead, she daydreamed of Riki, Elsie, and Jane. She had talked briefly with Jane a few weeks before and felt a surge of nostalgia at the sound of pans banging in the background.

Riki had been increasingly reserved in their sparse phone conversations. His e-mails were nonexistent. Since March she'd felt the distance pushing them further and further from the course she had hoped to set. She wanted to ask if he was seeing someone else, but was afraid of the answer. Everyone seemed to have moved on but her. It was ironic. She'd finally reached her big city dreams and felt more stunted than ever.

The ship blew its horn, long and mournful. Reba wished she could join its cry, and she might have if a sudden burst of yips hadn't sounded from the adjoining balcony. Tethered to the neighbor's wrought-iron café table was a black Chihuahua.

"I hear you, fella," said Reba.

The dog's triangular ears perked in her direction. She stepped forward and it leaped at her, the leash choking every other bark.

"Hush now. I'm not going to hurt you."

Riki had brought home a lost Chihuahua when they first moved in together. He named it Nacho and bought a minisombrero for it to wear. He would have kept it had the owners not come a week later. At the time, Reba had been up against deadline and was annoyed by both Riki and the puppy-pawed visitor prancing about their kitchen. But Riki had loved the idea of raising a pet together. She smiled at the memory, though it stung of so many regrets.

She went inside and retrieved the leftover Chinese takeout. "You like shrimp?" She held up a curly tail.

The dog sat on its haunches and cocked its head to the side. "Good boy," said Reba, tossing the shrimp over the six-inch balcony divide. He caught it midair.

Reba took another saucy shrimp and popped it in her own mouth. "You know," she mumbled, "I just came from your neck of the woods. Have you ever been to Chihuahua?"

Suddenly conscious that she was conversing with a dog, she leaned over the railing to make sure the neighbors weren't sitting in their living room getting a good laugh at her expense. The lights were off, the door securely closed.

The dog stood up on its hind feet and overlapped his paws; a practiced trait, she could tell.

"Very nice!" Reba threw him another shrimp, and the dog eagerly noshed on the reward. "You got a name?" She searched his collar for a tag but found none.

"That's all right. How about a nickname?" She pulled another shrimp from the container, deep in thought. He didn't look like a Rover or Max.

The dog stood on his hind legs again, pencil tail thwacking the wooden balcony.

She held up the food. "Shrimp?"

He excitedly bobbed his paws like panning for gold.

"Hey—that's not a bad idea. What do you say, Shrimp." It seemed to fit. She threw the tail to him and licked hoisin from her fingers.

Docking, the ship blew its horn again, but the sound seemed to echo less than before. The sailor on the deck was gone.

"Do you like kreppels?" Reba asked. "Some people say they're kind of like churros. Maybe I'll make us a batch."

Shrimp licked his chops and let his tongue loll out in something like a smile.

-----Original Message-----
From: deedee.adams@gmail.com
Sent: April 14, 2008 5:43 P.M.
To: reba.adams@hotmail.com
Subject: RE: It's raining here . . . AGAIN

Reba,

Forget the flowers, you sound like a drowned cat! I hate hearing you so gloom and doom. It's not healthy. Get your head out of the puddle. Remember what I said: Look up, kitty, or you'll miss the rainbow! I wish for a second you could see the Reba I see. You're a fighter, strong and determined. I've always admired that about you. Don't let yourself crumble from within.

Yes, Momma is going with the Richmond Junior League to Washington, D.C., for Independence Day. The ladies are honoring Vietnam Vets with red, white, and blue garlands made out of recycled clothing. (Don't ask me—it was some big "material drive" for our "brave men in uniform" a month back. They've been channeling Betsy Ross ever since.) So it's no use you flying in. She won't want to talk anything but apple pies and John Philip Sousa then. There's no other time this summer you could come? How about in the fall—Labor Day or Columbus Day? Try, Reba. Please.

I'm sorry to hear that you and Riki are in *another* rough patch. Long-distance relationships are difficult. Not that I know, but none of my girlfriends have been able to keep them up. I'm rooting for this Riki, though. If you and he make it work, an introduction is long overdue. Yet another reason to get on a plane. This is your big sister speaking: no more excuses. Bring Riki home with you. Maybe you need to get away together. We can make the weekend one big therapy session. ;)

Smile, baby sis. Whether we're standing on the shores of the Pacific or the Atlantic, the water is the same.

Love you, Deedee

forty-one

*E*lsie balanced heavy plates of meatloaf on the serving tray. Following the departure of the Ninth Air Force squadron, the R&R Center was notably quiet. Robby declared the kitchen crew on a minihiatus and announced "Mom's Meatloaf Special" as the set menu. Late the previous evening, they'd mixed, baked, and frozen over two dozen meaty bricks in preparation. The gigantic bowl of ground beef had nearly sent Elsie running for the toilet, but she wouldn't risk vomiting Mutti's tea.

For the past week, Mutti had brewed batches each morning and bound the herbs in petite cheesecloth sachets for Elsie to take to work in the evenings. Purple puffs of pennyroyal and leafy cohosh hung from the kitchen window to dry. Papa had nearly made himself a cup, mistaking the pennyroyal for lavender, so Mutti tied the stems with red yarn as an indicator.

This was Elsie's fifth and final day on the tincture. So far, the tea seemed to do little more than give her a yellow complexion and full bladder.

"Last order up for Table 2!" called the line cook. He handed Elsie a plate slathered in extra ketchup and wilted onions, and she hoisted the loaded tray onto her shoulder.

Five soldiers drank frothy steins at the table. Hungry eyes brightened with her approach, but before she reached them, something between her ribs and pelvis spasmed, then knotted hard. She doubled over. The plates slid forward to a crash.

Unable to collect herself from the pain, two of the men lifted her off the floor. A third brushed slimy vegetables and tomato sauce from her apron while the remaining pair picked up broken plates. Their faces contorted; their mouths moved, but she heard little. The sound of crashing still echoed. The knot twisted tighter inside. She clutched her stomach and closed her eyes. When she opened them again, Robby held her chin and strained to see the pain Elsie could not and would not tell him. He spoke to someone behind him, and then everything began to swirl like cinnamon mixed in cake batter. She was going to vomit but remembered the tea and leaned her head back to keep it all down. Quickly, she realized the room wasn't spinning. She was moving, being carried out of the dining hall through the kitchen into the back linen closet.

Robby made a long bed of stacked cream tablecloths and a pillow of folded napkins. She pulled her knees to her chest and begged to have her dirndl undone. Robby hurried the men out and did as she requested.

"Elsie, we've got to call a doctor," he said.

She gripped his arm, digging her fingernails into his wrist. A doctor would alert him of her pregnancy. "Nein." She understood what was happening. She only wished Mutti was there to validate her symptoms. "My mother," she whispered, but then remembered where she was and where she was supposed to be. She still hadn't told her parents about her job with the Americans. "Never mind."

Another cramp kicked so hard, she knew it could only be the baby writhing within.

Robby put his hand to her belly. "It hurts here?"

The pressure of his palm relieved some of the pain, and she wondered if the child felt his pulse through her thin skin. Her eyes stung and blurred, and she prayed for forgiveness.

"A new guy just arrived with the last recruits. He came to play pickup football the other day. Said he was a doc. I could get him. Nobody would know," said Robby.

Before she could refuse, he was gone, and she was alone. The closet lightbulb dangled from a cord above. A fat moth flew round, occasionally touching the hot white, then fluttering back, touching and fluttering, touching and fluttering, desperately diving into the brightness. Its powdery wings pattered against the round glass barrier. Elsie wished she could catch it in her palms and release it outside, so the true moonlight might set its path straight. Her cramps began to ease with each passing minute.

There was a knock and though she gave no permission, it opened. A tall man with russet hair falling over his brow entered. He stood out from the other soldiers with their tight regulation crew cuts; his face was older but softer by the framing.

"This is Doc Meriwether. I told him you've been feeling bad for weeks. He's going to fix you up," said Robby.

"Fräulein Schmidt." Doctor Meriwether nodded, then knelt by her makeshift bed and opened his Red Cross rucksack.

"Nein." She pulled away and tried to stand, but the pain returned.

Doctor Meriwether felt her forehead. His fingers so tender and careful, she immediately lay back.

"A little warm." He turned to Robby. "Mind stepping out while I examine the lady?"

Robby shifted his weight on either foot. "Elsie?"

She nodded, and he left.

"How's about you tell me where it hurts," said Doctor Meriwether.

Elsie couldn't distinguish what was different in his voice. There was a slow twang to his English, like honey drizzled off the comb.

"Woman's business." She hoped he'd leave it at that and be done. Instead, he put a palm to her lower belly and pressed down firmly. She gasped as something inside came loose. A warmth spread between her thighs.

"Uh-huh." He widened her eye between his fingers and peered. "Look right at me." And she did.

In fact, Elsie couldn't remember the last time she'd looked so closely into another person's eyes. Yes, she met the gaze of everyone she spoke to and sometimes remembered that their eyes were very light or very dark, but there was more she'd never noticed until Doctor Meriwether. His eyes weren't merely brown; they were gold flecked and gave way to green and yellow near the perimeters. His pupils were no ordinary darkness either; their centers glimmered light and reflected an entirely different world. She wished she could fly straight into them. Her heart beat fast.

"Sergeant Lee says you've had chronic vomiting, lack of appetite, fatigue." He paused and waited for a response.

Elsie nodded.

"When was your last menstruation?" He turned his face away when he asked, and she knew he knew.

She bit her lip to hold back the tears.

He moved to the end of the bed. "I'm sorry, Miss Schmidt, but would you allow me?" He gestured to her skirt.

She closed her eyes and lifted it to her knees. It only took a moment before he pulled it down again.

"You've miscarried a child. Did you do anything to yourself?" His voice was gentle. "I only ask because I need to know if there's a puncture wound. You'll die if you bleed out or develop an infection."

"I drank tea," said Elsie.

He frowned with concern.

"Pennyroyal and cohosh." Her voice broke. Another cramp seized her, and she pulled her knees up again.

"Stay here." He left the room for a moment, returning with a slice of bread and two glasses of water, one clear and one gray.

"First, drink this." He handed her the gray.

Elsie sipped and spat back in the glass. The water was gritty and tasted of charred wood.

"What is it?"

"Carbon. I promise it won't hurt you. It doesn't taste good, but you have to drink it all. Pennyroyal's got a mean bite if you use it wrong. This will help carry the poison out of your body."

"Poison?" Elsie gulped down the bitter drink. "I thought I was losing the baby."

"You did." He gestured with his chin for her to finish the silty bottom of the glass.

She swallowed hard. The charcoal bits scraped her back molars and sent goose bumps down her spine.

"The herbs. They poisoned you both." He took the glass from her. "I can't do much about the child now, but I can help you." He set the glass to the side and pulled a pillbox from his rucksack. "This will help the pain and cramping." He handed her a chalky tablet and the clear glass.

She drank them down together and swore water never tasted so sweet.

"Now eat something or that'll tear a hole in your stomach." He passed her the bread.

It melted in her mouth, and she was thankful to find comfort in familiar tastes.

"The pain should be better in a few minutes, but the bleeding could go on for a while." He sat on the ground beside the makeshift bed and studied her thoughtfully. "How old are you?"

"Seventeen."

"Ha." He scratched his head. "Just a kid."

"I am not," she contested and sat up the best she could.

Doctor Meriwether pushed a hand through his wavy hair, and it fell back like apple tree leaves shifted by the breeze. "When I was seventeen, I was mucking the stalls of my daddy's barn, still wet behind the ears with a milk mustache. You're too young to be mixed up with all this—war and these fellas," he said, reminding Elsie that Robby waited outside.

Sweat trickled between her breasts. "With respect, Doctor, I have lived through more than you could ever imagine. I thank you for your help, and if I may ask for one more kindness: do not tell him. Please." She looked to the door.

Doctor Meriwether followed. "Oh. I see."

"No one can know."

Their eyes met and held. The moth overhead pattered against the bulb. He smiled sympathetically, and she knew he'd keep her secret.

"I'm sure he's eager to know how you are." He stood.

Surprising them both, Elsie grasped his hand. "Thank you." She didn't want to let go, and he didn't pull away. His fingers in hers felt as natural as her own body. She released before she grew too accustomed to his steady pulse.

Doctor Meriwether opened the door. "Alive and kicking," he announced.

Robby came in rubbing sweat from his temples. "She okay?"

Elsie didn't flinch. She trusted the answer before it was given.

"The little lady just needs rest and good food. You boys here will have to do without her pretty face for a week," said Doctor Meriwether.

Robby patted him on the shoulder. "Thanks, Doc. I'll cook up some chicken noodle soup ASAP. And uh—" He turned them so their backs were to Elsie. "Command might get the wrong idea so . . . I was hoping this could stay between us. Patient-doctor confidentiality and all."

Doctor Meriwether slung his rucksack over his shoulder. "I am well aware of the rules, Sergeant." He turned to Elsie. "Stay off your feet until the cramping stops. Tonight and tomorrow, rest," he instructed. "You'll need to drive her home after you close up the kitchen," he told Robby. "I'll be around if you need me."

The light of his eyes shimmered, and her breath caught. She wanted to follow him. She didn't care where. But the tenderness of her belly and the moistness of her skirt shamed her still.

forty-two

EL CAMINO VILLAGE
APARTMENTS
2048 EL CAMINO REAL
SAN FRANCISCO, CA

MAY 5, 2008

*A*fter a long Monday, Reba sat on the balcony with a full glass of cheap white wine, a can of tuna, and two buttermilk biscuits baked from scratch the day before. The recipe was called "Shoofly Biscuits." Deedee had clipped it out of one of Momma's southern hospitality magazines and mailed it with the note:

> *There's a lot of wisdom in that old song. I can't help smiling when I'm eating these. Thought I'd share. Skip to my Lou, my darlin'.*

Reba was willing to give anything a shot. The little blue devils of April had matured to full-grown doldrums come May.

She sipped her wine. "Freelancers have to understand that a deadline is a deadline," she explained. "When they're a day or two late, it means I have to cram all my work into the week before it goes to press, so there's *bound* to be oversights." She pulled the crusty top off a biscuit and threw it over the balcony railing to Shrimp. "I'm not superwoman! And where was Leigh? Shouldn't she be double-triple-checking all our work before it goes to press? Isn't that the job of an editor in chief? No, no, she's too busy shaking hands and going to luncheons at Chez Panisse Café. Meanwhile

I'm editing these ignorant, fluff-ball pieces about celebrity diets, fashion footwear, and restaurants using organic butter! Where are the real stories about real people?" She took a bite of bread, pulling hard with her teeth. "Hmm . . . a little dense. What'd you think?"

Shrimp had finished the biscuit and had proceeded to sniff the ground for misplaced crumbs.

"Of course you like it. You lick your balls too." She ripped off another piece and tossed it over. "What was I saying?"

It was her fourth glass of wine. The day had been particularly hard: Leigh had admonished her in front of the whole office for allowing the May issue to be published with the profiled celebrity chef's name incorrectly spelled; Riki hadn't returned her call from over a week ago; Deedee e-mailed that she'd met an attorney named Davison and though she'd never ascribed to it before, she now believed in love at first sight; and to top it off, her kitchen sink had a leak that flooded the linoleum with an inch of standing water. She was convinced the cosmos was out to get her, so she prescribed herself a bottle of wine and escaped to the balcony.

"The take-home message for you, my little friend, is work sucks, love sucks, life sucks. I was better off in El Paso." She set the glass down and forked tuna from the can. "By the way, where are *your* people? You live alone over there? No, somebody's got to be cleaning up after you. Lord knows I feed you." She retrieved her glass to wash down the fishiness. "God, I hope I can't get sued for feeding the neighbor's dog. Hey, how about you run some laps round the balcony. Work off those biscuits. Can't have you getting tubby—like that guy who sued McDonald's for making him fat. I'm no McDonald's." She nodded to herself.

The night sky was coppery from the city lights. Artificial white, yellow, and orange stars globed together around the bay. She missed the moon, among so many things in El Paso.

"Here." She threw Shrimp the rest of the bread and listened to him lick and chew. "Glad somebody's enjoying those things. I don't know what I did wrong. Maybe I overmixed or maybe I didn't mix enough. Who knows!"

Suddenly, Shrimp came to attention on all fours, ears perked high, tail lifted like a radio antenna. The sliding glass door on his balcony slid open and a man walked out from the dark apartment. Shrimp scurried to him doing crazy eights between his feet.

"Hey, Jerry-G, looks like you already got dinner." The man held a bowl of kibble in his hand. A half-eaten crust lay beside his wing-tipped shoe.

"Crap," Reba whispered to herself and gulped the last of her wine. "Uh, hi," she said as she rose from her rickety lawn chair. "I'm Reba. I just moved in—well, back in February—so I can't really say *just*. But considering we've somehow managed not to meet until now, I might as well have just moved in. But your dog and I are old friends. I kind of got the impression that he's alone a lot too, so I thought we'd keep each other company. Anyhow . . ." She took a deep breath. "Hi, neighbor!" She stuck her hand across the divide. It looked more like a wobbly butcher's knife than a welcoming hand.

He laughed, set the kibble on the ground, and flipped on his balcony light. "Reba, you said?" He shook. "Jase DeLuca."

Any relation to Dean and Deluca? She almost asked, but the fraction of her that was semisober exercised restraint.

Jase looked like something off the cover of *GQ* magazine. He had to be near her age, perhaps a little older. His collared shirt and tailored slacks remained pressed and neat even at the late hour; his rolled-up sleeves exposed tanned, tight forearms; his chiseled jaw hadn't even a hint of shadow; and his sandy blond hair was casually coifed to perfection. The guy was tall and debonair as a movie star. A crème brûlée on her doorstep!

Reba's stance swayed, and she wondered if this was how it felt to swoon. Maybe Jane and Deedee were right and love came at you like a lightning bolt—BAM—hello, love.

"I'm new myself. We must've moved in around the same time." Jase lifted Shrimp with one hand. "This is Jerry Garcia. But I guess you've already met."

She laughed to herself. A Chihuahua named Jerry Garcia?

"Jerry-G for short." The dog had retrieved the remaining hard crust and gnawed furiously on it.

"Oh! I shouldn't have, uh, given him that." She swallowed hard.

Jase held Jerry-G so the dog's beady eyes were level with his own. "So this is why you've been stinking up the place for weeks, eh?" Then he turned to Reba. "You know you owe me."

"I'm so, so sorry." She flushed a sweat and smelled the booze in it. "Whatever you want—I mean if he got sick or something because of me."

"An air freshener." Jase smiled.

Reba rubbed away the moisture on her upper lip. "You want the plug-in or the spray?"

"A plug-in offer? Fancy." Jase laughed. "You know what, I take it back. It's been a hell of a day. You share a glass of whatever you're drinking and we'll call it even." He set Jerry-G back on the ground.

"Umm..." Reba turned to the bottle, embarrassed to admit it was empty. "I've got more in the fridge. Do you want to come over?"

She'd momentarily forgotten about her plumbing problem. Catching a glimpse of her swamped kitchen through the glass door, she wondered if she should ask him to bring galoshes. Could that come off sultry? Her head was fuzzy. She really shouldn't have any more wine, but she owed him. It was neighborly. Plus he made her stomach cartwheel. It was the first happy feeling she'd had in months. She didn't want to let it go so fast.

Jase ran a hand through his mane. "I would, but I ordered a pizza from North Beach," he explained. "Have you eaten?"

The can of tuna and the remaining hockey puck biscuit sat beside her chair.

"Kind of . . . not really," she said.

"I got the Coit Tower: mushroom, sausage, salami, and pepperoni. Tell me you aren't a vegan, raw foodie, or one of the thousands of California dieters."

"Pshaw—not me! No, no, no." She wagged her finger like a flirty schoolmarm. "These days I'll eat anything you put in front of me. No holes bar—holds barred, I mean." She rubbed her eyes to focus.

"Good, then grab the wine and come over to my place." Jase opened his condo door and Jerry-G tried to follow. Jase nudged him back with his foot. "You know you aren't allowed inside, bud."

The dog gave a weak whine.

Reba briefly wondered what good an air fresher would do outdoors, but then Jase said, "Meet you in five minutes?"

"Cinco minutos," she echoed while Jerry-G walked in tight circles on the balcony.

When Reba awoke in Jase's apartment the next morning, he was already gone. It was quarter till noon. Panicked and with a hangover to beat all hangovers, it seemed a colossal task to steady her fingers and dial Leigh on the phone by the bed.

"I'm sick," she told her, and she wasn't lying.

After hanging up, she stumbled to Jase's toilet and vomited spicy bits of salami and cheese. When she went to rinse her mouth, the confetti of russet hairs ringing the sink made her dry heave once more.

"Oh, God," she swore. "Never again."

Trembling from head to toe, she gingerly made her way around Jase's bedroom, a precautionary hand towel under her chin, covering her nakedness.

She wore only her underwear: a fact that partially contributed to her queasiness. Her head pounded like a ticking clock. A countdown to what, she dared not imagine. She found her pants tangled in the sheets falling over the side of Jase's bed; her shirt on a cushioned chair; a single pink flamingo flip-flop in the middle of the floor. She gathered her things as quickly as possible without disrupting her stomach, slipped into her button-down shirt and decided to make a fast, pantless dash home.

She cracked the bedroom door. Though she knew he was gone, everything about the morning felt like a violation, and she didn't want to get caught. She'd never experienced the collegiate "walk of shame" and had always raised an eyebrow or two at those who did. Now, over a decade later, she was the one tiptoeing down the hall and praying to escape without notice.

Outside on the balcony, Jerry-G rested his head on his front paws like a daydreaming child. He didn't notice her behind the reflective glass door. The empty wine bottle sat on the mahogany coffee table beside the pizza box with one last slice of congealed cheese and diced meats. She looked away, imagining the smell of peppermint to keep from gagging. Her flip-flop twin lay haphazardly under the table. She had to retrieve it or risk Jase bringing it over. The last thing she wanted was that conversation, though at this point any conversation would be awkward.

Careful not to attract Jerry-G's attention with brisk movement, she reached beneath the table, pinched the sandal's thong between her thumb and forefinger, and did a fluid pirouette back around, nearly knocking into the bookshelf: a Bobby Kennedy biography, a worn copy of *How to Win Friends and Influence People,* a blue vase with fake cherry blossom twigs, and a photograph of Jase holding two little girls. The picture was too small for its four-by-six frame, cut with scissors to square off the trio.

Reba picked it up and examined closer. A silver band on his left hand. She winced at the girls' gleeful smiles and fat bows tying back blond locks. They took after him—like child models in a Macy's catalogue. A husband. A father. Her stomach lurched.

"Oh God," she whispered and put the frame back on the shelf.

Fleeting memories of the night returned: Jase inviting her over for pizza;

grabbing a chilled bottle of pinot grigio; laughing over dewy glasses; the smell of baked bread and cheese; the taste of saucy kisses; his hands on her bare back; the bedsheets twisted round her ankles.

"Oh God, oh God, oh God." Still clutching her belongings, she sat down on the coffee table, knocking the empty bottle to the jute rug beneath. It rolled off onto the oak floor with a clink. Jerry-G sprang up and furiously yapped at the sliding glass door.

The tabletop stuck to her thighs, sticky with residue. She thought she'd be sick again, so she stuffed her face into the rumpled folds of her pants. They smelled like home, like the springtime laundry detergent Riki liked to use: *all* with bleach. She missed him so much. Even in the midst of betrayal, she wanted him there; to hold her and say he still loved her despite all her flaws, present and past.

"Riki," she whispered. "I'm sorry." Instinctively, she reached for the ring at her chest, but her fingers grazed her collarbone. She'd taken it off the day before and left it in the little bottle of blue jewelry cleaner to soak. No doubt it'd sparkle like a star now. She grasped at the invisible, pressing her fist against her breastbone.

Without warning, the front door swung opened.

"Oh, hey, I thought by now—" Jase checked his watch, then took a big breath. "I guess you didn't make it to work." He laughed nervously. "I barely made it myself. I came home during lunch to grab a few things I forgot in the morning rush. What a night, huh?" He cleared his throat and jingled his keys.

The only thing within reach was her clothing and the pizza, and she sure as hell wasn't going to sacrifice her Tommy Hilfiger sandals at his expense. So she flung the take-out box as best she could. The cardboard did a lacka-daisical flap in the air with just enough volition to slingshot the pizza slice facedown onto his shoes. Reba couldn't have been more gratified.

Seething, she stood tall. She couldn't take back whatever had happened between them, but she could be responsible for this moment. With every ounce of composure she could muster, she marched toward the door.

"Wa-wait a second!" He lifted both palms in front of her without touching. "Nothing happened, Reba. You totally passed out before . . ." He smirked.

She lifted her chin. "You are a royal dickhead."

He flipped his coiffure. "Baby, if you're going to call anybody names, you better start with Señorita Wine-O."

It was meant to be a joke. Reba didn't think it funny. She punched him square in the gut. He lurched forward.

"You"—she pointed to the photograph across the room—"should be ashamed! Tell me. Is that your wife? Are those your children?"

"It's complicated," he said as he coughed, still at a ninety-degree angle.

"It's what? Compli—" She dropped her clothes to the floor and pummeled his ribs with both hands. "Complicated my ass! Yes or no!"

"We're divorcing," he said, then grabbed her wrists and held them at bay. "That's why I moved here."

"I may be a lousy drunk, a shitty girlfriend, a neglectful sister, and a second-rate daughter," she raged and wrenched free. "Hell, I might even be a rotten neighbor, but at least I know exactly who I am and who I'm not! I am Reba Adams, damn it!" The words burned her lips. "And I shouldn't be here." Her eyes brimmed. "You—you are"—she pointed back at the photo again—"not the kind of man I deserve."

Jase frowned.

"I had better!" She squatted down and snatched her fallen pants and shoes, sniffling back emotions she hadn't meant to spill. Jerry-G stood with paws on the glass, ears erect. "Shrimp deserves better, too! You can't keep him locked out because it makes your life easier. It's cruel!"

She stomped to the sliding door and opened it. Like a wound top, Jerry-G leaped inside, bounding over the living room carpet and skittering down the wooden hallway.

"Hey, that's my dog!"

"Then start acting like it!"

She left Jase chasing Jerry-G and slammed her apartment door behind her. Through the wall came strings of profanities and furniture thuds. Reba put on a James Taylor CD and the shower and sang her heart out when "Fire and Rain" played.

Feeling more herself afterward, she latched Riki's ring back around her neck and slipped into a faded pair of jeans and a worn Richmond Flying Squirrels jersey. She mopped the kitchen, straightened the apartment, and called the superintendent for a maintenance appointment. She felt better. Inside, everything was neat and orderly. Outside on the balcony sat the sour can of tuna and a stale biscuit. She left them where they were.

"The flies can have 'em," she whispered, tossing back two Aleve and nestling into her couch with a glass of cucumber water and *Gone with the Wind* on TV.

Just after Scarlett threw the vase at Rhett, Reba's cell phone jangled in her purse. She dug through change and peppermint stars, lipsticks and pens, old business cards and crumbled rolls of antacids until she felt the familiar rectangle, buzzing and singing. One missed call from Jane Meriwether. She muted the television and redialed.

On the third ring, Jane answered. "Reba?"

Reba hadn't been able to eat all day, and her head felt light at the familiar sound of Jane's voice. She lay back on the couch.

"Oh, Jane, I'm so glad you called." She rubbed her forehead, trying to count up days and weeks since they'd last spoken. The numbers jumbled, so she gave up. "I've missed you—I've missed all of you so much."

"Mom's in a coma."

Everything stopped, as though the words carried bolts of electricity.

"She's in the hospital," Jane continued. "I wanted to take her in last Friday when her hands started shaking, but she refused to go until after Cinco de Mayo. She wanted to surprise Sergio with *conchas*. Stubborn woman."

Reba listened to Jane breathe over the line and realized she wasn't.

"Then this morning, she was rolling dough and dropped. Just like that. When I went to help her up, she was a rag doll, babbling in German. Scared me so bad I closed the bakery on the spot and drove her over to Thomason's ER. The doctor says she had a stroke."

Reba turned onto her side and buried her face in the cushions.

"I should've taken her when I saw her hands. I should've made her go. I should've done more," lamented Jane.

"It's not your fault," Reba mumbled, then righted herself on the couch. "You can't force a person to do what you want—even if you think it's for their best." Her breath caught. "You are a good daughter. You love her. That's what counts."

Reba was speaking to Jane and herself.

"Sergio and Riki are with me," said Jane. "The doctor doesn't think Mom'll . . ."

Reba brought her knees to her chest, wishing she were there and not here, wishing she'd never left in the first place. She couldn't put the phone down after Jane hung up. So she scrolled through numbers until she came to her momma's, then she dialed.

"Hello?" came her momma's southern lilt.

How Reba had missed her despite everything. She sighed long into the receiver. She had so much to say but couldn't seem to form the words.

"Reba, honey, is that you?"

Reba nodded and hugged the phone close, love and hope stretched tight across the miles.

————Original Message————
From: reba.adams@hotmail.com
Sent: May 6, 2008 11:50 P.M.
To: deedee.adams@gmail.com
Subject: Leaving for El Paso

Deedee,

Elsie had a stroke. She's in a coma, and the doctors don't think she's going to make it out. I wish I weren't so far from home. Riki's with Jane now, and I can't help but love him even more for never ceasing to be there—even when I didn't ask or expect him to, even when I think he isn't, he is. You were right when you said you couldn't force someone to see your truth. I assumed you were talking about Daddy, but I was the one who needed to open her eyes. I've made so many mistakes. I should never have left. I called Momma. She told me to book myself on the first flight back to El Paso.

I leave in six hours, but I can't sleep. My bags are packed and looking around my apartment, I could leave for good and not miss a thing. I thought I was finally reaching my dream in San Francisco, but that was my head lying to my heart. I know where I'm supposed to be—whom I'm supposed to be with. Momma says love can forgive all things. I think I believe her, or at least I want to, and that's a start.

I know you're a praying person, D, so could you say one for Elsie? One for me too.

Love, Reba

forty-three

*I*t was her first night back on shift, and though she felt physically recovered, she declined Robby's offer to help him bake Moravian Lovefeast
Buns. She wasn't in the mood. Besides, she'd never been completely taken
with his recipes—too rich to have routinely. So she claimed she was still
under doctor's orders to rest, which was partly true.

The summer night was clear enough to make out each wink in the Milky
Way and to witness a star burst like corn from its kernel. Its lunar tail
streaked the sky as it soared, and Elsie wondered if anyone else had seen
the celestial flight. She walked with eyes cast heavenward to the mercu-
rial constellations, feeling light and pain free for the first time in months.
So stark and new was the sensation that she believed at any moment, she
might rise up on hidden wings and join the angels. How nice that would
be, she thought, and sighed to herself, knowing too few nights like this
remained before winter returned. So she slowed her gait, relishing the
warmth on her skin.

Her bicycle was parked beside a stack of rain-warped milk crates in the
kitchen staff parking lot. She backed it out, but stopped when the wheel
caught on something—or rather, someone. Doctor Meriwether.

"Oh! My apologies." Her cheeks flushed hot.

"No, it's my fault. I shouldn't have snuck up on you." He wore civilian clothes: a white, open-collared shirt and wide pleated trousers. Elsie thought she'd never seen a more handsome man in all her life.

"I was walking. Beautiful night. Moon's out." He pointed up.

The moon hung bold and glistening above, like a silver coin fixed in the sky.

"While I was over this way . . ." He scratched his head. "I figured I'd check in on you. Sergeant Lee said you were back at work."

Elsie nodded. For one of the first times she could recall, she was shy for reasons that had nothing to do with fear.

"So how're you feeling?"

"Better."

"No complications after our visit? The bleeding stopped?"

Elsie nodded and looked away, his words astringent and the miscarriage still too raw in her body and memory.

"I'm glad to hear that." He stepped closer.

Her heart sped up.

"Well, you look mighty improved. Not to say you didn't look beautiful before." His Adam's apple bobbed. "Are you on your way home?" He gestured to her bicycle.

"Ja."

"Being your doctor, I don't think I can let you exert yourself like that yet."

"It is very close," she explained.

"That may be the case but still. How's about you let me drive you? The medic jeep's over there, and I got the keys." He jingled his pocket. "I can fit your bike in the back, no problem."

The jeep was parked in the R&R Center's guest lot around front of the building. She could have ridden home in the time it took to get there and load the bicycle, but that didn't matter. The ride would be a relief to her feet, and she liked being with the handsome Doctor Meriwether. He smelled clean of mint and shirt starch, scents that whispered of better days.

Their fingers overlapped when he reached for the handlebars. Elsie smiled.

"So," Doctor Meriwether began as he lifted the bike into the trunk. "How did you and Sergeant Lee get introduced?"

Elsie pushed a loose strand back into her braid. "When the Amis— Americans came. He was outside my family bakery. We had bread that would go stale anyhow." She shrugged. "I gave it to them."

"Very big of you." He swung open the passenger door and she climbed in. "Most people around here would've given the bread to the pigs before an American."

"We don't have pigs," quipped Elsie.

Doctor Meriwether came round to the driver's seat. "Fair enough." He winked and sputtered the ignition. "So you're the daughter of a baker?"

"Ja, and I am a baker, too," she corrected.

They started down the road. "I'll have to try your goods. Where I'm from, it's most only skillet cornbread."

Elsie had never heard of such a thing, but thought perhaps it was an English–German misinterpretation. "Where are you from in America?"

"A little state called Texas."

A flash of lightning zipped from her navel to her chin. "Texas oven-baked beans?"

"Yeah, you heard of 'em?"

While cleaning out Tobias's crawl space, she'd found her secret items thoughtfully lined along the interior. Such trivial tokens of her child-hood now took on meaning far beyond the material—because Tobias had guarded them, slept beside them, shared in them. She moved all the items, including the American advertisement, into a corroded cacao tin under her bed. The only thing missing was the Robert Frost book. She'd run her hands over every nook in the crawl space, but it was nowhere to be found. God is a poet, Tobias had told her once, and she believed.

"Made in the USA," she recited. "You must be a Texas cowboy."

"I guess so," he said, then laughed so true and unbridled that she couldn't help joining.

They drove faster down the lane. The wind whipped over their faces, smelling of nearby honeysuckle and glacier water. He turned down the wrong road, but Elsie kept quiet. They'd get home eventually. She liked being at his side. He made her feel more than she was, bigger than Germany or America or all the war between.

When they finally arrived on her street, Elsie had him pull up to the bäckerei doors.

"Doktor Meriwether," she began.

"—Albert. Al," he said.

"Al." Even the sound of him was pleasant, like a music note. "I very much appreciate you . . ."

"My pleasure," he said while unloading her bike.

"Not only for the ride." Elsie looked down at her shoes. "I thank you for everything."

"Elsie." It was the first time he called her by her first name. It rolled off his tongue, slow and lyrical. "You and uh—Sergeant Lee. Is he your . . . I mean to say, are you two—" He stopped and gently kicked the bike tire with his toe. "Aw, never mind."

Elsie faced him. His eyes sparkled in the moonlight. "No," she said. The foreign word rang out open-ended. "We were but . . ." She shook her head. "It is difficult to explain."

Robby embodied independence: strange, youthful, and exhilarating. But in the many months that she'd known him, she'd never felt the way she did in five minutes with Doctor Meriwether. With Al, she felt freedom, and that was vastly different from all that had come before.

A lazy breeze blew the overhanging bäckerei sign. It squeaked on its hinges, and they both looked up.

"Would it be all right if I came by tomorrow—to grab a bite to eat and visit a spell?" asked Al.

She knew her papa would never approve of this dark-eyed American, but not one part of her cared. She was being true to herself. The time for hiding was over.

Silhouetted under the starry sky, Al's face was patient and earnest.

"I would like that very much," she said and decided she'd make him sunflower seed rolls the next day. The first new harvest had just come in.

forty-four

Dear Mutti,

Texas is a strange place. Different from Garmisch. The mountains rise naked against the blue and when the sun sets, it paints the sky every color you can imagine and many you cannot. It is never cold or dark. Even in the night, the moon is so full and bright you'd think it was the face of God. I like it, though I miss you and Papa most desperately.

We have settled into our house on the military grounds. Fort Bliss, they call it. I hope it lives up to its name. The people are friendly and help me around as best they can. There are no bäckereis or metzgereis in town. I heated canned baked beans every night for the first two weeks, but man cannot live on beans alone! My neighbor is from a place called Merry-land and she says that the women buy their meats and food supplies at "The Commissary." She is taking me to this place tomorrow so I may buy flour, butter, and yeast. I plan to bake rolls as soon as I can. My stomach growls thinking about them now.

I went to the Post Exchange today to purchase wooden bowls, mixing spoons, and a baking tray in preparation. We haven't anything to our name. When I paid for the items, the man at the till said, "Thank you, Mrs. Meriwether" and for a moment, I'd forgotten that was me. Mrs. Meriwether. It has a nice sound, like a greeting. Don't you agree? It rings of newness, and I can't wait for the first time I introduce myself as such.

How is home? No word from Hazel still, I suspect. A week ago, Al and I were at the fabric store picking material for curtains when I swore I heard Hazel's voice beyond the linen bolts. I raced around expecting to find her but, of course, it was not. My disappointment was so great, I set to trembling on the spot, apologized profusely to the woman, and dragged Al out as fast as my legs could carry me. I have not given up that we will one day be together again.

How is Papa? I deeply regret our harsh parting. I pray for his forgiveness and acceptance of us. I miss him and wish he understood that the world has changed and Germany with it. No one is good or bad by birth or nation or religion. Inside, we are all masters and slaves, rich and poor, perfect and flawed. I know I am, and he is, too. We love despite ourselves. Our hearts betray our minds. Al is a good man and I love him, Mutti. That is a gift I do not take for granted.

I'll write you as often as I can. I hope you reply, though I will hold no ill feelings if you do not. I understand. Still, you are my mutti. I love you, and so I will continue to put pen to paper.

Eternally yours, Elsie

SCHMIDT BÄCKEREI
56 LUDWIGSTRASSE
GARMISCH, GERMANY

FEBRUARY 27, 1947

My dear Elsie,

Enclosed is a photograph of us. Papa had old film developed. He told me to throw this one in the garbage, still bitter over everything, but I could not. You are my child, and I will not lose both my daughters. It is too much in one lifetime. I send it to you instead.

I was happy for your letter from Texas, USA. On the same day, we received news from Hazel's friend Ovidia. She claims that Hazel's daughter was taken to the _Waisenhaus_ orphanage in Munich. They call her Lillian. Papa and I are going there next Saturday, though I am unsure of the outcome. The whereabouts of the twin boy and Hazel continue to be a mystery.

Dear, I understand that love makes us do things we can't explain or justify. So I write and hope that you will return to us someday. I often think of you and Hazel as girls whispering secrets and playing dress-up in your room. Too quickly those days went. Only in heaven will we all be together once more. This is certain.

With great love, Mutti

MARCH 8, 1947

Dear Elsie,

We have collected Hazel's daughter, Lillian, from Waisenhaus. She closely resembles you and Hazel when you were young. It is a strangeness to find ourselves here once more—two young children in our keep. It brings me great joy to have her with us. Even your papa's spirits have improved since her arrival. She is a pleasant child, strong and of a happy nature.

We have decided not to tell Lillian of her paternity since we have no documentation of the man's identity. Although Peter Abend is Julius's known father, the Lebensborn Program listed him under Hazel's surname. Thus, both children will be Schmidt. It is easier this way. The truth is far too cumbersome. While Julius is at an age of remembering, I pray Lillian never knows. The matter is irreparable, and no good can come of acknowledging it. The Thousand-Year Reich was a fantasy to which your papa still clings. I see it more clearly now and am ashamed of my past foolishness. What Papa and I do agree on is that these are not children of the Fatherland. They are ours.

With great love, Mutti

forty-five

*L*illian sat reading *The Fellowship of the Ring* by J.R.R. Tolkien. A British pilot on winter holiday had given it to her. He'd read it twice and was looking to free up space in his pack before returning home to London. Lillian was a perpetual bookworm and wanted the novel desperately as an early Christmas present. Her opa agreed to the gift for educational purposes only—so Lillian could improve her English. She was the lone family member who could properly communicate with the American and English patrons shuttling in and out the bäckerei door.

"Lillian, put that book down and help Opa finish up," instructed her oma. "Strong, young hands like yours might be exactly what he needs."

Lillian sighed and shut the book. Frodo and his friends had just set off to Rivendell. She was heavyhearted to leave the grand adventure and return to her mundane world of rising yeast dough and day-old bread.

Oma covered marzipan sugarplums with dainty strips of parchment so they wouldn't be peppered with dead fruit flies by morning. In the kitchen, Opa still worked by dusky candle; some of the wax had splashed against the glass luminary, further marginalizing its light. She slid her fingers to the electric wall switch for the overhead bulb but then thought better and let it be.

She watched him from the shadows as he rolled the molasses dough into a smooth, thick skin across the baking board. He took up a giant heart-shaped cookie cutter, positioned it precisely, and pressed down.

For the last-minute Christmas customers, they already had over a dozen lebkuchen, iced with frilly edges and piped with Christmas greetings. But the ones he made now were not for anybody with a deutsche mark to spare. These were special hearts—the gingerbread Opa made each Christmas with their names embroidered in icing.

Opa hummed "Silent Night" as he cut and laid the cookies on the baking sheet. The names of her family: Max, Luana, Julius, Lillian, Hazel, Peter, Elsie, and Albert. He always made eight, though the last four stayed high up on the tree, uneaten and growing hard as slate.

Her parents, Hazel and Peter, had died during the war, or so her Oma told her. But children talk as children do, especially in small towns like Garmisch. When she was still in bloomers, the truth of her paternity was already being whispered about on the playground. It was her schoolmate Richelle Spreckels, the daughter of Trudi Abend Spreckels, who finally broke the news in a rage after being tagged out in a high-stakes game of *Fangen.*

"It's not fair!" Richelle cried. "You're not supposed to be here! Nobody even knows who your papa is!"

The group of children had hushed around Lillian. The game of chase abruptly ended.

"My papa is Peter and my mother is Hazel!" Lillian defended.

"Your mother may be Hazel Schmidt, but my mamma says Peter Abend is not your papa! She knows. She is his sister!" And with that, Richelle had scooped up a wad of soft mud and flung it, streaking Lillian's smocked, pink dress. A handful of surrounding children had tittered.

She walked home muddy and shamed, and while Oma cleaned the dress as best she could, the stains remained.

"Who did this to you and why?" Oma had asked, but Lillian refused to tell, not wanting to call Oma a liar and afraid to hear the truth come from her mouth. It pricked her deep within, the way the truth does, and she didn't want to believe until she had facts to back it up.

But from that day forward, Richelle's accusation remained in the back of her mind—"You're not supposed to be here." This became her quest: to find out exactly who she was and where she was supposed to be. Lillian made few friends in school, preferring the company of her oma and opa, the friendly customers of the bakery, the faraway characters in her storybooks, and her tante Elsie's letters.

Elsie and Albert lived in the United States, a place called Texas where cowboys rode white stallions and Indians made colorful shawls dyed with berry juices. Those were the stories from Elsie's letters. They were full of adventure and word pictures: the desert sun oozing into the horizon like a giant fried egg; lizards with iridescent green scales lounging in the shade of porcupine cacti; the Rio Grande River snaking through the sand dunes, alive with reptiles and water fowl come to quench their thirsts in the only basin for miles. When she was very young, Lillian begged Oma to read from the letters at bedtime. Under the whispered spell of storytime, she dreamed of Elsie and wondered how the small *vanillekipferl* moon hanging over her Zugspitze could possibly be the same great spotlight in the Texan sky.

Everything Elsie described sounded bigger and more wondrous than anything she'd ever seen in Germany. Sometimes Lillian could barely contain her excitement when Elsie wrote about galloping on horseback across the plains, a dust storm at her back and thunder clapping above. She'd squealed aloud under her eiderdown, and Oma would shush her not to wake Opa. Early on, Oma warned Lillian not to mention the letters to anyone. "Some things are secrets," she explained and Lillian agreed. She treasured this confidence between them.

Opa never spoke of Elsie, and before her brother Julius went off to boarding school, he told Lillian that he doubted Elsie would ever set foot in Germany again. A stern young man, she'd always been afraid of crossing him. He rarely came home from Munich anymore, and though she'd never say it aloud, Lillian didn't miss him. She did miss Elsie, though. An aunt she'd never met in the flesh. She confessed to Oma that one of her nightly prayers was for Elsie to walk in the bäckerei door. Oma said she prayed the same thing.

Whenever an unknown woman entered the shop, Lillian's heart would pitter-patter so that she could barely take the order; inevitably, the customer would smile at her flightiness, pay, and leave. Lillian wished she knew what the adult Elsie looked like so she could avoid such crescendos of hope. There was only one photograph of her mother and aunt in the house—a picture Oma kept of the girls sitting beneath the branches of a cherry tree. Lillian had studied the image so thoroughly that she knew the exact count of freckles on her mother's cheek, the exact number of teeth in Elsie's smile. For the rest, she relied on the letters.

In them, Elsie was kind, loving, and fearless; and she knew more stories about her mother than anyone in the world. She wrote about the cherry tree photograph, sharing Hazel's secret wishes and how they came to be; of Hazel's love of music and beautiful dresses; how she was the most graceful woman in Garmisch and the most faithful sister. It made Lillian long for a sister of her own, and she often pretended the Toni doll Elsie sent from America was her younger sibling. Oma told her to be grateful for her brother Julius, and she would've found that easy to do if he had shown an ounce of sibling affection. So she clung to what she knew for certain: half of her was unquestionably Schmidt.

Opa put cheesecloth over the cutouts and set the tray aside. Though he never spoke their names, Elsie and Albert appeared on the tree branches every year, reminding Lillian and everyone else that despite it all, they were family.

Opa turned. "Ach, Lillian! You surprised me."

"I'm sorry, Opa. Oma told me to help you."

"Doch!" He clapped his hands together. "As you can see, I'm finished. We just have to put away these scraps." He began to pull the remnants of the gingerbread into a ball. "Come, help me."

Lillian went to his side. He smelled of cinnamon, ginger, and cardamom, and she leaned close to his side; he smelled like Christmas.

"Here, have a taste." He pinched a piece of dough and popped it in her mouth.

Molasses sweet and spicy. Lillian let it dissolve on her tongue and slip down her throat. "It's good."

He kissed her forehead. "Don't tell Oma. She'll be cross with me for giving you treats before bed."

She smiled. She was good at keeping secrets.

That night, Oma sat up in Lillian's room darning her wool school stockings. Lillian's feet were cold beneath her bed covers, and she wanted to hear a story.

"Would you lie with me a little, Oma? I can't sleep yet," pleaded Lillian. She knew she was too old for bedtime stories, but hoped Oma would relent.

Oma sighed, set down her needle and thread, and slipped beneath the covers.

Lillian laced her feet between hers.

"You're freezing, child!" Oma fluffed the blankets around them.

"Are you excited for Christmas?" asked Lillian.

"Ja," said Oma. "Are you?"

Lillian tucked the covers under her chin and nodded. "Do you think we'll get a letter from Tante Elsie?"

Oma pulled Lillian into the crook of her arm. "She always writes on Christmas."

Lillian knew that to be true but wanted Oma's reassurance.

"I bought the carp today. Fat as a giant pinecone. Did you see?"

Lillian shook her head. "But I did see Opa making our lebkuchen hearts." She giggled and buried her face against Oma.

"Did you now." Oma took a deep breath, her body rising and falling heavily.

"Do you think Julius will mind if I have his, since he's staying at school this year?"

"You'll have to ask Opa," replied Oma. "Now, all warm. It is time for sleeping." She leaned forward to stand, but Lillian stopped her.

"Don't go yet, please. Would you read to me—the letter about the day Tante Elsie helped Onkel Albert at the hospital? The one where she gave a candy stripe to the boy with a broken arm."

"Candy striper. In America, they are like nurses, but their job is to comfort the sick," explained Oma. She reached beneath the mattress for where they kept the wad of letters. "What was the date?"

"It was summer," said Lillian. "Because she said they had their first summer storm that cracked flaming icicles across the sky." Her heart sped up reciting Elsie's words. "The boy had been so scared, he fell off his chair and broke his arm."

"Ack ja," said Oma. "It was August, I believe." She flipped through the envelopes until she found the one. "August 3." The pages crinkled against her fingers. "Dear Mutti and Lillian," she began.

Lillian closed her eyes, snuggled down close, and let her imagination drift across the ocean.

forty-six

56 LUDWIGSTRASSE
GARMISCH, GERMANY

OCTOBER 5, 1967

Dear Tante Elsie,

Thank you again for the McCall's dress pattern and the Beatles album you sent. We got a new radio station here. It is called the British Broadcasting Corporation. Have you heard of it in America? It plays all the good music, even Jim Morrison. And today, Tony Blackburn (the announcer on Radio 1) was talking about everything that's going on over there with you. Is it true that American mobs are protesting in the streets? It is hard to imagine, but Oma says it's the way of war. She worries about you. I explained to her that Vietnam is where the fighting is and that is far away from Texas. Still, she tells me to write you to keep baby Jane and Onkel Albert close by and the doors locked tight.

She would write you as well, but she's already gone to bed. For the past couple months she's been sleeping much more than is customary. She didn't want me to mention it to you before—claiming it was allergies from the change of season and drinking her teas for this or that—but it's well into fall now and she's more tired than ever. She fights me about visiting the doctor. I tell her they have pills for almost everything these days, but she refuses. Maybe you could talk to her. Ask Onkel Albert what he thinks.

Other than that, we are well here. Opa is good. Still insisting on making the first batch of brötchen himself even though we've hired two trained bakers and one chocolatier. Hugo is the best of the three and the most recently employed. He apprenticed with a pastry chef in the Bishopric of Liège, Belgium, and has added waffles to our menu. I've gained five pounds since his arrival and loved every bite of it! In a perfect world, I'd enclose one of Hugo's waffles with this letter. I'm positive you would love them as much as the rest of us. Business has increased almost 20 percent, and Opa couldn't dote on the man any more. He loves him like the son he never had.

A gelato shop opened next door—the American tourists and military are crazy for the stuff. So Hugo and Opa are discussing plans to sell waffle cones to the gelateria. Business is booming, and we're all glad for that.

I asked Opa last night if we turn a good profit by the end of the year, if I might go to university in the spring. I believe I would like to study history or literature. I'm not sure which. In either case, I've put it off too long already. In my dreams, I'd come to the United States. There are so many wonderful schools there, but I couldn't leave Oma and Opa. I'll probably apply to LMU Munich. Opa said that was a good plan. So now I just need to get in. Pray for me. I want this more than just about anything.

I must go now. I have to sweep the kitchen before bed. It's not so bad now that I can listen to the radio while I do it!

My love to you, Jane, and Onkel Albert,

Lillian

P.S. I nearly forgot! Julius has finally wed! He sent us word last month. Her name is Klara and she is from Lübeck. Her father is a banker, and so they have moved to Hamburg for Julius to manage the Hamburg Bank. We didn't get any more detail than that. You know Julius.

56 LUDWIGSTRASSE
GARMISCH, GERMANY

OCTOBER 19, 1967

Dear Tante Elsie,

So much has happened in such a short time, I don't where to begin. Opa refuses to let me send a telegram or call long distance, so I am mailing this and pray you receive it as fast as humanly possible. We have just returned from the hospital. Oma took a turn for the worse. For three days, she lay in bed without a crumb to eat or sip of tea. I was so frightened that I called the emergency Krankentransporte.

They say it is cancer. Oh, Tante Elsie, if only I had done something months ago! If we had caught it sooner perhaps-.-.-. but now, it is too late. They sent her home, and Opa and I are at her bedside every hour.

I am inconsolable and would never ask this unless it was as dire as it is. Please, come home. The doctor says she could be with us for weeks or a handful of days. Opa refuses to accept the gravity of her prognosis. I don't think he can imagine his life without her—or will let himself. It will break his heart and mine. I can't endure this alone. Come back to us.

Faithfully,
Lillian

forty-seven

*A*rriving two hours ahead of schedule, Elsie had taken a taxicab from the bahnhof and had it drop her on Ludwigstrasse. It'd been over twenty years since she'd stepped on that street. The clip of her heels against the cobblestone was a cadence her body took to instinctively. The autumn air was crisp and clean as the evergreens, and she breathed it in as deeply as she could. The sky was piebald with thick, gray clouds shrouding the Zugspitze. A single drop of rain wet her cheek but no more. Soon enough the heavens would open up, and she was glad she'd taken the earlier train from Munich.

A young couple exited the bakery with a fat rye loaf wrapped in brown paper. The familiar sign, Schmidt Bäckerei, above the door rocked gently in the Alpine breeze.

"Guten abend." The cabby handed over her luggage.

"Guten abend," replied Elsie. The words felt clunky and hard to her ears. It'd been a long while since she'd spoken German outside of whispered lullabies to baby Jane.

A bell chimed as the bakery door opened, but the smell greeted her far before the threshold. A toasty blanket of yeasty goodness. Papa's recipe. Only his bread made the air so decadent and satisfying. She'd tried to replicate it for years in her own bakery but never quite succeeded, too much vanilla and cinnamon lingering about.

Despite all the years and a handful of modern updates, the Schmidt Bakery was almost exactly as she remembered. The dill had been replanted in a larger pot but still sat in the front window. The breadbaskets lined the shelf exactly as she had organized them. Formica tables replaced the two wooden ones but in the same cramped spots. Here it was again, like a dream restored, and yet not.

"May I help you?" asked a young man behind the register.

Suddenly, she felt awkward and foreign. Her indigo daisy-print blouse and flip hairdo didn't belong. The part of her that had been Elsie Schmidt remembered this place with tenderness and sorrow, but that girl was like a storybook character in a Grimm fairy tale. Now, she was Elsie Meriwether with a loving husband, a beautiful baby daughter, and her own bakery in the sunny West Texas desert. This was no longer her home, and surprisingly, that realization brought her great comfort and strength.

"Are you Hugo?"

"Nein. I'm Moritz. Hugo is in the back." He rearranged sweets on a tray—mandelkekse, almond bar cookies, Elsie recognized.

"Is Lillian here?"

Moritz paused, then slid the tray into the glass case. "Are you a friend of the family?"

Elsie felt a twinge. "I am Elsie. Max and Luana's daughter."

Moritz's eyes opened as wide as the bonbons on display. "Ack ja! You are early! Please, please." He came round from the register. "I am Moritz Schneider." He extended his hand.

"Schneider?" Elsie smiled and shook. "Any relation to Bitsy Schneider?"

"My mother!" He put a thumb to his chest. "I am her youngest son."

"I knew her well," said Elsie. "You kicked her a lot, as I recall." She patted her abdomen, and Moritz laughed.

"That's what Frau Schmidt tells me." At the mention of Mutti, his countenance dropped. "It is good you have come."

Elsie's heart stammered beneath her ribs.

"Here," he said, taking her suitcase. "They are with her."

He escorted her to a doorway she didn't recognize; a new wall had been erected officially partitioning the bakery storefront from the kitchen and the stairwell to their living quarters. The second floor had been renovated. The bedroom wall where she'd hidden Tobias had been torn down and the space expanded into a common area with a large television. Mutti and Papa's bedroom remained as it always had been, but an extension had been added to the far end of the floor. A plank step led up to two opposing doors. Lillian's and Julius's bedrooms, Elsie guessed.

She stood by the television's flickering black-and-white images and thought, *This is where I slept and played dress-up with Hazel.* She took a step: *Where I celebrated my seventeenth birthday with Tobias.* Another: *Where Major Kremer stood.* And another: *Where Mutti told me her secrets.* This place held so many moments she could never forget and yet, nothing was as it had been.

Moritz set her luggage beside a sofa where the door to her bedroom once arched. He went to Mutti and Papa's door. "Lillian?" He knocked.

The door cracked open, and Lillian's face appeared. .

"She is here," said Moritz.

"Tante Elsie?" Lillian whispered and slipped out the opening. "Tante!" She embraced Elsie as though they had lived side by side for all their days. Her shoulders trembled. "I am so grateful to have you with us."

"There, there," soothed Elsie. "How is she?"

"No better, but you made it in time." Lillian wiped the tears away with the back of her hand.

Lillian had sent a handful of snapshots over the years, but this was the first time Elsie had seen her niece in the flesh. The resemblance to Hazel was so extraordinary that the old stitches of Elsie's mended heart pulled at their seams. Her eyes stung at the vision of her sister reborn.

"You look so much like your mother." She gripped Lillian—ensuring she was made of matter and not spirit.

Lillian turned her chin down. "I am but a shadow of her."

"Nein," said Elsie. "You are the brightest parts." She wrapped her arms around Lillian again to hide her budding tears.

Lillian took Elsie's hand in hers. "Come. They've been waiting."

Inside Mutti's room, the curtains were drawn tight. A small lamp on the night table cast a pink glow over the bed.

"Elsie is here," announced Lillian.

Mutti's delicate fingers moved over the edelweiss-embroidered coverlet. "Elsie?"

Elsie's knees turned to jelly with each step until she could no longer stand. She knelt by the bedside.

"Dear, let me look at you." Mutti cupped her chin and leaned forward from the shadows.

Her lips were sallow, her face gaunt, and her eyes so dark and tired that it pained Elsie to hold their gaze; but Mutti's touch was tender, and the smell of her buttery skin, ever the same.

"My beautiful daughter," she said.

Elsie turned her lips into her palm and kissed it.

"Isn't she, Max?"

Papa sat on the opposite side of the bed with bowed head.

"Ja, Luana. My girls . . . the most beautiful in Germany." He swallowed hard and laced his fingers tight.

"How is my granddaughter Jane?" asked Mutti.

"She is well." Elsie's voice broke.

"Strong and healthy?"

Elsie nodded. "She eats me out of lebkuchen."

Mutti gave a satisfied "Hmm." Then she said, "I am sorry to have made you leave her and Albert."

"They are fine. I wanted to come. So did Al, but we were afraid that . . ." She bit her lip and looked to Papa.

He cleared his throat and stood, his stature so much smaller than in Elsie's memory. "I will bring us soup. Lillian, help me please."

Lillian obeyed and followed him out.

Alone, Mutti stroked Elsie's hair. "I like it down," she said. "It reminds me of when you and Hazel were young, and I would comb your hair before bed, remember?"

"I have to iron it to get it this way," Elsie sniffled. "Otherwise it is wavy and crimped. Hazel's hair was like silk, so straight and fine."

"You have your papa's hair. When it makes up its mind to stand up in the morning, you will not get it to lie back down the rest of the day. Vitality." She grinned. "Hazel had my hair and look at it now"—she softly touched her temple—"limp and lifeless. All I can do is braid back and hide the bald spots."

Though she tried to keep it steady, Elsie's breath came in ragged snippets.

"That was not funny. I know, I know," Mutti comforted, and she opened the bedsheet a ways. "Come, lie beside me."

Elsie slipped out of her matching blue pumps and spooned Mutti. Her body was angular, reedy thin, and colder than it should've been beneath the wool comforter. Elsie hugged herself to her mother and rubbed stocking feet against Mutti's bare ones.

"I've missed my girls," Mutti whispered and kissed Elsie's head.

Against her chest, Elsie counted each heartbeat and prayed for the next, and the next, and the next. She could contain her grief no longer.

"I'm sorry I stayed away so long," said Elsie.

"Hush, dear. I never blamed you for doing what you felt was right and best. I have always admired that in you. I wish I had a cup of your courage. Perhaps things would have been different for our family."

"You are the strongest woman I've ever known."

"Doch, look in the mirror, and you will see the strongest Schmidt." She leaned in close to Elsie's ear. "And those are your papa's words."

Elsie hugged her tight and wished the moment could be suspended for all eternity.

"Before I go," said Mutti, "there are things I need you to know." She lifted Elsie's chin so their gazes met. "Your papa loves you deeply. Make amends with him. He sees how wrong he was about Albert and the war. His pride kept him from admitting it, but he knows."

Sorrow filled up Elsie's chest and spilled out. "Mutti, I was wrong too. I lied because I thought I was protecting you. There was so much I should have told you . . . so much."

"The past is a black, heavy thing. It will quietly smother our spirits if we let it. You must make peace with it and move forward. Promise me?"

Elsie nodded.

"The second . . ." Mutti breathed deeply. Her rib bones bowed in Elsie's embrace. "You must know that your sister, Hazel, is dead, as is her son Friedhelm."

"For certain?"

"Inside, we've both known for many years, ja?" She gave a sad smile of comfort. "I've kept in touch with Ovidia. In her search for her missing son, she came upon the Lebensborn birth and death register for the Steinhöring women." Mutti inhaled sharply, pressed her fingers to an unseen lower pain, then continued. "Hazel's twin boy. He was listed as disabled and part of something called Operation T4." She blinked hard. "A Nazi euthanasia program. Common practice, apparently."

A chilly draft swept through the room. Elsie rubbed her feet against Mutti's.

"The document also listed the deaths of Program mothers."

The lamplight thinned. A wave of rain pelted the roof. Below, men's voices carried through the floorboards.

"How?" asked Elsie.

"Suicide," Mutti whispered.

"Oh, Hazel." Elsie squeezed her eyes tight.

"I never told your papa. We each carry our own coffer of secrets. Some are best buried with us in the grave. They do no good for the living." She gripped Elsie's hand. "There is an unmarked headstone in our family plot at St. Sebastian's Cemetery. Will you see that Hazel's name is rightfully engraved on it?"

Elsie nodded.

"I will see her soon. That is my consolation. God is just and merciful in all things."

Elsie prayed Mutti was right. There was so much she wanted justice for and so much more for which she wanted mercy.

"Last," said Mutti, "is a secret I am ashamed to say I kept, though it did not belong to me."

They both had their secrets, some shared, some not, but Elsie could not imagine whose Mutti had to confess now.

"Reach under the bedside," instructed Mutti.

Elsie did as she said until her fingers grazed a stack of bound paper, leafy with age. She held them to the light and recognized her own handwriting.

"My letters to you?"

"Not the last two," said Mutti.

Elsie flipped the stack and pulled the bottom pages from the collection; the stationery was thin and more brittle than the rest. Carefully, she unfolded and at last read the words of Frau Rattelmüller:

> *Elsie, I heard the Gestapo was at your home so I went to see for myself. It was God's providence for I was outside the bakery when the soldiers came with Tobias. Upon seeing me, the boy let out a shout as mighty as the archangel Gabriel. In the confusion of the storm and panic in the streets, I was able to rush him to my home undetected. He is here now. I have packed and plan to leave with him at nightfall with all those fleeing the city. I believe he will pass as a son of Germany on the journey to the Swiss border. Old as I may be, these bones will have to manage. I promised I would do what I could to help you. I make good on that promise now. Before we take our leave, I wanted you to know of the boy's safety. Do not worry. I will protect him with my life. I hope this note reaches you without consequence. I leave it at your back door and pray you are the first to cross the threshold. May God bless and protect you and your family, dear Elsie. I will try to contact you again when it is safe.*
>
> *—Frau R.*

Elsie, I hope this letter finds its way to your good hands. Tobias and I are among friends in Zurich. The news of the Allied invasion of Garmisch is bittersweet. Though we are German, our Fatherland is no longer a welcoming place. The Jewish families I hid for over a year—the Mailers and the Zuckermanns—lost nearly all their extended family members over the course of these wretched years. Thanks to your engagement ring, we were able to bribe the SS guards and smuggle Nanette Mailer, her friend, and the Zuckermanns' niece, Tabita, from KZ Dachau before the march. Unfortunately, Tobias's sister, Cecile, succumbed to the camp's harsh conditions mid-January. I have broken the news to him and am deeply sorry we were not able to help her and so many others.

The Mailers and Zuckermanns have decided to leave Europe. The Mailers are bound for Israel. The Zuckermanns for the United States of America. I am too old to undertake such extensive pilgrimages. My sister-in-law lives in Lucerne. I will go to her instead and have offered Tobias a home with me there, should he choose. However, he has formed a strong kinship with the Zuckermanns. Having lost their nine-year-old son in the KZ Dachau, Tobias is a balm to their hearts. They have asked him to join their family in America. This proposition brought a smile—the first since the news of Cecile's death—so I pray it is a sign that he plans to accept. I believe he would be happy with the Zuckermanns. They are among the finest people I have ever been blessed to know. Tobias would be provided for and loved the rest of his life. He is so young with so much living yet to do. I hope this knowledge brings you comfort.

Tobias and I will be at this address until the second week in July when we all take our leave from Zurich. He is anxious to hear from you and to write to you, but until we know for certain you are receiving these letters, it is safer for me to correspond. I pray daily for your safety and the safety of your family.

—Frau R.

Elsie's eyes welled and ran wet and unabated. Tobias lived! She *had* saved him. She consumed the words like a starved captive, pressing them so close that she left pink lipstick smears on the fragile pages. Tobias was in America, like her. She might've walked right by him at the grocery store and never known. The Zuckermanns? Had she heard the family name mentioned over the years? Though she had not, her joy ballooned, threatening to lift her from the bed.

But Mutti's face remained dark and doleful. "I'm sorry I kept these from you." She clasped her hands together. Her wedding band slipped down her finger. "I was afraid. I found the first letter at the back door the night after the Gestapo had . . ." She swallowed. "I didn't want them returning to hurt you again. I didn't want them to harm Frau Rattelmüller, either. When the second letter arrived and the Americans were here, I still feared for us. I couldn't risk the only daughter I had left." She put a feeble hand on Elsie's cheek. "I hid the letters and prayed for Frau Rattelmüller to stop writing. I thought it best if we all forgot those hard years. Whatever you did, whatever you were involved with, I didn't want to know." Her fingers had gone clammy against Elsie's skin. "I simply wanted to move on. And you did, though not in the way your papa or I expected." Her forehead shimmered with fever sweat. "He was so angry with you for agreeing to marry an American. I didn't want to bring any more strife to our house by exposing the letters. So I kept them hidden and you moved to America. And year by year, they seemed less important, less relevant to our lives." Her hand dropped to the bed. "But I was wrong. Wrong to keep them from you and wrong to be afraid of their contents. I should have been proud." She turned, her countenance intense and bolder than it'd been since Elsie arrived. "I *am* proud—of everything you did to help that Jewish child. I'm proud of everything you have done in your life," she said, her body collapsing inward from the force of it.

Footsteps echoed on the stairs; a slice of light fell across the bedroom floor followed by the tangy aroma of onion and caraway seeds.

"*Schwarzbrotsuppe,*" said Papa. He and Lillian each carried two bowls.

Mutti squeezed Elsie's hands still clasped round the letter bundle. "These are yours and always were," she whispered.

"Bread soup warms the soul," said Lillian. "Isn't that what you say, Opa?"

Mutti ran her hand over his arm. "My Max. A finer husband a woman could not have prayed to have. Thank you."

Papa cleared his throat twice, but his voice failed him.

"Eat, Elsie," she instructed. "It's been a long trip, and I want to hear about Jane and Albert and your bakery. Can you believe it, Max? Our daughter is a baker and businesswoman. The girls today." She smiled at Elsie and winked at Lillian. "The world holds so much promise for them."

Papa looked to all three; his chest expanded with approval.

They sat around the bed together clinking spoons in bowls, laughing and listening to Elsie's stories of home. But while they filled their stomachs warm, Mutti ate nothing, her soup congealing on the night table.

forty-eight

SUNSET FUNERALS
9400 NORTH LOOP
EL PASO, TEXAS

MAY 11, 2008

*T*he funeral parlor was crowded and balmy hot from too many bodies pressed against one another. In the center was a stone urn containing Elsie's ashes and beside it, an ornate gold plaque inscribed: IN LOVING MEMORY OF ELSIE SCHMIDT MERIWETHER, BELOVED WIFE AND MOTHER, TRUE FRIEND AND BAKER. JANUARY 30, 1928–MAY 7, 2008. The simplicity of the urn and the opulence of the plaque contrasted. Reba figured the funeral home had supplied the latter. It matched the gold thread curtains and brocade rug.

Reba had taken the first flight from San Francisco to El Paso, but it made little difference. By the time she had seen the Franklin Mountains out the plane window, Elsie was gone.

While Jane arranged for the cremation and funeral, Reba wrote up and sent out the obituary to every newspaper in Texas. She knew it only mattered locally, but somehow that didn't seem enough; besides, it gave her something to do, unlike now. She paced between the memorial wall and the urn, bumping elbows and hips and making awkward conversation with strangers.

When she spotted Riki on the funeral home's burgundy couch, she made a beeline for him.

"How are you holding up?" he asked.

She sat heavy in the cushions. "So many people. I don't know anybody." There was a bowl of butterscotch candies on the side table. She reached across Riki to them and caught a whiff of his spicy aftershave. Her heart leaped in her chest. She missed everything about him.

He scanned the crowd. "Are all these folks customers?"

"Maybe." She unwrapped an amber disk and popped it in her mouth. "Kind of wonderful to think something as simple as bread can mean so much to people."

A towheaded woman walked toward them and gestured to the couch. "Hallo, may I join you here?"

"Of course," said Reba. Her candy bobbled on her tongue.

The woman pulled a program from her purse. The funeral home generously printed a dozen in German and the rest in English. She read the German.

"How did you know Elsie?" Riki asked in casual conversation.

"I am her niece, Lillian."

"Her niece?" Reba crunched the candy and swallowed jagged pieces. "I had always thought Elsie was an only child."

"No," said Lillian. "My *mutter*—Elsie's sister, Hazel—died in Germany during the war. Tante Elsie was, in her way, the mother I never had."

"Have you come all the way from Germany?" asked Riki.

"No, Vich-ita."

"Wichita, Kansas?" asked Reba.

She laughed. "Ja, a German fräulein in the American heartland. I moved to the US for university studies and met my husband during my thesis work on the Lebensborn Program. He's a professor of German history. Tante Elsie is how I came to America. My opa passed nine months after Oma. Our family bakery was willed to Elsie, but she asked me to sell it to our head baker and use the money for school. It would not have been possible without her generosity. I would not have met my husband or had my children. It is because of her that I am who I am."

"I understand," said Reba.

An elderly man and his wife entered. Their gazes moved across the room and settled on Lillian.

"Excuse me. I'm looking for Miss Meriwether, Elsie's daughter. Might that be you?" asked the man.

"No, unfortunately not," said Lillian.

"This is her niece," Reba explained.

"The family resemblance is great."

In the crowd's center, Jane's head bobbed. "That's Elsie's daughter." Reba pointed and the well-wishers moved on.

Lillian smiled. "I could not receive a higher compliment than that." She rose. "Would you please pardon me? I must pay respects to the memorial."

"Of course," said Reba. "It was a pleasure to meet you. I consider Elsie and Jane family, so that would include you, too. I hope we meet again."

Lillian nodded appreciatively and left. Alone, Reba leaned into Riki's shoulder and looked out over the crowd. People were laughing and smiling, telling stories of Elsie and remembering her as more than a friend, as family.

"The only other funeral I've been to is my daddy's. Everything was different. It was like being locked in a closet of a burning house. Not like this." She shrugged. "It feels . . . nice."

Riki took her hand in his. "She'd have liked it this way. She made people's lives better."

Reba nodded, then slipped her hands behind her neck and undid the chain. "A while ago, Elsie told me to either wear your ring or give it back." She fingered the gold band.

Riki frowned and reached out his hand, but Reba held the ring tight.

"She had me pegged at the beginning. She saw right through my talk." A lump caught in her throat. She dropped her chin to her chest. "I've made so many mistakes, Riki. I don't know how you'll ever forgive me for them, but I hope you do." She had to get it out now while she had the courage. "San Francisco was awful. I was so lonely and then there was this guy. A stupid, stupid guy." She shook her head. "But I'm not going back. I know for sure what I want. I see myself clearer now than ever in my life."

Jane interrupted with a whistle. "Listen up, folks! Mom couldn't have stood to have everybody weeping and wailing round her grave. So I want to invite ya'll over to the bakery. We can celebrate Mom's life proper—with a mouthful of food!" She laughed, wiped her eyes, then picked up Elsie's urn.

It didn't take long for the room to empty, leaving only Reba and Riki.

"I know it's asking a lot, but I'd like to give it another try." Reba bit her lip and turned the ring over and over. "Third time's the charm?"

Riki gently took the ring from her. "I quit my job." He cupped her hand in his. "Everything was wrong."

Reba tried to breathe, but her lungs pinched. She knew there was a possibility he wouldn't forgive her—that he'd moved on. "Wrong," she repeated. She tensed her forearms. She didn't know what she'd do if he turned her away.

"I see my life clearer too, and I want something else. Something that's right." He squeezed her hand.

"Okay. So"—a hot flash swept from her ears to toes—"what feels right? I understand what I told you about San Francisco is probably a shock. But I'm in love with you and I want to be with you for the rest of my life—if you want that too. Still. But if you don't feel that's right"—she gulped—"for you then . . ." Her voice pitched upward, and she had to stop before she talked herself to crying.

His scowl softened. "I didn't say *you* weren't right for me. I said my job wasn't."

"Oh," she said and realized she'd pulled out of his grip and was wringing her hands. She laid them palms down in her lap. "I'm sorry. I'm a mess."

"We both have things we're not proud of, Reba. You say you've made big mistakes? Well, I've made them too. I let people get hurt. It's hard for me to live with that fact."

She understood. Her daddy carried a similar burden. Only this time, she wouldn't stand by and pretend it didn't exist. They could find forgiveness together, and that possibility made her heart bloom.

"Do you still want to marry me? Because I still want to marry you," she said firmly.

He looked over her face, smoothed a wavy lock behind her ear, then slipped the ring on her finger. "If you'll have an unemployed Chicano."

The fault line running through her core shifted, and she collapsed forward onto his chest, burying her face in his neck and the comforting scent of him. "Yes," she whispered and pulled herself closer. "A hundred percent, yes."

Tenderly, Riki pushed her back so they were face-to-face. "We got a long road. Both of us."

Reba nodded. "Tell me."

He dug in his pocket and retrieved a worn copper penny.

"A little boy named Victor gave this to me. He was part of a family we detained and then deported to Juárez." He smoothed his thumb over the face. "They shot him—*we* shot him. He's dead for being in the wrong place at the wrong time. He's dead because nobody did anything to save him from drowning in violence. *I* didn't do anything, except kick back under the current."

Then Riki told her the story, the way he saw it. The story the rest of the world didn't know or didn't want to or maybe a little of both. As he spoke, Reba threaded her fingers through his. The white diamond on her hand fractured the light into a perfect rainbow on the wall.

forty-nine

ST. SEBASTIAN CHAPEL
CEMETERY
GARMISCH, GERMANY

NOVEMBER 6, 1967

*D*ead leaves blanketed the cemetery in a patchwork quilt of umber. Briefly disrupted by spade strikes, and mourners' cries overhead, the sleepy tenants soon returned to rest, the grounds silent and empty once more, the new mound of dirt settling inch by inch, hour by hour, as the living pressed on, press on.

During the burial, Elsie had taken Papa's hand in hers, their rolling pin calluses aligning perfectly.

"I love you," she'd whispered.

He'd pulled her close with trembling arms and kissed her temple. "My Elsie. Forgive me."

She'd only the strength to nod and weep until all the stale years and regrets crumbled under the weight of his embrace.

"I'll take Opa home," Lillian had offered at the end of the funeral. "You stay as long as you want."

And Elsie had, hours after everyone else; after even the priest had gone inside, his hands red and raw from the wintry wind.

The chapel bell rang out five strokes. The sun began to set, dissolving into the Black Forest ridgeline. In less than an hour it would be dark, and she'd be forced away from this spot, and night would come and go, and she'd board her plane in the morning, flying a half a world away, back to her daughter's smile and her husband's kiss, and tomorrow would follow tomorrow leaving behind this moment and all within it.

So she hung on, reading the granite headstone over and over, trying to make it feel the way she thought it ought, trying to brand it inside herself. *Luana Schmidt, Beloved Wife and Mother, 1897–1967. Luana Schmidt, Beloved Wife and Mother. Luana Schmidt, Beloved. Luana Schmidt. Luana.* Mutti.

It was a modest epitaph. The way Mutti would have wanted. Yet so small in comparison to the life it eulogized. In the spring, blades of grass and wildflowers would bloom anew without ever knowing the life that nurtured them. For years to come, those who came and went would never perceive what depth of love lay beneath their tread.

To the far right was Peter Abend's grave, a garland of holly berries hung round the stone. *Oh, Peter,* Elsie thought, *how much you missed.*

Beside Mutti was Hazel's marker. Papa agreed to the engraving without question or explanation, and Elsie was relieved. HAZEL SCHMIDT, LOVING DAUGHTER AND SISTER. Elsie had left off the dates, unsure of what to put, and unwilling to add to Papa's heartache.

Elsie balled her gloved fists. Death shouldn't be so unremarkable, she thought. Mutti, Hazel, Friedhelm, Peter, the born and unborn. They were loved and deserved more. Not in worldly stone, marble or gems, but in memory and celebration; they deserved the heavens to open up for a moment for all that had been and was gone.

In a nearby tree, a finch took flight singing *seep, seep, seep* as it went. *Just and merciful,* Mutti had said of God. The bird climbed high, its song fading in the wind.

Twilight cast an amber glow. The tombstones' shadows stretched long. It was time. Elsie turned to leave and as she did, a small gravestone stood out, alone and apart from the neat familial lines of the cemetery. Her eyes grazed the name, and she stopped.

JOSEF HUB. No inscription. No dates.

Elsie went to it, pulled off her gloves, and traced the print: Josef. She sighed. He deserved remembering as well. His life had been as much a part of her story as the others. She had no flower to leave him, so she pulled loose the blue ribbon from her hair and tied it round the headstone.

She tried to remember Josef without the Nazi uniform, but she'd never really known the man beneath—the secret burdens he carried. So she said a prayer for his soul: that he might find forgiveness and love. She had to believe that was possible, even for the dead.

fifty

*R*eba held her hat as Riki rumbled down the ashen streets to Panteón San Rafael Cemetery. She wore his Stetson rimmed with the reddest geraniums she could find in the shop. It was Día de Los Muertos.

A morning haze drifted over the ramshackle buildings, smelling of sulfur and copper smelting from the ASARCO plant on the US side. In the front yard of a weather-beaten Mexican adobe, a pile of debris burned; small Chihuahuas circled the fire pit, children still in pajamas baiting them on. Across the horizon, plumes of gray ash tunneled to the heavens from small homes clinging to the sandy mountainside.

"Are those Día de Los Muertos bonfires?" asked Reba.

Riki leaned over and studied the mottled sky. "Nope. Juárez folks burning trash to keep warm."

Reba had heard such rumors but had never seen it done. It made the morning look as apocalyptic as the holiday.

They drove on, past the neighborhoods, to the southern outskirts of the city where the cemetery stretched out in long shunted plots, row upon row, like land tilled for seeding. The canals between the burial columns were already crowded with family members tending to a bounty of white crosses, candle altars, food, and flowers. The harvest of graves extended far into the rugged desert.

"So many," whispered Reba.

"They come to honor their loved ones—to remember the past," said Riki.

But Reba hadn't meant the living; she'd meant the dead. Panteón San Rafael opened in 1995. Brand new in comparison to most, yet there were tens of thousands already buried beneath its sacred ground.

Riki led her through the labyrinth of mourners and shrines, past old women praying to Virgin Mary *retablos,* younger women singing lullabies, men inscribing names on sugar skulls, and children arranging marigolds along the perimeters of buried caskets. They pressed farther in, past the newly buried, to where the mounds had seemingly shrunk, their occupants planted back into the earth.

Riki stopped at the foot of an unadorned stone marker: BETO CHAVEZ, 1933–1998. NATALIA CHAVEZ, 1936–1998. DEVOTED AND FAITHFUL ALWAYS. His parents. Reba put an arm round his waist, not for herself but for his comfort.

She'd agreed to come though she was unsure of what to expect. Standing there now, the affection she felt for people she'd never known surprised her. She thought of her daddy's large, black marble tomb, glossy and ominous in the middle of the manicured Richmond Baptist Cemetery. She'd hated it—feared it—and the sea of gloomy family and friends who gathered to watch him be lowered into darkness. But this place was entirely different. The sandstone memorials were whitewashed bright; the sun haloed everything in gold; flowers and decorations transformed the catacombs into colorful bursts of revelry.

Riki unfolded a rainbow wool *rebozo* and laid it over the grave. Then he took a handkerchief from his back pocket and cleaned the sand from the stone inscription.

"Mom, Dad," he whispered, "meet Reba." He looked up to her.

Reba knelt down on the shawl and took from her bag a stained-glass Madonna candle and a box of homemade churros—Jane's modified recipe based on Elsie's kreppels.

"A pleasure to meet you," said Reba. "I'm not much of a baker, but I brought the best I could do from the best I know." She set the box on the tombstone and opened the top; the aroma of cinnamon and fried dough rose up sweet. "Riki says these were your favorites."

He smiled and pulled her into his arms. They sat picnic style for over an hour, Riki telling her stories of his parents, his childhood, his history. As the sun rose higher, more people arrived with garlands and guitars, basket lunches and laughter, and the cemetery bloomed even further with song and savory smells. Reba thought it one of the most beautiful events she'd ever witnessed, a celebration of death, a celebration of life. She wondered if the angels had indeed spread their wings over them all. She liked to think so.

At half past noon, they packed up but left behind their offerings and two geranium blooms from Reba's hat. On the walk back to the parked car, Riki stopped suddenly before a grave decorated in a blanket of orange marigolds and children's toys: a worn soccer ball, a plastic airplane, a stuffed tiger with fuzzy stripes. The day before had been Día de los Inocentes, the day of remembrance for lost children. Riki's hand dropped away from Reba. The block stenciling on the wooden white cross read VICTOR GARCIA.

Riki's Victor, Reba thought, and clasped Riki's hand tight in hers. She wanted him to know she was there with him—in good times and bad, in joy and in sorrow.

Though it was Sunday, Jane opened the bakery from 2:00 to 5:00 p.m. so customers could visit Elsie's dedication altar. Riki and Reba were there at quarter till two, rapping on the glass door.

Jane opened it with a welcoming laugh and tinkling bell above. "Mom would be so pleased!" She gestured to Reba's scarlet-flowered hat and ushered them in. "I can't say Sergio and I dressed with such flair, but we did our part."

A large baking tray of glazed bone-crossed buns cooled beside the register.

"We baked all night." She snatched one up and offered it to Riki. "You're the expert. Don't pussyfoot. Tell me if they're up to snuff."

Riki took the pan de muerto, turning it round. "They sure look like Mom's." He bit in. "Taste like them too," he mumbled.

Reba winked at him and skimmed her hand down his back. Stumbling on Victor's grave at Panteón San Rafael had been a surprise. Riki confided that he hoped to make some reparation to the Garcia family one day. Not that he could change anything. But perhaps in the acknowledgment of their suffering and loss, they could all find healing. Reba agreed. She'd learned that the past was a blurry mosaic of right and wrong. You had to recognize your part in each of those and remember. If you tried to forget, to run from the fears, the regrets and transgressions, they'd eventually hunt you down and consume your life like Daddy's wolf did his. Reba was not her daddy. She was stronger, and she'd met people who showed her how to forgive and be forgiven. She was glad to be by Riki's side at Victor's grave. He would do the same for her.

"Good!" Jane clapped her hands. "That's what I was aiming for."

In front of the pastry display case was a café table turned makeshift altar. A picture of Elsie and a teenage Jane stood center, their faces oddly similar to the black-and-white photo on the wall. Beside it was a photograph of Doctor Albert Meriwether, dressed in his army Class-A uniform. Around the pictures were sugar skulls, candles, a white rose, letters tied with baking twine, an Edelweiss pin, a cowboy cartoon, a weathered book, and two lebkuchen hearts.

"You've got quite a spread," said Reba.

"I decorated with all her favorites." Jane fingered the wooden frame of Al. "So my dad, of course, and then some things I found in an old tin in Mom's dresser. This pin, a cartoon ad for baked beans, and letters—mostly from my grandma and Lillian, but there are others too."

Reba nodded. "No explanation needed for the lebkuchen. Specialty of the house."

"Mom would come back from the dead and snatch me bald if I didn't have gingerbread." Jane smiled.

"What about this?" She lifted the book, vaguely making out the worn title on the coverless page. "*A Boy's Will*. Frost? I read this in high school."

"Lillian gave it to me at the funeral. She said about a year before, a man named Tobias Zuckermann mailed it to Elsie at the Schmidt Bakery in Garmisch. Of course, Mom wasn't there. The new owner mailed it to the only address he had—Lillian in Wichita. She had it in mind to mail it here, but Mom passed before she had the chance. She brought it to the funeral," explained Jane. "But here's where the story gets good. He wrote a letter to Mom with the book. He was a Jew detained at Dachau during World War II. Apparently, Mom and one of her neighbors saved him from the Gestapo. Mom hid him in her bedroom wall, and somehow, they got him out of Germany. Can you imagine? Mom never said a word about it to me." Jane shook her head. "I guess she used to read this book of poetry to him. He marked his favorites."

Reba opened the book to a down-turned corner, "The Trial by Existence":

> *Even the bravest that are slain*
> *Shall not dissemble their surprise*
> *On waking to find valor reign,*
> *Even as on earth, in paradise.*

She cradled the flimsy copy, feeling the gravity of age, hope, and fear pressed into the willowy pages.

"Tobias wrote that he immigrated to California, got married, and had a bunch of kids. He even named one of his daughters after Mom. It's all right over there in the letter." She pointed to the stack tied with twine. "I figured she might want to read her mail today." She winked.

"Amazing." Reba considered the stack, her curiosity eating away at her.

"You can read it later if you want," said Jane. "Mom wouldn't mind. I think it says a lot about the kind of woman she was, then and now. She broke the mold."

"She sure did," said Reba.

"Jane—Reba," Sergio called. "Would you like something to drink?"

"Yes, a celebration toast! You bring the libations, and we'll bring the food." Jane snapped a set of tongs together.

Riki smiled wide at them and followed Sergio into the kitchen.

"Riki's in fine spirits," said Jane. "I'm guessing Citizenship and Immigration Services has been a nice change of pace for him, eh?"

Reba nodded. She was sure that played a part. "The work is good. Bert Mosley's brother-in-law is the acting deputy director. With all of Riki's Border Patrol experience, they were more than happy to have him and he was glad to be on the other side—welcoming people in, instead of kicking them out." She traced the soft edges of the book in her palm. "So much has changed since a year ago. Sometimes I look in the mirror and can hardly believe how good I have it. Riki is going to meet my family at Thanksgiving. Finally!"

"That's right, you two are eastbound for a spell." Jane carefully peeled a sticky bun off the tray. "Did *Sun City* have any objections? You been back now what—five months?" She placed the bone-crossed bread on a pewter platter.

"Those are the perks of being the managing editor. It isn't like I'm a stranger. It's a new hat on an old head. Plus, I'll only be gone a week." Reba swiped her finger across the pooled sugar on the tray, licked it clean, then continued. "I don't want to be away any longer than that. Riki's mapping out all kinds of travel plans, but I want us to hurry back home so we can snuggle up on the porch and start living—*really* living."

"Sounds like you're a new head in an old hat, if you ask me." Jane clapped her tongs approvingly. "I hear you, lady. The winds have changed these days. I hardly notice the trains and planes anymore. I guess when you're happy where you are, the grass don't seem so green on the other side of the fence. Maybe it never was." She shrugged with a smile. "Y'all flying or driving east?"

"It's a road trip." Reba drew a clumsy outline of the United States in the sugar icing. "Up across the panhandle"—she walked her fingers along the tray—"through Nashville and over to Virginia." She licked the frosting clean. "It's been too long, and there are things I have to discuss with my family. I want Riki with me when I do. It's important he know the whole truth of me." She moved the tray aside for Jane. "The last stop is Virginia Beach. Riki's never seen the ocean."

"He'll love it." Jane winked. "Every part." She balanced the last bun on the pile and set the silver platter on a café table swathed in skull polka-dot fabric.

Sergio returned with bottles of Bitburger. Riki followed close behind. Pausing at Elsie's altar, he dug in his pocket until he found Victor's penny. He laid it beside a red-white-and-blue sugar skull. Reba joined him.

"Looks like we're ready," said Jane. She raised her bottle high. "To you, Mom. And all those looking down on us from above."

The flames of the altar candles danced in wavy undulations.

Reba sipped, the pilsner tasting of new dough rising in the oven heat.

fifty-one

124 EDEN VALLEY LANE
ESCONDIDO, CA

MAY 8, 2007

Dear Elsie,

For years, I have anticipated writing this letter. At first, I re-
frained out of apprehension and what I imagined the consequences
might be to you and your family. Over time, I admit, I did not
write for selfish reasons. Remembering those last days in Germany
brings such vivid memories. I sometimes wake in the dark and believe I'm still hiding inside your bedroom wall, a small boy again.
The Gestapo's gunshots haunt me. Even now, I am startled at the
sound of a popped birthday balloon, a hit baseball, a lit firecracker—
childish amusements meant to entertain, but my heart freezes cold
in my chest, and I am back in Garmisch praying for a miracle. Then
I see my children at play with their children, my wife smiling over
them, and I know that God provided just that. And I do not mean
only on that spring day in 1945. No, he was watching over us both
for all our lives. Alongside the difficult memories of those years are
the ones I have of you, Elsie. Whenever I pass a pâtisserie on a city
street, a café in an airport, even my own kitchen, warm with my
daughter's baked cookies, I am halted and can barely keep from
weeping. Not out of sadness, but out of joy and thanksgiving. I pray
the <u>Birkhat</u> <u>HaGomel</u> for you, my guardian angel. The first true

and trustworthy friend on my path to salvation. You were my first. Frau Rattelmüller came next and then the Zuckermanns.

Frau passed away not long after arriving in Lucerne, and I never knew if her letters successfully arrived to you. In those last days of the war, so much was lost—of the living and the dead. Having escaped the Gestapo at your bakery, Frau Rattelmüller hid me in her cloak and we ran through the backstreets to her house where she quickly packed, fed me brötchen, dressed me in bundhosen and a wool travel coat, and told me I was to pass as an Aryan child. We left that very hour, sitting on the back of farmers' wagons and walking great distances. We did not sleep until we reached the Swiss border where her friends greeted us with transportation to Zurich and happy news of Germany's ultimate surrender. The war had ended, but none of us dared go back. We spent two months in Switzerland.

In July 1945, when the Zuckermanns chose to set off for the United States, I joined them. A Jewish family hidden in Frau Rattelmüller's attic for many arduous years, they lost their son, Johan, at KZ Dachau where my own parents and sister, Cecile, perished. At the age of seven, I believed my life to have ended, but now, I know that it had truly just begun. The Zuckermanns were my new family in America, both of us grieving our losses and rejoicing in each breath we had together. I went to school and then on to San Diego University where I earned my Ph.D. in music composition and taught courses. I kept my promise to you. I sang. And later, I wrote my own orchestrations and lyrics. Poetry in notes.

Today, my granddaughter Jacquelyn asked if I could write a song for the Jonas Brothers. She plays them on her electronic player. I told her they reminded me of the Monkees. She looked at me incredulously and said, "I didn't know there were singing monkeys a long time ago." I laughed but realized how old I am to these young ones. How new and unknowing their minds are to the world's history. I wonder if it is better for them to remain that way—innocent and naive. Should we bury our memory barbs to keep them from piercing budding hearts? No doubt they will encounter their own tragedies in due time. Or should we warn our children that the world is harsh and men can be wicked? Warn them so that they take care to guard each other and seek out compassion? These are the questions that consume me these days. I ponder them as Jacquelyn holds her iPod like a microphone and performs "pop" music for me. I can't help smiling. The youth have a way of transforming even an old man like myself. I told Jacquelyn I'd write a song for her instead of the Jonas sons. I have not composed or taught professionally in over five years, retired to enjoy the company of my wife, children, and grandchildren.

I married Kelly, a pianist from San Diego, in 1970; and we had the first of our four children in 1971. My daughter Elsie, your namesake, gave birth to my eighth grandchild last month. He already shows a great affinity for meter, responding to Mother Goose rhymes with inquisitive eyes and fluttering feet. He is named Robert after our favorite poet. This enclosed copy of "A Boy's Will" has been on my bookshelf for six decades. I was reading it when you called me from my hiding place our last hour together. I slipped it beneath the drawstring of my trousers, not knowing the events that would quickly transpire. It has stayed with me all these years as my only tangible proof that you existed and were not simply a spirit of my mind's making. It has brought me great comfort and inspiration.

On this anniversary of the war's end, I think it time I return it to its rightful owner. Thank you, Elsie. Never doubt that you saved me. Never doubt that it was more than enough. I do not know if you are still in Garmisch or Germany or this world, but I like to think that wherever you are, my voice will reach you.

    With great love and sincerest thanks,
    Tobias

epilogue

Reba,

In honor of you and Riki finally setting a wedding date, I'm sending you a dozen of Mom's recipes. These have been the Schmidt bakers' secrets for generations, but I know Mom wouldn't mind my sharing with you and Riki. Y'all are practically family. She'd be pleased as punch to have you and yours carry on her legacy in the kitchen.

I'm sure she's smiling in heaven to see you finally take the plunge, and I can't wait to bake the biggest, sweetest celebration cake I can muster!

Guten appetit!

— Jane

Elsie Schmidt Meriwether's German Bakery Recipes

Reba's Bread (no dairy)

In honor of Miss Reba Adams. (Soon to be Mrs. Reba Adams Chavez!)

1 cup warm water
1 packet active dry yeast (rapid)
3 tablespoons white sugar
½ teaspoon salt

1 teaspoon cinnamon
2 tablespoon oil
3 cups all-purpose flour
¾ cup raisins

Sprinkle yeast over warm water. In separate bowl, combine sugar, salt, cinnamon, and oil. Stir in mixed yeast. Beat in 1½ cups flour. Add raisins. Stir in remaining flour. Knead on floured wooden board until the dough stops being sticky—about 10 minutes.

Form into ball and place in greased bowl, turning to coat. Cover with a dish towel, set in a warm spot, and let double in size. Once it has, punch it down and shape into a loaf. Place in greased bread pan. Cover and let rise again, only 30 minutes this time, then bake 30 minutes at 400°F until the crust is golden brown. Cool and slice up to serve.

Note: Now that you eat dairy, I suggest you spread a heap of butter over while it's still blazing. That'll put this bread over the top!

Thomasplitzchen Buns

Mom always said these could make your enemies your friends or your friends your enemies. I put on five pounds every St. Thomas Day because of them, so I'd say they're my friendly enemies. Too good to eat just one.

2 cups all-purpose flour
½ teaspoon salt
½ cup butter
½ cup sugar or brown sugar
2 teaspoons baking powder
½ cup milk

Filling
3 teaspoons melted butter
1 cup currants, raisins, cranberries,
  or whatever small, dried fruit you
  have on hand
¼ cup sugar

Icing
3 tablespoons melted butter
Few drops vanilla extract
2 cups powdered sugar

Mix up all the ingredients for the buns. Get a rolling pin and press out the dough to one-eighth-inch thick on a floured board. Mix together the filling: butter, dried fruit, and sugar. Spread it on the dough. Roll it up like a fat sausage, and make one-inch slices. Put them pinwheel side up on a greased cookie sheet and bake off in a pre-heated 350°F oven until barely suntanned on top. For me, that's about 12 minutes on a hot day and 15 on a cold one. To make the icing, mix together butter, vanilla extract, and powdered sugar. When the buns are out of the oven, give them a good sugar smothering and let cool.

Lebkuchen Hearts

These puppies will keep for months in the freezer and still taste like heaven! Shh—don't tell the customers.

½ cup honey
½ cup dark molasses
¾ cup packed brown sugar
3 tablespoons almond oil
1 large egg
2¾ cups all-purpose flour

2 teaspoons ground cinnamon
1 teaspoon baking powder
½ teaspoon baking soda
½ teaspoon salt
½ teaspoon ground cardamom
½ teaspoon ground ginger

In a pan, boil honey and molasses. Let it cool, then add brown sugar, almond oil, and egg. In another bowl, mix flour, cinnamon, baking powder, baking soda, salt, cardamom, and ginger. Pour wet into dry ingredients. Make sure it's good and mixed. (Sometimes we add chopped hazelnuts or almonds, but Mom likes them the plain old-fashioned way.) Cover dough, and chill in refrigerator overnight.

In the morning, roll out the dough and cut into heart shapes—or spread in a pan for squares. Bake until it springs back to the touch. Careful not to burn yourself! Usually takes about 15 minutes at 350°F. Glaze top with icing (recipe below). Let cool until it doesn't drip. Cut into squares if you're making them that way, and decorate with almond slices or colored icing or really anything you fancy.

Lebkuchen Icing
1 cup white sugar
½ cup water
½ cup powdered sugar

Boil the white sugar and water for a good 5 minutes, so the sugar is dissolved. Take off the stove and mix in powdered sugar. Brush on warm lebkuchen.

Brötchen

There's nothing more German than this recipe. A staple for all true Schmidt bakers. These are best hot out of the oven with butter or cherry jam. That's the way Mom did it. Here, I'll give you Oma's cherry jam recipe too.

2½ to 3 cups all-purpose flour
1 packet active dry yeast (rapid)
1 teaspoon sugar
1 cup warm water

1 tablespoon oil
1 teaspoon salt
1 egg white

Put 2½ cups flour into a large bowl and make a well in the middle. Pour yeast, sugar, and two tablespoons of warm water (the water comes from the 1 cup) into the well. Mix yeast, sugar, and water in the well, but don't mix in the flour yet. Cover the bowl with a cloth and set it in a warm place for 15 minutes until it proofs. Add the rest of the water and oil, and beat in the salt and flour good. Turn out the dough on a floured wooden board, and knead. Add the remaining ½ cup flour as needed to make it smooth. Put dough in a greased bowl, cover, and let it rise until it doubles in size. About an hour in that same warm spot.

Punch down, then split it into 12 pieces. Shape into rolls and place 3 inches apart on a greased and floured baking tray. Cover and let rise one more time until they double again.

Cut a cross on top of each. Beat egg white and 1 teaspoon water with a fork until frothy and brush the rolls. (Oh, I forgot—you should have preheated the oven to 450°F already.) Then you bake for 15 to 20 minutes until the tops are golden.

Oma's Cherry Jam

Mom would've insisted that you eat this on brötchen to cut the sweet and sour. She claimed it could rot your teeth otherwise. But I used to sneak spoonfuls right out of the jar as a kid, and I still got a full set of chompers.

> 2 lbs (6 cups) pitted cherries, chop them up or keep them whole
>   according to your preference
> 5 cups white sugar
> ½ teaspoon butter
> A splash or two of Kirschwasser (German cherry liquor—very good!)

Note: Some recipes use lemon juice, but Oma didn't often have a lemon hanging around. You can make this without the butter and Kirschwasser, too, if need be. The jam is just as tasty.

Place cherries in a large, heavy-duty pot. Stir in sugar. Let this sit together for 2 to 4 hours. Add the butter now (if using). Bring it all to a rolling boil, being sure to stir it good, until it gels on the back of a spoon. Then take it off the heat and skim away the foam. Add the Kirschwasser to taste. Spoon the cherry preserves into one-pint steilized jamming jars. Screw on the lids as tight as you can. Let stand inverted for 5 minutes then turn over. These will keep for as long as you like.

Schnecken Sticky German Snails (Cinnamon Rolls)

These are similar to Thomasplitzchen buns, only the ingredients are more expensive with messier results. Their decadence borders on sinful. They make a person want to gobble without a care for who's watching! And Mom never discouraged folks from doing just that.

Dough
3⅓ cups bread flour
3 tablespoons sugar
½ teaspoon salt
¼ ounce fast rise yeast or
    1 tablespoon fresh yeast
⅓ cup unsalted butter
½ cup milk, plus 2 tablespoons
2 eggs

Syrup
½ cup unsalted butter, plus
    1 tablespoon
2 tablespoons white sugar
½ cup maple syrup
1 cup nuts (walnuts or pecans or
    whatever you got in the pantry)

Glaze	Filling
1 egg	3 tablespoons white sugar
2 tablespoons milk	½ cup brown sugar
1 tablespoon cinnamon	

Grease a 13- × 9-inch pan. Mix flour, sugar, salt, and yeast in a large bowl. Melt butter in the ½ cup milk over very low heat and beat in eggs. Stir the milk-n-butter mixture into the dry ingredients to make the dough. Knead for 10 minutes. When it's soft but springy, form a ball and put in a greased bowl. Turn to coat and cover. Leave in a warm place for an hour until it doubles in size. While that's rising, go ahead and make the syrup.

Cream the butter until smooth, and add the sugar. Beat in maple syrup, and then pour the whole sticky sweet mess down in your baking pan. Top with the nuts.

Give the bloomed dough a good punch or two, then roll it into a large rectangle with the long side closest to you.

Time to glaze. Beat egg and add milk. Using a pastry brush or your fingers, spread the glaze over the rolled-out dough. Mix the sugars and cinnamon in a little bowl and sprinkle over glazed dough.

Roll it up from the long side, pushing away from you firmly. Cut into 12 even slices, and lay each slice swirly-side up on top of the nuts in the pan.

Let the oven preheat to 350°F while the buns rise for 20 minutes, then slide them into the hot oven. Bake for 20 to 25 minutes until they're golden on top but gooey in the middle. (Oh, I forgot a good tip: Mom always put a baking sheet underneath to catch all the sugar drippings so they don't muss up your oven. Burnt sugar is a devil to clean.)

Take the buns out and let them cool a spell; 5 to 10 minutes should be plenty of time. Then get a baking sheet or big plate, and turn the pan over on it. Carefully dump the cinnamon buns upside down and spatula out all the syrup and nuts and good stuff.

Ready to eat whenever they're cool enough to handle without burning your fingers. I dare you to wait any longer!

Matschbrötchen (Mud Bread Roll)

Tried and true.

    1 schaumkuss (foam kiss) or a Mallomar from the store
    1 brötchen or white bun

Pull or cut bread in half. Place chocolate foam kiss between pieces. Smash together and eat immediately. Preferably with a friend.

Schwarzwälder Kirschtorte (Black Forest Cake)

Mom fancied a strong cup of coffee with a slice of this. She said it brought out the rich chocolate flavor. I think it's delicious with or without!

Cake

1²/₃ cups all-purpose flour
²/₃ cup unsweetened cocoa powder
1½ teaspoons baking soda
1 teaspoon salt
½ cup shortening
1½ cups white sugar
2 eggs
1 teaspoon vanilla
1½ cups buttermilk or regular—
   whatever is on hand
½ cup Kirschwasser

Filling

1 cup heavy whipping cream
½ teaspoon vanilla
1 tablespoon Kirschwasser (Not optional
   in this recipe. You must have it!)
1 cup powdered sugar
Pinch of salt
1 cup pitted cherries chopped

Topping

1 square semisweet chocolate, or remaining crumbles
10 whole cherries (candied maraschino cherries work fine too)

Preheat (I remembered!) oven to 350°F. Grease and flour two 8-inch round pans. Sift together flour, cocoa, baking soda, and salt. Set aside.

Cream shortening and sugar until fluffy. Add eggs and beat. Add vanilla. Add flour mixture, alternating with milk until combined.

Pour into pans. Bake for 35 to 40 minutes, or until a toothpick inserted into the cake comes out clean. Cool completely. (Very important!) Cut each layer in half, horizontally, making four layers total. Sprinkle layers generously with ½ cup Kirschwasser.

In a separate bowl, whip the cream stiff. Beat in ½ teaspoon vanilla and 1 tablespoon Kirschwasser. Add powdered sugar, and a pinch of salt. Beat again. (Note: This recipe is exercise.) Spread first layer of cake with ¹/₃ of the filling. Top with ¹/₃ of the cherries. Repeat with the remaining layers.

Decorate the top and sides of cake with leftover cream filling and chocolate curls. I use a potato peeler on the chocolate square or whatever chocolate crumbs are around. Sprinkle the cake generously. Place ten cherries around the top—these help you know where to cut the slices.

Sonnenblumenkernbrot (Sunflower Seed Rolls)

*My dad was partial to these, so they're one of my
favorites too. You can bet Mom had no trouble finding loads of sunflower seeds
in this town, and neither will you.*

2½ cup all-purpose flour	1 package sourdough extract (optional)
1½ cup rye flour	1⅔ cup lukewarm water, divided
1½ teaspoon salt	½ cup dry-roasted sunflower seeds 1 packet
active dry yeast (rapid)	plus more for decoration

Start by mixing together the white flour, rye flour, and salt. Dissolve yeast in ¼ cup of the water. Add the yeast water, the sourdough extract (if you're using it) and the rest of the water to the flour mix. Stir until it clumps into a ball. Knead on a floured board for 5 minutes. The dough should be firm and a little gummy.

Knead in the sunflower seeds, shape into a ball, place in a greased bowl, cover, and let rise in a warm place for about an hour.

When it's doubled in size, punch it down, knead for a minute, and shape into 12 buns. Brush the tops with water (if you still didn't eat dairy) or milk (now that you do!), and load them up good with extra sunflower seeds. Place the rolls on a greased tray, and let them rise until they almost doubled again.

Preheat your oven to 500°F. (Yeah, I know it's awful hot to start, but trust Mom, it makes the best crust.) Put an old baking pan on the bottom rack, and let it get hot too. When the oven reaches 500°F, slash the tops of the rolls with a knife, pour a cup of water into the old baking pan, and put the rolls on the rack above. Then close up the oven as fast as a jackrabbit and turn it down to 400°F. Bake for 15 to 20 minutes until they're as golden as the Texas sunflowers in the fall.

Spiced Crumb Cake

Mom's favorite and sure to please a crowd!

This cake is made in steps.

Step 1

1 cup white sugar	1 cup softened butter
1 cup packed brown sugar	1 teaspoon cinnamon
3 cups all-purpose flour	¼ to ½ teaspoon salt

Mix all ingredients to crumbs with hands. Put aside 1 packed cup.

Step 2

1 teaspoon vanilla extract
2 well-beaten eggs
1 cup buttermilk to which 1 teaspoon baking soda has been added

Add these items to the rest (minus the packed cup). Mix well, and pour into a greased baking dish. I use a 9- × 11-inch pan.

Step 3

Sprinkle remaining crumb mixture plus ½ cup chopped hazelnuts on top.
    Bake at 325°F for about 40 minutes. Easy as 1-2-3!

Pan de Muerto courtesy of Riki Chavez's Mamá

I'm still perfecting this one. But like Mom said, we got to learn the recipes of our people so we can pass them on to the next generation of bakers and their sons and daughters.

½ cup good butter	1 teaspoon salt
½ cup milk	2 packets active dry yeast (rapid-o)
½ cup water	1 teaspoon aniseed
1½ cups all-purpose flour	4 eggs
½ cup sugar	4½ cups flour (extra)

In a saucepan over medium flame, heat the butter, milk, and water until it's hot but not boiling. While it's doing its business on the stove, mix up the 1½ cups of flour, sugar, salt, yeast, and aniseed. Take the liquid mixture off the stove, and beat in the dry mix until it comes together nice. Add the eggs. Add 1 cup of extra flour. Mix. Continue adding flour until it comes together like a dough should, soft but not sticky. Knead on a well-floured board for 10 minutes.

    Grease up a big bowl, and put that dough inside, cover it up, and let it rise in a warm place. It should bloom in about 1½ hours. Punch it down, and shape it into round buns. Roll out some smaller pieces, and make them look like bones. Cross the bones on top of the buns and let them rise again for an hour.

    Preheat your oven to 350°F when you're finally ready, and bake 40 minutes. Remove and glaze immediately. That recipe is below.

Dead Bread Glaze

½ cup sugar
⅓ cup fresh orange juice
2 tablespoons grated orange zest

Bring everything to a boil for 2 minutes, then brush over the buns.

Churros/Kreppels

Same as Mom's sugar-cinnamon kreppels, only shaped different. Ain't no matter where they come from, the ingredients is all the same.

Vegetable oil for frying
½ cup butter
1 cup water
¼ teaspoon salt

½ cup sugar
1 cup all-purpose flour, sifted
3 eggs
¼ teaspoon cinnamon

Note: You're going to need a candy thermometer for this one.

Heat at least 2 inches of oil to 375°F. Stick the candy thermometer in it to check.

In a pot, simmer the butter and water together. Add the salt and 1 tablespoon of the sugar. Stir until dissolved. Bring to a boil. Mix in the flour, stir it fiercely to blend well. Continue mixing until mixture forms a doughy ball, about 1 minute, but take it off the heat after 30 seconds or they won't puff up like they should. (I ruined two batches until I figured out the timing.)

Add eggs one at a time, mixing after each. Make sure all the eggs are incorporated and the dough is shining pretty. Let it cool for about 5 minutes. Mix up the remaining sugar and cinnamon in a brown paper bag and set aside.

Here's where it gets tricky, so make sure your patience hat is on tight. Spoon the dough mixture into a plastic baggy—one of them Ziplocs will do. Squish the dough into one of the bag corners. Cut that corner tip. Squeeze out 4-inch strips of dough into the hot oil, 3 or 4 at a time in the pot, otherwise they'll crowd up and make a heap of a soggy mess. Fry 2 minutes, then flip them with a fork. Fry another 2 minutes till golden and crispy. Use the fork to fish them onto paper towels. Let them drain for a few minutes, but get them in that brown paper bag quick as you can. You want them hot to make the sugar stick. They say these are best warm, but I've had them a day old, and they still taste dang good.

Acknowledgments

*E*normous thanks to my editor, Kate Kennedy, whose masterful editorial skills, boundless support, and friendship fostered my creativity and helped the book bloom. To my publicist, Nora O'Malley, who jumped in banging the drum and never ceased. My Crown family is unparalleled.

Thanks to my agent team, Doris Michaels and Delia Berrigan Fakis, for loving this story from the start and for sharing it with German family members, survivors of this onerous period in Germany's history. Their enthusiasm for the book was the ultimate stamp of approval. As well, many thanks to Paul Cirone and Molly Friedrich for friendship and wise counsel. Your generosity continues to astound me.

Thank you to the staff of Marina's Germany Bakery in El Paso, Texas, and the German Community Center at Fort Bliss for graciously allowing me to visit, ask questions, and poke around. In researching this novel, I'm indebted to the countless World War II websites that kept me awake nights, horrified, fascinated, and unable to forget. To the survivors of this war, thank you for having the bravery to live. To their children, grandchildren, and great-grandchildren, thank you for having the courage to share your history. As well, deepest appreciation to my students at the University of Texas at El Paso who trusted me with their personal immigration stories. Your words did not fall on deaf ears.

To my "person," Christy Fore: no words can express how treasured your friendship is to me. Thank you for reading this and all my writing. Your insight and ability to graciously manage my obsessive-compulsive nature have been my Balm of Gilead on many a day.

I'm blessed and entirely beholden to my family. You are my lamps in this world. Thank you to my parents, Eleane and Curtis, my baby brothers, Jason and Andrew, the Norats, the McCoys, and everybody in between. Your infinite love, encouragement, prayers, and ability to make me laugh so hard I lose my balance have given my life a joyful and necessary equilibrium. Thanks for shepherding me through the good days and bad. Mom and Dad, thank you for reminding me that I can always "come home."

Last, but most important, I thank God for my husband, Brian Waterman. Garmisch, Germany, is woven into both our childhoods and adult lives. Thank you for ceaselessly being my champion and my German translator; for reminding me that we all need a little holiday sometimes (preferably at a Deutschland B&B); for encouraging me to climb to St. Martin Hütte even though I thought it too high; for patiently cheering me up the rugged alpine path and providing celebration drinks at the summit. Every day you do the same. May we grow old greeting each dawn with, *Guten Morgen, coffee drinkin'*?

Reading Group Guide

The discussion questions and list of book club activities are intended to enrich your reading group's conversation about *The Baker's Daughter*, Sarah McCoy's absorbing and compelling new novel. In order to provide reading groups with the most informed and thought-provoking questions possible, it is necessary to reveal important aspects of the plot of this novel as well as the ending. If you have not finished reading *The Baker's Daughter*, we respectfully suggest that you wait before reviewing this guide.

Discussion Questions

- The epigraph pairs two quotes. The first is from Mark Twain, and the second is from Robert Frost's poem "The Trial by Existence." Why do you think McCoy put these quotes together? Which characters do you believe they reference?

- The concept of baking, sharing, and passing on recipes is woven throughout the book. What are a couple of your favorite family recipes? Have you shared those with your children and/or friends? How have recipes played a part in your own childhood and adult life?

• Epistolary storytelling in the form of letter writing is a vital way the characters directly communicate with each other and express many of their innermost feelings. Do you have friends or family members with whom you frequently exchange letters, cards, or e-mails, though you rarely see them in person or talk on the phone? If so, do you find yourself being more or less open in those written communications?

• Reba is continuously reinventing herself, trying on new personalities and fictitious lives. Why does she engage in this behavior? Why does she think running away from her family's problems will help her achieve a new beginning? How do you believe discovering Elsie's story changed Reba?

• Considering Elsie's true feelings for Josef, why does she take his gifts, accompany him to the ball, accept his proposal, and wear his ring? Why does she pretend to be engaged to him? Do her circumstances make her betrayal right? If you were in her position, what would you have done?

• When Reba finds her daddy's therapy notes, she wishes she had never read them. She wants to remember him differently. She doesn't want to believe that the facts are true. Have you ever felt this way about something? Looking back, do you feel remorse or gratitude for the decision you made regarding it?

• Both Elsie and Reba are confronted with the issue of blind obedience. At what point must we question the governing regulations? At what point must we act on our own convictions? Is this a slippery slope?

• Though generations apart, Elsie and Reba are both empowered women. How does this manifest in Elsie's story? In Reba's? How does McCoy depict gender roles? How do all the women characters claim or reclaim their power (Mutti, Hazel, Frau Rattelmüller, Jane, Deedee, Reba's momma, Lillian, etc.)?

• Does Josef's personal suffering justify his public actions? Do you sympathize with Josef's struggle between duty to country and his individual feelings? Why or why not? Similarly, how does Riki justify his daily work with the U.S. Customs and Border Protection? Have you ever participated in something you didn't believe in?

- Collective ownership is a central tenet of the Lebensborn Program. What might you see are positive attributes of communal living? What are the negative? Discuss the importance of personal identity and/or possession to Elsie and society as a whole.

- Do you believe Mutti was right to keep Frau Rattelmüller's letters from Elsie? Discuss her motivations and the possible outcomes if she hadn't kept the secret.

- In the Epilogue, Jane gives Reba a recipe cookbook in honor of her "setting a wedding date." Do you think they followed through? Where do you think Riki and Reba are today?

Book Club Activities

- Ask each book club member to bring a family recipe for a book club recipe swap or a prepared dish for a potluck of family foods. Go around the group sharing the history of each dish/recipe.

- Pull out pretty stationery or a lovely card and write an old friend. Say anything that comes to mind as if he or she were sitting beside you and see what comes to the page. Mail it as a surprise to that individual.

- Elsie and Hazel watched Jean Harlow's *Libeled Lady* (1936) as girls. Consider renting the film and hosting a movie night with your book club. How do you see the female starlets resonating in Elsie? How would you cast *The Baker's Daughter* as a movie?

- Have a baking party using Elsie's German recipes from the novel's Epilogue. Pick one as the theme (say, a Lebkuchen Bake-Off) or try them all.